D0276801

ed or before th

AFTER THE DANCE IS OVER

AFTER THE DANCE IS OVER

Joan Jonker

HEADLINE

First published in 2001
by HEADLINE BOOK PUBLISHING

10 9 8 7 6 5 4 3 2 1

British Library Cataloguing in Publication Data

Jonker, Joan
    After the dance is over
    1. Liverpool (England) – Social life and customs
    2. Domestic fiction
    I. Title
    823.9'14 [F]

ISBN 0 7472 7250 6

Typeset by
CBS, Martlesham Heath, Ipswich, Suffolk

Printed and bound in Great Britain

HEADLINE BOOK PUBLISHING
A division of Hodder Headline
338 Euston Road
London NW1 3BH

www.headline.co.uk
www.hodderheadline.com

Dear Readers

This is a story of love, laughter and friendship. The fans of Molly Bennett and Nellie McDonough will be delighted because this is the hilarious duo at their very best. Laughter is in abundance and guaranteed, so pull up a chair and treat yourself.

Warmest regards to all my readers

Take care

Joan

Chapter 1

'Molly Bennett, will yer slow down, girl, before me heart gives out on me?' Nellie McDonough was red in the face as she tried to make her eighteen stone move faster to catch up with her friend. 'What the hell's the hurry?'

Molly turned around, put her hands on her hips and tutted. 'I'm only going to the bread shop. I used the last of the loaf for Ruthie's breakfast and there's not a crumb in the house. Anyway, where are you off to?'

'I'm following you to see what ye're up to! What's the big idea? Yer never go to the shops without me.'

'Oh, aye? Well, who was it passed my window on her way to the shops about an hour ago, sunshine? Yer never knocked to ask if I wanted to come with yer.'

'Ah, but there's a difference, girl. Yer see, I don't mind going to the shops without you, but I object to you going without me! If I'm not with yer, God knows what yer'd get up to on yer own. So now yer know.'

'Nellie, ye're with me more often than me shadow. By the time I get back with me loaf, yer'll be knocking on the door for yer morning cup of tea.'

'I won't, yer know, girl, 'cos you'll be letting us in with a key. I might as well stay with yer now, it's no good wasting good shoe leather going home and then coming out again.'

'If I thought yer'd understand, sunshine, I'd explain that ye're wasting more shoe leather coming to the shops with me now than yer would walking the few yards from your house to mine. But yer'd only talk yer way out of it, so I won't bother.'

'Yer know something, girl, yer talk too much. Yer mouth is never still. We're wasting good time standing here doing nowt when we could be back in your house and I could be dunking a ginger biscuit in me tea.'

Molly's mouth gaped. 'You cheeky article, Nellie McDonough!

What makes yer think ye're getting a ginger snap? I've kept yer in cups of tea for the last twenty odd years, now yer expect to get biscuits with it! And yer know everything's still on ration so yer've got a flaming nerve.'

'Ay, yer've got a short memory, girl. What about the packet of custard creams I gave yer that time?'

Molly was dying to laugh at the expression on her best mate's face. At the moment she was playing the drama queen, but any second she'd be a petulant child with a quivering bottom lip. 'And aren't you forgetting who ate that packet of biscuits? If my memory serves me correct, by the time I'd had two, you'd scoffed the rest!'

'I don't know why ye're raking that up, girl, 'cos it was years ago!'

'You're the one what raked it up, not me! And you're the one what ate the biscuits!'

At four feet ten inches, Nellie had to look up at Molly. 'I'm getting a kink in me neck, so are we going for yer bread or not? It'll be ruddy stale by the time yer get it, and I'm not very partial to stale bread.'

'You should worry, yer won't be the one eating it!'

A sly smile spread across Nellie's chubby face. 'I would be if yer asked me to have a bit of lunch with yer. After all yer wouldn't begrudge a member of yer family having a round of toast?'

'How many times do I have to tell yer that ye're not one of the family? Just because your Steve married my Jill, that doesn't make us blood relations!'

'As near as damn it, it does! Anyway, me tummy heard me mention a round of toast and it's starting to rumble, so can we get our skates on?' She linked her friend's arm. 'Come on, girl, and don't talk so much.'

'Oh, no, yer don't.' Molly moved her arm away. 'Me other arm, sunshine, I'm not walking on the outside and ending up in the gutter.'

'I can't help having wide hips what sway, girl. Anyone would think I was pushing yer on purpose, and I wouldn't do that, not to me very best mate.'

'Flattery won't get yer a round of toast, Nellie, so don't be trying it on. I've got a stack of washing to put out on the line, and if you hadn't come along I'd have been to the shop and back by now and me washing would be wafting in the breeze.' She squeezed her friend's arm. 'Still, the sun's going to shine for another few hours so I'll get me clothes dry.'

'I put mine out at eight o'clock and they're dry now,' Nellie said, her face the picture of innocence as she purposely threw the cat amongst the pigeons. She'd been up since seven and hadn't had a decent laugh yet. 'I've got them all folded up ready for ironing.'

Molly pulled up sharp. 'Yer've what! Got all yer washing dried and ready for ironing! Well, you cheeky so-and-so! Yer've got yerself all organised, with time on yer hands, so yer think yer'll do some socialising in my house, do yer, drinking my tea and eating my biscuits?'

'I thought yer said yer had no biscuits, girl?'

'Oh, sod off, Nellie McDonough!' Molly stuck her nose in the air and thought of how to get one back on her mate. She'd found this word in the dictionary a couple of weeks ago and had been waiting for the opportunity to use it. 'Whether I've got any biscuits or not is really inconsequential – and none of your ruddy business.'

'Temper, girl, temper! Remember that bad heart of yours. I don't want yer pegging out on me in the middle of the main road.'

'That's my mate for yer, full of sympathy. Never mind that I've conked out in the middle of the tram lines, all yer thinking about is how soft you'll look. Ye're as hard as nails, Nellie, with a swinging brick for a heart.'

The two friends were walking towards the main road, with Nellie chatting away oblivious to the fact that Molly was getting pushed nearer to the wall with each step. 'Yer might know a lot of big words, girl, but ye're not that bloody clever. I said I didn't want yer pegging out on me, not conking out. Conking out means passing out if yer've had too much to drink, or fainting with the heat. But pegging out means finito, yer haven't got a return fare, yer've gone for good.'

'Very nicely put, sunshine, with just the right amount of delicacy and sympathy for which ye're well known.' They were standing at the kerb and Molly looked both ways before leading her friend across the wide main road. 'I may as well get all me shopping in now, save coming out later. Yer've turned me whole day upside down, Nellie McDonough, but then I should be used to it 'cos I always end up giving in to yer.'

Tony Reynolds was putting a tray of minced meat in the window of his butcher's shop when he saw them crossing the road. He shouted to his assistant, 'Ay out, Ellen, here come the terrible twins. They should brighten the day for us, they usually do.' He smiled as his two favourite customers entered the shop, with Nellie having to come through the door sideways on. 'Good morning, ladies, how are you this fine day?'

Nellie swaggered over to the counter. 'Morning, Tony. Morning,

Ellen. I'm feeling very well meself, but I wouldn't ask Molly if I were you 'cos she's got a right gob on her. Nearly bit me head off she did because I asked her if I could have a bite to eat with her! I mean, yer wouldn't see a beggar in the street starve, would yer, never mind yer own flesh and blood?'

'So help me I'll clock her one of these days.' Molly winked at the butcher she'd known since the day she moved into the area as a newly married woman, and to his assistant who was her next-door neighbour and good friend. 'And I didn't have a gob on me until I found *her* following me down the street. I only came out for a loaf, 'cos as yer know we don't usually do our shopping until later, but me bold Nellie changed all that just 'cos she's too ruddy nosy.'

'That's a load of cobblers.' Nellie's vigorously shaking head sent her layers of chins flying in all directions. 'The real reason she's got a cob on is because I've got all me washing dried ready to iron and she hasn't even got hers on the line yet. Now is it my fault if she's too bloody lazy to get out of ruddy bed in the mornings?'

'I'm not getting involved,' Ellen said, knowing full well the two women had never had a proper falling out in the twenty years she'd known them. And if they didn't leave here laughing their heads off, she'd eat her hat. 'Fight it out between yerselves.'

'Ye're a wise woman, Ellen,' Tony said, beaming. 'Never take sides between two friends.' He rubbed his hands together. 'What can I get for you, ladies?'

'I haven't got me ration book with me, Tony, 'cos I wasn't expecting to do me shopping now,' Molly said. 'So can I have half of mince and I'll bring yer the coupons tomorrow?'

'Yer certainly can, Molly. And I'll throw yer a bit extra in for good measure 'cos the bloke at the abattoir was in a good mood this morning and gave me over the odds.'

'I'll have the same as me mate.' Nellie wasn't going to be left out. 'Especially that extra bit ye're throwing on for good measure what yer got off the bloke at the . . . er . . . the . . . er . . . the place what yer get yer meat from.'

Tony chuckled. 'The abattoir, Nellie, that's what the place is called.'

She walked around the shop in a circle while she considered how best to find out what she wanted to know. Then she had a brainwave. 'Ay, ye're good with words, Tony, but I bet my mate can lick the pants off yer.' She jerked her head at Molly. 'Go on, girl, tell him what it is when ye've either got biscuits or yer haven't.'

Molly kept her face straight but she was laughing inside. She'd wondered when her friend would get round to it. 'It's none of your ruddy business!'

'Yeah, I know yer said that. But what did yer say before?'

Molly held her chin in her hand, her blue eyes thoughtful. 'Let's see if I can remember. Oh, yes, I said whether I had biscuits or not was inconsequential.'

Nellie folded her arms and hitched up her mountainous bosom. 'There yer are, Tony, how's that for a word? I bet yer a tanner yer don't know what it means.'

'Oh, yer shouldn't have bet me a tanner, Nellie, 'cos yer've lost. It means something of little importance. So hand yer money over.'

Nellie was flummoxed. Her eyes darted around the shop seeking a way out. And she found it. 'I'll only believe yer, Tony, if yer write it down for me. Go on, spell it out.'

It was the butcher's turn to be flummoxed. He hadn't got a clue how to spell it. But he found a way out, too! At least he thought he had. 'I'll tell yer what, I'll weigh yer mince while Ellen writes it down for yer.'

Ellen's eyes and mouth were wide. 'Spell it? I can't even say it, never mind write it down. No, I've got a better idea, Tony, I'll serve the ladies while you find yerself a nice clean piece of paper what hasn't got any blood on.'

'Ha-ha.' Nellie's shoulders shook with mirth. 'Yer can't spell it, can yer, Tony? Come on, be a man and admit it.'

'Nellie, you bet me a tanner and the bet stands. Just make sure yer have it with yer tomorrow when I bring in a nice clean piece of paper with the word written on it.'

'Bugger off, Tony Reynolds, yer must think I just came over on the banana boat!' Her shake of head and chins signified her disgust. 'Yer haven't got a ruddy clue! Fat chance yer've got of getting a tanner off me. If I want to see it written down I can get me mate to do it for nowt!'

'Yer know what you can do, don't yer, sunshine?' Molly said. 'I can say it, and I know what it means, but I'd have a job spelling it. Yer bet Tony a tanner he didn't know the meaning of it and he did, so pay up and look happy.'

Nellie wasn't having any of that. Her head shook so fast her chins didn't know which way to turn. 'Tony stands as much chance of getting sixpence off me as my George has of winning the football pools.'

'But George doesn't do the football pools!'

Nellie spread her hands. 'See what I mean, girl? Tony doesn't stand

5

a snowball's chance in hell. Anyway, him being a fine upstanding Catholic, he knows it's a sin to gamble. So I'm doing him a favour by leading him down the path of rightussness.'

Molly and Ellen covered their mouths, bodies shaking with laughter, while Tony tilted his head back to enjoy a loud guffaw. In the process his straw hat fell off, landed on the sawdust-covered floor, and brought a fresh burst of hilarity from them. As he bent down to retrieve it, he used the counter as a screen while he tried to wipe the smile off his face. 'Oh, aye, Nellie, what path is that, then?'

'You heard me, yer haven't got cloth ears.' Nellie knew exactly what she was doing and saying, she always did. But she was game for a laugh, too. Mind you, she'd learned about the path of righteousness at school, the priest had made sure of that, so she was on safe ground there. It was that big word of Molly's that had her beat, she couldn't even get her tongue around it. 'I don't know what the three of yer are laughing at, yer silly sods. Have yer never heard of the path of rightussness?'

'I'll tell yer what I'll do, Nellie, so we'll be quits. I'll take a chance on God not minding anyone having a little flutter, and I'll bet you a tanner yer can't spell it. Now I can't be fairer than that.'

Nellie's mind went back to the priest who used to take them for religious instruction every morning. Where was he now when she needed him? He used to drive it home to them every morning about the path of righteousness, but he'd never asked them to spell it! 'Not on yer life, Tony Reynolds. I don't think much of me chances of getting to heaven as it is – I'm not going looking for trouble!'

Molly put an arm across her friend's shoulder. 'Yer know I'm going to put in a good word for yer, I've told yer that. When we get to the pearly gates I'll tell St Peter of all the good things yer've done in life which might have slipped his notice.'

'I don't know about slipping *his* notice, they've slipped mine as well! I can't for the life of me think of any good things I've done.' Then a gleam came into her eyes. 'I know, I'll get George to give me a reference! He's always telling me how good I am in the bedroom.'

Molly's hand shot out to cover her friend's mouth. 'Tony, will yer serve us quick and let us get out of the shop while I can still look yer in the face?' She glared at Nellie. 'I don't want to hear another word out of you, just hand over yer money so I can pay for yer meat.' When there was no response, she took her hand away. 'Did yer hear what I said, sunshine? I want some money off yer to pay Tony.'

'I heard yer, girl, but yer had yer hand over me mouth and yer didn't give me a chance to tell yer I haven't got no money on me! I didn't know we were coming shopping, did I? I only followed yer to see what yer were up to. So you pay the man and I'll settle up with yer later.'

Molly shook her head. 'I don't believe this, I only came out to buy a loaf of bread. Now I'm lumbered with paying for me mate's dinner! When we get to the greengrocer's I'll have to fork out for the spuds and veg as well! I just can't win!'

'Holy sufferin' ducks, girl, don't be making a song and dance about it! I've said I'll pay yer later, and I will!'

'How much later, sunshine? This year, next year, sometime, never? I wouldn't mind if I got it back the same day, but getting money off you is like getting blood out of a ruddy stone. I think I'll have to start learning this trick meself. All it needs is to act daft and pretend I've come out without me purse.'

'It wouldn't do yer no good, girl, 'cos as they say, every dog knows its own tricks. Yer wouldn't get away with it, not with me.'

'Then I'll have to get into the habit of making sure yer've got yer purse on yer before we set foot out of the house.' Molly didn't mean what she was saying, and Nellie and the two behind the counter knew it, because this sort of banter went on every day. They enjoyed it, their friendship thrived on it and it brought laughter to a lot of people. 'Ye're a scrounger, Nellie McDonough, that's what yer are.'

Nellie raised her brows, curled a hand to examine her fingernails and feigned a yawn. 'Go on, girl, tell them about the one thousand two hundred and fifty-three cups of tea I've had off yer while ye're at it. Oh, and don't forget the custard creams and ginger snaps, I bet yer know exactly how many of them I've had, too. It's a wonder they didn't choke me they were that begrudged.'

'Well, there was no fear of me choking on the cups of tea and biscuits I've had in *your* house, sunshine, 'cos I've had none.' Molly slapped an open palm to her forehead. 'Ah, I tell a lie. The day me mangle broke down and yer said I could use yours, well, yer made me a cup of tea that day. It was the first time in twenty-four years, and the last.' She rooted in her purse, brought out half a crown and passed it over the counter. 'Here yer are, Tony, there's two customers coming in so we'll get out of yer way. I bet yer'll be glad to see the back of us.'

She took the meat off the butcher and linked her mate's arm. 'Come on, sunshine, or it'll be dark before I get me washing out. Ta-ra, Ellen, I'll see yer later.'

Tony and his assistant watched them walk through the door and burst out laughing when they heard Nellie say, 'I did buy yer a cream slice one day, girl, have yer forgotten? And I always mind yer table when ye're having a party . . .'

'They're priceless,' Tony said. 'I wish all me customers were like them.'

Ellen didn't answer as she went to attend to the customers. If she'd had time, she'd have told her boss that women like her neighbours didn't come along very often. She wouldn't be where she was today but for them. Once married to a violent, bullying drunkard, she hadn't been sorry when, blind drunk, he'd staggered into the path of a tram and been killed. It was a relief for her and her children who were beaten black and blue by him almost daily. But she was left penniless with no money for food or rent, and the prospect of being turfed out of her home was looming large when Molly and Nellie took her and the kids under their wings. Thanks to them her children were now happy and well nourished, and she was married to Corker, the most loving and caring person in the world. She would never forget her debt to the two women who'd made it possible.

'Am I coming in for a round of toast, girl? Go on, don't be mean.'

'Go home and get yer purse then, sunshine, I need me money back today. Yer owe me for the meat, spuds, onions, carrots and turnip. So poppy off while I make a start getting me washing on the line.'

'Anyone would think I was going to do a bunk to hear you talk. I'll give yer the money tonight, scout's honour.'

'No, Nellie, I want it now! I'm counting me coppers these days and trying to put a few to one side each week for something special. So scarper before I reckon up what it'll cost me to give yer a round of toast with margarine on, and two cups of tea.'

'What are yer saving up for, girl?'

'I'll tell yer while we're having our lunch, as long as yer promise to keep it a secret.'

Considering her weight, Nellie was very light on her feet and she covered the distance from Molly's to her own house, three doors up, like a ballerina. She grabbed her purse from the glass bowl on the sideboard and was back before Molly had time to get her pegs out. 'My God, ye're not half slow, girl, I thought yer'd have yer washing out by now!'

'It won't take me five minutes, sunshine, and for yer cheek yer can fill the kettle and cut a few slices off the loaf. And I don't want them like doorsteps, either, so don't be too heavy-handed.' Molly slipped her pinny on, filled the pocket with pegs and draped a sheet over her arm. 'Oh, when the kettle's boiled, pour some hot water in the teapot to warm it up. Swill it around and empty it out before yer put the tea in.'

Nellie saluted. She couldn't see her feet, but she hoped that, like her bosom, they were standing to attention. 'Aye, aye, sir! All present and correct, sir!'

Molly was grinning as she pegged the sheet on the line. She'd been glad of Nellie the last two months to take her mind of losing her two daughters. They'd married in a double wedding ceremony and Molly and her husband Jack had been so proud that their beautiful daughters had wed decent men who loved them dearly and would be good to them. Jill, the eldest, had married Nellie's son, Steve. They'd been sweethearts practically since they were toddlers. Doreen had married Phil, with whom she'd fallen head over heels in love the night they first met at Barlow's Lane dance hall. But although Molly had cried at the wedding, knowing her girls were leaving home, she'd had no idea then she'd miss them so much. Mind, she had a lot to be thankful for because they still lived in the street and she saw them every day. Doreen and Phil lived in the house facing with Miss Victoria Clegg, who had taken Phil in as a lodger when he had nowhere to live. He'd become like a son to her, the family she'd never had, and he adored her. So Doreen was lucky, walking into a fully furnished house and living there with two people she loved. And Jill, the gentle one of the family, only lived at the top end of the street with Corker's mam, Lizzie, who had offered to share her home with the newly weds until they could afford to buy the furniture for a place of their own. Molly saw her girls every day and knew they were happy. But even though she still had her son Tommy, and daughter Ruthie at home, she missed the two fledglings who had flown from her nest.

'What the hell are yer doing, girl?' Nellie stood on the kitchen step looking very impatient. 'Are yer blowing that sheet dry?'

Brought out of her reverie, Molly grinned. 'Pass the other sheet out and a few pegs. I don't mind as long as I get them dry, I can put the smaller things on the ceiling rack.'

Ten minutes later they sat facing each other across the table, and there was margarine trickling down Nellie's chin as she asked, 'What's the secret, girl, what are yer saving up for?'

'Nellie, if yer tell a living soul I'll never speak to yer again. I want it to be a surprise.'

'Cross my heart and hope to die, girl, I won't breathe a word.'

'Well, yer know our Tommy said he wouldn't marry Rosie O'Grady unless her mam and dad could be at the wedding? He's not on full pay yet and his wages are lousy so him and Rosie are going without things to save up for the wedding and pay for her parents to come over from Ireland. I want to help them as much as I can. It cost me and Jack a packet when the girls got married, and I really don't begrudge a penny of it because we wanted to give them a good send off, but now I think it's only fair to do what we can for Tommy and Rosie, with her parents not being here. He's me only son, and he's a good lad. Never given us any trouble and always bright and cheerful. He must be worrying about where the money's going to come from for the wedding, but he never says a word.

'I've told Jack we can't give him less than we gave our daughters, it wouldn't be fair and would look as though we didn't love him as much. And I do, Nellie, I love the bones of him. So me and Jack are going to put a bit by each week. It won't be much because I'm missing the girls' wages, but we'll do our best.'

'They're not getting married for a while, are they, girl?'

'Not until next summer, but the weeks fly over, sunshine, so we can't afford to hang about. He won't be out of his time then, not for another few months, but they'll be living with me ma and da after the wedding, so they won't have a lot to lay out each week. And Rosie is a very good manager.'

Nellie reached into her pocket and brought out her well-worn purse. 'I'll give yer what I owe yer now, before yer have me crying in me tea.' She put a handful of change on the table. 'Help yerself, girl, but leave me enough to pay the rent man.' She watched her friend carefully picking out the right amount of coins to cover what was owing to her. 'Talking about the rent man, girl, remember I told yer I asked him to consider Archie's mam for the first house what came empty in the street, and he said he'd got someone lined up who'd been waiting a long time? Well, I've heard this morning that old Mrs Harwick from next door but two is leaving to go and live with her daughter in Maghull. She's getting too old to look after herself now, and her daughter's frightened of anything happening to her and them not able to get to her in time. So I believe she's moving the week after next.'

'Ah, she's a nice little thing,' Molly said. 'A good neighbour, keeps her house spotless and doesn't have a bad word to say about anyone. I think after Miss Clegg she's the oldest resident of the street. We'll miss seeing her around.'

'Yeah, she's a little love. But if she was my mam I wouldn't want her living so far away from me, not at her age. Yer never know, she could easy fall over and not be able to move and then lie there for days without anyone knowing.'

'That's right, sunshine, cheer me up! Anyway, what's all this got to do with the rent man and Archie's mam?'

'Well, it means that Ida can have the next house what comes empty. And I'm going to remind Mr Henry he's not to promise it to anyone else.'

Molly curled her hands around the cup and held it near her mouth. Peering over the rim, she studied her friend. When Nellie's son Steve got married she was left with two other children, just like Molly herself. Except that Nellie's were both grown up, Lily had just turned twenty-one, and Paul was nearing twenty. 'Is your Lily going serious with Archie, or are they just good friends?'

'He's dead serious, girl, but yer can't get to the bottom of our Lily. I think she's frightened of showing her feelings because of what that bastard Len did to her. She's got over him all right, but it's going to take a while before she trusts another feller completely.'

'Pity, really, 'cos Archie's a smashing bloke. If I was twenty years younger – no, twenty-five years more like – and I didn't have Jack, I'd be running after him meself,' Molly said. 'He's our Tommy's hero, he really looks up to him. He says if it wasn't for Archie, him and a lot of other soldiers would have been blown up. Led them through a minefield, he did, without any thought for his own safety. That takes guts, that does. And I'm very fond of him, which is why I'm wondering if yer think it's wise to be asking Mr Henry to let Ida have the next house what comes empty? It's not that I wouldn't like her and Archie as neighbours, 'cos I would, but what if they get a house in the street and then your Lily decides he's not the one for her? It would make things very awkward all round.'

'I have thought of that, girl, I'm not daft. But yer know how often a house comes empty in this street. Every blue moon. Plenty of time for our Lily to make up her mind. I'd lay odds she already has, really, but is frightened of showing her feelings in case she gets hurt again.' Nellie nodded to the two framed photographs standing proudly one at either end of the sideboard. They were wedding photographs of Molly's two girls with their brand new husbands and it brought a lump to Nellie's throat to see her Steve smiling broadly with his arm around the girl he'd loved all his life. 'Looking at them photographs, girl, yer wouldn't know which of the girls was which 'cos they're so alike.

11

Anyone would take them for twins.' She put on her hard-done-by look. 'Ye're lucky having two photographs, I've only got the one.'

'Don't start that again, sunshine, ye're beginning to sound like a broken record. It's only natural I've got two, 'cos two of my daughters were married. When your Lily gets wed, you'll have another one to stand on yer sideboard.'

'Ah, but when your Tommy gets married, yer'll still be one up on me.'

Molly tutted. 'Yer'll catch up with me when your Paul decides to settle down. And before yer bring our Ruthie into it, may I remind yer she's not thirteen until next week? And anyway, it's not my fault I've got four children and you've only got three.'

'Of course it's your fault! Ye're a dark horse, Molly Bennett, telling me off every time I mention what goes on in me bedroom, when you and Jack must go at it hammer and tongs! And don't look at me like that, 'cos the fact that you've got one more child than me speaks for itself.'

'Let's change the subject, sunshine, shall we? What about your Paul, is he settling down at all? I know he's going out with Phoebe 'cos I see them passing the window, but d'yer think it's the real thing?'

'Your guess is as good as mine, girl, I wouldn't have a bet on it. She's tamed him a lot, but whether he'll stay tamed is another matter. I think Ellen and Corker have told the girl to let Paul do all the running, and I wouldn't blame them if they had because all he thinks about is having a good time. She's got him on a string now, but whether the day will come when he wants to cut the string I wouldn't know.'

'She's a lovely girl is Phoebe, he'd go a long way to find one better. But he's only twenty so he's got time to grow up.'

'I thought the army would have changed him, but it hasn't,' Nellie said, putting her hand out to see if there was any more tea in the pot. 'But like yer say, time's on his side.'

'Don't be looking for another cup of tea, sunshine, 'cos I'm going to throw yer out now. I've got a stack of work to do and I want the dinner ready for when the family come in. I'm going round to me ma's tonight for a game of cards and I want to be out by half-seven at the latest.'

'Can I come with yer, girl, I wouldn't mind a game of cards?'

'No, sunshine, 'cos I'm going across the road before I go to me ma's, to see how Victoria is. I haven't been for a few days and I feel mean because our Doreen won't leave her on her own even to slip to the shops, which means the poor girl doesn't get out much. She never complains 'cos she loves the old lady, but her and Phil should get out on their own now and again, they're too young to be tied to the house all the time. And the old lady is ninety now, she does need someone to keep an eye on her. So I'm going to suggest I sit with Victoria tomorrow night while they go to the pictures.'

'I'll come with yer to keep yer company, eh? Victoria would enjoy that 'cos we make her laugh. So how about it, girl?'

'On one condition, sunshine. That yer don't use the word bedroom, not even once.'

Chapter 2

'Mam, can I go over to Bella's when I've had me dinner?' Ruthie threw her coat on the couch and made her way to the kitchen. 'Her mam's bought her a new box of dominoes and we want to have a game.' She waited until her mother nodded, then smiled and rubbed her tummy. 'Ooh, that smells nice.'

'I've done the best I could with what I had, sunshine, that's all yer can do these days.' Molly smiled at her daughter, and as she never failed to, could see her two eldest girls in her youngest one. They had the same blonde hair and vivid blue eyes, except that Ruthie was more forward than Jill and Doreen had been at her age. You could blame the war for that, with the bombing and everything else. The kids missed their childhood years, which was a shame. 'There's plenty of goodness in it, sunshine, but yer'll need a magnifying glass to find the meat. I'll be glad when rationing is over and we can get back to normal.'

'Yeah, I'm looking forward to buying sweets with me pocket money.' The young girl twisted a lock of the blonde hair that was hanging down over her shoulders. 'The first thing I'm going to buy when rationing is over is a great big slab of Cadbury's chocolate.'

'D'yer know what I'm looking forward to?' Molly asked. 'Going into the butcher's and asking Tony for a pound of thick sausages, a pound of lean bacon and a black pudding.'

Ruthie giggled. 'What about a dozen eggs?'

'Oh, I don't get me eggs from Tony, sunshine, I get them from Irwin's. Nice brown ones that look as though they've just been laid.'

'Mam, can I go over to our Doreen's for half-an-hour? I promised Aunt Vicky I'd call and comb her hair for her.'

'Doreen does her hair, she does it a treat!'

'I know that, but I like doing it, too. And I'm ever so gentle with her, I don't pull on it or comb it too near the scalp.'

'Oh, go on then, but don't make a nuisance of yerself. And keep an eye open for yer dad and Tommy coming home from work, I want you back here at the same time as them.' Molly followed her daughter to the front door. 'Will yer tell Doreen I'll be slipping over tonight before I go round to yer nan's?'

Ruthie gave her a cheeky grin before saying in a very good imitation of Nellie's voice, 'I'll do that for yer, girl, but what's in it for me?'

'Very good, sunshine, but not perfect yet. Yer'll have to practise a bit more to get the nod right, and the way she stands. But I'll give yer eight out of ten.'

Molly was smiling as she went back to the kitchen. Her whole family loved Nellie and thought she was the funniest thing on two legs. And she was, too! She never told a proper joke, but she didn't need to 'cos she had plenty of her own tricks up her sleeve.

It was half-past five and Molly was setting the table when there was a tap on the window. She knew it wasn't Nellie because her friend didn't tap, she rapped hard enough to shake the window frame. A peek through the curtains showed Ellen standing outside. 'Hello, sunshine, come on in!'

'No, I'll get home and see to the dinner. Tony let me leave when the shop closed, he said he'd clean up tonight to give me a break. I'm only calling to tell yer Corker's ship is due in at the weekend, he's hoping to be home on Saturday.'

'Oh, that's good news! Did yer know when me and Nellie were in this morning?'

Ellen shook her head. 'No, there was a letter on the mat when Peter got home from school and he brought it down to me. I'm made up, I can't wait to see him.'

'I bet yer can't. We'll all be glad to see him, too. He's one of my favourite people is Corker, a man yer could trust with yer life.' Molly smiled at the woman who had changed over the years from the downtrodden wife of a bully to a woman who could hold her head high now she was married to a man who loved and cared for her and the children. 'I'll tell Jack to be ready to go for a pint on Saturday night and I'll let George know as well. They'll be over the moon.'

'I just thought I'd let yer know.' Ellen handed over a small parcel. 'I got some dripping for yer to share with Nellie. It's not much, but it'll help.'

'Ye're a pal, sunshine, and I won't forget yer in me will.' Molly watched her neighbour put the key in the lock of the house next door. 'I'll see yer, Ellen, ta-ra.' There was a spring in her step as she put the dripping in the kitchen. There'd be enough there to make a pan of chips, so that was tomorrow's dinner taken care of. She had a packet of dried peas in, so she'd put them in steep tonight, then tomorrow morning she'd get out early enough to make sure she was first in the queue for pies from Hanley's. She'd better let Nellie know, though, 'cos if she went off on her own there'd be blue murder. Whatever the Bennetts had for their dinner, the McDonough family had to have the same.

Molly was stirring the pan of stew to make sure it didn't stick to the bottom of the pan when she heard the key in the lock. Her face lit up. This would be Jill who never failed to call in every night for a few minutes on her way home from work. Her daughter had kept her job on after she got married so she and Steve could save more money each week.

'Hello, sunshine.' Molly held her arms wide and Jill walked into them. 'I look forward to these few minutes every night when I've got yer all to meself.' She stepped back and looked with pride at the pretty girl smiling back at her. 'How did work go?'

'Same as usual, Mam, nothing exciting,' Jill said, her eyes going to the table set for four. 'The thing I miss most is us all sitting down together every night for our dinner. I miss you other times, but that was somehow special. We used to have some good laughs, didn't we, Mam?'

'We did that, sunshine, but don't forget that the person who gave us something to laugh about is now yer mother-in-law. And I think yer'll agree that yer hopped in lucky there 'cos mother-in-laws like Nellie don't come along very often.'

'I know that, Mam, and I really love her. And Steve takes after her for being funny, he has Mrs Corkhill and me in stitches every night. I think he makes up half the stories just to make us laugh. But I still miss me family.'

'Yer wouldn't be natural if yer didn't, sunshine, I was the same meself when I got married. But yer'll get over it – I did. Mind you, for the first few months, every time yer dad looked sideways at me I burst out crying and said I was going back to me ma.'

'I haven't gone that far yet, Mam.' Jill turned when she heard the door opening and before she knew what was happening her brother's hands had circled her waist and she was lifted high in the air. She grinned down into the handsome face which was so like their dad's, and in a voice as prim and proper as she could muster, told him, 'Put me down, Tommy, or I'll tell me husband on yer.'

He lowered her to the ground and kissed her cheek before releasing her. 'Marriage must agree with yer, Jill, 'cos yer look prettier every day.'

'Move out of the way, son, and give yer dad a look in.' Jack locked his arms around his first-born and gave her a hug. 'He's right, sweetheart, yer look like a million dollars.'

'And you're still the most handsome man in Liverpool.' Jill's vivid blue eyes rolled. 'But don't tell Steve I said that, or Uncle Corker.'

'Ay, Corker's coming home on Saturday, yer'll all be glad to hear. Ellen called before to tell me. So yer'll have yer drinking buddy to go for a pint with, Jack.' Molly gazed from father to son. She could clearly remember the first night she'd met Jack, and he'd looked exactly as Tommy looked now: dark hair, deep brown eyes, strong jaw and well built, except her son could give his dad a few inches in height. 'Or should I say buddies, 'cos we mustn't leave George out.'

'Auntie Nellie would have yer life if yer did.' Jill put the straps of her bag over her shoulder. 'Anyway, I'd better be going, I like to be in when Steve gets home.'

'Oh, hang on a second, sunshine, I've got something to tell yer. I'm calling in to see Victoria later, and I'm going to suggest that me and Nellie sit with her tomorrow night while Doreen and Phil go to the pictures. Wouldn't you and Steve like to go with them? It would do yer good to get out and enjoy yerself. All work and no play makes for a very dull life, especially when ye're young. Make the best of it while yer can.'

'Yeah, I'd like that! But I don't want to make arrangements without asking Steve first, so I'll see how he feels about it and nip down later and tell Doreen. It would be nice, though, 'cos we haven't been out as a foursome for ages.'

'Has there ever been a time in yer life, sunshine, when Steve refused yer anything? He'd take the stars out of the sky for yer if he could.'

'I know that, Mam, but I'd still rather ask. I know he'll say yes, but I'll wait until he says it before making definite arrangements with Doreen. I'd hate to disappoint her.'

'You do what yer think best, sweetheart,' Jack said. 'It's right that yer should talk it over with yer husband first.'

Molly chuckled inside. In all the years they'd been married Jack had never once stopped her from doing something. He might have put up an argument to begin with, but after some gentle persuasion he always came round to her way of thinking. 'You make tracks, sunshine, or Steve will be in before yer. And if our Ruthie isn't in here by the time I get the dinner on the table I'll have her guts for garters.'

'I heard that, Mam!' The young girl came in like a gust of wind. 'I didn't see me dad coming 'cos I was combing Aunt Vicky's hair and I had me back to the window.'

'Oh, eye, buggerlugs, yer must have had yer back turned for quite a while 'cos yer missed Jill and Tommy as well. And the Lord knows Tommy's too big for anyone to miss.'

'Well, I'm here now, and I'll thank yer to leave my guts alone 'cos I'm attached to them.'

Jill ruffled her hair. 'You're here, and I'm about to make meself scarce. Enjoy yer dinner and I'll see yer all tomorrow.'

All eyes were on the window as she passed, and they returned her wave. 'Now,' Molly said, 'you lot get yer hands washed while I put the dinner out. And don't take all day about it or the meal will be ruined.'

A little while later, when they were all seated, Jack said, 'I still can't get used to those two empty chairs. I feel as though there's something missing.'

'I'll ask Nellie and George to come in if ye're feeling lonely,' Molly said. 'Would that make yer feel better?'

'I'll have Nellie as a dessert, but not as the main course. She'd be fine for just after the meal when we can relax with a cigarette, a cup of tea and Nellie as the entertainment.'

'Now that's what I call having yer cake and eating it! Ye're not soft, are yer? If yer want to be entertained by Nellie yer'll have to throw a party or take a day off and come shopping with us.' Molly chuckled as in her mind's eye she pictured the comical expressions on her friend's face in the butcher's that morning. 'Oh, and a bit of advice. Learn a big word and throw it casually into the conversation. Something like inconsequential.'

Three mouths gaped before asking in unison, 'Yer what?'

'Well, yer can't expect Nellie to be funny all the time, can yer? Not without some help, anyway. Like today, me, Tony and Ellen all got a jolly good laugh out of her, just because of that one word.'

'That's some word, though, that is,' Tommy said, thinking he must have been to a different type of school from his mother. 'I can't even say it, never mind spell it or understand what it means.'

'Ah, well, yer see, son, a few years ago I indulged meself by buying a dictionary, and I've certainly had me money's worth out of it. All I've got to do is look for a big word and see what it means. I don't have to learn how to spell it 'cos neither Nellie nor you lot would know whether I'd got it right or not.'

'It's a wonder she hasn't twigged by now and bought herself a dictionary to get her own back. She must be slipping.'

'Is she heckerslike! Nellie's got more nous than the lot of us put together. Her one aim in life is to make people happy, to see them with smiles on their faces. And if she has to act daft to do that, then she couldn't care less what people think about her. And that's why she's me best mate and I love the bones of her.'

'I've been practising, Mam, with our Doreen.' Ruthie's chair was pushed back with such force it nearly toppled over. She righted it before standing in front of the grate and taking up her position. With her arms folded and hoisting an imaginary bosom, her eyes narrowed, she mimicked, 'Ah, that's real nice of yer, girl, I'm glad somebody loves me. That's apart from my feller, of course. I know he loves me 'cos he tells me every night how pretty I am, and what a lovely figure I've got. I've got a feeling he's having me on, though, 'cos I've noticed he only tells me when he's taken his glasses off, and the silly sod's as blind as a bat without them.' Once again the imaginary bosom was hitched. 'But it was real nice of yer to say I was yer best mate, girl, and that yer love the bones of me. Who knows? If yer play yer ruddy cards right, one day I might be able to say the same about you.'

Jack and Tommy thought it was hilarious, but Molly didn't know whether to laugh or reprimand her daughter for swearing. 'That was an improvement, sunshine, but I don't want a girl of your age to be coming out with swear words. It's not on, so remember that in future.'

'How can I impersonate yer best mate, and the woman yer love the bones of, when I'm not allowed to use her words?' Ruthie wagged her shoulders like Nellie and hitched up the bosom. 'Well, it's like this, yer see, girl, I'm not really swearing – I'm just expressing me feelings, like, if yer see what I mean.'

A smile was playing around Molly's mouth when she said, 'Ye're a little tinker, you are. Yer sisters were never as cheeky as you.'

Ruthie was determined to have the last word. 'Our Jill wasn't, but Doreen was. Yer were always saying what a cheeky article she was.'

'All right, that's enough now. Sit down and finish yer dinner so I can clear away and get the dishes done. I want to get out handy 'cos I'm going round to me ma's after I've seen Victoria.'

'I'll do the dishes, love,' Jack said. 'You get yerself ready.'

'I'll give a hand,' Tommy offered. 'And when yer've been over the road we can walk round to me nan's together.'

'No, don't wait for me, you go when ye're ready. I don't want to rush in and out of Victoria's and I'd be on pins if I thought I was holding yer back. I'll see yer at me ma's.'

Ruthie had gone across to her friend Bella's, and the washing-up had been done by the time Molly was ready to go out. Jack was sitting in his fireside chair enjoying a Woodbine, the unopened *Echo* on his knees. 'I won't be late, love.' She bent to kiss his cheek but he quickly turned his head so her lips landed on his. He grinned up at her and when she looked into those deep brown eyes her heart turned over. All these years and she was still madly in love with him. She glanced into the kitchen to make sure Tommy was still getting washed before pursing her lips and saying softly, 'I'll have another one of those, please.'

Jack was more than happy to oblige. 'Try and not be late back, love, 'cos I miss yer when ye're not here. And we haven't had an early night for a long time.'

'Yer never know, sunshine, tonight could just be your lucky night.'

Tommy couldn't help but overhear, and he kept wiping his face with the towel to give them a bit of time and privacy. He hoped when he married Rosie that they'd always love each other like his mam and dad did.

Phil opened the front door. 'Aunt Vicky has been watching that window like a hawk. She's looking forward to seeing you.'

Molly treated him like she would if he were her own son. He had no family of his own but she and Nellie, and Corker, had welcomed him into their families and Phil was happier now than he'd ever been. 'Give us a quick kiss then, son-in-law.'

'Ay, I heard that,' Doreen called. 'Get in here where I can see yer. It's coming to something when yer can't trust yer husband with yer own mother.'

Phil beamed. 'Well, ye're so alike, I thought it was you for a minute.'

'Yer thought it was me? Well, yer cheeky beggar! Me mam's twenty-five years older than me, if yer haven't noticed.'

'All right, so I was getting in practice for when you're her age. In twenty-five years yer'll look just like she does now. And that's a compliment to yer mam.'

'Oh, give over, the two of yer.' Molly made her way across the room to where Miss Victoria Clegg sat in her favourite chair with cushions at her side and back. She looked so frail Molly felt a catch in her throat. 'Are these two always like this, Victoria? Yer want to put yer foot down with them. Show them who's the boss.'

Victoria lifted her face for a kiss. 'There's never a cross word between them, Molly, they're as good as gold. I don't know what I'd do without them.'

Doreen and Phil were standing with their arms around each other's waist. 'I think it's the other way round, Aunt Vicky,' he said. 'Heaven alone knows where I'd be if yer hadn't taken pity on me on that day seven years ago. Yer gave me a home and treated me like a son, and now yer've allowed me to bring my lovely wife into that home. I must be the luckiest bloke alive to have two such beautiful women in my life.'

'Ay, don't you be leaving my mam out,' Doreen said. 'The very idea!'

'All right, love, I've got three beautiful women in me life.'

'For heaven's sake, will yer both knock it off! And sit down, yer make the place look untidy.' Molly sat facing the old lady. 'Have yer heard we're losing one of our old neighbours, Victoria? Nellie tells me that Mrs Harwick is leaving to go and live with her daughter in Maghull.'

'No, I hadn't heard. But then I never go out these days to see anyone. I used to be quite friendly with Vera Harwick, she came to live in the street about the same time as me.' There was a note of sadness in the soft voice. 'We were both in our prime then, and it doesn't seem like fifty years ago. It just shows how quickly time passes, and how fleeting life is.'

'That's why I say yer should make the best of it while yer can,' Molly said. 'Which is why I'm going to suggest that me and Nellie keep yer company tomorrow night, sunshine, while Phil and Doreen have a night out. At their age they should get out more. And me and Nellie will be made up to sit with you and have a good jangle.'

The pale, watery eyes smiled. 'I'd like that, Molly. And I'm glad ye're giving the young ones the chance to spend some time on their own, enjoying themselves.'

'What about you two lovebirds, does it meet with your approval?'

'Oh, yes, Mam, that would be great!' Doreen turned to smile into her husband's face. 'It will be like courting again.'

'I mentioned it to Jill, so her and Steve might make up a foursome. It's not definite, but I think Jill will be coming to see yer tonight to make arrangements. It'll be nice for the four of yer to get together again, won't it?'

'Yeah, I don't see much of our Jill so we've loads to catch up on.' Doreen gave Phil's hand a squeeze before leaving his side to kiss her mother. 'Thanks for thinking about us, Mam, ye're a cracker.'

'Ay, what's this about you teaching Ruthie to impersonate Nellie?' Molly decided she wanted to sit nearer to Victoria because the old lady's sight and hearing weren't too good. She pulled out one of the dining chairs and placed it as close as she could. 'She's really good at it. If yer closed yer eyes yer would think it was Nellie yer were listening to. She had Jack and Tommy in stitches.'

'Don't tell us, Mam, show us! No matter how good our Ruthie is, she'll never be as good as you. Go on, be a sport.'

'Well, I'll have a go but I probably won't remember it word for word. I'll do me best for yer, though.' The chair was scraped back and after squaring her shoulders and hoisting up her boson, Molly assumed the facial expressions of her best mate. Because she'd faced her across the table every day for so long, she knew exactly when the eyes would be narrowed, when the head would shake or nod and the contortions her mouth would go through. And because the frail old lady, who was loved by everyone, was shaking with laughter, Molly put everything she had into her performance. She felt well rewarded when a thin, veined hand reached out to grip hers.

'That was very funny, Molly, it could have been Nellie standing there except for the difference in size. It reminded me of all the times the two of you have made me laugh when I thought I had nothing to laugh about.'

'Then make sure yer have a good snooze tomorrow afternoon, sunshine, so ye're bright eyed and bushy tailed for when Nellie comes. Yer'll get plenty of laughs then, 'cos yer'll have the real genuine article here, and she never fails.'

'Perhaps we'd be better off staying in,' Phil said. 'We'd probably have more fun.'

'No, we're not staying in!' Doreen was quick to say. 'I haven't had the chance to have a really good talk with our Jill for ages, and we'll have loads to tell each other.'

'I know yer will, love, and I've got loads to tell Steve.' Phil's blush went unnoticed as he added, 'All about work, of course.'

'Oh, it's yerself at last, Auntie Molly.' When Rosie O'Grady hugged and kissed you, you knew you'd been hugged and kissed. She was enthusiastic in everything she did. 'Sure, we thought yer weren't coming.'

'I stayed a bit longer at Victoria's than I intended, sunshine, but I'm here now.'

'I'd just about given you up, Mam,' Tommy said. 'I thought yer'd have been here ages ago.'

'Good grief, I'm not that late, son.' Molly's eyes went to her ma and da who were sitting in their own fireside chairs either side of the grate. Although in their seventies now, they were a handsome couple. Her mother, Bridie, had kept her slim figure, and although there were wrinkles to be seen on her face, it still bore the signs of the beauty she'd once been. Her hair was snow white now and she wore it in a bun at the nape of her neck. 'Hello, Ma, have yer been behaving yerself?' Molly put a hand on each of the chair arms and leaned forward to give a kiss to the mother she adored. 'Not been giving me da a hard time, have yer?'

Bob Jackson chuckled as he tilted his head for a peck on the cheek. 'I'm waited on hand and foot, Molly, by yer ma and Rosie. I think they'd spoon feed me if I'd let them.'

'Yer look well on it, Da, I'll say that. As Rosie would say, it's a fine figure of a man yer are.' Molly's father was very precious to her and all the family because about seven years ago he'd had a heart attack and they'd thought they were going to lose him. But although he was never the same robust man after, he'd pulled through. Bridie had watched him like a hawk ever since. She fetched and carried for him, made sure he was never sitting in a draught and wouldn't even let him carry a shovelful of coal. They adored each other, their love as strong as it was on the day she first met him at the Pier Head. She'd left Ireland as a young girl to work in Liverpool and had found a job as skivvy in the home of a rich family. She was very lonely and missed her family so much she used to cry herself to sleep. Until the day she'd gone down to the Pier Head on the one Sunday she got off every four weeks. A gust of wind had blown her hat off and Bob had come to her rescue. He always said they'd fallen in love at first sight, and they'd married as soon as he had enough money to rent a house. That love had lasted as strong as ever for nearly fifty years.

'I'll put the kettle on,' Bridie said, 'and we'll have a cup of tea before we get down to the serious business of playing cards.'

'Yer'll do no such thing, Auntie Bridget.' Rosie jumped to her feet. 'It's meself that'll make the tea while you talk to Auntie Molly. And me ever-loving intended will give me a hand.'

A wide grin covered Tommy's face. 'Ye're a forward wench, Rosie O'Grady. Yer only want to get me on me own so yer can steal a kiss.'

'Sure, doesn't everyone know that!' Rosie O'Grady wasn't just pretty, she was a real Irish beauty. With an abundance of jet black curly hair, deep blue eyes and a perfect heart-shaped face that was never without a smile, she was a joy for the eye to behold. She too had come to Liverpool to find work but was lucky that a cousin of Bridie's had written to ask her if Rosie could stay with them until she found her feet. Everyone in the family agreed it was the best thing that could have happened for Bridie and Bob. Their lives were enriched by Rosie's presence, and her Irish brogue was like music to Bridie's ears, reminding her of her homeland. 'If it's too lazy yer are, Tommy Bennett, then I can just as easily kiss yer in front of everyone.'

His grin became even wider. 'She would, too, yer know, Mam.'

'I know that! And I'm surprised ye're still sitting there when yer could have had half a dozen kisses by now. Yer dad was never as slow as you.'

'Oh, no, he couldn't, Auntie Molly.' Rosie's curls bounced when she shook her head. 'As me mammy always says, if yer have too much of anything then yer soon lose interest.'

'I don't think yer mammy had kissing in mind, Rosie,' Bridie said. 'If yer truly love someone, then yer can never have too much of kissing, nor would yer ever lose interest. Sure, haven't I been kissing the same man for over fifty years, and it's meself that can never get enough.'

'Rosie, yer've got everyone at it now.' Tommy got to his feet, his huge frame dwarfing everything in the room. 'As yer ever-loving intended, it will give me the greatest pleasure to accompany yer to the kitchen and partake of yer ever-loving kisses.'

Rosie tossed her head. 'Yer've got as long as it takes for the kettle to boil. But because yer are me ever-loving intended, I'll put the gas on a very low light.' Her bonny smile encompassed them all. 'Now if yer'd all be so kind as to keep on talking, me and my beloved husband-to-be can do a spot of courting.'

Bridie shook her head when they heard the young couple giggling in the kitchen. 'Ah, what it is to be young, eh? Especially when yer meet the man of yer dreams.' Her eyes met her daughter's and she smiled that gentle smile. 'We seem to be a lucky family in that respect, sweetheart. First yer da and me, then you and Jack. And now Jill and Doreen are happily married to good men who adore them and will always care for them.' She jerked her head towards the kitchen. 'And if ever two people were meant for each other it's your son and Rosie O'Grady. It does me poor old heart good to see them, so it does.'

'Me and Jack feel the same. She's given us many laughs over the years has Rosie, and my son would have to go a long way to find someone with all the gifts she has.' Molly raised her voice to call,

'Are you two making a meal out of it? It'll be time to go home before the cards are even on the table.'

'Don't blame me, Mam, blame me ever-loving intended. I've told her to put me down but she doesn't take a blind bit of notice.'

'Rosie, take yer hands of my son right this minute! And put him down 'cos yer never know where he's been.'

They could hear Rosie's infectious giggle and it warmed their hearts. 'Sure, isn't it meself that's being manhandled, Auntie Molly? What chance does a slip of a girl like meself have against a big strapping lad like yer son?'

'If that tea isn't on the table in five minutes I'll come out and see to it meself,' Molly said licking her lips. 'Me throat's parched, and I'm sure yer mammy would have a saying to suit the occasion, Rosie O'Grady. Something along the lines of, "If yer see a man dying of thirst, give him water".'

'We can give yer a cup of water right away, Mam,' Tommy said, laughter in his voice. 'But tea will take a few minutes longer.'

Rosie came in carrying a laden tray. 'I wouldn't have been so long, Auntie Molly, but yer have a very masterful son. I'm putty in his hands, so I am.'

'I'll take over now, me darlin',' Bridie said. 'You and Tommy sit down while I pour and yer Auntie Molly passes the cups around.'

'I see yer've got custard creams, Ma.' Molly stood up ready to take the cups as they were filled. 'It's a good job Nellie's not here or she'd scoff the lot. They're her favourites. Mind you, the cheeky beggar told me the other day that at a push she'd make do with ginger snaps if there was nowt else.'

'She doesn't change, does she?' Even the thought of the woman brought a smile to Bob's face. She was a great favourite with the Jacksons, was Nellie. 'You always know where you are with her.'

Molly sat down carefully with her cup and saucer in her hand. You always got your tea in real china cups here, no thick muggen ones for Bridie. But Molly thought it was a mixed blessing. Oh, the tea tasted better out of china, no doubt about that, but the fear of dropping the cup and saucer took away some of the pleasure. 'Are you two still saving up hard?'

'Oh, yes, Auntie Molly, every penny we can spare goes away. And it's mounting up, isn't it, Tommy, me darlin'?'

'Yeah, it's mounting up.' The smile had left Tommy's face and he became serious. 'The trouble is, time is going faster than our savings are growing. I can't see us having enough by next summer to get

26

married. We would if we were having a little hole in the corner affair, but we're not! I want Rosie to have as good a wedding as anyone. One she can look back on as being the best day of her life. I don't mind for meself 'cos it'll be the best day of my life no matter what sort of a wedding we have. But I want to do it in style, with all the trimmings, for Rosie. Especially as her mam and dad are coming over for it. I want them to be really proud of her.'

Tommy seldom showed his serious side, and his words brought silence for a few seconds. Then Molly said, 'Yer'll make it, son, I know yer will. You and Rosie will have the best send-off anyone's ever seen. And her parents will be proud of both of yer. You mark my words, son, it'll all come right in the end.' Mentally she told herself it would come right if it was the last thing she did. She wouldn't tell them now and build their hopes up, but she'd make sure she and Jack had enough saved to pay for the reception and the fare for Rosie's mam and dad to come from Ireland.

No one noticed the look exchanged between Bridie and Bob. They too were putting a bit by each week to help the grandson they adored and the girl who'd found her way into their hearts.

Chapter 3

It was seven o'clock the following night when a pane of glass rattled in the window frame to herald the arrival of Nellie. 'What time d'yer call this?' Molly asked as she opened the door to her neighbour. 'I said half-past seven!'

'Better to be early than late, girl!' Nellie brushed past and waddled to the living room. 'I could have turned up late and missed a piece of world-shattering news.'

Jack looked up from his paper and chuckled. 'Oh, aye, Nellie, and what would yer call world-shattering news?'

Nellie gave a quick glance into the kitchen to make sure neither of the children was there before saying, 'You could be in the family way again.'

'That certainly would be world-shattering news, Nellie, especially to me. After all, our Ruthie is thirteen now.'

'That don't make no ruddy difference 'cos there was seven years between her and Tommy.' She pulled a chair from the table and carefully lowered herself down, all eighteen stone of her. 'It wouldn't surprise me what hanky-panky you and Molly get up to in yer bedroom. She's a dark horse is yer wife, never says nothing. But I can always tell by the smile she's got on her face some mornings. She thinks I'm thick,' Nellie tapped the side of her forehead, 'but I'm all there up here.'

Molly, still wearing a pinny as she leaned back against the sideboard with her arms folded, tapped her head. 'If ye're all there up here, how come ye're half an hour early? Yer might have known I wouldn't be ready 'cos we're not due over the road until half-past.'

'Well, it's like this, yer see, girl, our Lily and Paul were upstairs getting ready to go out, and my feller was asleep in the chair. Now that sounds very nice and homely, doesn't it? A scene of domestic bliss. And it would be if my feller didn't snore so loud. Honest to God, he'd be a blessing to the Salvation Army. They wouldn't need no feller on the drums or trumpeters if they had George, he can make all those sounds with his nose and mouth. It drives yer crazy just sitting listening to him.'

'One of these days I'm going to tell your feller what yer say about him behind his back. I bet yer making it up and he doesn't snore at all,' Molly said. 'Anyway, Mrs Talk-a-Bit, I'm surprised he can get to sleep with you talking fifteen to the dozen and not even stopping for breath.'

'You're a fine one to talk, girl, ye're not exactly a shrinking violet yerself. Sometimes I can't get a word in edgeways with yer.' Nellie leaned back in the chair and ignored the wood creaking in protest. 'I'll have yer know that at one time I was so shy and quiet I seriously thought of entering a monastery.'

Even as the words were leaving her mouth, Molly knew she was walking into a trap. 'Yer couldn't have gone to a monastery, soft girl, 'cos only men go in there.'

'I know, I know! I told yer I wasn't daft, didn't I?' Nellie shuffled her bottom and the chair groaned and creaked ominously. 'Anyway, go and get yerself changed instead of standing there yapping.'

'Will you sit still on that ruddy chair, sunshine, 'cos yer've got me heart in me mouth. And anyway, I'm not getting changed just to go over the road.'

'Well, that's nice I must say!' Nellie spread her hands. 'Did yer hear that, Jack? Me and Victoria are not worth getting changed for!'

'I'm keeping out of it, Nellie,' Jack said, enjoying every minute of the exchange. His wife and her best mate went through something like this a couple of times a day, and had done for the last twenty years. And never once had they repeated themselves. 'I'm just an innocent bystander so forget I'm here.'

'I don't know why ye're getting on yer high horse 'cos I'm not getting changed,' Molly said. 'You haven't got changed.'

'That's where ye're wrong, girl, 'cos I have got changed.'

'You have not! Yer had that dress on this morning and this afternoon so don't be trying to kid me.'

'I have got changed, clever clogs. I changed me knickers.'

The only one who didn't see the joke and wasn't laughing was the chair. With Nellie shaking with mirth, the seat, the back and the four legs were really under pressure. They didn't think they could hold out much longer, but Molly came to their aid. She grabbed her mate's arms, pulled her up and led her over to the couch. Plonking her down, she said, 'Now we can all breathe easier, sunshine. You sit there like a good little girl while I swill me face and comb me hair. And no, I am not changing me knickers. Not for you or anyone else.'

'I'll tell Victoria yer've got dirty knickers on, girl, and she won't like that.'

'Tell who yer like, I don't care. Knock next door if yer want, it won't bother me.'

'Nah, she's a jangler that one. It would be all over the street in no time if I told her. And anyway, I don't want no one to know my best mate wears dirty knickers. They say yer can judge a person by the friends they keep, which means they'd think I was a dirty bugger as well.'

'If you use the word knickers one more time, sunshine, so help me I'll throttle yer. Now you just sit there nice and quiet and behave yerself.'

'Are yer going upstairs, girl?'

'No, I'm not! I'm swilling me face in the kitchen sink, why?'

'I was thinking if yer were going upstairs, instead of me behaving meself, I'd be in with a chance of misbehaving with your feller. I'd like to know if he could put a smile on me face like the one what you have on yours every Monday morning.'

'Nellie McDonough, the older yer get, the worse yer get! Honest, I don't know where to put me face sometimes, the things yer come out with.'

'Right this minute, girl, I suggest yer put yer face under the tap and get yerself ready. We'll be late the way ye're going on,' Nellie muttered disdainfully under her breath. 'I'm surprised she wasn't late for her own bloody wedding! I know one thing, if she's late for her own funeral I'm not going to stand around waiting, not if it's raining. She can bury herself when she turns up.'

'This is a very pleasant conversation, I must say! But what makes yer think I'll be going first, sunshine?'

'Well, yer've got a dicky heart, haven't yer, girl? Now I'd be the last one in the world to want to worry yer, but, well, yer never know the minute with a dodgy ticker.'

'There's nothing wrong with my heart at the moment, Nellie McDonough, but that could all change if I exert meself too much. And putting my hands around your neck and strangling yer might just do the trick.'

Nellie grinned. 'In that case we'd both go together, wouldn't we, girl? And I'd get me wings and harp before you, 'cos Saint Peter wouldn't take kindly to you, not when he heard yer choked me.'

Molly was chuckling as she made her way to the kitchen. 'That's the only thing that's stopping me, sunshine.'

Molly stood on Miss Clegg's step and watched as her two daughters and their new husbands walked down the street in a line, arms linked and faces beaming. She could hear their laughter and thought how lucky she and Jack were that the girls had fallen for boys they got on so well with. It would have broken their hearts if they'd brought someone like Lily McDonough's old boyfriend into their lives. He was a real rotter, was Len Lofthouse, and Molly could understand Nellie's worry. But that was in the past and Lily never even mentioned his name now, thank goodness.

Molly was closing the door when she heard Nellie's voice. She was telling Victoria about the knickers incident, and although she was supposed to be whispering she was speaking loud enough for Molly to hear. So she stood perfectly still and cocked an ear.

'Don't let on I've said anything, Victoria, and pretend to be shocked, like.'

You crafty article, Molly thought. Well, I'll have to put you in your place. So she made a noise when she closed the door to warn them she was on her way in. 'It's lovely to see the young ones going out together again, they looked like courting couples.'

When Molly stood by the table, Victoria said, 'Sit yerself down, Molly, and take the weight off yer feet.'

This was what Nellie was waiting for, but Molly put a spoke in her wheel by answering before her mate could get the words out, 'Have yer got an old cloth I can put over the seat, Victoria? Yer see, I haven't got no knickers on.'

Nellie gaped, and her chins got ready to go their separate ways. 'Yer've got no knickers on? Well, yer dirty bugger! What did yer take them off for?'

'Because you said yer were going to tell everyone I had dirty knickers on. I wasn't going to give yer the chance to do that so I took them off. They're in steep now, in the dolly tub.'

'I don't believe yer,' Nellie said. 'Show me!'

'Show yer! The only way I can show yer is for yer to go over to our house and look in the dolly tub. Go on, me and Victoria don't mind yer leaving us for five minutes.'

'Sod off, Molly Bennett! I meant prove to me that ye're knickerless. I won't believe yer until I see yer bare backside.'

'Yer know what you can do, don't yer, sunshine? Yer can go and take a long running jump into a lake. Preferably a deep one.'

Nellie could hear Victoria laughing and knew it was time to give in. 'She's a proper sneak, Victoria, she was listening outside. It's a shame, really, 'cos we could have had a good laugh.'

'Yes, at my expense, sunshine! Well, yer'll have to think of something else.'

'I'm trying to, girl, I really am. Me head is going round and round trying to come up with something. In the meantime, can I just say yer wouldn't get rid of me if I jumped in a lake, 'cos I wouldn't drown, I'd float on top until someone came to me rescue.' Nellie tried to snap her fingers but it didn't work. Three times she tried, but they just wouldn't click. Holding the offending finger and thumb close to her face, she growled, 'You two are not a ha'porth of good and if I didn't need yer for using me knife and fork I'd consider giving yer away.'

'I've always thought yer were tuppence short of a shilling, sunshine, but I never thought yer were that far gone yer'd end up talking to yer fingers.'

'Ah, well, yer see, girl, I was buying meself time while I thought of something to make yer laugh.' Nellie turned a beaming face to Victoria. 'My mate Molly Bennett would fall for the cat. She believed me when I said I'd changed me knickers. Now just watch her face when I tell her I didn't.'

'Yer didn't fool me for a second,' Molly said. 'It's only the other week yer told me that yer had to lie on the bed with yer legs in the air before yer could get them on. And I knew yer wouldn't go through that performance just to come over here. So now we've got that out of the way, I'll put the kettle on, shall I, Victoria?'

'Yes, please, Molly. And Doreen's left a plate of biscuits for us. They're in the pantry.'

'Did she say how many?' Nellie asked. 'I wouldn't trust my mate not to pinch a couple while she's waiting for the kettle to boil.'

'Every dog knows its own tricks best, sunshine. Now you keep Victoria amused while I see to a cuppa.' When the tray was set, Molly leaned back against the sink waiting for the kettle to boil. And while she waited, she listened.

'I believe Vera Harwick's leaving, Nellie? Molly told me yesterday.'

'Yeah, she's going to live in Maghull with her daughter. There's a family moving into her house when she moves out. Mam, Dad and two grown-up children. Their name's Mowbray, so Mr Henry told me.'

Molly moved away from the sink and popped her head around the

33

kitchen door. 'You didn't tell me all that, Nellie McDonough, yer just said the house was spoken for. How come?'

'I can't remember to tell yer everything, girl! Yer should ask if yer want to know more.'

'Yer usually tell me everything without me having to ask! I spend most of me time trying to shut yer up! Anyway, how am I to know that yer know more than ye're telling me? I'm not a ruddy mind-reader.'

'Keep yer hair on, girl, there's no need to raise yer voice to me. It's not my fault if ye're not nosy enough to want to know everyone's business. Yer should keep yer ear to the ground, like me, then anything I missed, you'd pick up and between us we'd know everything what goes on in the street.'

'I don't want to know everything what goes on in the street! I'm only interested in me own family and me friends, the rest I couldn't care less about.'

'In that case yer may as well go back and make that tea. Yer won't be interested in what I'm going to tell Victoria about Mrs Harwick selling some of her furniture because it won't all fit in her daughter's house.'

Molly sat down on the arm of the couch. 'Is she? Ah, I bet she'll be sad to do that 'cos she takes a pride in her furniture.'

Nellie winked at Victoria before turning with a look of surprise on her face. 'Oh, are yer still here, girl? I thought yer were making the tea seeing as ye're not interested.'

'So help me I'll clock yer one if ye're making all this up, Nellie McDonough. And I wouldn't put it past yer, either!'

'Now why would I make it up, girl? I only make things up to give people a laugh and there's nothing funny in an old lady selling her furniture. At least, I don't think so.'

'But why didn't yer tell me? I mean, there might be something there our Jill and Steve would like! Yer know they haven't got a stick of furniture to their name.'

'I know that, girl. After all, Steve is me son. And that's why I asked Mrs Harwick to let us know when she makes up her mind what is for sale.'

Molly flew off her perch and wrapped her arms around her best mate. 'I take everything back that I've said about yer, sunshine, 'cos ye're a little smasher.' Then she stood back and put a frown on her face. 'How come I'm not allowed to go to the shops without yer, yet you can go sneaking around without me?'

Nellie tapped her nose. 'Well, it's like this, yer see, girl, if I had you with me yer'd hamper me investigations. Yer'd get embarrassed, go all red in the face and tell me to mind me own business. I'd never hear any gossip if I took yer everywhere with me.'

Molly looked at the old lady who was taking it all in and really enjoying herself. 'She's past the post, isn't she, Victoria? I don't know what I'm going to do with her.'

'My old ma used to say if yer want a job doing, do it yerself. And she was right, too! So I'm going to make the ruddy tea meself.' Nellie managed to push herself off the chair on the third attempt. When she stood up she squared her shoulders, pushing her bosom forward and putting a great strain on the seams of her dress. The two front buttons were trying valiantly not to pop. Taking a few seconds to compose herself and get the words sorted in her mind, she put on her posh voice. 'When we've finally got a cup in our hands, with a biscuit in the saucer, we can discuss the situation further. Until then, I would be grateful if you'd keep those gobs of yours shut.' With a shake of her head and her chins swaying, she made her exit.

'She's very genteel, my mate, isn't she, sunshine?' Molly sat down close to the old lady and covered her hand with her own. 'I've got to say yer look very well, Victoria, with yer hair all waved and that nice blue blouse you're wearing. Yer put me and Nellie to shame.'

'I've got your daughter to thank for that, sweetheart, she really looks after me and won't let me have a hair out of place. I am so lucky having her and Phil in my life. I used to worry about growing old and being alone, but both of them wait on me hand and foot. And they do it in such a way I don't feel like I'm a burden to them.'

'Ye're not a burden, sunshine. Both of them love the bones of yer. And I've got to say our Doreen's turned out to be a daughter to be proud of.'

At that precise moment, Doreen was telling the two men to walk on ahead because she had something to tell Jill. 'Go on, ye're not missing anything, it's just girl talk.'

After a quick glance at his wife, Phil took Steve's arm. 'Come on, let's leave them to it and we'll indulge in men's talk. How's work going?'

Doreen waited until they were out of earshot before giving her sister a nervous smile. 'I'm going to go all red and embarrassed now, sis, but I want yer to know and the only way is to blurt it out – I'm expecting a baby.'

Jill came to an abrupt halt, her eyes wide with surprise. 'Ye're not, are yer?'

'Well, I haven't been to the doctor's yet, but I missed last month's period and I've missed this months' too. And I know I am 'cos I feel different. Me and Phil are over the moon because it's what we wanted.'

'You haven't given yerself much time, have yer?'

'We could have waited, but we decided to have one quickly, for Aunt Vicky's sake. She's very old, Jill, and we wanted her to see our baby before anything happens to her. We haven't told her yet, but she'll be so happy.'

'Have yer told me mam and dad?'

'No, and I don't want you to, either. I'll go to the doctor's in a few weeks and if he confirms it, I'll tell everyone then. But for now I'd like yer to keep it under yer hat. Phil will be telling Steve as I'm telling you, that's what we planned, but I want yer to ask him not to mention it to anyone. Will yer do that for us, sis?'

'Of course I will.' Jill was beginning to feel excited. It would be lovely having a baby in the family. 'I can just see me mam's face, she'll be so happy to be a grandma. And me dad, of course, he'll be over the moon being a granda.'

'What about you, Jill, are yer happy for us?'

'Happy and jealous at the same time. Me and Steve will have to wait until we get a place of our own, but I don't mind 'cos we're lucky that Mrs Corkhill took us in as lodgers. Not that we feel like lodgers, she's given us the run of the house and we're really at home there.'

Doreen grinned into her sister's face and put on a baby voice. 'Hello, Auntie Jill.'

The two burst out laughing and flung their arms around each other. 'We'll be old married women with a tribe of kids before we know it.'

'Ay, you speak for yerself,' Jill said. 'I'm never going to be an old married woman. I'm going to take after me mam, she's never grown old. She keeps herself young, and so does me dad. That's how they've kept the flame of love burning all these years, and that's how me and Steve are going to be.'

The boys walked back towards them, both with self-conscious smiles and faces tinged pink with embarrassment. After all the couples had only been married two and a half months and what went on in their bedrooms was not usually talked about. But this was different, it was something that should be celebrated.

They linked arms and as they neared the picture house, Steve said,

'This is my treat tonight. The best seats in the front stalls and a box of chocolates. It's not breaking eggs with a big stick, I know, but just a little way of saying that me and Jill are very happy for yer.'

When Doreen tilted her head to gaze into Phil's face she knew exactly how her mother and father felt when they exchanged that special look which told of the great love they had for each other. A love that didn't need words. 'We'll do the same for them when their turn comes, won't we, love?' Then she giggled. 'That's if we can get someone to babysit.'

A few days later, when Nellie arrived for her morning cuppa and a chat, she had an air of excitement about her. 'Good morning, girl! I see yer've still got yer working clothes on. Yer should have the good manners to look respectable when yer know I'm coming.'

Molly closed the front door then looked down at herself. She was wearing her working clothes, but that was because she hadn't finished the housework yet. 'What's got into you, sunshine? D'yer expect me to get changed just to have a cuppa with yer, and then change back to finish me work off? You know what yer can do, Nellie McDonough, yer can take a running jump.'

'Oh, well, if that's the way yer feel about it, girl, I won't bother telling yer me news.' A chair was pulled from under the table and Nellie plonked herself down. 'It's coming to something when me best mate tells me to sod off.'

'I never did tell yer to sod off! Anyway, what's got into yer this morning? Did yer come with the intention of starting a fight?' Then Molly narrowed her eyes as she took in her friend's combed hair and, if she wasn't mistaken, there was even a trace of lipstick. 'What are you all got up for?' She took a closer look. 'No tidemark, hair neat and a spot of Lily's lipstick. What are yer up to?'

'Nah, yer wouldn't be interested, girl.' Nellie was having great difficulty in keeping her face straight. 'Just make me the usual cuppa and then I'll go about me business. And yer needn't bother about a biscuit, I'll get one where I'm going.'

Molly took a deep breath, thinking, She's dying for me to ask where she's going, but I'm not going to. 'I'll stick the kettle on.' She lit the gas under the kettle and watched the flames flicker for a while as she stuck to her resolution. She would not ask her mate what was going on, she was blowed if she would. But as the seconds ticked by and there wasn't a peep out of Nellie, Molly couldn't control herself any longer. Popping her head around the living-room door, she asked, as casually as she could muster, 'Where are yer off to, then?'

Nellie raised her eyebrows in a condescending manner. 'I thought I'd take Mrs Harwick up on her offer to allow me to view the furniture she'll be selling.' She curled a hand and gazed at her nails as though she'd just had them manicured. Each finger was lifted and closely inspected by eyes that were dancing with devilment. Then, when she raised her head, nail inspection over, she feigned surprise at seeing Molly. 'Oh, are you still there?' The expression on her face as she slowly pronounced each word was comical. 'I thought you were making me a cup of tea before sending me about my business?'

'If this is one of yer little jokes, Nellie McDonough, so help me I'll swing for yer. Now I want the truth so come on, spit it out.'

Spreading her hands with a look of innocence on her face, Nellie said, 'So I'm a liar now, am I? Well, it's nice to know what yer really think about me.' She put her palms flat on the table as though to push herself up. 'I won't bother with the tea, thank you very much. It would be like supping with the devil.'

'You ain't going anywhere, sunshine, so don't be pretending. And if yer push that chair back and the legs come off, I'll be suggesting yer ask Mrs Harwick to sell yer one of hers to make up for it.'

Nellie's lips clamped together. 'D'yer know what, girl? I felt like a little ray of sunshine when I left the house. So happy, in fact, I wouldn't have called the King me aunt. I only had to pass two doors to get here, and in that short space of time I've been made to feel as miserable as bloody sin. And it's all your fault. I should have known when yer opened the door and I saw yer had a face on yer like a wet fish that I'd be better off turning around and going back home.'

'Tut, tut, tut. You poor little thing, so badly done to! But what can yer expect when yer come here hoping I'll be dressed to the nines at this hour of the morning? How was I to know about Mrs Harwick?' Molly put both hands on the table and pressed her face as close to her friend's as she could. 'Anyway, when did yer see the old lady? Yer didn't go out visiting after yer left here yesterday, did yer?'

When Nellie shook her head her chins went haywire. 'Now yer know I wouldn't go visiting without you, girl! I wouldn't do a thing like that, not to me best mate.'

'Then how did yer see her?'

'Well, this is how it happened, girl. George reminded me that there were only a few matches left in the box so I said I'd slip up to the corner shop to make sure we'd have enough for the morning. Anyway,

Mrs Harwick was standing on her step, waving her daughter off, so I stopped to talk to her. Just being friendly, like, girl, same as anyone would be. And that's when she told me that the bedroom she'd be having in Maghull was quite big so she was taking her own bedroom suite. There is furniture in the other bedroom, which is what she asked me if we'd like to have a look at before anyone else has the chance.' Nellie took a deep breath and blew it out slowly. 'That's how it happened so are yer satisfied now, nosy poke?'

'Of course I am, sunshine, I never doubted yer for a minute. But let me make the tea and then we can talk.' Molly was back in minutes with two cups of tea and two custard creams. 'They're the last of the biscuits until I can scrounge some more off Maisie in the shop.' She put them on the table and then sat facing her friend. 'I had a word with our Jill about the furniture and her and Steve are not keen on buying second-hand furniture. They said they wouldn't like to sleep in a bed that someone else had slept in.'

'Oh, it's a pity about them, then! Yer'd think they'd be glad of the opportunity to get some good, solid furniture. And anyway, they're sleeping in a bed now that Corker used to sleep in! So what's the difference?'

'Well, for a start, one difference is that the bed they're in now isn't a permanent thing. When they get a place of their own they want everything new. And the other difference, sunshine, and it's a big one, is that you and me are not Jill and Steve. It's for them to say what they want, not us.'

'Yeah, ye're right, girl, as usual.' Nellie looked disappointed. She'd been looking forward to rooting in Mrs Harwick's house. Not that she was nosy, like, it was purely out of interest. 'We can still have a look, can't we? Yer never know, we might see something we like for ourselves.' She turned her head so Molly couldn't see the laughter lurking behind her eyes. 'Didn't Victoria say she had a beautiful dining-room suite? That's something you could do with, girl, 'cos this one's on its last legs.'

Molly gasped. 'You cheeky beggar! This dining suite isn't very old!'

'Yes, it is, girl, I remember yer getting it when Jack came up on the pools that time!'

'That's not so long ago! Six or seven years at the most, and a good suite should last about twenty years if it's well cared for. And I'll have yer know this suite has been very well cared for.' It was Molly's turn to have a twinkle in her eye now. 'It's all in good nick except for the chairs what have had a battering over the years. They'll be the first things to give out.'

Nellie managed to flare her nostrils and grind her teeth before saying, 'Are yer hinsinuating that I'm to blame for yer flaming chairs going wonky?'

'The chairs can answer that for themselves, sunshine. Every morning when yer knock, they creak and groan. I'm sure if they could they'd hide until yer'd gone.'

'Ho, ho, ho, very funny. I've a good mind to bring one of me own chairs with me when I come. Yer never hear them complaining when I sit on them. In fact they're very fond of my backside.'

'They've told yer that, have they?'

'Yeah, every time I sit down they sing a song of welcome.'

'I've never heard of a chair singing, sunshine, what does it sound like?'

Nellie's chubby cheeks creased with mirth, and her shaking tummy had the table moving up and down. 'They haven't got good voices, girl, I'll grant yer that. It's more like creaking and groaning, but I know they're saying hello to me backside.'

The two mates looked across the table at each other and the room rang with laughter.

'Come in, ladies.' Vera Harwick held the door wide. She was a frail woman in her late-eighties, but she could teach the younger generation a thing or two about keeping a nice house. She might be slower in her movements now but she still stuck to the daily routine she'd started when she first came to this house as a new bride. 'I've had the kettle on a low light waiting for yer. Sit yerselves down and I'll wet the tea.'

Not for the world would Molly or Nellie say they'd just had two cups of tea because they knew the old lady would be disappointed. But as soon as she disappeared into the kitchen, Nellie mouthed, 'I'll be running to the lavvy all day.'

'Shush!' Molly shot her a warning look before rolling her eyes to the ceiling. 'Do us a favour and behave yerself for once. I know it'll be hard, but please try, at least until we're out of this house. Otherwise yer'll put me to shame.'

'It's a pity about you, now! Yer needn't be going all lah-de-dah on me 'cos it won't work, I've known yer too long.' Nellie shuffled to the edge of the chair and pushed herself up. Then she glared at Molly before waddling out to the kitchen. 'I was just saying to my mate that there's nothing I hate more than a snob. What do you think, Vera?'

'Oh, I couldn't agree more, Nellie! I can't stand folk that think they're a cut above the rest when we all know damn' well they're no better than anyone else.'

'Them's my sentiments entirely, Vera.' Nellie's nod was one of satisfaction as she sauntered back to the living-room door, allowing her chins to enjoy a nice slow waltz. 'Did yer hear that, girl? It's a pity that everyone isn't as down to earth.'

'Take no notice of her, Mrs Harwick,' Molly called. 'She's having her funny half-hour and 'cos there's no one else around she picks on me, soft girl. But I don't mind, me shoulders are strong enough to take it. Besides, I'm beginning to feel a bit sorry for her 'cos I think she's going funny in her old age.'

'If she's in her old age, Molly, then it's God help me!' Vera put the teapot on the wooden tray with the cups and saucers, sugar bowl and milk jug. 'You can carry that in for me, Nellie, while I see if I've got any biscuits. And yer'll have to excuse the old tray and the even older crockery, all me best stuff has gone to our Val's. Every time she comes she takes something back with her so it's less for me to worry about a week tomorrow.'

'We'll all miss yer, sunshine, yer know that. I hope yer don't leave without saying goodbye to Miss Clegg 'cos she'd be upset.'

'Vicky is one person I won't forget to say goodbye to. We've been friends for a long time, must be over forty years. I'm glad she's not on her own now or I'd worry meself to death about leaving her.'

'She's well looked after, Vera, so yer can put yer mind at rest. And yer'll be able to say farewell to Corker, he's due home tomorrow.' Molly held out her hand for the cup and saucer Nellie was passing over. 'We'll drink this tea, then yer can show us what furniture yer want to sell. Not that we could buy it even if we wanted to 'cos we've both got a house full. Still, there's no harm in looking, is there?'

'Ye're under no obligation, Molly, so don't be worrying.'

'If our Jill and Steve had a house, I know they'd ask about this dining-room suite 'cos it's beautiful. Better than that ruddy Utility rubbish they're selling now.'

'I've already got a buyer for this suite, Molly. A friend of our Val's jumped at it. So there's really only the back bedroom to clear now.'

'You two go up first, I'm not as agile as I used to be.' Vera Harwick stood to one side to let them pass. 'Yer know where the back bedroom is, in the same place as yours.'

Nellie's impish grin appeared. 'Shall I give yer a piggy-back, Vera?'

41

'Yer'll do no such thing!' Molly said. 'Ye're walking behind me, sunshine, so that if I fall I'll have something soft to land on.'

Nellie feigned horror. 'Did yer hear that, Vera? And she's supposed to be me best mate.'

'Stop gabbing and let's get on with it.' Molly began to mount the steep, shallow stairs. She could hear her friend puffing and panting behind her, and when she got to the top she turned round and held out a hand. 'Grab hold of it, sunshine, and I'll pull yer up.'

Nellie's face was red with exertion, but she still managed a smile. 'Yer see, yer do love me, don't yer, girl?'

Molly looked with affection at the little woman who had stood by her side through thick and thin, during the good times and the bad. And she couldn't resist cupping the chubby face and planting a kiss on each cheek. 'I love every inch of yer, sunshine, bones, flesh and hair. I wouldn't part with yer for a big clock.'

Nellie was well pleased. She turned to ask Vera if she'd heard what her mate said, and found the old lady standing on the next to top stair waiting for them to make room for her on the tiny landing. 'Ah, look, we've left yer stuck there, and in yer own house, too!'

'Well, if we move, she won't be stuck, will she?' Molly pulled on her friend's arm. 'Into the back bedroom with yer.'

'Ooh, ay, look at that, girl!' Nellie walked over to a straight-backed dining chair. Only it was nicer than any dining chair she'd ever seen. It was a carver, with polished arms and the seat covered in rose-coloured velvet. 'Ay, this is the gear, girl, look at it. Wouldn't it be nice in your room standing by the sideboard?' Her body began to shake with laughter. 'Yer could keep it just for when I come and I'd look like the Queen of the May sat in it.'

But Molly wasn't paying any attention, she was too taken up with a tallboy standing in front of the window. It was so highly polished you could see your face in it and there wasn't a mark on it. There were three deep drawers and the top lifted up to reveal a shallow drawer where small things like socks and hankies could be kept. 'This is beautiful. Nellie, come and have a look. It's in perfect condition and a lovely piece of furniture.'

Nellie ambled across. 'Yeah, ye're right, girl, it is beautiful. I bet Jill and Steve would be made up with that.'

'If they didn't want it, I'd keep it for meself.' Molly looked to where Vera was standing. 'How much are yer asking for this, sunshine?'

'I don't know, Molly, I'm not very good at this. What do you think?'

'It's up to you to say, love, you're the one what's selling. There's no need to be embarrassed, we're all friends here and we're not likely to fall out over it.'

'Would five shillings be all right, or is that too much?'

'It's not enough, sunshine, yer'd be diddling yerself. How about seven and six?'

'Oh, that's ample, Molly, I'd be very happy with that.'

'Right, the deed is done. But I'll have to bring yer the money up later 'cos I've only got enough on me to do me shopping. Don't let anyone see it in the meantime, though, 'cos I definitely want it.'

Vera was very pleased with herself. Her daughter had told her to ask for seven and six because the tallboy was worth that, but she didn't have the nerve. 'It's yours, Molly, so don't worry about giving me the money today.'

Molly shook her head. 'No, I'll bring it up this afternoon.' She grinned at Nellie. 'Come on, sunshine, let's get to the shops.'

Nellie's face was set. 'Ay, just hang about, girl! What about my chair?'

'I'm not buying a chair to put in my house just for you to sit on! Yer must think I want me bumps feeling!'

'And what happens if I break one of yours? Yer'd be a chair short then.'

'I don't believe I'm hearing this!' Molly was beginning to see the funny side but wasn't going to let her mate see. 'The obvious answer is to say yer better hadn't break one of my chairs or I'll have yer guts for garters.'

'But just say I did, then yer must see that yer wouldn't have enough chairs for all the family to sit on. Anyone with half an eye could see that.'

Molly's mind was working overtime. It was a lovely chair, no doubt about that. And she was sure Jill would jump at the tallboy, which meant she wouldn't have to find the money for that. But there was Tommy's wedding to think of, she was trying to save for that. Then she thought, Oh, blow, what the hell? 'How much for the chair, Vera?'

'Say three bob, Molly, would that be all right?'

'That would be fine, Vera, I'll take it.' And when Molly saw the smile on Nellie's face she decided it was well worth three bob. 'Come on, sunshine, let's be on our way to the shops before they close for dinner.'

'Anything you say, girl!' Nellie cast her eyes to the chair. 'D'yer know, I've got a feeling that chair and my backside are going to get on very well.'

Chapter 4

Jill was admiring the tallboy when Jack and Tommy came in from work. Her father raised his brows. 'Oh, aye, where did that come from?'

'I bought it off Vera Harwick.' Molly was feeling good inside because her daughter had fallen for the piece of furniture right away. 'I took a chance on Jill liking it, 'cos it was a bargain if ever there was one. But if she doesn't want it I'll keep it for meself.'

'No, I'll be glad of it, Mam. I think it's lovely and we could do with a few extra drawers. I'll bring the money down later.'

Jack hung his cap on the hook behind the door before walking around the tallboy and nodding his agreement. 'It's in very good nick, the old lady's looked after it well. How much did she ask for it?'

'Seven and six, and well worth it.' Molly had been standing in front of the chair and she now moved away. How she kept her face straight she'd never know. 'Oh, and the chair was three bob.'

'Oh, that's nice,' Tommy said, moving closer and rubbing a hand over one of the arms. 'It's a good chair, this, must have cost a few bob when it was new. Is this for Jill as well?'

Molly had to bite on the inside of her mouth to keep the laughter back. 'No, that's for Nellie.'

Jack pushed forward for a better view. 'Yeah, it's a good chair, that. D'yer want me to take it to Nellie's for yer?' Then he frowned. 'How did yer get them here in the first place?'

'Me and me mate laid in ambush for Ken Weston.' Molly laughed at the memory. 'We waited for him coming home from his six to two shift, and he was quite happy to give me a hand getting them down Vera's stairs and into here. Though if the truth be told it was the other way around. I gave him a hand, and Ken did all the hard work. I wouldn't attempt it with Nellie, although she did offer, 'cos she'd have dropped the ruddy things.'

'Why didn't yer wait for me and Tommy?' Jack asked. 'We'd have done it for yer, save yer asking Ken.'

'Well, yer know I'm not blessed with patience. I wanted the tallboy here for when Jill came, to see what she thought of it. But yer can carry it up to Mrs Corkhill's later, when yer've had yer dinner. Come to think of it, it'll be better to wait until it's dark, save filling the neighbours' mouths.'

'I'll get Steve to come down and help me dad to carry it,' Jill said. 'Tommy will be wanting to go out before it's dark, I imagine.'

'You imagine right.' Her brother grinned. 'My dearly beloved intended will have the police out if I'm not there before it gets dark. But I can drop the chair off at Auntie Nellie's on me way, I've got to pass the door.'

'Ah, well, yer see, the chair isn't going to Nellie's, it's staying here.' Molly looked at each of the faces that she loved so dearly. 'Sit down and I'll give yer a good laugh. My mate was at her very best today and I still can't believe it's happened.' Molly remained standing and took on the pose of her best friend. She went through the whole rigmarole of the chair, with eyes, mouth and bosom playing the part of Nellie. When she was playing herself, she moved away, then once again reverted to the little woman who was the cause of the loud guffaws and high-pitched laughter coming from her audience.

Jack wiped the tears from his eyes. 'So that chair is for the sole use of Nellie?'

'She only mentioned her backside.' Molly pressed at the stitch in her side. 'Oh, dear, oh, dear, I've never laughed so much in all me life. And yer know her feet don't touch the floor when she sits in one of these chairs? Well, she stands no chance with the new one 'cos it's about three inches higher! She'll need a stepladder to get on it!'

'She's a cracker is Auntie Nellie,' Tommy said. 'I've never known anyone as funny.'

'I think you're just as funny, Mam, you and Auntie Nellie bounce off each other.' Jill stood up to give Molly a hug. 'I'm lucky to have you as my man and Auntie Nellie as my mother-in-law.'

'And don't be forgetting that handsome husband of yours, sunshine. I think yer've done very well for yerself all round.' Molly patted her daughter's bottom. 'Now go on home and see to his dinner. And tell Mrs Corkhill to put her best togs on for her son coming home tomorrow. Yer could even offer to do her hair for her, sunshine.'

'That's all been sorted out, Mam. I'm putting her hair in rollers tonight and I'll comb it out for her in the morning. She's really looking forward to seeing him, she's so excited she can't sit still. Her best dress has been on a hanger for days now, and her shoes all shine.'

46

'And Corker will be just as excited, sunshine, 'cos they love the bones of each other.'

'I know that, Mam, and yer couldn't help but love Mrs Corkhill 'cos she's so nice. Me and Steve are very happy with her.'

'Yeah, yer hopped in lucky there, sweetheart.' Jack gave his daughter a kiss as he made his way to the kitchen to wash his hands. 'Yer'd go a long way to find a nicer family.'

Tommy bent his six foot two inch frame to say, softly, 'But never forget yer came from a very good family yerself.'

At that moment the door burst open and Ruthie came flying in. 'I beat Bella again at dominoes, Mam, that's the third time in a row.' Her eyes lighted on the chair and she slipped between her mother and Jill to plonk herself down on it. 'Ay, this is the gear.' She swung her legs and ran her hands over the smooth arms. 'I bags this for me very own.'

Amid the laughter, Molly could be heard saying, 'Yer'll bag more than that if yer Auntie Nellie catches yer.'

Three doors away, Nellie was holding forth. 'I'll lay odds that it came from Buckingham Palace, and that it's been sat on by nobility.'

'I can't get over you having the cheek to ask Molly to buy it for yer, and her being daft enough to be talked into it!' George, Lily and Paul had had a good laugh when Nellie was telling them the story, but now George was shaking his head in bewilderment. 'She's bought a chair just for you to sit in? She must have a screw loose!'

'You're going to pay her for it, surely?' Lily said. 'If you're the one what wanted it then it's only right yer should fork out, yer can't expect Auntie Molly to be out of pocket.'

'Nah, she's not out of pocket, love! Her purse may be a bit lighter, but there's nowt wrong with her pocket.'

'If it's as nice as yer say, I can't see her letting yer sit in it,' Paul said. 'Anyway, if yer liked it so much, why didn't yer buy it yerself?'

'Well, it's like this, son. If yer look at it from all angles, there wasn't much point in bringing it here when I spend more time in the Bennetts' house. And I can't see meself putting it on me head and taking it down with me every time I go there.' Nellie appealed to her husband. 'That makes sense, doesn't it, love?'

George shrugged his shoulders, his fork halfway to his mouth. 'Nothing you or Molly does makes sense to me, I've given up trying to understand yer.'

'That's because ye're ignorant, yer see, love, not taught proper. If yer'd been to a good school like what me and me mate did, yer'd understand us then. And, if I may say so, yer'd be enjoying life a lot more.'

Paul chuckled. 'Somehow I can't see me dad getting a kick out of buying a second-hand chair, it wouldn't be up his street.'

'That's his tough luck then, isn't it? If he looked on the bright side, laughed at the little things instead of moaning, he'd be a much happier man.'

'Nellie, if I was any happier, they'd be carting me off to a loony bin for having a permanent smile on me clock.' George had a very dry sense of humour, and unlike his wife could tell a joke without laughing. 'Mind you, yer could come and visit me once a month and bring yer chair with yer. I believe the chairs in those places are as hard as hell.'

Lily laid her knife and fork down and pushed her plate away. 'That was nice, that, Mam. Although how yer had the time to cook a dinner with yer social life being so busy is beyond me.'

'I can move meself when I want to, girl, I'm not just a pretty face.' Nellie reached for the empty plate. 'Is Archie coming tonight?'

'Yeah, we're going round to the Jacksons' with Tommy to have a game of cards. I'm getting quite a dab hand at it now, I won tuppence last week.'

'Good for you!' Nellie looked at her son. 'What about you, Paul, are yer seeing Phoebe tonight?'

'I sure am, Ma! We'll be shining our shoes and going jazzing.' Paul was a handsome lad, just on six foot with jet black hair and deep brown laughing eyes. His dimples weren't as deep as his brother Steve's, but they were very attractive. Many a girl had lost her heart to this young man who had a zest for living. He'd been the love 'em and leave 'em type until he noticed the girl next door but one had grown into a very attractive young woman and she'd taken his fancy. Whether she'd stolen his heart was something his family weren't quite sure of as yet. 'We'll be tripping the light fantastic at Blair Hall tonight.'

'Is Phoebe as keen on this dancing lark as you are?' Nellie asked. She was afraid of her son hurting Corker's daughter. 'Or is it you who likes having yer own way all the flaming time?'

Lily was about to push her chair back when she heard the question being asked. She remained seated, waiting for his answer, and George's face showed that he too would be interested in his son's reply. Both of them were very fond of Phoebe who was gentle and very softly spoken, the exact opposite to Paul.

'I don't get all me own way with her, Mam! Oh, I know she's quiet and looks as though butter wouldn't melt in her mouth, but believe you me she can stick up for herself.' His deep brown eyes twinkled and his white teeth gleamed. 'She's got a temper, too, and wouldn't think twice about clocking me one if I looked sideways at her.'

'Yer still haven't answered me question, soft lad. Which, in case yer've forgotten was, is Phoebe as crazy about dancing as you are?'

'Yeah, she is!' Then Paul pulled a face before having the grace to admit, 'Well, perhaps not quite as crazy as me. She'd just as soon go to the pictures and watch Cary Grant kissing Katharine Hepburn.'

'Then yer should take her to the pictures more often,' Lily said. 'Yer can't expect to have everything yer own way all the time. Phoebe's a nice girl and yer don't know when ye're well off.'

'Ay, I'm not a bad catch meself! She could do a lot worse than me.'

George moved from the table to his fireside chair, picking up his cigarette packet from the mantelpiece before sitting down. 'Are the pair of yer courting serious, like?'

'Well, we're not talking marriage, if that's what yer mean. Phoebe's only eighteen, I'm only twenty, and that's far too young to think of settling down. But we are going out together, there's nobody else on the horizon for either of us.'

'Until the day I see yer with me own eyes, standing at the altar putting a ring on a girl's finger, then I'll take anything yer say with a pinch of salt.' Nellie reached out. 'Pass me the plates, girl, and I'll get them done before you two take over the kitchen to get washed and titivate yerselves up.' Stacking the plates on top of each other, she chuckled. 'Now if yer had a chair like mine I could understand yer dolling yerself up to the nines because yer'd have something to swank about.'

'This must be some chair, I can't wait to see it,' Paul said, winking at the mother he adored. 'And before we let the subject drop, I'd just like to set the record straight. Phoebe has been my girlfriend for over two months now, so I suppose yer could say we're courting, but marriage hasn't been mentioned and isn't on the cards. Ask me again in a year's time and the answer might be different.'

'I'll give yer a hand with the washing-up, Mam, then we'll be finished in no time.' Lily raised her eyebrows at Paul as she followed her mother to the kitchen. 'Yer better watch yerself, kid, or Phoebe might not be around in a year's time.'

He looked at his father and held up his hands. 'What did I say to bring all this on, Dad? I never said a dickie-bird, then suddenly I'm

49

the worst in the world and everyone is ganging up on me!'

'Don't bring me into it, son, I'm just watching from the sidelines.' George lit his cigarette and watched the smoke swirling upwards. 'But I think what yer mam is trying to say is that it's time yer grew up.'

Never one to take offence, Paul chuckled. 'I can just see me mam's face if I came in one night and told her I was getting married! She'd lay a duck egg and tell me I was far too young to think of settling down.'

Nellie's head appeared around the door. 'I can do a lot of things, son, but laying a ruddy duck egg isn't one of them. And while ye're too young to be thinking of marriage yet, I hope yer don't leave it too long or me fine three-guinea hat what I had for Steve's wedding will be either motheaten or green mouldy.'

George sat forward in his chair. 'Three-guinea hat! Yer never told me yer paid that much for it! Yer said yer got it from TJ's for thirty bob!'

Nellie's face was a picture. 'I didn't, did I, love?' She put a finger on her chin and pretended to look thoughtful. 'Oh, yeah, it's coming back to me now. I remember thinking that if I told yer the truth, yer'd do yer nut.'

'Ye're right, I would have done. In fact I'm doing it now! What on earth possessed yer to fork out so much for a ruddy titfer?'

'Didn't yer like me hat then, love?'

'Of course I liked yer hat, I told yer so! But if I'd known it cost more than a week's wages I would have liked it a lot less. In fact, I'd have made yer take it back.'

The thought of his mam taking the hat back brought a loud chuckle from Paul. 'Oh, yeah, I can see me mam doing it, too!'

Looking all angelic, Nellie tried to reason with her husband. 'Well, it's like this, yer see, love. If yer find something yer like and it's expensive, then yer've got to pay the price. It's like that chair I was telling yer about. If yer want something, yer've got to fork out.'

'But the chair didn't cost yer anything, Molly paid for it!'

'Don't be changing the subject and bringing Molly into it, George, 'cos yer only get me all confused.' Nellie rubbed her forehead. 'Where was I when yer put me off track?'

'Yer were supposed to be washing the dishes with me,' Lily called, smiling at the plate she was putting on the draining board. She didn't know why her father bothered because he'd never get the better of his wife. Mind you, he was more aware of that than anyone. But he wouldn't ever want to get the better of her. 'I'll finish drying them, then I'll get washed. It won't take me long, Paul, so keep yer hair on.'

Nellie went to stand in front of her husband's chair and her chubby face creased into a beaming smile. 'Yer did me a favour there, love, got me out of washing the dishes. Yer see, yer do have yer uses.'

George smiled back at her. If Paul hadn't been sitting there watching, Nellie would have been pulled forward and kissed soundly. 'Oh, I have me uses all right. Such as slaving away for five and a half days a week so me wife can throw me wages away on expensive titfers.'

'I'll get me money's worth out of that hat, love, don't worry. I can wear it for Tommy's wedding, it'll still be like new.' Nellie raised her voice. 'And I can put it away for when our Lily gets married.'

'I heard that, Mam!' Lily held the flannel from her face and popped her head around the door. 'Yer've had a go at our Paul so it's my turn now, is it? Well, I wouldn't hold me breath if I were you 'cos yer'll have a flipping long wait. And don't yer ever come out with anything like that in front of Archie 'cos I wouldn't know where to put me face.'

'Oh, I wouldn't say it in front of yer face, love, I'd wait until yer were upstairs. I'm not that thick I'd want to embarrass me own daughter.'

'Mam!' Lily looked horror-stricken. 'I've only been going out with the lad for a few months, I'd die of humiliation if yer even breathed the word marriage.'

'Well, yer can't afford to hang around, girl, 'cos ye're twenty-one and me and yer dad don't want to see yer left on the shelf.'

'All right, Nellie, that's enough,' George said. 'A joke's a joke as long as it doesn't go too far. That's when it stops being funny.'

The frown left Lily's face and she grinned. 'It's all right, Dad, I'm used to me mam now and I don't take no notice of her.'

Nellie shook her head and clicked her tongue against the roof of her mouth. 'I don't know, love, it looks as though we'll never have the house to ourselves.'

'Mam, yer wouldn't know what to do with yerself if we all left home,' Paul said. 'Ye're fretting over our Steve leaving, and he's only living up the street! So what would yer be like if me and Lily decided to up sticks as well? Yer'd be broken-hearted.'

'I know that, big head, and yer dad knows that. But I'm not ruddy well going to tell you that 'cos ye're cocky enough as it is.'

'Oh, I wouldn't say I was cocky, Mam! Sure of meself, perhaps, but not cocky.'

Lily jerked her head as she came through from the kitchen. 'The sink's all yours now, Paul, I'm going upstairs to get changed. Archie will be here in fifteen minutes.' She winked at her father. 'Keep a rein on yer wife's tongue, will yer, Dad, 'cos it runs away with her sometimes. I'd hate to look through the window and see Archie hot-footing it down the street with me mam chasing him with a shotgun.'

Lily was combing her hair in front of the mirror over the mantelpiece when the knock came. 'I'll answer it, save you getting up.'

'If it's Archie, which it's bound to be,' Nellie said, a crafty look in her eye, 'tell him there's only one bullet in me shotgun so he's safe if I miss him first time.'

'Mam, will yer behave yerself?' Lily narrowed her eyes and glared, and her mother glared back. Then they burst out laughing and Lily was looking very happy when she opened the door because she intended to catch her mother out by playing her at her own game. 'Hello, Archie, how are yer?' She was barring his way and he could tell by the look on her face that something was in the wind. 'Before yer come in I'd better warn yer that me mam is sitting with a shotgun on her knees. But don't worry too much 'cos there's only one bullet in it and she's a lousy shot.'

Archie's face broke into a smile. He was a handsome lad who would stand out in a crowd. Tall and raven haired, his nose was on the large size but the rest of him was so pleasing to the eye you didn't notice. 'What's she up to now?'

'You'll find out, come on in.'

'Hello, Archie, lad.' George lowered his evening paper. 'How's the world treating yer?'

'Can't complain, Mr McDonough, life's pretty good at the moment.' Archie glanced at Nellie. 'Ah, have yer put yer shotgun away?'

'Yeah, no one wants to play with me. They're a right shower of miserable buggers. Don't like to see anyone having fun and enjoying themselves.'

'Ah, I'll play with yer, Mrs Mac! You get the gun out and I'll draw a target on the yard door. A tanner to the first one to get a bull's-eye.'

'How soft you are, lad,' Nellie huffed. 'Yer've been in the army for two years, carrying a gun with yer everywhere and shooting everything in sight! And here's little me, can't even hold the ruddy thing it's that big and heavy.'

Archie was well into his stride now. 'I'll teach yer! It's easy when yer know how. With your sharp eyes yer couldn't go wrong.'

'Excuse me for interrupting, lad,' George said, 'but it's not Nellie's eyes what are sharp, it's her flipping tongue.'

'I still say she could learn. Three tries and she'd have mastered it.'

'I've only got one bullet, soft lad, so that puts paid to your little game.'

'That's a shame, I was really looking forward to teaching yer. Where is the gun, anyway?'

Nellie got up, pretending she didn't hear. 'That cloth on the sideboard is always skewiff, it gets on me nerves. About fifteen times a day I have to straighten it. The contrary so-and-so's got a mind of its own.'

'Archie asked yer a question, Nellie,' George said. 'It's manners to answer when ye're spoken to.'

'Oh, I'm sorry, lad, I didn't hear yer.' She looked all contrite. 'What did yer say?'

'I asked where the gun is?'

'What gun?'

'The gun yer've been talking about.'

'Ah, no, lad, yer've got it wrong. I haven't been talking about no gun, it was you what mentioned it. Never mind if yer've forgotten, though, 'cos we all forget things sometimes. I wasn't so bad until I got married, then it took me all me time to remember me own name. Yer'll find the same thing will happen to you when yer get wed.'

Lily managed to keep her gasp silent. Well, the crafty so-and-so had really turned the tables on her. The best thing to do now was beat a hasty retreat before her mother said something that would really embarrass her. 'Come on, Archie, Tommy will be waiting for us.'

After saying goodbye, Archie followed Lily to the door. There he hesitated for a second before turning back. 'Where d'yer keep the gun, Mrs Mac?'

'In me ruddy head with all me other fantasies, lad.' Nellie grinned into the face of the boy she hoped would one day be her son-in-law. What a happy woman she'd be if that day ever came. 'Yer might as well be dead if yer have no dreams or fantasies. They're what keep me going.'

'You hang on to yer dreams, Mrs Mac, don't let anyone take them away from yer.' He chucked her under the chin. 'I'll see yer later.'

'Sure, that was a long game, right enough,' Bridie said. 'It's nearly our bedtime, sweetheart.' She put her hand over her husband's who was sitting next to her. 'One more hand and we'll call it quits before the bedtime fairy sends us to sleep.'

'If it's tired yer are, Auntie Bridget, then we'll not play any more.' Rosie cast an anxious eye over the elderly couple. 'I'll make a drink and then we can just sit quietly and talk. I'm sure me beloved intended can think of something to amuse us, can yer not, Tommy?'

'Nothing very exciting happens, love, except I go to work and come home.' Then he remembered the chair. 'Oh, yes, something did happen today which you'll find very funny, Nan, and you, Granda. And of course it's all to do with Auntie Nellie.'

Lily clapped her hands, her pretty face coming alive. 'I know what it is, Tommy, and ye're right, it's hilarious. Go on, I'm going to enjoy this.'

'Did you get the whole story, word for word?'

'Yeah, and the actions,' Lily said. 'Why?'

'Well, I'll make a fool of meself if you will. You be your mam, and I'll be mine.'

'Oh, I don't know about that. Laughing at me mam is one thing, impersonating her is another.'

Archie started the clapping, followed by Bob and Bridie and Rosie. And he had them chanting, 'We want Lily, we want Lily!'

'Come in the kitchen and we'll rehearse.' Tommy suggested. 'And don't forget, it'll be easier for you than for me. After all, I'm a man taking a woman off.'

'Well, fancy that now,' Bridie said, her eyes bright with laughter. 'Sure, we wouldn't have known if yer hadn't told us, and that's a fact.'

'Oh, I don't know,' Archie said, tongue in cheek. 'He's taller than Mrs Bennett but there is a resemblance – I think it's the nose and the chin.'

'If ye're going to make fun of us we won't do it.' Lily's nod was emphatic. 'So it's up to you, suit yerselves.'

'We'll not be making fun of yer, Lily, and it's meself that'll make sure of it.' Rosie's face was straight but there was a twinkle in her beautiful blue Irish eyes. 'We'll laugh with yer, so we will, but we'll not be making fun of yer.'

Tommy and Lily retired to the kitchen, and although the listeners couldn't hear what was being said they could hear the laughter and knew they were in for a treat. And they weren't disappointed. Lily had made use of Bridie's wraparound pinny which she'd noticed hanging on the hook on the kitchen door, and Tommy had used a tea towel to wrap around his head turban style. They really excelled themselves, encouraged by loud hoots of laughter. Bob and Bridie were clinging to each other, using Bob's handkerchief to wipe away the tears that were running down their faces, and Rosie was bouncing up and down on her chair, her dark curls swirling and her rich, infectious laughter ringing out. As for Archie, he was in stitches. But there was more than laughter in his eyes as he watched Lily, and if Nellie had been there she would have been heartened by the look that held more than mere affection for her daughter. He was crazy about Lily but had managed to keep his feelings to himself for the last few months because he was afraid of scaring her off. She'd been badly hurt by Len Lofthouse and he wasn't sure she was ready to trust another man.

'Anything you say, girl!' Lily had her mother's expression off to perfection as she brought the performance to an end. 'D'yer know, I've got a feeling that chair and my backside are going to get on very well.'

Tommy took hold of her hand and they bowed to their audience before doubling up with laughter themselves. 'You were great, Lily, yer had yer mother spot on.'

'Yer didn't do so bad yerself. It's a pity our mothers weren't here to see it, they'd have been made up.'

'Yer were both brilliant,' Bob said. 'It's a long time since I laughed so much.'

Rosie rounded the table. 'Tommy Bennett, will yer let go of Lily's hand right this minute before I take the poker to yer? As my dearly beloved intended, sure ye're not supposed to look at another girl, let alone hold her hand.'

Tommy put two hands around her waist and lifted her up. Twirling her round, he laughed into the face he thought the most beautiful in the world. 'Sure, isn't it enough that yer have me heart, Rosie O'Grady?' His Irish lilt was perfect, but then hadn't he been listening to his nan since the day he was born? 'And it's me heart that's full of love for yer, so it is.'

'My mammy always said that yer should beware of the man with a smooth tongue, 'cos he can't be trusted. So I'll not believe a word ye're saying unless yer give me a kiss.' When she was lowered to the floor, Rosie said, 'I'll have me kiss in the kitchen while we're waiting for the kettle to boil. That should take a few minutes, and sure, if ye're half the man I think yer are, Tommy Bennett, I'll have been well and truly kissed a dozen times by then.'

'Will I have time to come up for air, 'cos I don't want to die just yet?' Tommy had his hands around her waist as he followed her to the kitchen. 'Mind you, I'd die with a smile on me face if I was kissing you.'

'Those lovebirds have got no shame, so they haven't,' Bridie said with a smile. 'In my day yer kissed in the dark and didn't tell anyone. Bob's mother would have had a fit if I'd asked him for a kiss in front of her. She'd have said I was a shameless hussy.'

'Yer didn't go short for all that, though, did yer, sweetheart?' The love between Bob and his wife was so strong it made an onlooker feel as though they could reach out and touch it. 'We have had a wonderful life, you and me. Our marriage was made in heaven, sweetheart, and we've got the best family and friends anyone could ask for.'

'Don't be going all sentimental on me, Bob Jackson, or yer'll have everyone in tears, so yer will. We've just had a good laugh so can yer not think of anything cheerful?'

'I can't, sweetheart, I was never any good at jokes. But perhaps Archie has some tales to tell about that lazy workmate of his.'

'Oh, yer mean Fred Berry!' Archie grinned. 'He's still at it, taking at least one day a week off through some mishap. But he must be running out of ideas because he's resorted to using the same old lame excuses. The one where he slips in the dog dirt, he's used that one three times. The boss was being sarcastic when he asked if it was the same dog every time, but Fred's got no sense of humour at all and his face was dead straight when he said no, it wasn't the same dog, it was three different ones. But that didn't satisfy the boss 'cos he was hoping for a laugh and hadn't got one. Then he asked how did Fred know it was three different dogs each time.' Archie chuckled at the thought. 'I told yer Fred had no sense of humour, but he sure can think up excuses. He had it all off pat in a matter of seconds. "Well, yer see, boss, one had a collar round his neck, one had a piece of string, and the third one was cross-eyed."'

Rosie came in carrying the teapot, followed by Tommy with the tray. That both their faces were pink, and he had more lipstick on his lips than Rosie did, didn't seem to bother them at all. They were in love and didn't care who knew it. 'Oh, will yer look at that now! See what yer've done, Tommy Bennett? While you were keeping me prisoner in the kitchen, weren't they all having a good laugh.'

'Don't be trying to put the blame on me, Rosie O'Grady, I asked yer to put me down and yer wouldn't.'

'Archie's been telling us about the man he works with,' Bob told them. 'You know, the lazy one who's always taking days off.'

Tommy slapped his old army mate on the back before sitting down. 'Come on, what's he been up to now?'

'I've just been saying he's gone a bit dull. The best I can think of is about three dogs.' Archie repeated the story. 'Then the week before last he was just closing the door behind him when next door's cat came running past and he just couldn't stop himself from tripping over it. He hurt an elbow when he fell and it was dinnertime when the bleeding stopped so it wasn't worth turning into work then, apparently. The lads pulled his leg when he came out of the boss's office and we asked to see the wound. And sure enough his elbow was bandaged with a piece of sheet, but would he take it off to let us see? Would he hell!'

'I've got one I bet he's never thought of.' Tommy was chuckling at what he was about to come out with. 'He could say he was sitting on the tram coming to work when suddenly it came to a screeching halt. All the passengers were thrown forward and he banged his head on the seat in front.'

'And would he say why the tram had come to an abrupt halt?' Lily asked. 'There must have been some reason for it.'

'Oh, there was! There was a man lying across the tram lines wanting to commit suicide and no one could budge him 'cos he said he didn't want to live any more. And the man turned out to be your boss, Archie, driven to the deed by none other than Fred Berry!'

'That's a cracker, that is,' Archie said when the laughter had died down. 'I'll charge him tuppence for that, it's well worth it. And if yer can think of any more, pal, let me know 'cos I could be on to a good thing here.'

'I'll rack me brains if there's something in it for me.'

'How does fifty-fifty sound?'

'Ye're on.' The two men shook hands and burst into laughter. 'We should be so lucky,' Archie said, while Tommy told Rosie that any money he made would go in their savings box and was rewarded with a noisy kiss.

'I always enjoy going to the Jacksons'.' Archie was cupping Lily's elbow as they walked the short distance to her street. 'It's better than sitting in a picture house any day.'

'Yeah, they're the salt of the earth. Rosie's only nineteen, but she does a fine job of looking after the old folk and going out to work as well. She's got a good head on her shoulders, that's for sure.'

Archie bent his arm. 'Stick yer leg in, kid, so people will know we're together.' When he felt her arm entwined with his, he had to steel himself not to draw her closer. 'She's also got a good bloke in Tommy, they don't come any better.'

'Ye're right, they're very suited to each other. They'll have a happy marriage like Auntie Bridie and Uncle Bob.'

'Making good marriages seems to run in the Bennett and McDonough families. Look at yer mam and dad, and Mr and Mrs Bennett. And we mustn't forget the young newly-weds, they're blissfully happy.' Dare I go any further? Archie asked himself. Then decided that rather than jeopardise the relationship he had with Lily, he'd be wise to tread carefully. So he sounded light-hearted when he said, 'Yer never know, we might end up as happy as them, one day. Yer never know yer luck in a big city.'

'Only time will tell, kiddo, only time will tell.'

Archie was well satisfied with that. Not so long ago, still bitter from the pain Lofthouse had caused her, her answer would have been very different. So he considered a little progress had been made, and dared to put a hand over the one linked to his arm. And the goodnight kiss he'd get when he left her outside her house might not be as passionate as those of Rosie and Tommy, but at least they were on kissing terms.

Chapter 5

Molly and Nellie watched the removal van move away from Vera Harwick's old house and both had lumps in their throat. 'I'll miss the old lady, we've known her a long time,' Molly said. 'Since the day we moved into the street.'

'Yeah, I remember she came and knocked on the door to see if we'd like her to make a pot of tea to keep us going until we'd unpacked.' Nellie sniffed and ran the back of her hand across her nose. 'She was a good neighbour.'

'Never mind, sunshine, she's going to be better off where she's going.' Molly linked arms with her friend. 'She's left her address so we can write to her.'

The pair set off down the street, headed for the shops. 'I hope the fish shop haven't sold out by the time we get there. Everyone eats fish on a Friday.' Molly was using all her weight to keep Nellie walking in a straight line. It was hard going 'cos pushing against eighteen stone is no joke. But better that than ending up in the gutter. 'If I'm lucky enough to get a piece of cod, we can have it with peas and chips. The family will love that.'

'Yeah, I'll have the same, girl.' Nellie's chins agreed with her nodding head. 'I'm going to the butcher's, too, to get meat for the weekend. And I'm getting all me veg and spuds in 'cos I don't want to go out tomorrow.'

'Why not? We always go shopping on a Saturday!'

'Well, I'm not going tomorrow, girl, 'cos the new family are moving into Vera's house and I don't want to miss that.'

Molly stopped in her tracks. 'I don't believe it! Are yer telling me ye're changing yer habits just so yer can be nosy and spy on people yer've never seen in yer life?'

Nellie wasn't the least bit put out. 'Of course I am! I wouldn't miss it for the world! When I see what's being carried in, I'll know what sort of neighbours we're getting. Whether they're posh or riff-raff.'

'Yer'll soon find that out without spying on the people. It's a pity yer haven't got something better to do, sunshine, that's all I can say.'

'It's all right for you, girl, yer won't be as near them as we are. If they're noisy buggers we're the ones what'll have to put up with it.' Nellie pulled on Molly's arm. 'Are we going to the shops or not? Anyone would think I'd told yer I was going to rob a bank tomorrow, the state of yer ruddy face.'

'I'm just surprised ye're so interested in other people's business! What would yer do it they knocked on your door and asked if they could come in and see what furniture you had? I know what yer'd do – yer'd clock them one and send them packing with yer foot up their backside.'

'Well, that would be a different kettle of fish, wouldn't it, girl? I mean, all the neighbours what lived in the street when we moved in, well, they saw what we had. And everyone what's moved in since has been watched, 'cos I've seen the neighbours lurking behind their lace curtains. It's only natural to be curious, girl.'

'Don't you mean nosy?'

Nellie sighed as they plodded along. 'I was going to suggest yer come up to ours, 'cos yer won't see anything from your house. I was even going to make yer a cup of tea and mug yer to a cream slice. But if yer won't come I'll have to sit on me own.'

'I never said that.'

'Never said what, girl?'

'That I won't come. Yer shouldn't be so quick to jump to conclusions, sunshine.'

Nellie kept her face straight but she was grinning inside. I knew she'd come, she said to herself, there's not a woman breathing who isn't nosy. Or one who could resist a cream slice. 'So are you getting all the food in for the weekend, then?'

'What time are the new people moving in?'

'Now I know I'm a mine of information, girl, and usually know all what goes on in the street. But I'm not a clairvoyant so I don't know what time the ruddy removal van will be coming. I imagine, with Vera moving out today, they'll want to get in as early as possible to get as much sorted out as possible.'

'I'll get everything in today except bread. Our Ruthie can get that for me in the morning and she may as well get yours while she's at it.' Molly couldn't believe she was doing this, she'd never been one for peeping through curtains. 'If Jack knew what we were up to he'd say I'd lost the run of me senses. And he'd be right, an' all.'

60

'Oh, go on, girl, yer only live once so be a dare-devil and live dangerously.'

'Spying on people is hardly living dangerously. I know one thing: whoever the people are, I won't be able to look them in the face without feeling guilty.'

'Yer'll feel less guilty when ye're sitting nice and comfortable, looking out of my front window, with a cup of tea in one hand and a cream slice in the other. I'll let yer sit in George's chair 'cos it's very comfortable, which will help if we're keeping watch for very long.'

'Oh, aye, and where is George going to sit?'

'I've got it all figured out, girl, so there's no need for yer to worry. If Liverpool are playing at home he will be going to the match with Paul and Tommy. If there's no match he can have my chair and you can bring the one from your house for me.'

They were turning the corner into the main road and Molly had her mouth open ready to call Nellie a cheeky so-and-so when they walked headlong into a man the size of a house. 'Corker! It's nice to see yer.' Molly smiled into the weatherbeaten face of one of her favourite people. He stood six foot four inches tall, and was built like a battleship. With his sea-cap set at a jaunty angle, bright blue laughing eyes and bushy beard and moustache, it was easy to see why the local children called him Sinbad the Sailor.

'Good morning, ladies! Off shopping, are yer?'

'Yeah,' Molly said. 'We're getting in as much as we can 'cos the shops are murder on a Saturday.' She looked down at the bunch of flowers he was carrying. 'They're for yer ma, are they?'

He nodded. 'I'm going to spend the rest of the day with her. I'm due back on the ship on Sunday, so I want to see as much of her as I can. Mind you, I don't have to worry about her when I'm away now, not with Jill and Steve looking out for her. They've taken a load off my mind 'cos I did worry about her when I was away for weeks on end.'

'Yer leave seems to have flown over. But you and Ellen are coming in for a drink tomorrow night, aren't yer?'

Nellie put her hand to her mouth and gave what she thought was a discreet cough. 'I'm here, yer know, Corker. I know I'm little but I'm not that bloody little that yer can't see me.'

Corker let out a loud guffaw. 'There's good stuff in little parcels, Nellie, me darlin', and I wouldn't leave yer out for the world. I'll be seeing yer tonight 'cos I'm going for a pint with George and Jack.'

Nellie bristled. 'Never mind that now, I'm more interested in the invitation yer've just received from my mate. All lah-de-dah, she was. "You and Ellen are coming in for a drink tomorrow night, aren't yer?" Not a dickie bird about me, her best mate, what's standing right beside her. And after I've invited her to come to my house tomorrow morning for a cup of tea and a cream slice! That's gratitude for yer.'

Oh, my God, Molly thought, she's going to tell him what I'm going to her house for. She can't keep a thing to herself. So before her friend had time to drop her in it, she said, 'I had every intention of inviting you and George, sunshine, so don't be getting yer knickers in a twist.'

'I'd have a job,' Nellie said, her eyes dancing. 'I haven't got none on.'

Molly grabbed her arm. 'Corker, we'll love yer and leave yer before my mate here comes out with something else to embarrass me. We'll see yer!' She dragged a reluctant Nellie along to the shops and Corker's laughter was still ringing in her ears when they entered the butcher's.

'Good morning, Tony. Morning, Ellen. We've just seen Corker, he's off to his ma's.'

'Yeah, I know, he called in.' Ellen smiled at her two neighbours. 'How's things?'

'This one's got a cob on,' Nellie said, jerking her head and chins towards Molly. 'Just because I told your feller I had no knickers on.' She spread her hands and put on her innocent face. 'I mean, what's the harm in that?'

'No harm at all, Nellie!' Tony was dying to laugh but kept his face straight. 'Unless yer get run over by a bus or tram, then yer'd be in a right pickle. Laying on the ground with a crowd of people looking down at yer, and you with no knickers on! Yer'd be the talk of the wash-house.'

'Well, if I'd got killed by this bus or tram, I wouldn't be worrying about what I looked like, would I? And if I hadn't got killed, I'd ask the nosy buggers what they were looking at and tell them to sod off.'

'That's very ladylike, I'm sure.' Molly rolled her eyes to the ceiling. 'No knickers and swearing like a trooper. I'd just pretend I wasn't with yer and walk away.'

'Well, if yer did that, girl, I'd tell the nosy people to run after yer 'cos it was you what had pushed me under the bus just so yer could steal me knickers. And the men would catch yer and hang on to yer tight until the bobby came.'

'Ooh, er, the men would hang on to me, would they?' Molly puckered her lips. 'Ay, if I could be sure of that, it'd be worth pushing yer under a ruddy bus.'

'That's charming, that is.' Nellie let her mouth droop at the corners. 'I've a good mind not to get yer that cream slice I promised.'

'Oh, aye, what cream slice is that, then?' Tony asked. 'I'm a bit partial to them meself.'

'Take no notice of her, she's having yer on.' Molly's eyes sent daggers and warnings to the little woman who was enjoying her discomfort. 'I'll have three-quarters of stew for now, please, Tony, that'll do tomorrow's dinner. And what can yer do for us for Sunday?'

'Unless yer've come into some coupons, the best I can do for yer, Molly, is a breast of lamb. But if I pick yer a lean one, it'll be nice rolled and stuffed and done slowly in the oven.'

'That'll do a treat, Tony, thanks. I won't take it with me now, though, I'd rather yer kept it in your cold room until tomorrow. I'll send Ruthie down for it.'

'I'll have the same as her now, lad, and yer can give Ruthie a breast of lamb for me. And make sure it's as lean as me mate's or there'll be trouble.'

'Nellie, they'll be so much alike yer'll think they're twins. If I can possibly manage it, I'll get two that come from the same lamb. Now I can't say fairer than that, can I?' The butcher pushed his straw hat to the back of his head. 'In fact, I think that's deserving of a cream slice.'

'Oh, you can sod off, Tony Reynolds, there's not enough room at me window for you.'

There was curiosity in the butcher's eyes and he was just about to ask what Nellie's window had to do with a cream slice when Molly took matters into her own hands. 'I'm in a bit of a hurry today, Tony, so could yer serve us, please?'

'I'll serve yer, Molly,' Ellen said, taking a tray of chopped stewing meat out of the window. 'And I'll see to Nellie while Tony puts the breasts of lamb away before all the lean ones go.'

Nellie was having the time of her life. She'd get a good telling off from Molly when they got outside, but it was worth it just to see her going all of a dither. Why her mate didn't want people to know they were going to watch new neighbours moving in tomorrow Nellie couldn't make head nor tail of. I mean, what harm was there in it? It passed an hour or so away, and yer got some idea of what yer new neighbours were like.

'Two bob each they are, ladies,' Tony said. 'D'yer want to pay me now or in the morning?'

'We'll pay now and get it over with.' Molly reached into the basket for her purse. 'Come on, slow coach, get yer money out for the man. How much is it with the stew, Tony?'

'Three bob each and we'll call it quits.'

Molly held out her hand. 'Cough up, sunshine, and we'll be on our way.'

'I'll settle up with yer when we get to the greengrocer's, save getting me purse out now.' Nellie gave the butcher a sly wink. 'How much did yer say I owe?'

'Three bob, Nellie, and cheap at half the price.'

'Did yer hear that, girl, I owe yer three bob. Remind me in case I forget.'

'Yer don't owe me anything, sunshine, 'cos I'm not paying Tony just 'cos you're too ruddy lazy to get yer purse out. If I let yer get away with it yer'd pull the same stunt in the greengrocer's, and I'd end up having to fight for me money. Besides, I've only got enough to buy what I want, it's not pay day until tomorrow.' Molly looked at Ellen and tutted. 'For some reason this one thinks I'm made of money. The best of it is, there's three working in her house so she should be loaded instead of crying poverty all the time.'

'I don't cry poverty, I'm just careful with me money.' Nellie pretended to be hurt as she counted what was in her purse and handed over the exact money. 'Yer've really upset me now, girl, I'm cut to the quick.'

'It's not me what's upset yer, sunshine, it's just that yer hate parting with money. But now it's all been sorted out, can we get on our way before the day's over?'

Molly left the shop first and didn't see the sly wink Nellie gave to the two behind the counter which told them that it was all in fun. And she had more up her sleeve.

'Are we going for the spuds now, girl, or to Hanley's for our bread?'

'Bread first, in case they run out.' Molly glanced sideways and thought her friend looked downcast so she held her arm out. 'Stick yer leg in, sunshine, and cheer up.'

'I'm all right, girl, it's me corns what are playing up on me.' This was far from the truth for Nellie was concocting her next trick. 'While we're at Hanley's, I'll ask Edna to put two cream slices away for us in the morning.'

'That's a good idea, sunshine, 'cos the cream cakes sell out in no time.'

'I was thinking, girl, that Ruthie could pick them up after she's been to the butcher's and I could settle up with yer later.'

Molly came to a standstill. 'Why, you crafty monkey! Yer tempt me to your house with the offer of tea and a cream slice, and I end up paying for the blinking thing meself. And yours into the bargain! If yer think I'm falling for that, sunshine, then yer've got another think coming.'

'Yeah, ye're right, girl,' Nellie said, looking contrite. 'Especially as ye're bringing the chair up for me to sit on.'

'Who said I'm bringing the chair up?'

'You did, girl!'

'I never said no such thing! I think you just hear what yer want to hear. It was you what suggested me bringing the chair, I never said I would.'

'Ah, but yer never said yer wouldn't so I thought yer were in agreement.'

They joined the queue outside the confectioner's and smiled at the neighbours who were in front of them. Then Molly carried on, 'Yer know what thought did, don't yer, sunshine?'

Before Nellie could answer, the two women in front spoke as one: 'He followed a muck cart and thought it was a wedding.'

'Then he must have been as blind as a bat and had no sense of smell.' Nellie saw an opening and took it. 'Ay, Bessie, did yer know the new people were moving into Vera Harwick's house tomorrow?'

'Ooh, are they?' Bessie folded her arms under a bosom not much smaller than Nellie's. 'I wonder what they'll be like?'

'Me and Molly were saying just the same thing about five minutes ago. Weren't we, girl? I mean, it's only natural to be curious. Nosy, even!'

Molly looked at her best mate and wondered how it was she always turned a conversation round to where she wanted it. Then she saw the chubby face crease and the eyes dance with mischief, and she put back her head and roared with laughter.

Bessie and her neighbour never did find out what Molly was laughing at because the queue began to move and they all shuffled forward.

'Ah, ay, Mam!' Ruthie pulled a face. 'Why can't you go to the shops? Yer always do on a Saturday, with Auntie Nellie.'

Molly breathed in through her teeth. It was no good telling her daughter a lie because she'd be playing in the street with Bella and would soon realise her mother wasn't in. Anyway, it was wrong to tell a child a deliberate lie unless there was a good reason for it. 'If I tell yer something will yer keep it to yerself? Scouts honour?'

Ruthie grinned. 'Is it worth a penny?'

'Oh, go on, then.' Molly pulled a chair out. 'Sit down for a minute.' When her daughter was seated facing her, Molly started at the beginning and left nothing out. Halfway through, Ruthie was laughing so much the tears were rolling down her cheeks.

'Auntie Nellie should be on the stage, she's so funny. Go on, Mam, tell us the rest.'

By this time Molly could see how hilarious it was and her own chuckles were loud. She ended with the queue moving up and Nellie's eyes dancing with mischief. 'So there yer have it, sunshine. A morning in the company of yer Auntie Nellie.'

'Have yer told me dad?'

'No, I haven't, but he'll find out if that furniture van doesn't turn up before him and Tommy come in from work at one o'clock. I can just imagine what he'll say: that I've got a screw loose. He'd be right, too, I have! Anyway, I'll have to come back for half-twelve to see to their dinner. I made the stew last night and it only needs warming up.'

'Ye're going to have to tell him, yer won't be able to keep it to yerself. Besides I bet he wouldn't say yer had a screw loose, he'd see the funny side.'

'Aye, well, I'll see how the land lies first. If the van has been and gone by the time him and Tommy get home, I'll tell them.' Molly pushed herself to her feet. 'You put yer coat on, sunshine, and get down to the shops. I've got to carry that ruddy chair up to Nellie's and I'm taking it the back way so nobody will see me.'

'I'll be out in the street with Bella, so we'll be watching the van getting unloaded, too.' Ruthie had her own streak of devilment. 'We'll wave to yer through the window.'

Molly looked horror-stricken. 'Don't you dare, yer'll give the game away!'

'Only kiddin', Mam, but I gotcha there.'

'And I'll get you, you young madam, if yer don't hurry up to the shops. Ask Tony to wrap the meat separately, leave one here in the pantry and bring the other to Nellie's, with the two cream slices.' A memory flashed through Molly's head and she grinned. 'Ay, remember the last time yer went for cakes for me? Yer licked all round the edges and left hardly any cream inside. Well, see that doesn't happen today.'

'Oh, that'll never happen again 'cos I've got more sense now. Instead of licking the sides, I'd take the top off and pinch the cream from the middle so no one would ever know.'

'You do that and I'll marmalise yer! Now don't forget the meat's been paid for and yer've got sixpence in yer pocket for the cakes. There'll be tuppence change, I want a penny back and you can have the other one. On yer way now before Nellie comes to drag me up.'

'And the chair, Mam, don't forget the chair.'

'Sunshine, a snowball stands more chance in hell than I do of Nellie ever letting me forget that ruddy chair.'

Nellie heard her entry door open and rushed to the window to see Molly carefully carrying the chair up the yard. She opened the kitchen door, saying, 'Trust you to be late! The van's just arrived and we're not settled in our seats yet.'

'Have they unloaded it?' Molly asked, manoeuvring the chair so it didn't get scratched. 'If they haven't, what's all the fuss about?'

'I don't want to miss anything, that's what!' Nellie had moved the small table from the front window and George's fireside chair was strategically placed to afford a good view. 'Put it down there, girl, and we'll both be able to see everything.'

'I don't believe I'm doing this,' Molly said. 'I must be barmy.'

But when the removal men began to carry the furniture out, both women were on the edge of their seats. 'Ay, I like that sideboard, girl, it's a good one.' And the moquette-covered couch was also to Nellie's liking. 'No springs sticking up there, girl, not like my old thing which leaves marks on me backside.'

'So, the new neighbours seem to be meeting with yer approval,' Molly said. 'Which is just as well as yer'll be seeing plenty of them.'

'Early days yet, girl, early days.' Nellie's nose twitched as she moved too close to the net curtains. 'As my old ma used to say, yer can never judge a book by its cover.'

Ruthie came in the back way with the cakes and Nellie's meat and placed them on the table. 'I'm going, Mam, I don't want to miss anything.'

'Turn up the gas under the kettle on yer way out, sweetheart,' Nellie called, not taking her eyes from the window. 'I'll make yer mam a drink in a minute.'

Ruth did as she was asked, then popped her head round the door. 'Have they got any children, d'yer know?'

'We've seen a boy of about fourteen, sunshine, but whether he's with the removal men or one of the family, we wouldn't know.'

'Was he nice-looking?'

'He didn't look bad from where I'm sitting, but we're not close enough to see if he had pimples or blackheads.'

'I'm going before Bella gets her eyes on him first. Ta-ra, Mam. Ta-ra, Auntie Nellie.'

Nellie pulled a face. 'She takes after you, that one. Man mad.'

Molly gave her a gentle dig. 'I'm going to make the tea to stop meself from clocking yer one. But if anything exciting happens, give us a shout.'

Twenty minutes later nothing of interest had happened and Molly was getting fed up and thinking of going home. Most of the furniture had been carried into the house now, and there were only tea chests and boxes left. Then Nellie said, 'This must be the woman of the house – Mrs Mowbray.'

Leaning forward for a closer look, Molly saw a woman of about her own age and build, with mousy-coloured hair. She couldn't see her face because the woman had her back to them, talking to the young lad who was trying to lift a heavy box. Anyone with half an eye could see he wouldn't be able to carry it, and Molly's heart was in her mouth when she saw him dragging it to the edge of the van. 'He'll never manage that,' she said, just seconds before an ornament of some description fell to the floor and smashed into smithereens. And it was then that the excitement started.

'You stupid bugger!' the woman screamed. 'Just look what yer've done now. Put that bleedin' box down before I break yer bleedin' neck.'

'I couldn't help it, Mam,' the boy wailed, 'it wasn't my fault.'

'Whose bleedin' fault was it then, yer stupid sod?' The woman's voice was loud and coarse. 'Christ, I could kill yer with me bare hands.'

Nellie jumped to her feet. 'Can yer hear that, girl? Just listen to the language out of her, it's enough to make yer blush. She's definitely no lady.'

Molly glanced at her friend to see if it was a joke, but no, Nellie's face was straight. And so she wouldn't see the laughter bubbling up, Molly hung her head. That had to be the funniest thing her mate had ever said. Because there wasn't a swear word Nellie didn't know, she could beat anyone at it. In fact, she'd probably invented most of them. She modified her language when she was with Molly, having been warned early in their friendship that she mustn't use bad language in front of the children. But on her own, arguing or fighting with someone in the street, she could turn the air blue.

'The whole street can hear her, yer know, girl, and she's not going to be very popular with a tongue like that.'

'Nellie, yer could outswear her any day. And so could a lot of the neighbours.'

Looking really put out, Nellie said, 'I don't swear that much, girl! Yer've never heard me saying some of the words she's using.'

'Yer don't in my presence, sunshine, but when I'm not around yer really let rip. The other day I heard yer talking to Mrs Plumbley in the entry and yer language was shocking. Yer could put the new neighbour to shame.'

Nellie's smile came slowly until her whole face was creased, eyes disappearing in the folds of flesh. 'If ye're going to sneak up on people, girl, then yer only get what yer deserve. Anyway, a good swear does yer good. It stops yer getting into a bad temper and taking it out on people. Telling them to bugger off is better than belting them in the mouth.'

'In that case the new woman feels the same as you. If she hadn't sworn at her son, she probably would have clocked him one.'

'That's true.' Nellie's head was nodding so quickly her chins didn't know whether to do a foxtrot or a quickstep. 'Perhaps the ornament he broke was special, sentimental, like, and she was upset.'

'Could be! So yer see, for you to criticise her is like the pot calling the kettle black.'

'Yeah, I see what yer mean, girl. I'll tell yer what, to show I'm not bad-minded, shall I go and ask if she'd like me to make a pot of tea for her?'

'That's a very good idea, sunshine, one of the best yer've had today. And while ye're doing that, I'll get home and see to the dinner for Jack and Tommy coming home.'

'Yer'll be coming back, won't yer, to see how I got on with Mrs Mowbray?'

Molly shook her head. 'Don't forget you and George are coming to ours tonight, and Corker and Ellen. I'm going to make a sandwich cake and a batch of fairy cakes. It's not going to be a party, just a gathering of friends with Corker going away tomorrow. I might nip up to the corner shop and ask Maisie and Alec if they'd like to slip down for an hour. We haven't seen much of them since the wedding.' She nodded to the chair. 'You can bring that down with yer, I don't feel like carting it back now but it'll come in handy for tonight. Oh, and I don't want yer to say a word about this morning to anyone, not even George. I won't be telling my two, 'cos it'll make a good subject for discussion with the gang. And a ruddy good laugh.'

'Yer can rely on me, girl, I know when to keep me trap shut.' Nellie waited until Molly was opening the back door before calling, 'Oh, remind me to pay yer for the cakes sometime, in case it slips me mind. Not that it would slip me mind, of course, but I wouldn't want yer losing any sleep over it.'

Molly never said a word about how she'd spent the hours before Jack and Tommy got home from work at one o'clock. As far as they were concerned it had been just like any other Saturday morning. But her youngest daughter, Ruthie, was the fly in the ointment. Her knowing looks and smirks as they sat around the table had Molly on tenterhooks, and she nearly jumped out of her skin when Jack said, 'I see the new people have moved in, the van was leaving as we walked up the street.'

After shooting Ruthie a warning glance, Molly asked God to forgive her before answering. 'I knew they were moving in today, Nellie told me. They got the job over early, didn't they?'

'Have they got any nice-looking daughters?' Tommy asked.

'Ay, I'll tell Rosie on you.'

'Don't do that, Mam, or she'll hit me with the frying pan.' Tommy grinned. 'She doesn't mess about, yer know, she uses both hands to get a good swing.'

'We'll know all about them tonight when Nellie comes down. Knowing her, she'll probably be able to tell us how many blankets they've got on their beds.' Molly got to her feet and picked up her empty plate. 'There's no rush, so take yer time. I want to make some cakes for tonight and I don't want to leave it until the last minute. You relax and I'll bring yer a cup of tea through.'

'Have yer got enough in for tonight?' Jack asked. 'I mean in the drink line.'

'Trust a man to ask about the drinks and not mention food.' Molly tutted. 'And don't bother telling me that beer is food, either, 'cos I've heard all that before. Anyway, starting with the real food, I've got a tin of Spam I can open for sandwiches and I'm making some cakes. With a packet of biscuits, that's going to have to be enough 'cos I don't want to dip into me savings.'

Tommy tilted his head. 'What are yer saving up for, Mam? Better days?'

She wasn't about to tell him the truth, that was going to be a surprise when the time came. 'Christmas, sunshine! It'll be on us before we know it.'

'Molly, what about drinks?' Jack asked. 'I'll feel a right fool if I can't offer them a drink.'

'There's half a bottle of sherry left, and I've bought four large bottles of milk stout. That's plenty for four ladies. Oh, I've asked Maisie and Alec, that's why there's four ladies. As for the men, Corker said to leave the beer to him. And he insisted, Jack, so don't be looking at me like that.'

'But he always supplies the beer, it doesn't seem right!'

'Jack, it's always us that have the parties, so it's only fair that the others chip in. I don't mind having them here, I enjoy it, but we couldn't afford to fork out for all the food and drink every time. I'm not tight, but yer have to draw the line somewhere.'

'Me mam's right, Dad, it's only fair everyone makes a contribution,' Tommy said. 'Just think of all the parties we've had in this house. Every Christmas without fail, birthdays and weddings. And every time Uncle Corker comes home on leave. No one could afford to keep that up, unless they were loaded.'

'No, if yer look at it that way, I suppose not.'

'Well, I'm glad that's sorted out! Now when yer've finished yer dinner, Ruthie will bring the plates out.' Molly got as far as the kitchen door. 'By the way, is Liverpool playing at home this afternoon?'

Jack looked surprised. 'Yes, they are! But why the sudden interest? Yer've never asked me that before?'

'I thought yer might like to go to the match with George and Paul for a change. It would get yer out from under me feet. Then when I've done the baking I could give the room a good clear out without having to ask yer to shift all the time.'

Jack eyed his son. 'D'yer feel like going to the match, Tommy?'

The lad shook his head. It might only cost a few coppers, but those coppers were needed to swell the money he and Rosie had saved. 'No, I'll go round and sit with me nan and granda for an hour, then walk to meet Rosie when the shop closes.'

'Right, that's you two sorted out. And Ruthie, I suppose you'll be going over to Bella's?'

Ruthie frowned as she swung her legs back and forth under the chair. 'Where am I going tonight? I don't want to stay in with all the old fogeys.'

'Yer can go next door to Ellen's and have a game of cards with Gordon and Peter. Ask Bella if she'd like to come.'

That brought a smile to the girl's face. She had her eye on Ellen's son, Gordon. He was a working lad now, and thought himself all

71

grown-up. But she'd be leaving school herself next year, so she'd be grown-up herself then. 'Yeah, that's the gear, Mam, I'll go over and ask Bella now.'

'Table cleared first, sunshine, then the afternoon is yer own.'

Nellie and George were the first to arrive, and as soon as Molly opened the door she could see by her friend's face she was bursting with news and excitement. And when Nellie wanted to talk it was very difficult to shut her up. So Molly dragged her out to the kitchen, closed the door so no one could hear, then warned, 'Not a peep, sunshine, until everyone is here. The events of yesterday and this morning are going to be the highlight of this party so I want yer to promise to keep yer mouth shut and not spoil it.'

'Are we going to give a performance, girl?'

'We sure are, sunshine, we're going to have them rolling in the aisles.'

Nellie wagged her shoulders from side to side. 'Ooh, I can't wait, girl! But I can tell you a bit about what I found out, can't I? Just the Christian names of the Mowbrays, that can't hurt.' Her arms were folded and her bosom hitched. 'The mother is called Beryl and she's not bad when yer get talking to her. I didn't see her husband 'cos he was at work but his name's David. The lad we saw, Jeffrey, is fourteen, and there's a daughter called Joanne. But from what I saw, she's a hard case, dead forward and cheeky.'

Molly cocked an ear. 'There's a knock, sunshine, yer'll have to leave the rest till a bit later.' When she heard Corker's voice booming, Molly opened the kitchen door wide and let her friend in first. 'Welcome, Ellen, and you, Corker.'

'Molly, me darlin', ye're looking as pretty as ever.'

'Don't mind me,' Ellen said, 'I'm only yer wife.'

'And the best one in the world, me darlin'.' Corker dwarfed his wife when he put an arm across her shoulders. 'But I've been telling Molly for twenty years how pretty she is, if I stopped now she'd think she'd turned ugly. And if I may say so, Mrs McDonough is also looking very smart.' His weatherbeaten face grinned at Nellie before he handed over a heavy bag to Jack. 'A few bottles of beer to whet the whistle. Will they go in the kitchen?'

'Yeah, thanks, Corker. I'll wait for Maisie and Alec to come before pouring any drinks.'

'Was our Paul late for his date with Phoebe, Corker?' George asked. 'He was upstairs getting ready when we left, and honest to God, anyone would think he was going to Buckingham Palace, the time he spends polishing his shoes and slicking his hair.'

'Yeah, he knocked for Phoebe just as me and Ellen were coming out. They'll be off now to enjoy themselves. They make a fine-looking couple.'

'There's the door,' Molly said. 'It'll be Maisie and Alec. Make yerselves comfortable while I let them in, and then me and Nellie are going to entertain yer for an hour or so. And if me mate's in good form ye're in for a treat.'

Chapter 6

As Phoebe walked down the street with Paul, she was kicking herself for not having the guts to tell him she'd rather do something else than go dancing tonight. Her heart sank when she saw his dancing shoes under his arm, but she didn't say anything because her mam and dad were just going out and she didn't want to have words in front of them. Even now, because he seemed so happy and carefree, she was reluctant to speak out. It wasn't that she didn't like dancing, she did, but not every night. There were other things she would have preferred to do, like going on one of the Mersey ferries over to Seacombe and then walking to New Brighton. Or going to the pictures to sit on the back row of the stalls holding hands.

'Ye're quiet, aren't yer?' Paul said, looking down at her. 'I know ye're never very noisy or talkative, but yer seem more quiet than usual.'

Phoebe looked into his deep brown eyes and was lost. He loved dancing and she couldn't disappoint him. 'I'm all right, I just don't have much to talk about.'

They turned the corner of the street and saw a tram trundling towards the stop. 'That's handy, we're just in time.'

'Where are we going?'

'Blair Hall.' Paul cupped her elbow and helped her board the tram. 'I thought we'd honour them with our presence tonight.'

'Don't yer think it would be a good idea to ask me where I'd like to go?' Phoebe knew they'd end up in Blair Hall no matter what she said, but her pride told her she really couldn't let him get away with having his own way all the time. 'What if I'd wanted to go somewhere else, instead?'

Paul fished a sixpenny piece out of his pocket and handed it to the ticket collector who'd followed them to their seat. Then he waited for his ticket and change before answering. 'Where else would yer rather go?' He sounded surprised. 'I thought yer liked Blair Hall.'

'I do, but I think it would be nice if we did something else for a change. I know ye're mad on dancing, but every night is a bit much.'

'All yer have to do is say the word and we'll go wherever yer want.'

'We'll leave it for tonight 'cos yer've got yer heart set on dancing. But in future I'd like some say in the matter.'

The smile was back in those brown eyes and the dimples reappeared. 'Okay, boss, whatever you say.' Paul was happy now they were still on their way to Blair Hall. If Phoebe had insisted he would have given in to her, but he'd have been disappointed. He was at his happiest when gliding across the dance floor, and he excelled at it. There were few boys at any dance who could better him. He went every night, even on the two he wasn't seeing Phoebe. She had a night in to wash her hair and on the other night she went out with a girl from work.

'Next stop's ours, kiddo.' Paul left his seat and stood aside to let her go first, then put his hands on her slim waist to steady her when the tram lurched to a stop. 'Drunk again, Miss Corkhill, I'm going to tell yer mam and dad on yer.'

'That'll be the day.' Phoebe smiled into his face as they waited to cross the busy main road. 'I bet both our parents are enjoying a drink now at Auntie Molly's. And I bet they're having a good laugh.'

'That goes without saying.' He took her hand when the coast was clear, and they ran to the side entrance of the dance hall. 'Whenever me mam and Auntie Molly get together there's always high jinks.'

Paul paid the man at the door, then waited until Phoebe had checked her coat into the cloakroom. 'They're playing a tango, let's get cracking.'

They danced well together and made an attractive couple. Phoebe had a pretty face, slim figure, nicely shaped legs and long mousy-coloured hair which had been brushed until it shone. She was also the envy of many of the girls who had eyes for the tall, dark-haired boy who could set their hearts fluttering.

When they announced the next dance as a ladies' excuse-me quickstep, Phoebe groaned inwardly because they would no sooner take to the floor than some girl would touch Paul's shoulder and she'd be left to return to the edge. And it wasn't just one girl excusing him, it would be one every minute or so. Not for the world would she tell him she objected because then he'd think she was jealous. Which she was, of course, but that was something she'd never let him see. Her mam had warned her when she became old enough to date that she should never run after any boy as that was the quickest way to lose him.

It was only with reluctance that Phoebe allowed herself to be led on to the dance floor, and it was hard to keep a smile on her face. Her fears were realised when, after they'd covered just half the floor, a pretty dark-haired girl tapped Paul on the shoulder. He didn't think anything of it because he was used to it . . . it was an excuse-me, after all. But Phoebe was left to walk away, to stand on her own and watch. Then her mind rebelled and a voice in her head told her to find a chair and sit down instead.

She'd turned to walk towards the chairs lining the walls when she felt a hand on her arm. She looked sideways to find a tall blond boy smiling at her. 'Can I have this dance, please?'

When she opened her mouth to say she didn't want to dance, a voice in Phoebe's head told her not to be so soft. Why shouldn't she dance with a stranger? Paul was. And what was good for the goose was good for the gander. 'Yes, I'd like that.'

The boy was a good dancer and easy to follow. 'My name's Bill, what's yours?'

'Phoebe.'

'That's an unusual name but I like it.' He twirled her around with ease and she was happy she could follow his intricate footwork. 'Nice little dancer, too! D'yer come here often?'

'About once a week, usually. We go to Barlow's Lane and the Aintree Institute as well.'

'I notice yer said "we". Is the bloke yer came in with yer boyfriend?'

Phoebe blushed and lowered her eyes. 'Yes.'

'How long have yer been going out with him? Or am I being too nosy?'

'It's no secret, I've been seeing him for a few months now.'

The dance came to an end and she moved out of his arms. Smiling shyly, she said, 'Thank you.'

'It was my pleasure,' Bill told her, 'I'll see yer later.'

Paul watched her walking towards him. 'Who was the bloke?'

'How do I know? Except he said his name was Bill. Why?'

'Did yer tell him yer with me?' Paul looked very put out. 'I hope yer did.'

'I could ask yer the same thing, Paul. Did yer tell the dark-haired girl, or the blonde, that yer were with me?'

'That's different, that is! I didn't ask them to dance, they excused me!'

'And I didn't ask Bill to dance, he asked me!' Phoebe didn't usually have a temper and seldom raised her voice, but she was stung by the injustice. 'Would yer rather I sat like a wallflower while you enjoy yerself? That's a bit selfish, isn't it?'

Paul had the grace to blush. 'Yeah, it is, isn't it?' His smile reached his eyes. 'I'm not soft, am I? It's like me telling yer to sit and be a good little girl while I enjoy meself. That's dead selfish, and if I were you I'd tell me to get lost.'

'It's not worth falling out over, Paul, so just forget it.'

'Yeah, especially as they're playing a slow foxtrot, our favourite dance. Come into my arms, pretty lady, and let's get all romantic.'

After the interval they announced the next dance, a waltz, was to be a gentlemen's excuse-me. There won't be any problems here, Paul thought, as he lead Phoebe on to the dance floor. He'd never been excused by a bloke yet. But he found there was a first time for everything when Bill tapped him on the shoulder. 'Excuse me.'

The expression on Paul's face was difficult to describe. Surprise came first, then disbelief followed by a trace of anger. 'Can't yer find another girl? This one is mine.'

'It's a gentlemen's excuse-me, mate, and that's what I'm doing – I'm excusing yer.' Without further ado, Bill gently pulled Phoebe's arm free and waltzed off with her, leaving Paul standing scratching his head. But not for long. 'To hell with that,' he muttered, and gazed around for the nearest girl who was a good dancer. But all the time his eyes were following Phoebe and the bloke who was chatting away to her as they danced. As the strains of the waltz died away and Paul thanked his partner, he was not a happy man. Long-faced, he walked back to where Phoebe was standing.

'He had a bloody cheek, that feller! And you could have refused, yer know.'

'Paul McDonough, don't you dare swear at me! And if anyone's got a bloody cheek, it's you! What about the number of times I've been left like a lemon while you waltz off with some girl who's excused yer? I never hear you refusing to dance with them. But yer don't like it when the boot's on the other foot, do yer? Honest, ye're acting like a little boy who can't have what he wants, and it's about time yer grew up.'

Paul was taken aback. Shy, quiet Phoebe was actually shouting at him! And she looked so pretty with her flushed face, he wished he'd kept his mouth shut. 'I'm sorry, I was being very childish. Everything yer said is true, I was out of line. So now I've said I'm sorry, can I see a smile back on yer face, please?'

'Yer don't deserve to be forgiven because I'll be terrified now any time anyone asks me to dance. It's all right for you to laugh and joke with other girls, but heaven help me if I so much as look at another boy.' But looking into his deep brown, appealing eyes, Phoebe found herself weakening. 'Oh, forget it, we're both being childish. But I hope the same thing never happens again or I will lose me rag.'

'Yer look very pretty when ye're in a temper.' Paul put his arm around her slim waist. 'I'll be a good boy in future, I promise. Now, how about a rumba?'

He's a real charmer, Phoebe thought as they circled the room, and I'm a sucker for him. And with the thought came the memory of the man who had charmed her mother before they were wed, and had turned out to be a drunken rotter. A husband and father from hell. Thank God they had Corker for a father now and knew what a happy home was. But she would never forget Nobby Clarke, his foul language and his cruelty to her mam and the children. The way they'd starved and walked around with rags on their back. The memory of her father made her wary of all men. She didn't think for a second that Paul would turn out to be the same, and she was crazy about him, but it wouldn't hurt to keep him in check.

The last waltz was slow and dreamy, a good dance for singing softly and holding each other tight, upsets and tiffs forgotten for a while. 'Are yer friends with me again, Phoebe?' Paul whispered in her ear. ''Cos if ye're not, I won't be able to sleep. And I know yer wouldn't want to rob me of me beauty sleep, would yer?'

'Heaven forbid! We mustn't let Paul lose his beauty sleep.' She smiled her gentle smile before resting her head on his chest. 'Otherwise he might turn into a frog.'

'Yer'd still love me even if I was a frog, wouldn't yer?'

'Ooh, I don't know about that. I'd have to wait and see if my kiss would turn you into Prince Charming.' The dance was coming to an end and there would be a mad scramble for the cloakroom so Phoebe turned him towards the door. 'We can finish this conversation on the twenty-two tram or outside our front door.'

Paul grinned. 'There's always the side entry.'

'I'll tell me mam on you, Paul McDonough. Nice girls don't go down entries. Not with boys anyway. So yer'll have to be satisfied with a kiss outside our front door.'

With their arms around each other's waists, Phoebe and Paul walked up their street. They were a few doors away from the Bennetts' house when the door opened and a noisy, happy group of people spilled on to the pavement. And their laughter brought smiles to the young couple's faces.

'I might have known,' Paul said. 'Rotten drunk as usual.'

'Not quite, son, not quite.' Corker's loud guffaw carried the length of the street. 'Your mam has had us laughing so much there wasn't time for drinking.'

'Oh, aye, Mam, what have yer been up to now?' There was deep affection in Paul's eyes when he looked at his mother. 'Honest, ye're not fit to be let out.'

'I'll wager we had a better time than you, son,' George said. 'Yer mam and Auntie Molly entertained us with a play in three parts. The first act took place in the butcher's shop, the second in the queue at the cake shop and the finale had us looking out of your front window watching the new neighbours move in.'

'I've never laughed so much in all me life,' said Maisie from the corner shop. 'I thought Alec was going to choke, he laughed so much.'

'How about us all going into Auntie Molly's and doing it all over again?' Paul suggested. 'Me and Phoebe could do with a good laugh.'

'Yer know what yer can do with yerself, son, yer can sod off.' Nellie's nod was emphatic. 'If yer prefer to go jazzing instead of having some real fun, then that's yer own blinking fault.' She gave a loud hiccup, put a hand over her mouth and said in her poshest voice, 'Oh, pardon me, I'm sure. I don't know where that came from.'

'I don't know where it came from, sunshine, but I know where it's going – and that's in your house. It's time to call it a day 'cos we don't want to give the neighbours anything to complain about,' Molly said, her arm linked in Jack's. 'Besides, I'm bushed and ready for me bed.'

'Me too!' Maisie said. 'It's all right for you lot, yer can have a lie-in tomorrow. Me and Alec have to open the shop at eight o'clock. So while ye're lying there all snug and comfy, spare a thought for the poor beggars who have to work for a living.'

Corker slapped Alec on the back, catching him unawares and nearly sending him flying. A tap from the big man was like a blow from anyone else. 'I promise yer that as soon as I open me eyes, I'll start thinking about you two slaving away. I might even come up to sympathise with yer, say around one o'clock when the streets are aired off.'

Ellen gave him a dig. 'Let's make a move. Molly must be worn out. Her and Jack have done nothing but run around after us all night.'

'Ay, I did me whack,' Nellie said with indignation. 'Deputy hostess, that's what I was.'

Knowing his wife would be happy to stand there all night if she was let, George pulled on her arm. 'Come on, love, the party's over.'

Molly and Jack waved them off and closed the front door. 'Ooh, me feet are killing me,' Molly said, kicking her shoes off. 'I'll do without our usual cup of tea and go straight up.'

'Me too!' Jack pulled her close and hugged her. 'It was worth it though, love, 'cos it was a cracking night. The things you and Nellie get up to are unbelievable, and I bet yer don't tell me and George the half of it.'

She pecked his cheek. 'What yer don't know won't hurt yer, sunshine. And Nellie's the one who starts everything off. If yer knew some of the things she gets up to, you and George would have heart attacks. But I'll tell yer something, this street would be less friendly without her, and my life very dull.' She reached for his hand and pulled him towards the stairs. 'Come on, let's cuddle up nice and close and go to sleep.'

'That will be a very hard job,' Jack chuckled as he followed her up the stairs. 'If it's sleep yer want, I'd be better off sleeping with me back to yer on the very end of the bed.'

'Yer know what your trouble is, Jack Bennett? Yer've got no willpower.'

'That's only when I'm lying next to yer in bed, love. I've got loads of willpower when you're not around.'

Paul watched Corker insert the key in the lock and his heart sank. It looked as though he wasn't going to get his kiss tonight, 'cos Phoebe was bound to think she should go in with her mam and dad. But Corker hadn't forgotten what it was like to be young. 'Why don't yer come in for a cuppa, son? I'm sure my wife is going to make one.'

Ellen laughed. 'He's a proper tea-tank, my husband. He's had enough beer tonight to sink a ship but he still won't go to bed without his cup of char.'

Next door but one, George was opening their front door when he heard his wife behind him shout, 'Are we all invited for a cuppa, Ellen?'

'Nellie, are yer mad? Everyone is tired and can't get to bed quick enough. Surely yer've had enough entertainment for one night.'

'Well, why is Corker inviting our Paul in if he's as tired as yer say?'

'Because our son is going out with Phoebe, that's why. And if that doesn't sink in, get in the house and I'll draw yer a picture.' George stood back and waved her in. 'Go on, woman, get yourself inside.'

'Ooh, I do like me men to be masterful,' Nellie said. 'The strong silent type, like Gregory Peck or Randolph Scott. I could easy put a paper bag over yer head, George, and pretend it was Gregory or Randolph lying next to me.'

Much to the amusement of the Corkhills, George lifted his wife from the pavement and placed her in the hall. 'If it's the strong silent type yer want, I'm just the feller.' The only sound after that was the banging of the McDonoughs' door.

'She's quite a woman is your mam, son, one in a million.' Corker waved Paul to a seat on the couch. 'I've had more laughs out of her and Molly than I have out of Laurel and Hardy or Charlie Chase. Twenty odd years I've known them and their antics can still reduce me to tears.'

'Keep yer voice down, love,' Ellen said. 'Don't forget the children are asleep upstairs.'

'I think they're in the best place, I'm feeling tired meself now.' Corker could see his daughter hovering by the sideboard looking embarrassed and ill at ease. This was the first time Paul had been invited into the house as her boyfriend at such a late hour and he decided it would be best if he and Ellen made themselves scarce. 'I'll skip the tea tonight, love if yer don't mind.'

'I wasn't going to have one anyway,' Ellen told him. 'Three bottles of milk stout and two glasses of sherry are enough liquid for one night.'

'Yer won't think us rude if we leave yer, son, will yer?' Corker asked, trying to keep a straight face. 'Phoebe will make yer a drink.'

'That's fine, Uncle Corker. I won't keep her up too late, I promise. Just a cup of tea and I'll toddle off home.'

The big man curled the ends of his moustache and asked, 'What, no goodnight kiss?'

'That depends upon Phoebe.' Paul's eyes twinkled. 'We nearly had our first falling out tonight. All because a girl excused me in a quickstep, and a feller called Bill excused Phoebe in a waltz.'

'To me that sounds like a very good reason to fall out.' Corker stroked his bushy beard while his laughing eyes twinkled beneath his thick eyebrows. 'Hmm! What did yer say the feller's name was . . . Bill?'

'So Phoebe told me, I don't know the bloke from Adam.' Paul knew Corker was in a teasing mood and went along with it. 'I'll know him next time, though, and I'll tell him to get lost.'

'You will not!' Phoebe said. 'Yer'll not make a show of me in front of everyone. If yer do, yer'll be dancing on yer own the rest of the night.' As soon as the words left her mouth she realised how stupid they were. For Paul would never be short of partners. Still, she'd said it now and wasn't going to take the words back. 'So don't try it.'

'Did yer know yer daughter had a temper, Auntie Ellen?' Paul asked. 'She's got a real little paddy when she starts. She tore a strip of me in front of everyone and I thought I was back at school getting told off by the headmaster. I didn't half feel soft.'

Phoebe's mouth gaped. 'You fibber! Take no notice of him, Mam, he's acting daft.'

'We know he is, love, he's like his mam. Anyway, I'd be glad if yer did have a temper. I only wish I'd had one at your age.' Ellen jerked her head, 'Come on, Corker, I'm dead beat and bed is calling.'

When they heard the bedroom door close, Phoebe tutted and wagged her finger. 'You'll get me hung one of these days, Paul McDonough. Fancy saying that in front of me mam and dad.'

'It was said in fun, Phoebe, can't yer take a joke?'

She surprised him when she put a hand over her mouth to smother the sound of her laughter. 'I know that, soft lad. Now, d'yer want a cup of tea or not?'

'No, I want yer to sit down next to me.' He patted the empty space on the couch. 'D'yer realise this is the first time we've ever been in a room on our own? I'd rather not waste it by drinking tea.'

'Oh, and what would yer rather be doing?'

'Getting down to some serious kissing. All I've had so far from yer are a few pecks. I want to show yer what a real kiss is like.'

'Yer've had plenty of experience, then?'

Paul chuckled. 'No, I'm going to practise on you. I went to Connie Millington's to learn how to dance properly, but she wouldn't give me lessons in how to kiss.'

Phoebe twisted around to face him. 'Well, all yer do is pucker yer lips, like this.' She had her eyes closed when his lips touched hers, soft and tender. Her heart flipped and her tummy did somersaults. If she hadn't been sitting down she would have swooned.

'Was that nice?' Paul asked, his heartbeat racing. 'Will I pass the test?'

'It's hard to tell after one. Yer'd better give me another.' Phoebe puckered up again and waited for the thrill to run down her spine. She wasn't disappointed.

* * *

It was a Monday morning and Molly and Nellie were on their way to the shops when they saw their new neighbour walking towards them with a heavily laden basket. 'Hello, girl, ye're out early, aren't yer?'

'I thought I'd get me shopping in before I started on the bleedin' washing. I hate Monday, I always dread it.'

Nellie straightened her shoulders and pushed out her bosom. She felt really important 'cos her friend hadn't met their new neighbour yet so it was up to her to make the introductions. 'This is me mate, Molly, I told yer about her. And this is Beryl, girl, Beryl Mowbray.'

Molly held out her hand. 'Hello, Beryl, I'm pleased to make yer acquaintance.'

'Same here, queen, same here.' Beryl put the basket on the ground while she shook hands. 'I feel as though me arms are being pulled out of their sockets carrying that bleedin' thing. It weighs a ruddy ton!'

Molly looked down at the basket. 'Yer should have got some of these things on Saturday, save lugging this in one go. The likes of potatoes and washing powder, they weigh heavy.'

'Yeah, I know, queen! But I'm still sorting boxes out, finding places to put things, and I'm all at sixes and sevens. I spent all day Saturday knocking nails in walls to hang me pictures up, and unpacking crockery. My feller is useless, hasn't got a bleedin' clue.'

'Yer should have sent one of yer children to the shops, girl, save trying to do the lot on yer own. The kids are old enough to go to the shops for yer.'

'Nellie, me kids are worse than their father! Our Joanne is seventeen and she's one lazy cow. She won't do a hand's turn in case she breaks her bleedin' nails! All she's fit for is titivating herself up with powder an inch thick and bright red lipstick. She thinks she looks like a film star though she looks more like a tart. I've told her until I'm blue in the face but she doesn't take a blind bit of notice.' Beryl sighed. 'As for our Jeff, he started work a few months ago and thinks he's too grown up to be going on messages. Not long ago he'd have run to the ends of the earth if there was a penny in it. Still, there's folk worse off than me.' She bent and picked up the basket. 'I'd better be on me way, the bleedin' bedding and clothes won't wash themselves. It was nice meeting yer, Molly, and I'll see yer around.'

'D'yer want us to give yer a hand, sunshine? We could lighten yer load a bit.'

'No, thanks, queen, I'll manage. But the mood I'm in now, if either of me kids have any complaints about their dinner tonight, or even look sideways at me, I'll give them the rounds of the kitchen. And any cheek, I'll clock them one.'

The friends watched her as she walked away, leaning heavily to one side with the weight of the basket. 'We don't know we're born with our kids, sunshine, not after listening to that. Our Tommy's twenty, but he'd think nothing of running to the shops for me.'

'If they were mine I'd give them a bloody good hiding.' Nellie took her friend's arm and they turned around towards the main road. 'I told yer the girl looked a hard clock, didn't I? Yer can tell by her attitude that she's brazen.'

'I'm surprised Beryl lets them get away with it, she looks the type that could hold her own if it came to a fight. Still, sunshine, as long as they don't interfere with me or mine, they can get on with it.' Molly suddenly began to laugh. 'Here's me saying she looks the type to hold her own when I can't hold me own with you! I'm back in the gutter, Nellie!'

'What are yer doing down there, girl?'

'You pushed me here!'

'I never did no such thing! Now get back up here before I slap yer hand.' Nellie's chubby face beamed. 'Ay, girl, I'm not half glad you're me friend. I wouldn't like one what had kids who gave me cheek.' She tucked her arm in Molly's. 'Anyway, what are we having for dinner tonight?'

'I don't know, sunshine. What I do know is, if I give mine stew again they'll all leave home. I'm fed up with it meself. Fed up looking at it, fed up cooking it and fed up eating it.'

'What else is there? We haven't got enough coupons for a joint.'

'Let's work our charms on Tony, see what we can get out of him. I wouldn't mind sausages for a change, or a ham shank.'

'Yer'll have to do more than work yer charms for two ham shanks, girl. I think that would take the dance of the seven veils.'

'I don't need two ham shanks, sunshine, one will do me. So I'll work me charms and you can do the dance of the seven veils for your shank.'

If Molly could have seen the glint in her mate's eyes she would have taken her words back. But she didn't, and was in for the surprise of her life.

'Morning, Tony! Morning, Ellen!' Molly gave her brightest smile. 'How are yer both on this fine November day?'

The butcher looked suspicious. 'Oh, aye, what are yer after, Molly?'

'I'm working me charms on yer to see if I can wangle a ham shank.'

Nellie pulled on her arm. 'I'm just nipping down to the greengrocer's, girl, I won't be long.'

'Ay, hang on! I've got to go there, too!' But Molly's words were wasted because her friend had disappeared. 'I don't know what's suddenly got into her, she knows I've got to go for some spuds as well!'

'There's no accounting for Nellie's actions, Molly, yer know that. But she'll be back in a minute, you'll see. She won't stay away from you for long.' With it being Monday morning, Tony's white coat was spotlessly clean. He tried to keep it that way for as long as he could, but while he was talking to Molly, without thinking, he ran his blood-stained hands down the front of it. 'Oh, look what I've done now! That's what yer charms have done to me, Mrs Bennett.'

Ellen slipped out to the stockroom and came back with a navy and white striped apron. 'It's yer own fault, Tony, I told yer to put an apron on.'

'Don't you start, Ellen, ye're beginning to sound like me wife.' Tony tied the apron at the back and then grinned. 'Yer didn't happen to see a ham shank out there, did yer?'

'Yes, as a matter of fact I did!' Ellen gave her neighbour a broad wink. 'It's nice and lean, too, with plenty of meat on it.'

'How many coupons is it, Tony, 'cos . . .' Molly's words petered out when an apparition floated into the shop. It had Nellie's face, but the body was wearing a man's overcoat over a canvas apron. 'In the name of God, what have yer been up to now? Where the hell did yer get those things from, and why are yer wearing them? Yer look a sight!'

'Well, it's your fault, girl! Yer said I had to do a dance of the seven veils so Tony would give me a ham shank. And I counted up and didn't have seven things to take off! There was me coat, me dress, me knickers, vest and stockings. That's only five, girl, so I borrowed these off Billy at the greengrocer's to make up the seven.'

While Molly looked bewildered, Tony and Ellen were doubled up. What a lovely way to brighten up a dull Monday morning. 'And ye're going to do a dance for us, are yer, Nellie?'

She narrowed her eyes. 'Is me mate getting a ham shank?'

The butcher nodded. 'She hasn't got it yet, but yeah, she's getting one.'

'And if I do this dance, do I get one?'

'Ah, well, it all depends. The last time I saw a girl doing the dance of the seven veils, it was at the Metropole in Stanley Road. And blow me, didn't she leave one veil on! The place was in an uproar, everyone wanted their money back, saying they'd been had.'

'Well, if there's a ham shank at stake, this girl ain't going to leave a veil on.' Nellie moved Molly to stand by the window. 'I need plenty of room for this, girl. An artist can't give her best if the conditions are not right.'

'Nellie, as a bit of encouragement, if I think the performance is up to standard I'll let yer have the ham shank without coupons.'

'Tony, ye're going to see a performance like what yer've never seen before.' Nellie had to tilt her head back so she could look down her nose at Molly. 'As my best friend, and in appreciation of my talents, I want you to sing for me. I can't dance without music, yer see. So let's have something slow and smoochy.'

'I'm not standing in a butcher's shop singing, sunshine, not on your life! Besides the fact that I can't sing, I don't know any songs!'

'I know a slow smoochy song,' Ellen said. '"Girl Of My Dreams" would be great. And I know yer know the words, Molly, 'cos I've heard yer singing it.'

'Oh, all right, but you and Tony can help me out if I get stuck.' After clearing her throat and telling herself she must be mad, Molly began to sing softly. But she didn't get far before her laughter started.

Nellie had begun by slipping the greengrocer's overcoat off one shoulder and moving her body from side to side, her bosom swaying in time to the singing. Then she did the same with the other shoulder. Next, the coat was allowed to fall to the floor and she stood with her hands on her hips wiggling them from side to side with every ounce of her eighteen-stone body in motion. And the appreciative laughter she could hear egged her on. The canvas overall came off next, to be swung around over her head several times before being aimed at Tony.

By this time, Nellie was really enjoying herself. Down to her own coat now, she started undoing the buttons while swaying from side to side and smiling at her audience of three. Tony thought he was going to be sick he'd laughed so much, and the tears were rolling down Ellen's face. Only Molly was watching closely. Her laughter was loud, but knowing what her friend was capable of, she was ready to pounce if necessary.

With a smile on her face, Nellie was keeping her laughter to herself. She knew her mate inside out, and realised she'd be having kittens right now. So I'd better hurry up, she told herself, before Molly spoils me finale.

Still humming and swaying from side to side, Nellie let her coat fall to the floor. The dress she was wearing was buttoned to the waist and, taking her time, she undid the top button. Her fingers slid to the second button. It was then she started to get worried. What was Molly waiting for? A joke was a joke, but standing in a butcher's shop with her bosom exposed wasn't funny. Her George would have a duck egg if he knew!

'All right, sunshine, that's enough.' Molly picked up the coat from the floor and handed it over. 'I couldn't stand the sight of you, in yer nuddy, this time of the morning.'

'Ah, just as it was getting interesting,' Tony laughed. 'Ye're a spoilsport, Molly.'

'I'm mad, yer mean!' She turned her head to wink at him and Ellen. 'I must be to have a mate what takes all her clothes off in a shop. Just wait until I tell her feller.'

Nellie, dressed in her coat by this time, looked at her friend with disdain. 'Ye're only jealous 'cos yer haven't got a figure like mine. I bet Tony wouldn't give a ham shank to see what *you've* got under yer clothes.'

'I wouldn't be too sure about that, Nellie,' he said, his throat feeling hoarse from laughter. 'But I have to say you surpassed yerself today. It's the funniest bit of acting I've seen in me life. It's a pity yer didn't have a bigger audience.'

'She nearly did,' Ellen said. 'Here's two customers now.'

'Put those two shanks in a bag, will yer, before anyone sees them.' The butcher smiled at the two women who were regular customers. 'I won't keep yer long, I'm just finishing serving Molly and Nellie.'

Ellen came through from the back with a parcel wrapped in newspaper which she handed over to Molly. 'How much, Tony?'

'Two bob.'

'Is that a shilling each, Tony?' Nellie asked, looking hopeful. And when the butcher nodded her grin stretched from ear to ear.

'Ay, what are they getting for a shilling each?' one of the women asked. 'A flippin' big parcel like that, and only two bob? That's favouritism, that is.'

Nellie sidled up to the woman who was about eight inches taller than her. 'D'yer want to make something of it, Aggie Arkwright?'

'Any time ye're ready, Nellie McDonough.'

'For heaven's sake, grow up, the pair of yer,' Molly said. 'All this over a bag of bones!'

'Bones!' Aggie snorted. 'Pull the other one – it's got bells on.'

Nellie pushed her. At least, Nellie's bosom pushed her. 'It's you

88

what should have a bell around yer neck to let people know ye're coming so they can get out of the way.'

'Ooh, I'll have yer for that,' said Aggie Arkwright. She handed her basket to her friend, saying, 'Hang on to that while I go outside with this one.'

Tony looked at Ellen, his eyes asking if he should interfere. She shook her head, knowing that Molly wouldn't let the argument come to blows. And she was right.

'Ye're acting like kids, yer stupid nits.' Molly pushed the two women apart. 'All this because we wanted some bones to make a pan of soup! Yer want to get yer facts right, Aggie, before yer start throwing yer weight around.' She was asking God to forgive her for telling lies when she turned to Nellie. 'And you, you're just as bad. What I should do is let yer go outside and knock hell out of each other. But as I haven't got time to waste playing referee, will yer pay Tony and let's be on our way.'

'You pay him, girl, and I'll see yer right when we get home.'

'Don't push yer luck, sunshine, pay the man yerself. And don't forget Billy's coat and apron, 'cos I'm not carrying them.'

While Tony and Ellen had to wait for another quiet period before they could enjoy going over Nellie's version of the dance of the seven veils, it was not so with Molly and Nellie. They were no sooner out of the shop than they were doubled up laughing so loud that people passing wished they could share in the joke.

'Oh, dear, oh, dear, oh, dear!' Molly was holding her side. 'You were brilliant, sunshine, yer really were. And then Aggie Arkwright butting in was the icing on the cake. I can't wait for tonight to tell the family.'

'Can I come down?' Nellie asked. 'I could show them how I did it.'

'I'm sorry, sunshine, but I'm going round to me ma's. Tommy and Rosie are setting the date for their wedding, and they want to talk to me about it. If they don't book the church before Christmas, all the Saturdays in the summer will be spoken for.'

'When are they hoping to get married, girl?'

'I won't know until tonight. I would imagine July, but I'm not sure.' Molly linked her friend's arm and squeezed. 'I'll let yer know in the morning when yer can get yer posh hat out to dust.'

'And comb the feather, girl, don't forget the feather.'

'How could I ever forget the feather, sunshine?'

''Cos I won't let yer, that's why.' Nellie's chubby face creased.

'I've enjoyed meself this morning, girl, have you?'
'I have that, sunshine! It beats Monday morning blues any time.'

Chapter 7

'What date in July are yer hoping for, son?' Molly was seated at the end of the table in her parents' home with Jack facing her. At one side sat Bridie and Bob, and opposite them Tommy and Rosie. 'Yer'll have to get in quick because more couples want to get married in July than any other month of the year.'

'The last week would be the best. The firm closes down for two weeks' summer holiday and it would mean I wouldn't have to take time off.' Tommy gave his mother a wide smile of affection. 'I know I'm being optimistic, but it's better than being a merchant of doom. Anyway, there's another reason for wanting that date. It would mean I could spend more time with Rosie's mam and dad.'

'Ooh, isn't it exciting, Auntie Molly?' Rosie's beautiful face was aglow. 'It's meself that won't be getting any sleep from now until we've been to see Father Kelly.'

'Then it's yerself that'll have to get down to the church as soon as yer can, sweetheart,' Bridie said. 'If yer lose too much sleep yer'll be selling the customers odd shoes, and we can't be having that now.'

Tommy chuckled. 'Anyone walking with two left shoes on, we'll know they bought them from Rosie's shop.'

'Never mind shoes, let's get on with this wedding,' Molly said. 'Tell us what yer have planned so far.'

'Nothing definite, Auntie Molly, they're just wishes and hopes at the moment.'

'Then tell us about yer wishes and hopes, sunshine.'

'Hopes first, Auntie Molly, and top of the list is the priest saying we can get married on the last Saturday in July. I'm sure he will, 'cos isn't Father Kelly an understanding man? Then we pray and hope nothing comes along to stop me mammy and daddy from being here to see their daughter marrying such a foine upstanding man as Tommy. They'll be so proud of me, so they will.'

'It'll be a proud day for all of us, Rosie.' Jack smiled at the girl who had brought so much happiness into their lives. 'You'll officially become one of the family then.'

'Sure, hasn't she been one of the family since the day she set foot in Liverpool?' Bridie was inclined to get emotional when she thought of their beloved grandson marrying the girl they'd come to love so much. And that they would be starting their married life in this little house was like a dream come true for the elderly couple. 'We wouldn't know what to do without her, would we, sweetheart?'

'We certainly wouldn't,' Bob said. 'We'd have nothing to talk about if it wasn't for Rosie keeping us up-to-date with what's going on in the world. And especially what goes on in a certain shoe shop in Walton Vale. According to what she tells us, there's some queer folk in Liverpool and plenty of comedians.'

'We're getting off the subject,' Molly reminded them. 'I thought yer wanted to get as much sorted out as yer could?'

'Come on, Tommy Bennett, this is your wedding as well as mine, so don't be leaving it all to me.' Rosie's thick black hair bounced on her shoulders when she turned to face the boy she'd set her sights on the first day she saw him. They were both fifteen then and Tommy was at that awkward stage in a boy's life where he'd rather be with his mate, Ginger, than bothering with stupid girls who never stopped talking about stupid things. 'I've said my piece, now it's your turn.'

'D'yer think we could have the reception at Hanley's, Mam?' Tommy asked. 'They put a very good spread on for Jill and Doreen, and we'd be made up if they'd do the same for us.'

'You get me a definite date as soon as yer can, sunshine, and I'll have a word with the Hanleys. They'd be only too happy to do the reception for yer, I'm sure. Food isn't as hard to come by now that rationing is easing off so that won't be a problem. In fact, if yer've got the money there's nothing yer can't get on the black market.'

'Well, cash is going to be tight, Mam. The spivs won't be getting rich on our money. And, anyway, even if we were loaded I wouldn't buy off blokes who were making a good living while others were out there fighting a war. I know a lot of lads weren't called up because of ill health, and that wasn't their fault, but spivs really get up my nose.' Tommy's face creased into a smile. 'Right, now I've got that off me chest we can carry on where we left off. The next thing on our list is bridesmaids. D'yer think Jill, Doreen and Ruthie would be bridesmaids for us?'

'Yer sisters are married women now, sunshine, so they'd have to be matrons of honour. But I'm sure they'd jump at the chance. Ye're their only brother and they love the bones of yer, so they'll be delighted. Their bridesmaids' dresses will be as good as new, and I'm sure Lily and Maureen won't mind giving them back for yer sisters to wear. We could titivate them up so they look a bit different and it would save yer forking out for new ones which would be a complete waste of money. That's if yer wouldn't mind, Rosie? It's your wedding, the only one yer'll ever have, please God, so it's up to you entirely.'

'I wouldn't mind in the least, Auntie Molly. Sure there's no disgrace in being practical, as me mammy would say.'

'Well, I suggest yer go and see Father Kelly tomorrow night after work, and get the date fixed. Then come straight to ours and I'll have Jill and Doreen there, with their husbands of course, and leave it to you to ask them.' Molly looked across at her parents. 'Ma, you and Da come as well. Then we'll all know what's going on.'

'There's one other thing, Mam,' Tommy said, 'and that's me best man. I don't know who to ask because I can't choose between Ginger, who's been me mate since the day I started school, or Archie, who is, as yer all know, my hero.'

'That's a difficult one, sunshine, and only you can solve it. But yer don't have to do anything now. Leave it and give it some thought. I'm glad it's you who has to make the decision, not me, because I like both of them.'

Jack was glancing anxiously at the clock. 'Don't forget we've left Ruthie on her own, love, and we told her we wouldn't be long.'

'Bella's with her, she's not on her own. And they're not stupid kids, they're not likely to set the house on fire. Anyway, I want to give Ma and Da a damn good laugh. They like to be kept up-to-date with the exploits of my very best mate, Mrs Helen Theresa McDonough.'

Bob leaned his elbows on the table, laughter already showing in his eyes. 'Oh, aye, what's she been up to now?'

'It's not what she got up to, Bob,' Jack told him. 'It's what she got down to, and that was the top two buttons. Anyway, Molly's better at telling tales than I am.'

'I should hope so, sunshine, 'cos I was there, wasn't I? Which is just as well, 'cos God knows what she'd get up to if I wasn't at hand to keep an eye on her. She'd probably end up in the police station.' Molly's chuckle was deep in her throat. 'With my luck, I'd probably be put in the cell next to her!'

'I don't know where ye're all going to sit, there's not enough chairs to go round.' Molly was fussing, trying to seat everyone while thinking how big her family had grown. Her two eldest daughters were there with their husbands, her ma and da, Tommy and Rosie, and herself and Jack. There was only Ruthie missing; she'd been sent over to her friend's out of the way. 'The young ones can sit on each other's knees.'

When they were all seated, Molly leaned her arms on the table and raised her brows at Tommy. 'Well, sunshine, how did yer get on?'

The smile that he'd been keeping back now spread across the lad's handsome face as he tightened his arm around Rosie's waist. 'All fixed up, Mam! We are getting married on July the twenty-seventh at two o'clock.'

There were loud murmurs of approval as Molly left her chair to give her son and his future wife a big hug. There were tears at the back of her eyes, of joy mixed with sadness. She was so happy that he was marrying Rosie, the girl he adored and who would make him a very good wife. But she couldn't help thinking she'd soon be losing her only son, the third of her children to leave the nest in one year. 'I'm so happy for yer, sunshine, and for you, Rosie. Now yer can start planning yer wedding.'

'Have yer mentioned anything to Jill and Doreen, Mam?'

Molly shook her head. 'I thought yer'd rather ask them yerself.'

'What d'yer want to ask us, Tommy?' Jill asked, her pretty face aglow with happiness for her brother.

'As long as it's not a loan ye're after,' Doreen laughed, 'then the answer's "yes".'

'Will yer both be Rosie's matrons of honour?'

Jill didn't hesitate. 'Oh, I'd love to be, Rosie, thank you!'

When Doreen didn't answer, and Molly noticed the smile had left her face, she asked, 'What about you, Doreen, has the cat got yer tongue?'

Her face red with embarrassment, and gripping Phil's hand so tight her knuckles were white, the girl faced her mother. 'I won't be able to, Mam.'

'Why not?' Jack leaned forward. 'Yer can't let yer brother down.'

It was Phil who answered. 'Doreen wouldn't let Tommy down if she could help it, Mr Bennett. But, yer see, she's expecting a baby.'

You could have heard a pin drop. It was as though everyone had stopped breathing. Molly couldn't take it in, she stared at her daughter with her mouth gaping. Then she said, 'Is this yer idea of a joke, Doreen?'

Once again Phil stepped in to save his wife any more

embarrassment. 'It's not a joke, Mrs Bennett, Doreen is expecting a baby. We weren't certain ourselves until she went to the doctor's this afternoon. The baby's due in May.'

Doreen kissed his cheek before taking up the cudgels on her own behalf. 'We went in for the baby, Mam, for a special reason. Aunt Vicky is just on ninety and we both agreed that we'd like to have a child before anything happens to her.'

This time, when Molly left her chair, she didn't try to keep the tears back. Holding out her arms, she said, 'Come here, sunshine.'

Wrapped safely in her mother's embrace, Doreen felt at home. 'I'm glad that's over, Mam, I didn't know how I was going to tell yer.' When she felt her father's arms come around her, she sniffed up and managed a grin. 'Hello, Granddad.'

Jack cupped her face. 'Ye're making an old man of me already. But I'm very happy for you and Phil, and me and yer mam are over the moon.'

In the midst of congratulations, kisses, back slapping and hand shaking, a thought crossed Molly's mind. 'Steve, go and get yer mam.'

'Ah, no, Mam!' Doreen said, knowing what her Auntie Nellie was like for jokes. 'You tell her tomorrow.'

'I'm sorry, sunshine, but every time I was expecting, Nellie was the first to know and I was the first to know about hers. I'm not letting that tradition die. So go and get yer mam, Steve, but don't tell her what I want her for.'

Within minutes, Nellie waddled in. She took one look at the crowd and said, 'My God, what is this? A mothers' meeting for fathers only?' She jerked her thumb at Steve, whose dimples showed he was feeling very happy. 'This feller walked in, looking as though he'd lost a tanner and found half a crown! So I know whatever yer want me for, it isn't bad news.'

'No, it isn't, sunshine.' Molly was feeling so proud as she said, 'There's yer chair, so make yerself comfortable and we'll tell yer the wonderful news.'

Nellie's eyes narrowed with suspicion as she sat down. She wiggled her bottom backwards until she was resting against the chair back, and then put her hands on the arms. This left her feet dangling four inches from the floor, but a little disadvantage like that was the last thing on her mind. 'Well, don't all sit there staring at me as though I'm a dummy in a shop window! What the hell is going on?'

'There's a new baby on the way,' Molly said, beaming.

Nellie's legs stopped swinging and her mouth gaped. 'Ye're not in the family way again, are yer, girl?' She glared at Jack. 'What the hell d'yer think ye're playing at? Yer should be past that sort of thing now.'

'Nellie, I'm going to be a grandmother, sunshine, not a mother! Isn't that marvellous?'

It took a few seconds for it to sink in, then Nellie cast her eyes on her son. 'Why didn't yer tell me, yer silly nit! I'm yer mother, I should have been the first to be told.'

Steve chuckled. 'It's got nothing to do with me, Mam, so it wasn't my place to tell yer.'

'What d'yer mean, it's nothing to do with you! Yer've made a baby so it's got everything to do with you! Now just go home and tell yer dad.'

Molly touched her arm. 'Nellie, it's Doreen that's having the baby.' And she went on to explain why her daughter and Phil had tried for a baby so soon after getting married.

This really found Nellie's soft spot. As the tears started to trickle slowly down her chubby cheeks, she gulped, 'Look what yer've gone and made me do now, yer silly buggers. And I haven't got no hankie with me, either.'

Steve came to her rescue. 'Here yer are, Mam, use mine, it's clean. And I don't know what ye're crying for, it's supposed to be a happy occasion.'

'I know that, son, and as soon as I've blown me nose, I'll tell Doreen and Phil how happy I am for them. And after that I'll be reminding you of the little arrangement me and yer mother-in-law had when we first got married.'

Molly frowned and scratched her head. 'Oh, aye, what arrangement was that, sunshine?'

'Yer know very well what it was! A year after Steve was born, you had Jill. Then the year after, I had Lily and you had Doreen. The following year it was Paul and Tommy. I'm leaving Ruthie out of it 'cos I had nothing to do with yer having a baby after an interval of seven years.'

Not so long ago, this conversation would have had Jill blushing to the roots of her hair. But since marrying Steve, and getting used to her mother-in-law, she'd gained confidence and come out of her shell. 'What's this got to do with Steve, Auntie Nellie?'

'Well, it's like this, girl. Me and me mate will want it to run in the family. To be passed down, like, yer know? So when Doreen's baby is twelve months old, I'll expect to be a grandma to the latest edition to the McDonough family. And I don't mean fifteen months or two years, I mean dead on twelve months.' Nellie's eyes met her son's. 'D'yer think yer can manage that, Steve, or shall I buy yer a book on how it's done?'

The loudest laugh came from him. 'Me and Jill would like to oblige, Mam, but I'm afraid a house comes before a baby. We've got to get our priorities right.'

'Lizzie Corkhill wouldn't mind yer having a baby, she'd be over the moon! Ask her if yer don't believe me.'

'That's enough, Nellie, ye're going too far,' Molly said, thanking God Ruthie wasn't there. 'I should have left it till tomorrow to tell yer 'cos we've wasted a lot of time now. We were discussing Tommy and Rosie's wedding when Doreen dropped her bombshell and everything else was forgotten. My mind's in a whirl – I still can't get used to the idea of my daughter becoming a mother. It seems no time at all since she was at school. But for the time being, we'll have to put that aside and talk about the wedding. And when yer've all gone home me and Jack will sit quietly and talk about how much we're looking forward to the day when our first grandchild is born.'

'Oh, God,' Nellie groaned, letting her head drop into her hands. 'That's all I'm going to get off her for the next nine months. She hasn't got much of a chest, nothing worth talking about, but she'll be sticking it out as far as it'll go, and bragging to anyone who'll listen to her. Yer'd think she was the only one ever to become a grandmother. If she starts looking down her nose at me, so help me, I'll clock her one.'

Molly raised her brows. 'Have yer got it all off yer chest now, sunshine? Are yer finished?'

'Yes, I've finished, girl.' Nellie sounded very docile. 'You lot carry on and I'll just sit here taking it all in. But I'll be quite happy to help if yer need any advice. Molly won't be much use now, her head's in the clouds and she won't be thinking straight. But I'm here if yer need me, and yer all know I'm a dab hand at arranging weddings.'

Molly gasped. 'Yer've never arranged a wedding in yer life!'

'I got George to the church on time, didn't I? I wouldn't let him go with his best man in case he passed a pub on the way and decided he'd rather have a pint than get married. So to make sure, we went to the church together 'cos I didn't want to let him out of me sight until I had the ring on me finger.' Nellie hoisted her bosom and folded her arms under it before sitting back in the chair. 'And besides, Molly Bennett, who had the best hat on at yer daughter's wedding? I did, that's who! It's me what's got the best taste.'

Molly sighed. They'd never get anywhere while her mate sat there telling stories to make them laugh. This wasn't a party, they were all here to sort out the details of Rosie and Tommy's wedding. 'Nellie, will yer put the kettle on and make us a cup of tea?' Then she remembered how heavy-handed her friend was with crockery. 'Give us a shout when the tea's ready and I'll lend yer a hand with the cups.'

Nellie shuffled to the edge of the chair and pushed herself up with both hands. Then she glanced at Tommy. 'Am I invited to this wedding, lad?'

'Of course yer are, Auntie Nellie! Ye're top of the guest list.'

Looking very pleased with herself, Nellie smiled sweetly. 'For that compliment, lad, I'll put two spoonfuls of sugar in yer tea. But don't tell yer mam or she'll have me life.'

The next morning, Molly crossed the street to Victoria Clegg's house. She hadn't slept much, thinking about her daughter expecting a baby, and she wanted to have a word with Doreen to make sure the girl understood that in her condition she mustn't be shifting heavy furniture around, or climbing ladders to clean the high windows.

'Ye're an early bird, Mam,' Doreen said, holding the door wide to let her mother pass. 'Is everything all right?'

'Of course it is, sunshine! It's just that we didn't get much chance to talk last night, what with one thing and another, so I thought I'd nip over before Nellie calls for me to go to the shops.' Molly smiled at Victoria who was seated at the table finishing her breakfast. The old lady didn't come downstairs as early as she used to as it took her much longer nowadays to get washed and dressed. After giving her a hug, Molly asked, 'Well, what d'yer think of the news, eh? I bet yer were as surprised as we were?'

'Perhaps I'm being selfish, Molly, but I am so happy. I just pray that God spares me long enough to see and hold the baby.'

'Victoria Clegg, what sort of talk is that? The way you're going on, yer'll still be here to see the child starting school! And yer'd better be here for our Tommy's wedding, too, or he'll never speak to yer again.'

The faded blue eyes crinkled. 'I'd better pull me socks up then, hadn't I? I wouldn't like it if Tommy wasn't speaking to me.'

Molly pulled out a chair. 'Yer could have knocked me over with a feather when Phil came out with it last night. And as for Jack, he's gone to work in a daze. As I was waving him off, I heard him muttering,

"I'm going to be a granddad, I'm going to be a granddad!" And there was a spring in his step. Usually he has to walk quick to keep up with Tommy, but it was the other way around this morning. He is one very happy man.'

Doreen leaned back against the sideboard and folded her arms. 'I'm sorry it came out when it did, Mam, me and Phil were going to tell you and me dad before anyone else. But it couldn't be helped, I had to say I couldn't be a matron of honour 'cos the baby will be about two months old then. I feel a bit sad at not being there for Tommy and Rosie, but I'm not sad about the baby, I'm delighted. So is Phil, he's got a permanent smile on his face.'

Victoria was picking at the tablecloth and there was a hint of devilment in her eyes. 'I had an idea weeks ago that yer were pregnant, Doreen, because there was something different about yer. I couldn't put me finger on it at first, then I noticed yer face was filling out a little and yer seemed to be so contented with life.'

'Well, yer sly old thing!' Doreen moved to the back of the old lady's chair and put her arms around her. 'Yer probably knew before we did, 'cos we weren't really sure until I saw the doctor yesterday.'

'I hope he told yer to take things easy, sunshine,' Molly said. 'No lifting or moving heavy furniture or standing on ladders.'

Her daughter grinned. 'He told me to be careful, that's all. And to go back in a couple of months for an examination.'

Molly dropped her eyes. She wasn't going to mar her daughter's happiness by telling her what that examination would entail. And that if she'd thought telling her parents about the baby was embarrassing, then it was nothing to what was to come. It was something every expectant mother had to go through, but knowing that wasn't any consolation. 'I'll come with yer next time, sunshine, just to keep yer company. But in the meanwhile I'll be keeping me eye on yer.'

'So will I, Molly, so don't you worry,' Victoria said. 'I'll make sure she doesn't overdo it.'

'Blimey! Phil's at me all the time, and now you two! I suppose it is all right if I breathe?' Doreen was smiling when she spoke. Now the ordeal of telling her parents about the baby was over, she felt relieved and light-hearted. 'By the way, Mam, was anything settled about bridesmaids after me and Phil left last night?'

Molly shook her head. 'No, it got too late. I'm going into Hanley's this morning to book the reception, so that'll be one job done. Then I'll go round to see Tommy and Rosie tonight about bridesmaids.

We'll sort something out because I want them to have as nice a wedding as you and Jill had.'

'If there's any dresses to be made, Mam, I'll do them willingly,' Doreen said. 'I want to make up for not being able to be a matron of honour.'

'We'll see, sunshine, there's a long way to go yet.' Molly pushed her chair back and got to her feet. 'I'd better get going before Nellie comes looking for me. If she got settled down here I'd never be able to shift her.' She gave Victoria a kiss and whispered in her ear, 'Me mate's going mad because I'll be a grandmother before her.'

'Her turn will come.' Victoria patted her wispy white hair. 'She'll not be far behind yer.'

Molly chuckled. 'Poor Steve will be getting a dog's life off her. Thank God he can give as good as he gets and anything she says just rolls off his back. They want a house before they start a family and nothing Nellie says will alter that.'

Doreen happened to glance through the window then and she began to giggle. 'Auntie Nellie's looking through yer window, Mam. She must have knocked and got no answer so she's trying to see through the net curtains.'

'I'm off then. If she comes over here and plonks her backside down, there'll be no shifting her. I'll see yer later, ta-ra.'

Doreen held out her hand to the old lady. 'Come to the window, Aunt Vicky, and we'll spy on them. Just look at me Auntie Nellie. This should be interesting.'

Nellie was halfway across the cobbled street when Molly appeared. Folding her arms, the little woman asked, 'Where the hell have yer been? I've been knocking on yer door for the last half hour and nobody answered.'

'Well, they wouldn't, would they, seeing as there's no one in. I slipped across to see me daughter and I didn't think I had to ask your permission.'

'Don't be so sarky, smart arse! Why didn't yer knock for me and I could have come over with yer?'

'There was no reason for yer to come, that's why! And yer haven't been knocking for half an hour 'cos I've only been out twenty minutes at the most.' Molly had her back to Miss Clegg's window but she knew the old lady and Doreen would be watching. So she thought she'd give them something to laugh at. 'Anyway, I don't know what all the fuss is about. Yer wouldn't have been interested in anything that's been said.'

'How d'yer know I wouldn't?' Nellie put on her posh voice. 'For your hinformation, I might have been hextremely hinterested.' A sharp nod of her head set her chins swaying. 'So there, smart arse.'

'I can't imagine what would have interested yer. My daughter told me last night that she was expecting a baby so this morning I went over to see how she was. Okay?'

The chins weren't swaying now, they were really dancing. 'Oh, I might have known I'd get this this morning. I told my George yer'd be bragging. I suppose yer'll be stopping everyone in the street and telling them ye're going to be a grandmother while I stand next to yer, like a lemon, with a smile stuck on me gob. Well, to save yer the bother, and stop me from getting earache, I'll do the job for yer.' Without further ado, Nellie cupped her hands around her mouth and yelled at the top of her voice: 'Oyez! Oyez! Oyez!' Then she began to swing her arm up and down as though she was ringing an imaginary bell. 'Friends, Romans and countrymen, lend me your ears.'

Molly's feet didn't touch the ground as she made for her own house. After putting the key in the lock and throwing the door open, she dashed back and grabbed Nellie's hand. 'Yer'll have the whole street out if yer keep that up.'

The sharp tug on her arm took Nellie by surprise and she would have toppled over if Molly hadn't held on tight. As it was, her body was almost horizontal, except for her bosom and chins which followed the law of gravity. 'What the flaming hell are yer trying to do, Molly Bennett, kill me?'

'Stand up, Nellie, and stop acting daft.' Molly was holding her off the ground with one hand gripping her friend's, and the other supporting her upper arm. 'Use yer feet as a lever and push yerself up that way.'

'I can't, girl, yer'll have to pull me up.' Nellie was laughing silently. Her mate looked worried to death, but she didn't care if she fell on the cobblestones 'cos she only had her old coat on and it was ready for the rag and bone man anyway. 'Go on, girl, yer can do it.'

There was no way Molly could lift eighteen stone on her own. And she certainly wasn't going to shout for Doreen to give her a hand. But help came along in the shape of their new neighbour, Beryl Mowbray. She had just closed the door behind her when she saw this amazing sight, and it looked so comical she almost burst out laughing. But she remembered she was new around here and didn't want to make enemies.

'D'yer want a hand, queen?'

'Of course she does, soft girl,' Nellie said. 'Yer don't think I'm lying here for the good of me health, do yer?'

'From the position of yer, I thought yer were lying on a couch.' Beryl was having a hard time trying to keep her face straight. 'Yer remind me of Mae West, stretched out on a posh couch and saying, "Come up and see me some time".'

'Will yer leave the compliments until I'm standing up, girl, and then I'm sure I'll appreciate them more. Get me up quick, 'cos there's two women walking down the street.'

'Beryl, will you put yer arms around her waist, sunshine, and see if we can lift her between us?' It was a struggle because Nellie, enjoying herself no end, deliberately let her body go limp and was a dead weight. By the time she was upright, her two neighbours were red in the face and puffing like steam engines.

'There yer are, that wasn't too bad, was it?' Nellie was brushing herself down when the two women she'd seen came abreast. 'Good morning, ladies! Nice morning, isn't it?'

'Not bad, girl, not bad,' one of the women answered, curiosity in her eyes. 'Did yer fall over, Nellie?'

'No, did I heckerslike! I was doing me Mae West impersonation for me two mates. And they laughed so much they've worn themselves out.' Nellie gave them her most charming smile. 'I'll do it for yer some time, if yer like, Josie?'

Josie linked her friend's arm and began to hurry away. 'Yeah, that would be great, Nellie!' And the two women covered the ground to the main road in record time.

'Thanks for yer help, Beryl,' Molly said. 'I'd never have made it without yer.'

'Think nothing of it, queen, it was lucky I came out when I did. Now I'll be on me way to the shops to get something in for the dinner.'

'Oh, before yer go, Beryl,' Nellie said, 'Molly got some good news last night, didn't yer, girl? Her daughter's expecting a baby in May and my mate will be a grandma then.'

'Oh, that's nice, Molly, congratulations.'

'Thanks, Beryl, I'm really made up about it.' Molly turned and glared at her friend. 'Come in with me, sunshine, while I get me purse and basket.'

'Yea, and I'll use yer lavvy, girl, 'cos I'm dying to spend a penny. We'll see yer, Beryl, ta-ra for now.'

Across the street, Doreen let the curtain fall back into place. Her eyes were red after she'd wiped away tears of laughter. 'Have yer ever in yer life seen anything like it, Aunt Vicky?'

'Yes, sweetheart, I've been seeing it for nigh on twenty-five years now. Without yer mam and Auntie Nellie, I'd have been a lonely old woman with nothing in life to laugh about. They've given me so much enjoyment, and so much love as well.' Victoria let herself sink gently into her rocking chair. 'It's funny how life works, isn't it? If it wasn't for Phil stopping his rotter of a step-brother from trying to rob me one night, I would never have met him. And through him you've been brought into my life, giving me the family I never had. I'm a very lucky woman with a lot to thank God for.'

Doreen could feel a lump forming in her throat. 'Aunt Vicky, we've all got a lot to thank God for.'

'Jack, I'm slipping round to me ma's for half an hour,' Molly said that night as she came through from the kitchen drying her hands. 'Nothing was settled last night because we were taken off track by Doreen's news. Besides, there were too many here to have a serious talk.'

'Why didn't yer go round with Tommy, then?'

'I had a few things to rinse through and I didn't want to leave them until tomorrow. I've got some good news for Tommy and Rosie but I didn't tell him because I want them to hear it together.' She sat on the arm of the couch near her husband and after leaning forward to kiss him, said, 'I saw Edna Hanley today and booked their reception.'

Jack looked pleased. 'That's good, love, they'll be over the moon.'

'Yeah, she gave me a good price, too! If we keep putting some money away each week, we should be able to pay for it. I think that's the least we can do, and it'll be one worry less for Tommy. The main problem now is bridesmaids. And that's why I want to go round there tonight to see what we can sort out. I've got an idea, but I want to see what they think of it before telling anyone. So yer don't mind me leaving yer, do yer? I won't stay long.'

'You do what yer have to do, love, I don't mind in the least. And I'll bring Ruthie in when it's near her bedtime.'

'Ye're one in a million, Jack Bennett, it's no wonder I love the bones of yer.'

It was Tommy who opened the door to Molly. 'Yer didn't tell me yer were coming, Mam! I'd have waited for yer if I'd known.'

'I had a bit of washing to do, sunshine, and I didn't want to keep yer away from yer beloved any longer than necessary.' Molly was greeted by three pairs of eyes that showed surprise and pleasure. 'I can't keep away, can I?' She kissed her mother and father, gave Rosie a big hug then pulled out a chair. 'We didn't get very far last night, that's why I'm here.'

'Sure, ye're always welcome, Auntie Molly, so yer are.'

'I'll be earning me welcome tonight, sunshine, 'cos I come bearing good news. Molly's eyes rested briefly on each of the four faces eager with anticipation. 'I've booked Hanley's for yer wedding reception, and all they need is some idea of what yer want in the way of food.'

Rosie gave a squeal of delight. 'Oh, ye're a darling woman, Auntie Molly, and isn't it meself that's thinking I'll be the luckiest girl in the world to have yer for me mother-in-law.'

'That's great, Mam,' Tommy said. 'Do they need a deposit?'

'No, Edna never said,' Molly lied. She'd promised to hand five pounds over at the weekend but that was her secret. 'They've known us long enough to be sure we won't let them down.'

'That is good news,' Bridie said. 'The wedding booked, and the reception, the two main worries sorted out. It's proud I am of yer, me darlin'.'

'Yer can say that again,' Tommy said, his arm, as usual, around Rosie's waist. 'Ye're a mother in a million.'

'I wouldn't go that far, sunshine, but I have to admit I did feel pleased with meself when I saw Edna Hanley writing the date in her book. But there's another matter that is just as important and that's the question of bridesmaids. I was lying in bed last night going over it, and I've come up with an idea. If yer don't like it, don't worry, we'll think of something else.'

'Sure, it's good with ideas yer are, Auntie Molly,' Rosie said, 'so out with it.'

'Well, why not have the same bridesmaids as the girls did? Except for Maureen, of course, 'cos she's Doreen's friend. But the others have been friends of our family for more years than I care to remember. You've played with them in the street since yer were born, Tommy. That's Lily McDonough, and Phoebe and Dorothy Corkhill. They've still got the dresses and I'm sure they'd be as proud as Punch to be asked.' Molly held up her hand when Tommy opened his mouth to speak. 'Just let me finish, sunshine, then yer can tell me what yer think. The girls would be getting asked to the wedding and reception anyway so it wouldn't cost any more. That means yer'd have Jill as matron of honour, and four bridesmaids with all the dresses thrown in.' She sat back in her chair. 'It's up to you now. Tell me what yer think of me brainwave?'

'I think it's a brilliant idea, Mam, I really do.' Tommy could feel Rosie's excitement as she bounced up and down on his knee. And because he loved her so much and would give her the earth if he could, he thanked God for giving him such a loving, understanding mother.

'Me with a matron of honour and four bridesmaids, Auntie Molly!' There were sparks coming from Rosie's deep blue Irish eyes. 'Sure, me mammy and daddy will never have seen anything like it in all their lives, and that's a fact. They'll think I'm marrying the King of England, so they will.'

Bob winked and smiled across at his daughter. 'There's yer answer, sweetheart, I think they like yer idea.'

'It looks like it, Da, but I'll wait for an official answer.'

'We'd be made up, Mam, honest.' Tommy's face was one big smile. 'And we'd like to thank yer, wouldn't we, Rosie?'

'Thank you are just two words anyone can say, Tommy Bennett, and me Auntie Molly deserves more than that.' Rosie rounded the table to kiss Molly soundly. 'And me mammy and daddy will thank yer when they see yer, so they will.'

'Will you ask the girls for us, Mam?' Tommy asked.

Molly shook her head. 'No, sunshine, it's your place to ask them. I'll have a word with Nellie and Ellen, but you must ask the girls yourselves. Make up yer mind to do it tomorrow night and get it over with. But make it early 'cos Lily and Phoebe will probably be going out.'

It was Rosie who answered, her dark curls bouncing with her nodding head. 'We'll do that right enough, Auntie Molly.'

'All it leaves now are the cars and flowers.' Molly said. 'And choosing yer best man, of course. But I'm going to leave those things for you to organise Tommy, I've done my bit.' She looked at the clock. 'I'm not staying for a cuppa 'cos I promised Jack I'd only be half an hour. I'd better be making tracks.'

'I'll not keep yer but a few minutes, me darlin',' Bridie said, 'but me and yer da are thrilled about Doreen's baby. Our first great-grandchild.'

'Yeah, it shows we're all getting older, Ma. Imagine me a grandmother!'

'Have yer told Doreen she must look after herself now?' Bob asked. 'She mustn't overdo things.'

'I saw her this morning and she's fine. She seems very happy and contented and I find it hard to believe she's the same girl who used to answer me back and give cheek. I did tell her about taking things easy and not to be lifting or pushing furniture, but she said Phil and Victoria had already been on at her about it. I think me daughter's in very good hands, Da, I'm pleased to say.' Molly pushed her chair back and stood up. 'In fact, both me daughters are in good hands and that makes me a very happy woman.'

'Before yer go, sweetheart, how's Nellie today?' Bob asked. 'Still jealous?'

Molly looked at her father and thought, Oh, no, I'll be here all night if I start on that. So she screwed up her face and scratched her nose. 'She did something this morning I've never seen her do before. She had a lie down for a while. But she seemed all right after, I'm glad to say.'

'It's not like me Auntie Nellie to be sick,' Tommy said, concern showing on his face. 'What was wrong with her?'

'She just felt a bit down, sunshine, that's all. But she soon picked herself up.' As Molly was kissing them all goodbye, she told herself she'd tell them the tale next time she came, to give them a laugh. But not tonight, not when Jack was waiting for her.

Chapter 8

Nellie wasn't very good at keeping secrets, but she and Ellen had been warned by Molly that they weren't to say a word to their daughters until Tommy and Rosie asked them officially if they'd be Rosie's bridesmaids. Ellen could be trusted, and anyway she was working in the shop all day and had more on her mind. But Nellie didn't have anything of interest to keep her occupied and by the time Lily came home from work her mother was all keyed up. She was dying to blurt it out, but with Molly's dire warning ringing in her head she managed, with great difficulty, to put a rein on her tongue.

'Hurry up with yer dinners so I can get the dishes washed.'

George looked surprised. 'Give us a chance, love, I like to take me time when I'm eating. It's not good to bolt yer food down, yer get indigestion. Anyway, what's the hurry?'

'Yer never know who might come,' Nellie said. 'I want the place nice and tidy just in case we have any visitors.'

'There's only Archie coming, Mam, and yer can't call him a visitor.' Lily put down her knife and fork. 'He's not going to go around the furniture with his finger to see if yer've dusted.'

Paul grinned. 'I don't know, he might just happen to lift up the mat and discover that me mam has swept all the dirt underneath it.'

'Ay, buggerlugs, just you watch it!' Nellie appeared to get on her high horse. 'Yer've never seen me brushing dirt under the mat, so don't yer be spreading rumours about me.' Then her chubby face creased. 'Under the bed perhaps, but never under the mat.'

'Is that why the bed seems higher?' George asked, his face deadpan. 'I thought me legs were shrinking 'cos it takes me all me time to climb in these days.'

'Ha, ha, very funny, I must say. Now yer've all had yer little jokes at my expense, will yer use yer mouth to eat with and get that dinner down?'

'Nellie, if you hadn't started, we'd have well finished eating by now. The table would be cleared and the dishes washed, and it wouldn't

107

have mattered if the King had decided to get off the twenty-two tram and pay us a visit.'

Nellie wagged her finger. 'George McDonough, ye're not too big to have yer ears boxed.'

Paul swallowed the last piece of potato and pushed his plate away. 'Will yer stand on a chair to do it, Mam, or d'yer want me to lift yer up?'

'I don't need any help from you, clever clogs. I'm going to take a leaf out of Rosie's book, so there!'

'Oh, aye, what's this then?' George asked. 'Rosie's a bit young to be teaching an old dog new tricks, isn't she?'

'Are you saying I'm an old dog, George McDonough?'

'That's just a figure of speech, love, so don't be getting yer knickers in a twist. Anyway, I should have said an old female dog.'

Paul nudged his sister's foot under the table. 'What's the proper name for a female dog, Dad, it's just slipped me mind?'

George, his plate clear by now, pushed his chair back ready for a quick get away. 'They're called bitches, son.'

Nellie's chair went flying as she made a grab for him, but George fended her off with the chair legs. 'Now, now, love, stay calm or yer'll have a heart attack.'

'You'll have more than a heart attack when I get me hands on yer. Put that ruddy chair down and let me strangle yer.'

'Is that what Rosie does, Mam?' Lily asked. 'Is that the leaf ye're taking out of her book?'

'No, it's not, girl, 'cos she couldn't reach Tommy's neck to strangle him. And although he's besotted with her, he's not daft enough to bend down to make things easier for her.' Nellie waved a hand at her husband. 'Put that bloody chair down, yer soft nit.'

George chuckled as he set the chair down. Then he took a white hankie from his trouser pocket and waved it in the air. 'I'll call a truce if yer tell us what Rosie's secret is. Just so I can be prepared, like.'

'I'll tell yer if yer all promise to clear this place up after. 'Cos if the King does call, as yer dad said he might, I want everywhere spotless. I'm not having him going back to Buckingham Palace and telling the Queen we're an untidy lot in Liverpool.'

'It's a deal, Mam,' Lily said. 'But put a move on so I can get meself ready for when Archie comes. And I'm bagging the sink first tonight, Paul, so don't be making a dive for the kitchen before me.'

'Well,' Nellie said as she started to stack the plates, 'what Rosie does is, she stands on the second stair with the frying pan in her hands and hits Tommy on the head with it. And she says that's why he's got a flat head.'

'Don't be getting any ideas, Nellie,' George said as he made a bee-line for his cigarettes and easy chair. 'I wouldn't take that lying down.'

She narrowed her eyes and glared, thinking he was being funny, but her husband's face was straight. 'There'd be no ruddy point if yer were lying down, would there, yer silly sod? Honest to God, sometimes I think ye're not right in the head, George.' She got as far as the kitchen door and turned. 'Didn't yer once tell me yer used to get headaches and felt as though there was something loose rattling round in yer head?'

'What are yer on about, woman? I never said any such thing, and the only time I've had headaches is when yer keep nattering on about something of no bloody consequence.'

'Oh, I see,' Nellie said quietly. 'Only I was wondering about this thing rattling round in yer head, and I think I've got the answer to it. Yer've got a bloody screw loose, that's what it is!'

Before George could answer the knocker sounded. Lily gave a quick glance around, wishing they'd hurried their dinner like her mam had asked. 'Paul, will yer clear the table and take the cloth off,' she said, 'while I open the door?'

'Hello, Lily.' Archie was smiling and as immaculately dressed as ever. 'I'm a bit early 'cos I came on the tram with me mam to keep her company. She's gone to do a bit of ironing for me auntie.'

'Come in, then, but don't yer dare lift the corner of the mat up.'

'Why would I do that?'

'Well, apparently our Paul thinks that's where me mam sweeps the dirt when she's too lazy to go down the yard to the bin.'

'My mam does the same,' Archie nodded his head knowingly. 'Many's the time I've nearly broke me neck tripping on the lump in the mat. I'm wondering now whether they learned that at school, with my mam being in the same class as Mrs Mac.'

Nellie appeared at the kitchen door. 'Not only in the same class, lad, but sitting at the same desk! We must have copied each other's bad habits.' She smiled as she remembered those childhood days. 'I know we got the cane for talking more than any other girls in the class.'

'You haven't changed much, then,' George said. 'Yer've made a career out of talking.'

'I'll ignore that until the time comes to get me own back. I think Rosie said she stands on the second stair, but she's taller than me so

109

I'd better stand on the third to make sure.'

George chuckled. 'Nellie, yer'd never be able to lift that big frying pan over yer head, it weighs a flippin' ton.'

'Don't get cocky with me, George McDonough, or I'll show yer whether I can lift it or not.' Nellie saw two figures pass the window and waited for the knock. 'Oh, I wonder who this can be? If it's the King I hope he likes custard creams.'

Archie hadn't a clue what she was talking about, but he'd find out later from Lily. 'Shall I see who it is, Mrs Mac?'

'If yer would, lad. And if there's a horse and carriage there it'll be the King, so don't forget to bow from the waist down.' Nellie waited until she heard Archie greeting his old army mate then shouted, 'Whoever it is, bring them in, lad, don't keep them on the step.'

'It's only me, Auntie Nellie, with me ever-loving intended.' Tommy and Rosie were holding hands and grinning like Cheshire cats. 'We've come to ask a big favour of Lily.'

'She's in the kitchen getting washed but she won't be a minute. Sit down and make yerselves comfortable. Put yer feet on the mantelpiece if yer like.'

'Ooh, I wouldn't do that if I were you, lad,' George said. 'She's in a fighting mood is the wife.' He winked at Rosie. 'She's talking about standing on the third stair and hitting me on the head with the frying pan. I can't imagine where she got that idea from.'

'She didn't get it from me, Uncle George, and that's the truth of it.' Rosie's rich laughter filled the room. And there wasn't a person who wasn't affected by the sound and by the beauty of the young Irish girl. 'It's the second stair I stand on, not the third.'

The kitchen door opened and Lily came through drying her hands. 'I thought I recognised the laugh. It's nice to see yer both, are yer off out somewhere?'

'We came to see you,' Tommy said. 'Rosie has something she wants to ask yer.'

Lily sat on the arm of the couch. 'If I can help, I'll be only too glad to. What is it yer want to ask me, Rosie?'

'If yer'll be a bridesmaid at our wedding? Sure, yer'll make us very happy, for yer make a lovely bridesmaid, so yer do.'

Lily was taken by surprise. 'Are yer sure yer really want me?'

Tommy nodded. 'We'd be delighted, Lily. You've always been like family to us, and with Rosie not having anyone of her own here, she'd be over the moon if you'd agree.'

110

'Well, if ye're sure, then I'd be only too happy. Who else are yer asking?'

'Jill and Ruthie, of course, and we're going to see Phoebe and Dorothy when we leave here. If they agree, then it's one less thing to worry about.'

Nellie was sitting on the edge of her chair. 'Ay, yer'll be able to use the same dresses and that will be a saving for Tommy.'

George tilted his head as he looked at his wife. Well, the crafty so-and-so, he thought. She knew all about this, that's why she was so eager to get the dinner over. He chuckled quietly, thinking Molly must have told her not to say anything and she'd had to keep it bottled up inside her. With tongue in cheek, he said, 'This is a better surprise than the King coming, isn't it Nellie? Who'd have guessed Tommy and Rosie were going to call with such good news?'

'I wouldn't,' she said, wondering whether the frying pan was too heavy for her to lift? She'd try it when they'd all gone out, just in case she ever needed it. 'I'll be able to wear me posh hat again. It's never seen daylight since the wedding 'cos there's no call for it around here. I could hardly walk in the butcher's and ask for half a pound of sausages with that on me head, I'd be the talk of the wash-house.'

'I hope yer won't mind wearing the same dress again, Lily?' Rosie said, her blue eyes round and appealing. 'Only me and Tommy are saving up hard but, sure, we'd never be able to afford to buy five bridesmaids' dresses. And with me mammy and daddy coming, I want to have a fine wedding so they'll be proud of me.'

'And a fine wedding yer'll have, Rosie. I have no objection to wearing the dress again and I'm honoured that yer've asked me.'

'I know someone else who'll be happy,' Paul said. 'Phoebe will be over the moon. And Dorothy. I know for a fact that their dresses are hanging in the wardrobe covered in tissue paper, just waiting for the opportunity to be worn again.'

Tommy let out a sigh. 'That's a load of me mind. I thought yer might think I was a penny-pinching miser, and I'm not really. It's just that there's so many things to think of.' He gazed from Paul to Archie. 'Just wait until it's your turn and yer'll see what it's like.'

'Oh, I think those dresses are good for another two weddings,' Paul said, his dimples showing. 'What do you say, Archie?'

'I'll keep them in mind when the time arrives. Yer never know, I might come up on the pools before then and be rolling in it.'

'If yer luck's anything like mine, son,' George said, 'then ye'll be whistling in the wind for the rest of yer life.'

111

'Me and me dearly beloved intended have got each other, and that's far better than winning the pools.' Rosie didn't try to hide the love she felt for Tommy. 'If we've got each other, then it's a happy life we'll have.' Tapping her temple, she said, 'As me mammy would say, there's more to life than money.'

'She's a clever woman, is your mammy,' Lily said. 'And now I'll have to put a move on 'cos me and Archie are going to the pictures. But we'll sit and have a good talk soon, Rosie.'

'We'll be on our way, too,' Tommy said. 'We don't want to miss Phoebe and Dorothy.'

'Yer won't miss Phoebe because she's coming out with me.' Paul pulled a face when he looked at the clock. 'I'm late now. I just hope Rosie hasn't told her about the frying pan lark or I'm going to end up with a splitting headache.'

Archie was cupping Lily's elbow as they walked down the street. 'So ye're going to be a bridesmaid again, eh?'

'Yeah. I'm very fond of Tommy and Rosie and wouldn't let them down for the world. But if anybody else asks me, they've had it. Yer know about the old saying. "Three times a bridesmaid, but never the blushing bride"? Well, I'm not taking any chances on that happening.'

When they turned the corner of the street, Archie grabbed her hand and started to run. 'Quick, there's a bus coming, we'll just about make it.'

Later, sitting in the back row of the stalls in the Carlton Cinema, he put his arm across Lily's shoulders and whispered, 'Don't worry about being left on the shelf, Lily, because I'd marry yer meself before I'd let that happen.'

She turned her head to smile at him. 'Gee, thanks, Archie, that's the best offer I've had today. And it beats being an old maid with only a cat for company.'

'That's a back-handed compliment if ever I heard one, Lily McDonough. Yer've dampened me ardour now, just when I was beginning to feel romantic.' He could feel her shoulders shaking and asked, 'What's so funny about that?'

'I was just wondering what me mam would say about yer ardour being dampened. She wouldn't have let that pass without making a crack about it.'

'I bet Rosie's mammy has a saying for it.'

The lights in the picture house dimmed and Lily said, 'Shush, let me enjoy Clark Gable. I'll dream he falls madly in love with me and wants to marry me. And I'll consider me options between him and being an old maid with a cat.'

Archie growled. 'I hate Clark Gable.'

Lily smiled in the darkness. He really was a nice bloke to come out with. Attentive, funny and easy-going. Just the opposite from someone she was still trying hard to forget.

Paul was in such a hurry when he pulled the door closed behind him, he didn't see the girl until he bumped into her. 'I'm sorry, I should look where I'm going. I didn't stand on yer toes, did I?'

'No, I'm all right.' Joanne Mowbray had been lying in wait for the boy she thought was as handsome as any film star. 'I'm yer new neighbour, me name's Joanne. I know your name's Paul 'cos I've heard yer mam calling yer.' She nodded at the shoes under his arms. 'Going dancing, are yer?'

'That's the general idea.' Paul was a friendly person and smiled at her, as he would at anyone who spoke to him. 'But I'll have to go now 'cos I'm late. I'll see yer around.'

'Is she yer girlfriend?'

'Is who me girlfriend?'

'Her what lives next door but one to yer. I don't know her name.'

'Yes, she's me girlfriend and right now she'll be calling me everything for being late. And it's not manners to keep a lady waiting so I'll be on me way. Ta-ra, Joanne.'

She stood and watched him walk away, her eyes hard and scheming. 'Ta-ra, Paul.' Then she muttered under her breath, 'And yer'll definitely see me around.'

Phoebe opened the door. 'Where the heck have you been? I've been ready for ages!'

'Well, yer know Tommy and Rosie came, don't yer?'

She nodded. 'They've not long left here, but that's no excuse for yer being late. I'll do it to you sometime and see how yer like it.'

Ellen smiled when Paul walked in. 'That's not a very nice way to be greeted, is it?'

'I couldn't be rude to Tommy and Rosie, now could I? And blow me, when I came out of our house I nearly knocked a young girl over. The one that's just moved into Mrs Harwick's house. She must have been passing when I jumped off the step without looking and went slap-bang into her.'

Ellen had bent to poke the fire when Paul spoke and almost said the young girl had been hanging around when she'd come back from her mother-in-law's house. She'd wondered at the time if she was waiting for someone, and remembered thinking she'd be better waiting inside, out of the cold. 'Did she say anything to yer?'

'Only that her name was Joanne. I didn't have time to mess around because I knew Phoebe would be getting a cob on. But I got the impression that she certainly isn't backward in coming forward.'

'According to her mother she's not! I've only spoken to Mrs Mowbray once or twice in the shop, but she said her daughter was a hard clock.'

'Then next time she tries to talk to yer, Paul, just say yer haven't got time, ye're in a hurry.' Phoebe slipped her arms into her coat. 'And if she doesn't take no notice, tell her to get lost.'

'Aye, I'll do that, Phoebe, with knobs on! I'll say I'm in a hurry, but I won't tell her to get lost 'cos that wouldn't be very neighbourly.' When Paul rubbed his hands together one of his dancing shoes fell from under his arm and he bent to retrieve it. 'How did yer get on with Tommy and Rosie?'

Phoebe's face lit up. 'I'm thrilled and so is our Dorothy. She couldn't wait to get out of the door so she could go and tell her mate. She won't half be bragging.'

'She said she was going to see her mate, but I'd take that with a pinch of salt,' Ellen said. 'I think she's got a boyfriend on the sly.'

'Oh, I don't think so, Mam.' Phoebe giggled. 'Yer know what she's like for bragging, she wouldn't be able to keep it to herself.'

'I hope ye're right! I wouldn't mind her having a boyfriend if she'd bring him here to meet us so we'd know if he was decent and respectable. After all, she's only fifteen.'

'She's fifteen and three-quarters, Mam, as she keeps telling me. And she's not soft, she's well capable of looking after herself.' Phoebe could see Paul was getting restless. 'We'll go now, before me laddo here tells me how many dances he's missing.'

He grinned at Ellen, saying, 'Dorothy's not yer only daughter who can look after herself, Auntie Ellen. This one can be a real handful.'

Phoebe swung her handbag at him. 'You haven't seen the half of it yet. Just wait until the day I really lose me temper, then yer'll see.'

'Well, I hope yer let me know the day before, so I can take to me bed with a sore throat.'

'Will you two get going! It'll be time to come home before yer get there.' Ellen shoed them towards the door. 'Besides, I've been on me feet all day, I want to stretch out on the couch and relax while I've got the house to meself. Peace, perfect peace.'

'Are Gordon and Peter out as well?' Paul asked.

'Both round at their mates. I'm going to enjoy the quiet while I've got the chance. So be off with yer, and enjoy yerself.' Ellen closed the door after them and leaned back against it. She did feel tired. It was hard going working and looking after a house and children. Corker was always telling her to pack the job in, but she enjoyed her work and would miss it. Perhaps after Christmas she might consider it.

'So Tommy's all fixed up now, girl?' Her chubby hands curled around a cup, Nellie faced her friend across the table. 'I bet he's made up, is he?'

Molly nodded. 'Him and Rosie were delighted when they called in last night. Honest, I felt like hugging them to death I was so happy for them. They get pleasure out of little things that you and I would take for granted, and appreciate the help everyone's giving them. I'm glad the girls agreed to be bridesmaids, and I'm going to do everything I can to make this wedding day one that they'll be able to look back on all their lives, with pleasure. What we did for Jill and Doreen, I want for Tommy too.'

'They're a smashing couple, I'll grant yer that. I can't wait to see Rosie in her wedding dress 'cos she'll be a knockout. We won't be in the ha'penny specks with her, she'll put everyone in the shade.' Nellie eyed the last two ginger biscuits on the plate and then asked, 'Are yer going to leave those two little buggers all on their own or can I eat them?'

'Don't be greedy, sunshine, we'll have one each. And if ye're going to dunk it, will yer try to be ladylike and don't leave it in the tea until half of it falls in the cup? I hate to see yer fishing round with the spoon trying to find it.'

'I always do find it, though, girl.'

'Yer get bits of it, then leave the rest in the bottom of the cup for me to wash.' Molly helped herself to one of the biscuits and softened it by dipping it in the tea for a second. 'One thing, sunshine, the rationing should be a lot easier by next summer, so I won't have to go cadging off everyone.'

'Doreen will have had the baby by then, girl, and yer'll be a grandma. And yer'll have a christening party to think of.'

'Don't remind me of that, sunshine, 'cos it makes me sad.' Molly pulled a face. 'I can't help thinking that Phil won't have any family at the christening, not a soul. He's bound to feel it, even though he won't let it show.'

'He must have some family, somewhere. His dad must have had parents and perhaps brothers and sisters. All Phil was told by his mam after he left home, if yer could call living with the Bradleys home, was that his dad was killed in an accident three weeks before he was to marry his mam. And then she discovered she was in the family way. Then when the Bradley feller offered to marry her, she must have jumped at the chance. For all we know, both families might have disowned her 'cos of the shame, and Phil was left to be brought up by a rotter.'

Molly nodded. 'It's a miracle he's turned out to be such a nice bloke. Honest, decent and hard-working.'

'If yer remember, girl, we said at the time we'd do a bit of detecting and try and find him. I know it was years ago, but I can still remember us talking about it.'

'We wouldn't know where to start, Nellie! He told us his real father's name, but for the life of me I can't think what it was. I can remember him saying his mam lived in Bootle, down Marsh Lane way, and I think Bullen's Terrace was mentioned. But whether his dad came from the same area I wouldn't know.'

'Why don't yer ask him, girl? That would be the easiest way. He might know a bit more than he told us.'

'No, I don't want it mentioning to him! It would only rake up all the hurt and the bad memories, and for what? We might never be able to find any relatives now, not after twenty odd years.'

'We could try, girl, 'cos think of what it would mean to him. Remember how we talked once of opening our own detective agency. McDonough and Bennett?'

'No, I don't remember, sunshine.' Molly grinned. 'I do remember Bennett and McDonough, though.'

'Trust you! Yer always have to be in front of me.'

'Well, it was my idea in the first place, so that's only fair.'

'So are we in business, girl? Are we going to try and find Phil's family?'

'I'd like to try.' Molly's thoughts were racing ahead. 'Just think what it would mean to him to have someone related to him at the christening? A new baby and a new family. It would be wonderful for him, and for Doreen and the baby.'

Nellie rubbed her hands together. 'When do we start, girl?'

'Not until after Christmas, sunshine, 'cos I've so much to do. It's only a few weeks off and I haven't got a single present in yet. Not that anyone's getting anything special this year, I'm cutting right down so

116

I can put as much by as I can for Tommy's wedding.'

'After Christmas then, girl? When all the festivities are over, eh? It'll give us something to look forward to, and we'd be doing a good turn into the bargain.'

Molly banged a closed fist on the table, sending the cups rattling in the saucers. 'Nellie, I've just remembered the father's name. It was Bob Mitchell! It came to me in a flash, out of the blue.' She raised her eyes to the ceiling. 'Someone up there is on our side, sunshine, and we can't let Him down. So, right after Christmas, you and me are turning detectives and we'll keep on until we have some success. I'm determined about it now.'

'So am I, girl, and we'll be the best detectives in Liverpool. We'll get our man, or woman, if it kills us. And I think we should drink to it. So how about another cup of tea to seal our partnership?'

'Ye're a crafty article, Nellie McDonough, there's no keeping up with yer. But, yeah, what the hell? Let's have another cuppa.'

Chapter 9

Molly was waving Jack and Tommy off to work one morning when she heard her name being called. She turned her head to see Jill running down the street. 'You're going out early this morning, sunshine, it's only half-seven.'

'It's Mrs Corkhill, Mam, I don't think she's very well. Steve said I should take the day off in case she needs me, but I wouldn't know what to do if she really is sick.'

'Where is she now, still in bed?'

Jill nodded. 'She got up at seven, as she always does to have a cup of tea and a round of toast with me and Steve. But she only had a couple of sips of the tea and one bite of toast. Then she started to shiver and said she felt as though she was in for a cold so she'd be better going back to bed for an hour or so. She didn't look a bit well, Mam, her face was grey.'

'Come in for a minute, sunshine, while I get Ruthie out of bed and tell her to see to her own breakfast. She's old enough now to get herself ready for school.' Molly took her coat from a hook on the wall and was putting it on while she shouted up the stairs. 'Ruthie, yer'll have to make yer own breakfast, sunshine, and see yerself out to school. Mrs Corkhill's not well and I'm going up there with Jill. Did yer hear me?'

'Yeah, okay, Mam, I'll be all right.'

'Don't forget to bang the door after yer, I'm taking the key with me.' Molly could see the concern on Jill's face and squeezed her arm. 'Don't look so worried, sunshine, I'm sure Lizzie's right and it's just a cold. I don't think she's been sick in all the years I've known her.'

After making sure the door was securely closed, Molly took her daughter's arm and they walked quickly up the street. 'You go to work, Jill, and I'll see to Lizzie. Yer don't want to lose a day's pay when ye're saving up.'

'No, I can't expect yer to do that, Mam, I don't mind taking the day off. Besides, Mrs Corkhill's been so good to me and Steve, I'd feel mean if I went to work and left her.'

'We'll see how the land lies, sunshine, and take it from there. If it is only a cold, me and Nellie could manage to keep an eye on her between us. Now get the door open so I can see for meself what the situation is.'

Molly stood at the foot of the stairs and called, 'It's only me, Lizzie, so yer don't have to worry about making yerself respectable 'cos I've got everything you've got, only twice as much.' She motioned to Jill to stay downstairs. 'Leave yer coat on, sunshine, 'cos I think yer'll be going to work.'

'Jill shouldn't have gone for yer, Molly,' Lizzie Corkhill croaked. 'I told her it was only a chill and I'll be all right after a day in bed.'

'Better to be safe than sorry, Lizzie.' It was dark in the room because the curtains were drawn over, and Molly couldn't see the woman in the bed properly. 'I'm opening the curtains for a minute so I can see what I'm saying.' She tutted as she pulled back the curtains. 'That doesn't help much 'cos it's not broad daylight yet.' She walked to the bed and put a hand on the old woman's forehead. 'In the name of God, Lizzie, ye're burning! I could fry an egg on yer forehead it's so hot.'

'I'll sweat it out of me, Molly, so don't be worrying. I'll be all right tomorrow.'

'Like hell yer will, Lizzie, 'cos it's freezing in this room. I'm going down to make sure there's a fire up the chimney, then I'll get yer down and settled on the couch. Yer'll get pneumonia if yer stay up here. I'll be back in a minute.'

Jill was pacing the floor. 'Is she all right, Mam?'

'She won't be if she's left in that freezing cold bedroom. I'm going to put more coal on the fire to build it up, then I'll bring her down. I'll make a bed on the couch and make sure she's kept warm all day and drinks plenty of liquids. We'll manage, sunshine, so you poppy off to work. But do me a favour, knock at Nellie's on yer way down and let her know what's going on.'

Jill hesitated. 'Will yer manage to get Mrs Corkhill down the stairs on yer own?'

'Of course I can, yer daft ha'porth, she's as light as a feather. Now on yer way so I can get this place organised.'

There was plenty of coal in the scuttle at the side of the fireplace and Molly picked out several cobs and laid them carefully on the low fire. When they'd caught she put more on and in no time there was a bright fire roaring up the chimney and the room felt warm and welcoming. 'I'll wash me hands,' Molly said aloud as she made her way to the kitchen, 'then bring Lizzie down.' She smiled when she saw a bucketful of coal standing by the kitchen door. 'Ye're a good lad, Steve, a real gem.'

Lizzie Corkhill was sitting on the side of the bed when Molly went back upstairs. 'I'm trying to get me stockings off, girl, but I don't seem to have any energy.'

'Do it downstairs in the living room, where it's nice and warm. And before we go down, will yer tell me where yer keep yer nightdresses? If ye're going to lie on the couch yer may as well be comfortable.'

'They're in that chest of drawers, in the second drawer down. Me vests and knickers are in the top one.'

'Right, well, let's get yer down to the warm room, then I'll come back for whatever I need. Come on, hang on to me arm.'

'I'm being a nuisance, aren't I? Yer've got enough on yer plate without being lumbered with an old woman like me.'

'Lizzie Corkhill, yer'll never be an old woman, ye're just a slip of a girl! Anyway, what would Corker say if he knew I'd left his mam when she wasn't well? After all he's done for my family over the years, this doesn't even come near paying him back.' Molly stepped one stair down then put Lizzie's hand on the banister. 'I'll go down in front of yer, sunshine, and we'll take it nice and easy.'

'Ooh, that fire looks a treat, Molly, really homely.' The old lady couldn't stop shivering and shaking. 'It's just a chill I've got, that's all.'

Molly pulled the rocking chair near to the fire. 'Sit down there and yer'll soon warm yerself through. I'll nip up and get yer a clean nightie, some pillows and an eiderdown. We'll soon have yer as snug as a bug in a rug.'

'There's a cardi on the chair at the side of the bed, Molly, would yer bring that down with her so I can put it around me shoulders?'

'Will do, sunshine, will do.'

Fifteen minutes later, Lizzie was leaning back against three pillows, an eiderdown tucked in around her, sipping a cup of tea. 'I'll be all right now, Molly, so you go and get back to yer work. I know yer must be busy with Christmas being only a week way.'

'I'm in no hurry, Lizzie, so stop . . .' Molly's words were cut off when there was a rap on the window. 'I'll give yer three guesses who this is, Lizzie?'

The old lady managed a smile. 'It's too early for the rent man, girl.'

Molly opened the door and glared down at her friend. 'Don't you ever think of using the knocker, Nellie McDonough? Me and Lizzie nearly jumped out of our flaming skin.'

'I do think of using the knocker, girl, but I can't reach the ruddy thing! And don't tell me to stand on the step 'cos I've tried that, too! Me tummy gets in the way, yer see.'

'Well, come in so I can shut the door and keep the draught out. Lizzie's on the couch and she's got a cold as it is.'

Nellie waddled over to the couch and, shaking her head, put her hands on her hips. 'Oh, aye, Lizzie, swinging the lead, are yer?'

'That's right, girl, I just felt like being a lady for a day and getting waited on hand and foot.' Then came a bout of coughing and sneezing. 'Keep away from me, Nellie, I don't want to pass me germs on to yer.'

'Germs gave up on me a long time ago, Lizzie. They found that trying to get through me layers of fat was too much like hard work.' Nellie noted the flushed face, the watery eyes and the shallow breathing. 'Ye're in the best place there, girl, 'cos yer look full of it to me. Yer need a couple of Beecham's powders, they'd help.'

'I'll slip to the corner shop and get some,' Molly said. 'Seeing as you're here to sit with Lizzie. And I'll get some rice to make a pudding so yer've got something inside of yer. Is there anything else yer want, sunshine?'

'I've got plenty of rice in the larder, I always have it in for when Corker comes home. But the milkman's only left our usual pint, so we'll need more milk if ye're going to make a rice pudding. If yer pass me purse over, I'll give yer the money.'

'Yer can settle up with me later, there's no hurry.' Molly didn't say she'd come up without her purse and had no money on her. The corner shop would put it on the slate for her. 'I'll only be ten minutes.'

'I know your ten minutes, girl, they can turn into half hours.' Nellie took her coat off and put it on the back of a chair. 'Once you start gabbing, there's no stopping yer.'

'My God, just listen to Talk-a-bit! I'd have to go some to beat you, sunshine, 'cos you can talk when there's nothing to talk about! I've known you invent things, just so yer can keep yer mouth in motion.' Molly gave a slight inclination of her chin, then both she and Nellie looked to where Lizzie's head had fallen back against the pillows. She could hardly keep her eyes open. 'That's right, sunshine, you close yer eyes and snuggle up under that eiderdown. Me mate will see if there's anything wants doing in the kitchen while I nip up to the corner shop. I'll go out the back way, save letting a draught in from the front door.'

Nellie followed her to the kitchen. 'What d'yer think, girl?'

'I don't know what to think,' Molly told her in hushed tones. 'We'll see how she is later, after a couple of Beecham's. If her temperature doesn't go down I'd be inclined to get the doctor out. You stay out here until I get back, she might just go to sleep if she's left alone.'

'I'll wash those few dishes while I'm waiting for yer. But don't be long, girl, yer know I'm hopeless when anyone's sick.'

'Okay, sunshine, I'll fly there and back. I won't bother with me feet, I'll use me wings.'

Molly patted her friend's cheek before hurrying down the yard. She was just closing the entry door behind her when the door facing opened and out stepped one of the biggest gossips in the neighbourhood. She groaned inwardly while bringing a smile to her face. 'Morning, Elsie!'

'Morning, Molly!' Elsie Flanaghan's eyes showed her interest. 'What are yer doing here this early in the morning?'

'Me and Nellie often call on Mrs Corkhill at this time. Just for a natter and a cuppa, like. But she's running short on milk so I'm going to the corner shop for some.'

The eyes weighing her up and down were suspicious. 'Her milkman came ages ago! He does your street before he comes to us.'

'Oh, yeah, he's been.' Molly felt like asking what it had to do with her, but Elsie Flanaghan was the wrong one to cross. 'But by the time the three of us have two cups of tea it's half the bottle gone. So, as not to leave her short, I'm going to the corner for a pint.'

'She must use more of everything with yer daughter and her husband living with her. She must go through some money keeping two extra people, I don't know how she manages at her age with just a widow's pension.'

Molly was finding it hard to stem her rising temper. What a pity it was that some people had nothing better to do than nose into other people's business. Especially this one who wouldn't do anyone a good turn. 'I don't think it's my place to discuss Mrs Corkhill's financial situation with yer, Elsie, except to say yer've got yer sums wrong. And now I'll have to go or they'll think I've gone looking for a cow to get the milk from.'

'Hang on, I'll walk up with yer.'

'Sorry, Elsie, I'm in a hurry. Ta-ra!' Molly never stopped running until she pushed open the door of the corner shop.

123

Maisie and Alec Porter were both behind the counter serving. The shop was busy, but it didn't take the couple long to reduce the number of customers to three. It was then Maisie came along the counter to where Molly was standing. 'Alec can manage on his own now for a while. D'yer want to come through to the back, I'm going to put the kettle on for a drink?'

'I'll come through for a few minutes, Maisie, but I don't want a drink, thanks.' Molly lifted the hinged section of the counter, gave Alec a broad wink and followed his wife through to the stockroom. 'I've just bumped into that Elsie Flanaghan and she hasn't half made my blood boil. She's a real troublemaker and a bad-minded so-and-so.' After repeating the remarks made, and listening to Maisie give some suitable recommendations about what fate should befall the gossipmonger, Molly quickly explained how she happened to be in the entry in the first place. 'Lizzie doesn't look a bit well, so I need some Beecham's to try and get her temperature down. And a pint of milk to make a rice pudding for her. The trouble, is, Maisie, I was in such a hurry leaving the house, I came out without me purse. So I'm hoping yer'll be a pal and let me have the things on tick. I'll bring the money up later or send Ruthie with it if I can't get away.'

'Yer can have what yer like, yer know that, Molly. I'm sorry to hear Lizzie's not well, the poor dear. If there's anything I can do, yer just have to shout out. I could sit with her for an hour or two this afternoon, that would give yer a chance to do whatever yer have to do. The shop's not busy between one and three. Alec could easily manage on his own.'

'We'll see how things go, Maisie, but I think yer've got enough on yer plate with all the Christmas orders to see to. Me and Nellie will take it in turns to do our shopping, then Jill and Steve can take over when they come home from work.'

'They'll be a blessing to her at a time like this. Corker would be worried to death if he knew, he dotes on his ma. When's his ship due in, d'yer know?'

'Could be any time now, 'cos Ellen said he's hoping to have Christmas at home this year.'

Molly sighed. 'That's another thing I'll have to do, tell Ellen. It could be Lizzie will be all right tomorrow, but I'm not taking any chances and Ellen has a right to know.'

'I'll get yer the Beecham's and the milk. But don't forget I'm here if yer need any help. Me and Alec have got a soft spot for Lizzie.'

With the milk bottle in her hand, and the Beecham's powders in her pocket in case the Flanaghan woman was keeping tabs on her, Molly made haste down the entry. She'd been longer than expected and knew she'd get some stick off Nellie. And she wasn't wrong.

Nellie was leaning back against the sink with her arms folded and her lips set in a straight line. 'I'll tell yer what, girl, I'll never fly anywhere with you 'cos I'd be quicker getting the twenty-two tram. Who the hell have yer been gabbing to?'

Molly put a finger to her lips and popped her head around the living-room door. Lizzie was fast asleep, but it wasn't a restful sleep as she was breathing through her mouth and making noises which told of a blocked up nose. Very quietly, Molly closed the door. 'I was unfortunate enough to bump into Elsie Flanaghan, and she's so bloody nasty I felt like clocking her one. If I tell yer what she said, yer've got to promise not to repeat it to Steve or it'll cause ructions.'

Nellie stood to attention, hoisted her bosom and folded her arms beneath it. A sure sign she meant business. 'What did the flamer have to say about my son?'

'Oh, she included my Jill so ye're not on yer own, sunshine. Are yer going to give me yer solemn oath that yer won't repeat it?'

Nellie wondered whether a promise and a solemn oath meant the same thing. But she didn't know and gave up worrying. 'Go 'ed, girl.'

'Well, the queer one said Lizzie must go through some money every week keeping an extra two people. She didn't know how she managed it on a widow's pension. In other words, my Jill and your Steve are living off the old lady.'

Nellie's arms appeared from under her bosom and she began to push up her sleeves as though ready for a fight. 'Well, the bitch! The cheeky cow! Just wait until I see her, she won't know what hit her by the time I'm finished. She won't know what year it is, never mind what day.' Nellie paced the tiny kitchen floor, then stopped in front of her friend. 'And you just stood there and let her say that without clocking her one?'

'I've never clocked anyone in me life, sunshine, and I'm not about to start now. Especially someone who's not worth the effort.'

'So yer never said a dickie bird? Just let her get away with it?'

'I took her down a peg without resorting to blows, Nellie. I'll tell yer exactly what I said.' Molly took the powders from her pocket and laid them on the draining board with the milk. Then standing with her back straight, and looking down her nose, she said with an air of authority, 'I don't think it's my place to discuss Mrs Corkhill's financial situation with you, Elsie, except to say yer've got yer sums wrong.'

125

Nellie was impressed. In fact, Nellie was very impressed. 'Yer know, girl, ye're not half good with words. I'd say that was definitely taking her down a peg or two. I bet she's still trying to figure out what yer said. It was better than fisting her any day. But that's not to say she'll get off as lightly with me. I'll bide me time, but I'll get her when she's least expecting it. And don't worry, girl, I won't tell Steve 'cos he'd be really upset if he thought that's what people were saying about him and Jill.'

'Only bad-minded people like Elsie, and there's not many of them around here.' Molly opened the living-room door again. 'Lizzie's still asleep, but I'm afraid I'm going to have to wake her. She needs to take a Beecham's every four hours and the sooner we start the better. You mix one in a cup with water while I wake her up.'

Lizzie could barely open her eyes. 'I must have dropped off, Molly, what time is it?'

'It's only half-past nine, sunshine, and I wouldn't have woken yer up, but I want yer to take a powder. It'll make yer feel a bit better and yer can go back to sleep.'

Nellie came through carrying a cup. 'Get this down yer, girl, it'll do yer good.' She watched as the old lady shivered and pulled a face as she drank the potion. 'It's not very nice but it'll do the trick. A couple of those and yer'll be up doing a jig.'

'I hope so. Right now I feel as weak as a kitten.'

'Now comes a delicate subject,' Molly said, taking the empty cup. 'Yer'll need to go to the toilet, sunshine, so what do we do? I could put me coat around yer and help yer down the yard, or perhaps yer've got a chamber pot?'

'I've got one, Molly, but I'd have to be dying to use it. I'll go down the yard if yer'll help me.'

'That's no problem. Put yer cardi on properly and button it up, then I'll wrap me coat around yer. But make it the quickest penny yer've ever spent 'cos it's bitter out there.'

'D'yer want me to help, girl?' Nellie asked, wishing she was as efficient in times like this as her mate was. 'Or shall I build the fire up?'

'You see to the fire, sunshine.' Molly turned the collar of the coat up so Lizzie's ears were covered. 'There, that should keep the cold out. Open the kitchen door for us, Nellie, please.'

Five minutes later, Lizzie was tucked up on the couch. She couldn't control the shivering and yet her forehead was still burning. 'It's years since I had a cold, and never one as bad as this.'

'We'll see how yer are by tea-time,' Molly said. 'If ye're no better

I think we should call the doctor out, just to be on the safe side.' She saw a look of fear on the old lady's face and cursed herself for putting it there. 'I suggest the best thing yer can do now is sleep. Nellie's banked the fire up and it should last for hours. I'll put the rice pudding in the oven on a low light now, then, if yer do manage to drop off, me and Nellie will go home for an hour so we don't disturb yer. I'll have to take yer key, though, Lizzie, 'cos I never thought to ask Jill to give me hers.'

'It's in the dish on the sideboard. And thanks for everything Molly, and you, Nellie, I'd have been lost without yer.'

'No, yer wouldn't, sunshine, 'cos our Jill was going to take the day off. I had to chase her to work, she didn't want to leave yer. But stop talking now and try and sleep. Don't open the door if anyone knocks, stay right where yer are, in the warmth. We'll see yer later.'

'Nellie, we're going to have to split the shopping between us otherwise it'll take too long. If you get the spuds and cabbages, I'll see what Tony will give us in the meat line. I've got to go there anyway, to tell Ellen about her mother-in-law.'

'Ah, ay, girl, yer know I hate shopping on me own! I always end up getting the wrong things. Let me come with yer and we can run all the way.'

'No, sunshine, 'cos with the best will in the world, there's no way you won't stop and talk to everyone yer see. And I don't want to have to argue with yer in front of people or I'll be the worst in the world.' Nellie looked so forlorn Molly felt herself weakening. 'Look, you go to the greengrocer's, I'll go to the butcher's, and we'll meet up at Irwin's. How does that suit yer?'

'I don't know why we can't go together if I promise not to speak to anyone. It's not as though I can't walk as fast as yer.'

'Nellie, yer could have been at the greengrocer's by now! I don't want to leave Lizzie for too long, just in case she needs anything. So no more talking, be on yer way.'

When Molly walked into the butcher's alone and out of breath two pair of eyes kept watching the door. 'Don't tell me ye're on yer own, Molly?' Tony said. 'I thought you and Nellie were joined at the hip.'

'Not quite, Tony, but near enough. I've chased her to the green-grocer's while I came here, 'cos we're in a hurry. Lizzie's not too well, Ellen. I've been up there since half-seven when Jill came down to tell me. She was going to stay off work but I wouldn't let her.'

127

Ellen wiped her hands down her blood-stained apron. 'What's wrong with Lizzie?'

'She's got a very heavy cold, sweating and high temperature. And she's got no energy at all, which isn't a bit like her.'

'I'll nip up in me dinner hour, Molly, and thanks for seeing to her.'

'There's no need for yer to go in yer dinner hour, yer must be rushed off yer feet with all the Christmas orders. Leave it until tonight and go and see her then. Me and Nellie will keep a close eye on her. I brought her downstairs and put her on the couch with plenty of pillows and her eiderdown. It was too cold to leave her up in the bedroom, she'd have caught pneumonia as sure as eggs. She's got a nice fire and we've given her a Beecham's powder. We'll give her one every four hours and see if they bring her temperature down. But don't fret yerself, Ellen, if I was the least worried I'd send for the doctor.' Molly took a deep breath, 'Now, Tony, what goodies have yer in store for me and me mate?'

'How about some Cumberland sausage, Molly? I think yer families are partial to them with an egg and chips.'

'Ye're a pal, Tony, I don't know what me and Nellie would have done without yer. I'll be remembering yer in me will, that's for sure. And after all that flattering, can I ask yer to be quick before Nellie comes looking for me and more time will be wasted while she tells yer how she banked the fire up for Lizzie and gave her the Beecham's powder.'

Nellie was waiting outside Irwin's with the basket at her feet and a pained expression on her face. 'How soft you are, Molly Bennett! Leaving me to carry the heavy spuds and cabbage while you're carrying sweet bugger all!'

Molly grinned. 'Ah, yes, sunshine, but yer see, what you've carried might be heavy but it wouldn't be any good without what I've got in this small parcel.'

'I'm going to stay bad-tempered until yer tell me what it is. So go on, what have yer got?'

'Nothing much, only Cumberland sausage.'

'Ooh, ay, that's good girl! We haven't had Cumberland sausage for a long time. They're my George's favourite.' Nellie's chubby face beamed up at her friend as she rubbed her hands together before picking up the basket. 'I'll have one very happy husband tonight. I might even make him pay a forfeit for it.'

'How d'yer mean, pay a forfeit?'

'I thought yer didn't like me telling yer what goes on in our bedroom.'

'I'm not the least interested in what goes on in yer bedroom, sunshine, so keep it to yerself.'

'Then I can't tell yer about the forfeit, girl, 'cos George would be paying his forfeit in the bedroom. What I could do, to save yer blushing and wishing the ground would open and swallow yer up, is put it in a roundabout way. I could say, all casual like, that George had paid his forfeit much to my satisfaction.'

Molly turned her head and bit on her bottom lip. How could you fall out with someone who wouldn't let you? 'Get in the shop, Nellie, before I brain yer. And we'll get our bread from here today, save walking to Hanley's. We've been out long enough and I want to get back and see how Lizzie is.'

'Bloody slave driver,' Nellie muttered under her breath.

'What did yer say, sunshine?'

'I didn't say nothing, girl, I was humming.'

'That's a new one on me, then. I've never heard of a song what says "bloody slave driver". Mind you, I'm not very well up on the latest songs. Which is just as well if they've got swear words in. I'm more of a Bing Crosby fan meself. I like my songs romantic, sweet and wholesome.'

'Something like yerself, eh, girl?'

'I suppose yer could say that.' Molly smiled at the girl behind the counter and passed her ration books over. 'As much tea and margarine as I can have on those, sunshine.'

Nellie gave her a dig in the ribs. 'Eh, girl, I've come out without me ration books.'

Molly sighed. 'Trust you! Yer'd forget yer head if it was loose.'

'Don't blame me, it was the rushing out to get up to Lizzie's what did it. It didn't enter me head to bring me ration books.'

'Can yer let Nellie have some things and she'll bring her books in this afternoon?' Molly appealed to the assistant. 'I'll make sure yer get them.'

The girl pulled a face and nodded to where the manager was serving another customer. 'I daren't, Mrs Bennett, it's more than me job's worth. We've been warned that anyone found giving food without coupons will be sacked on the spot. I can't even do it for me own mam.'

'Ah, well, do us a favour, sunshine, and split my tea and marge in half. Then tomorrow my mate can bring her books and yer can halve them again so I get me own back.' Molly turned to Nellie. 'I'll pay for these, and two loaves. You pay tomorrow. And don't yer dare say yer've come without yer purse.'

'What a bloody palaver,' Nellie grumbled as they left the shop. 'All that for a few tea leaves and a square of marge that yer need a magnifying glass to see. It's enough to make yer spit. Just wait until rationing finishes, I'll be stuffing meself all day to make up for what we've missed. Bacon and egg for breakfast and real boiled ham for me sandwiches at dinnertime. I won't know I'm born!'

'Oh, will George be getting real boiled ham in his carry out, then?' Molly asked innocently. 'And Lily and Paul?'

Nellie had an answer ready, as Molly should have known she would. 'Ah, well, yer see, girl, that all depends. If George carries out his forfeit to my complete satisfaction, then he'll get boiled ham. If not, then it's brawn for him until he pulls his socks up.'

'I asked for that, didn't I ?' Molly said. 'I should know better by now.'

'Ye're too slow on the uptake, girl, that's yer problem. I've been telling yer that for nearly twenty-five years but yer still haven't learned.'

'I've learned enough, sunshine, a lot of yer bad habits have rubbed off on me. Not that I'm complaining, like, 'cos I've enjoyed meself along the way.' Molly reached out and took the heavy basket from her friend. 'I'll carry these now in part payment for all the laughs yer've given me over the years.'

Nellie's face wore a self-satisfied expression. 'Yeah, we've had some good times, haven't we, girl? And we've got a lot more to come. We've got Christmas next week, then after that we're going to play detective and see if we can find Phil's family. I'm not half looking forward to that, I can't wait to start.'

'First things first, Nellie, so just hold yer horses. We've got plenty to do before then, and Lizzie is a priority. We don't want Corker to come home and find his ma sick. Some homecoming that would be.'

Nellie's short legs moved faster. 'Yeah, let's put a move on and make sure she's all right. The poor old soul might be dying for a drink.'

'I'm hoping she'll still be asleep. That's the best medicine for a cold.'

'What are we doing with this shopping, girl, are we taking it up to Lizzie's with us?'

'No, we'll drop it off at home, there's no point in carting it up there. All being well, if she doesn't get any worse, we can take turns in coming home to get our dinners ready.'

130

Molly had taken Lizzie's back-door key with her, and the two women crept into the kitchen without making a sound. 'Not a peep, sunshine, 'cos I'd hate to wake her if she's in a good sleep.' Molly turned the knob on the living-room door and popped her head inside to find Lizzie curled up on the couch with her head buried in the pillows and the eiderdown covering her shoulders. She was breathing through her mouth and the sound was harsh as though her throat was dry. It's too soon for another Beecham's, Molly thought, but I think she should have a drink to clear any phlegm on her chest. She remembered having a heavy cold once and her mother telling her she must drink a lot or she'd never get better.

Molly closed the door quietly and stepped back right on to Nellie's foot.

'Bloody hell, girl, why don't yer look where ye're going! That didn't half hurt.'

'How can I look where I'm going when I back up? I'm really sorry, sunshine, but yer should have got out of me way! Does yer foot hurt?'

'Of course it does, soft girl! Yer stood on every one of me toes. I only see me feet once every blue moon, but I know I've got them now all right.'

'Lift yer foot and I'll take yer shoe off and rub yer toes better.'

That suited Nellie right down to the ground. She was practically purring with pleasure as Molly rubbed her toes gently. 'Ooh, that's the gear, girl, I could stand a lot of that.'

'So could I if I could find anyone daft enough to do it.' Molly lowered the foot. 'Leave yer shoe off for a while till the pain goes.' She turned the tap on and ran water over her hands. 'I'm not saying yer've got dirty feet, sunshine, but I'll enjoy me food better if I know me hands are clean.'

'How's Lizzie?'

'As snug as a bug in a rug, but she's breathing through her mouth and making cackling noises so after I've had a look at the rice pudding I'm going to wake her up for a cup of tea. If she doesn't seem any worse, you could go home and see to yer potatoes and cabbage.'

'All right, girl, then I'll come back and relieve yer so yer can see to your dinner.'

Lizzie looked dazed when Molly shook her shoulder. She couldn't make out what was happening at first. She tried to sit up but didn't have the strength. 'I must have been dead to the world, Molly.'

'Yer were, sunshine, and it was a shame to wake yer. But yer need plenty of liquid down yer when yer've got such a heavy cold, so I thought it best.'

When Nellie came in she was carrying a cup of tea. 'Here yer are, girl, I've put plenty of milk in so yer can drink it right off.'

The old lady looked flustered. 'I'm keeping you two from yer work and it's not fair. Yer've got families to see to.'

Molly held the cup to Lizzie's lips. 'Don't panic, we're very organised. We went to the shops while yer were asleep and got our dinner in. Nellie's going home for an hour to do a bit of work, then she's coming back to give me a break. So all you've got to worry about is getting better for when Corker's ship docks.'

'And for Christmas,' Nellie piped up. 'Father Christmas doesn't come down anyone's chimney if they're sick 'cos he's frightened of catching something.' Her brow furrowed in concentration. 'I thought that sounded awful mean of him when I heard about it. I mean, it's supposed to be a time of goodwill towards men, and there's not much goodwill if Father Christmas can't be arsed visiting sick people.'

'Nellie, yer don't half go on, sunshine.' Molly glanced at Lizzie and saw that although the old lady looked as though she was burning up, and her eyes were running, there was a trace of a smile on her face. 'But ye're worth yer weight in gold.'

'D'yer know, girl, that's the nicest thing yer've ever said to me.' Nellie looked as proud as a peacock. 'Just imagine how rich I'd be if someone would give me me weight in gold. Not that I'd be too proud to be yer friend, though, 'cos I'm not a snob. I'd still pass yer the time of day.'

'Nellie ye're generous to a fault. And now I'm going to be generous to you and tell yer to go home and see to the family's dinner. Try and get back for two o'clock, that's when Lizzie's due for another powder. Then I'll nip down and see to my dinner.'

'You go now Molly, I'll be all right.' Lizzie was feeling far from all right, but she didn't want to impose on their good nature. 'Honest, I will!'

'I'm staying, Lizzie, so don't waste yer breath. I'll see me mate out the back way and then plump yer pillows and make yer comfortable so yer can go back to sleep.' Molly jerked her head. 'Come on, Nellie, I'll see yer out.'

Chapter 10

Molly was darning a pair of Jack's socks which she'd brought with her to pass the time away while she was keeping an eye on Lizzie when she heard the front door being opened. It crossed her mind that Jill must have asked to be let off early because it was well before her usual time for getting home. But it wasn't her daughter, it was Ellen.

With a finger to her lips, Molly nodded to the sleeping woman. 'She's in a deep sleep, sunshine, so keep yer voice down.'

'How is she?'

'Just about the same. She's had two Beecham's and is due for another at six o'clock. She's slept most of the day, which is a good thing.' Molly raised her brows. 'What are yer doing here at this time, the shop doesn't close for another half-hour?'

'Tony told me I could go because he could see I was worrying meself to death. Anyway, we don't get many customers at this time 'cos most women are home cooking the dinner.' Ellen was speaking in a whisper, her eyes going constantly to her mother-in-law whom she adored. 'I've left him with all the cleaning to do, but he said he didn't mind 'cos I seldom ask for time off.'

'He's a good scout, is Tony, ye're lucky to have him for a boss.'

'I wouldn't have if it hadn't been for you and Nellie. I know it's years ago and me life is very different now from what it was then, but I'll never forget how you and Nellie helped me.' Ellen grinned. 'Yer pulled me from the gutter by the scruff of me neck and forced me to take stock of meself. And I've never looked back since.'

'That's what friends are for, sunshine, and yer've repaid us with interest.' Molly saw the figure on the couch stirring. 'I think someone is waking up.'

Ellen knelt down at Lizzie's side and stroked the wispy white hair which was wet with perspiration. 'What's all this, Ma? Yer can't be sick with Corker due home and Christmas just around the corner.'

'I'll be all right tomorrow, love, it's only a chill.' A bout of coughing had the old lady gasping for breath and Molly shot out to the kitchen to bring her a cup of water. It was gulped down quickly and Lizzie asked for another. 'Me mouth feels like sawdust, it's so dry.'

'Haven't the Beecham's powders done any good at all?' Molly asked. 'I thought they would have eased it a bit.'

'Me head isn't tight like it was. This morning I felt as though someone had put a band around it and was pulling it as hard as they could.' Lizzie closed her eyes for a few seconds when the effort to keep them open became too much. Then she reached for Ellen's hand. 'Molly and Nellie have been here since half-seven this morning, and they've waited on me hand and foot. Molly made a rice pudding, and although I felt more like flying than eating, she made me eat it and I enjoyed it.' Her head fell back against the pillows and all Lizzie wanted to do was sleep but things needed to be said. 'But I'm worried about them 'cos they've got families to see to.'

'Oh, dear, oh, dear, Lizzie Corkhill, it's a pity yer've got nothing better to worry about.' Shaking her head from side to side, Molly went to the chair she'd spent the afternoon sitting in and picked up Jack's socks. 'See these, sunshine? Well, my feller's been asking me to darn them for weeks but I never got down to it.' She put a hand in one of the socks where the heel had been darned. 'See how neat it is? That's because it was so peaceful here, no one to interrupt, that I was able to take my time and make a good job of it.'

'Well, go home now, Molly, and see to the family,' Ellen said. 'They'll be coming in from work soon and the men will expect their dinner after working all day.'

'I was going to stay until six o'clock to make sure Lizzie was given another Beecham's, it's important she has one every four hours. Jill and Steve will see to her through the night and I'll come down first thing in the morning.'

'Will yer stop talking and go home, Molly Bennett?' Ellen insisted. 'I'll make sure Ma gets her medicine, and I'll see if Jill thinks she can cope through the night. If not, I'll stay meself. But I'd be grateful if yer'd come in the morning, I daren't take a day off, we're too busy.'

Molly reached for her coat. 'I'll go then, if ye're sure. But will someone let me know later how things are? I don't want to be sitting there wondering what's going on.'

'I'll send Jill down, I promise. And I know yer've done me a big favour today, but can I ask yer to do one more? Give a knock at ours and tell Phoebe where I am, and ask her to make something for the kids to eat. Or she can get something from the chip shop if she likes.

It wouldn't do them any harm for one night.'

'I'll do that.' Molly bent down to look into Lizzie's flushed face. 'I'll see yer in the morning, sunshine, and you behave yerself till then.'

'I don't know how to thank yer, Molly, yer've been very good.'

'If yer want to thank me, then get yerself better.' Molly gave Ellen the eye. 'I'll go out the back, come and shut the door after me.' Standing on the kitchen step, she whispered, 'Will yer make sure someone takes her down to the lavvy? She won't use the chamber pot under any circumstances. But she wouldn't be too happy about Steve taking her, so before settling her down for the night, would you or Jill do the honours? She's got her pride has our Lizzie, and we wouldn't want to deprive her of it, not at her age.'

'Molly, ye're an angel. And I know Corker will appreciate what ye're doing.'

'He'll appreciate it much more if he comes home to see his ma fit and well. So it's all hands to the pumps for the next few days. Please God she'll be better by then.' With a smile, Molly walked down the yard. 'Ta-ra, Ellen. Yer know where I am if yer want me.'

Paul was whistling as he knocked on the Corkhills' door. 'Is Phoebe ready, Gord?'

'No, she's washing the dishes.' Gordon stepped aside and jerked his head. 'Yer'd better come in and wait for her.'

Phoebe appeared at the kitchen door, still in her working clothes and with her hands dripping. 'I'm going to be half an hour at least then I want to go and see me nan. So why don't you go on and I'll meet yer in the dance hall?'

'Why d'yer have to go to yer nan's? Yer mam's up there, and Jill and Steve, so why d'you have to go?'

Phoebe sighed inwardly. Paul could be very selfish at times. Life for him was a bed of roses and he didn't see why anything should spoil it. 'I don't have to go, Paul. I'm going because she's me nan, I love her, and right now she's sick. Yer can wait for me to get ready, if yer like, and come up with me. Or yer can go on to the dance. The chances are that it'll be too late for me to follow yer, but yer know enough people there, yer wouldn't be on yer own.'

The corners of Paul's mouth turned down in a sulk. 'I don't want to go on me own, I want to go with you. Can't yer go and see yer nan tomorrow night?'

'No, I can't, I'm going tonight.' Phoebe was adamant. 'I wouldn't enjoy meself knowing she was sick while I was prancing around a

135

dance floor. But there's nothing to stop you from going, she's not your nan.'

'Why can't Dorothy go?'

Gordon was sitting at the table next to his younger brother, Peter, and didn't see why his sister should have to go through this. 'Our Dot's up there now, and me and Peter are going after Phoebe's been. We can't all traipse in together when me nan's sick.'

Paul ignored him. 'We had a date, Phoebe.'

'Yes, I know, but sickness doesn't come just when it suits yer, it can happen any time. If it was someone in your family I bet yer wouldn't go dancing.'

'I'll wait till yer get ready, then I'll walk up with yer. We'll take it from there, eh?'

'Suit yerself, I'll be as quick as I can.'

Later, when Phoebe pulled the door behind her and they stood on the pavement, Paul tried once again to persuade her. 'It wouldn't hurt to leave yer nan until tomorrow night. Go on, do it to please me.' He was coaxing her with his eyes and soft voice. 'I don't want to go to the dance without yer, I'd miss yer.'

'We seem to have different priorities, Paul, I'm sorry. There's no way yer can talk me out of seeing me nan so don't waste yer time.'

'Then I'll wait outside for yer. It might not be too late to go to Barlow's Lane.'

But Phoebe wouldn't have given in to him if he'd gone down on bended knee. She'd been well warned by her mam about men who were as sweet as honey on the outside and a devil on the inside. Not that she needed any warning, she'd seen a good example in her father. 'No, I'd rather yer didn't. I'd be on pins knowing yer were waiting. You do what yer want tonight and we'll leave it at that.'

'I'll see yer tomorrow, then, eh?' Paul put a hand on her arm, knowing he'd gone too far and wanting to make amends. 'Ye're not going to fall out with me over it, are yer?'

'I'm not so petty or childish. Besides I've got more important things on me mind right now. Yer can give me a knock tomorrow.' Phoebe began to walk away. 'Enjoy yerself at the dance.'

Paul stood watching her, calling himself all the stupid, selfish articles going. He'd certainly blotted his copybook tonight! Even to his own ears he'd sounded a right prat, trying to talk his girlfriend out of going to see her sick grandma. But from what his mam had said, Mrs Corkhill just had a cold and that didn't sound serious to him.

But the situation brought a smile to the face of a certain young girl.

For, unbeknown to him, Joanne Mowbray was standing in the side entry only a few yards away, and she'd heard every word that passed between the boy she had her eye on and his girlfriend. She'd been waiting for ages with the intention of accidentally on purpose bumping into Paul and his girl. She'd thought they'd be off dancing 'cos she kept track of his movements and was expecting to just exchange a few words. A case of slowly letting him see she was around and interested. But luck was on her side tonight, and she was bent on making the most of it.

'Hello, Paul.'

He spun around. 'Oh, it's you! Yer gave me a start.'

'Not out dancing tonight, then?'

He shook his head. 'Phoebe's grandma isn't well and she's gone up to see her.' Pulling a face, he joked, 'She stood me up.'

'I bet that doesn't happen to yer often, not a nice-looking lad like you. Anyway, can't yer go to the dance on yer own? Ye're not engaged to Phoebe, are yer?'

'No, we're not engaged. She did tell me to go to the dance, and I was in two minds, but I've gone off the idea now and think I'll have a night in. Me mam will wonder what's hit me 'cos I can't remember the last time I stayed in but that's what I'm going to do.'

Joanne was seventeen in years but much older in worldly wisdom. She knew she needed to be patient to get anywhere with Paul otherwise she'd spoil her chances altogether. 'It's a shame really 'cos I'd have come with yer to keep yer company, but I've made arrangements to meet a friend and I can't let them down.'

Paul's eyes widened. He was about to say it was manners to wait until you were asked, then decided he was reading more into it than there was. Joanne looked as though she was well able to look after herself, but even she wouldn't be that brazen. The girl was probably only trying to be friendly. 'You'd better be on yer way, then, 'cos yer don't want to keep yer friend hanging around. There's nothing worse than standing on a corner waiting for yer girlfriend.'

'Oh, it's not a boy I'm meeting, it's a girl I've known since school.' Joanne tossed her long dark hair and flashed him a smile, showing a fine set of white teeth. 'I fell out with me boyfriend a couple of weeks ago so I'm footloose and fancy free.' She turned to face the main road. 'Anyway, I'll see yer around. Ta-ra.'

Paul stood for a while pondering. He certainly wasn't going dancing, he'd gone right off the idea. He knew Lily and Archie were staying in tonight to have a game of cards with his mam and dad, so should he go home and join them? Or should he hang around and wait for Phoebe? Then, feeling lighter in his mind, he decided to do both. A game of cards and then seek out his girlfriend and try and get back in her good books.

Nellie looked up with surprise when her son walked in. 'Have yer forgotten something? I thought yer'd be in the middle of a fandango by now.'

Paul smiled sheepishly. He wouldn't half get some stick off his mam if she knew how stupid he'd been. 'Phoebe's gone up to see her nan so yer've got the pleasure of my company for an hour or so.'

'Don't ell me yer've given the dance a miss?' Lily said, holding the hand of cards to her chest so Archie wouldn't steal a peek. 'They say there's a first time for everything and yer've certainly proved them right.'

'D'yer hear what I've got to put up with, Archie? A feller can't be in his own home without someone making cracks about it.'

'Well, yer must admit it's unusual, son, we're not used to having yer around,' George said. 'But now yer are, pull yerself a chair out. Yer'll have to wait for us to finish this hand and then we'll deal yer in the next.'

'And no crying if yer lose, d'yer hear?' Nellie gave him a broad grin. She knew her son better than he knew himself, and she'd bet a pound to a pinch of snuff something had happened to discommode him. 'It's serious stuff this, yer could lose as much as tuppence.'

Paul feigned horror. 'Tuppence! Ooh, I don't think me bank would stand such a loss. Are yer good for a loan, Mam?'

'I'm skint and happy, son, I'm afraid. All me spare cash has gone into me Christmas clubs at the corner shop, the butcher's and the greengrocer's.'

'Neither a borrower nor a lender be, son,' George said. 'I suggest yer use the money yer would have spent going to the dance.'

'He won't need any money the way we're going on.' Archie grinned. 'It'll be midnight before we finish this hand.'

'Yeah,' Lily said. 'Eyes down.'

Paul sat watching, feigning interest, but his thoughts were not on the game. His eyes kept straying to the window to see if he could catch Phoebe passing, and this didn't go unnoticed by his mother. He's had his hand slapped tonight, Nellie told herself, and it's not before time. He needs taking down a peg or two and telling that he wasn't put on this earth just to have fun.

She stuck it for another ten minutes then said, 'For heaven's sake, son, why don't yer go and call for Phoebe at . . .' Nellie glimpsed a familiar figure passing the window just then. 'Yer'll be happy to know she's just gone past. Which means she's doing us all a favour 'cos yer fidgeting is putting us off the ruddy game.'

But Paul didn't wait around to hear all his mam said. He caught up with Phoebe as she was putting the key in the lock. 'Good evening, Miss Corkhill.'

Phoebe's heart missed a beat. She was so glad to see him but afraid to show it in case he thought he only had to smile and all would be forgiven. 'I'm surprised to see you, I thought yer'd be at the dance.'

'I found I didn't want to go without yer. I was out of order before, acting like a selfish kid who wasn't getting his own way, and I owe yer an apology.'

'Then give it to me inside, 'cos the boys are waiting to go and see me nan. Come on in.'

Gordon and Peter were standing just inside the door. 'How's me nan?' Gordon asked. 'Is she very sick?'

'She is poorly,' Phoebe told him. 'But me mam said it might be just a heavy cold she's got. If not, they'll have to get the doctor in.' She turned to Paul. 'I believe your mam and Auntie Molly have been looking after her all day, which is very good of them. She's singing their praises to high heaven.'

'We'll go then, Sis.' Gordon put his arm across his brother's shoulder. 'Then I'm taking Peter to me mate's for an hour.'

'Don't keep him out late or me mam will go mad. Don't forget he's still at school.'

'Not for much longer I'm not.' Peter didn't like being treated like a child. 'I've only got another six months, then I'll be working.'

She ruffled his hair. 'I know, I'm looking forward to it 'cos I won't have to give yer pocket money every week. Anyway, don't stop out too late 'cos me mam worries about yer. And don't stay too long with me nan. Remember she's not well and needs to rest.'

When the boys had left, Paul asked, 'Where's Dorothy?'

'Out with her friend.'

'Then seeing as we've got the house to ourselves, will yer sit on the couch with me so I can tell yer how sorry I am?'

'Is that all yer want me to sit on the couch for, so yer can tell me how sorry yer are?'

'Ah, well, yer see, that's the excuse I'm most likely to get away with. If I said I wanted to put me arms around yer and kiss yer, I'm not sure whether yer'd clock me one or not. So, being a coward, I went for the safest bet.'

Phoebe tried to keep her face straight but found it impossible. Those deep brown eyes and the dimples did it every time. 'Okay, but ye're not out of the dog-house yet. Yer can't get around me that easy. So yer kisses will have to be better than yer excuses.'

'They say practice makes perfect. Let's start now before yer mam comes in and puts me off me stride.'

'She won't be in until ten o'clock 'cos she wants to see me nan bedded down for the night. Then Jill and Steve said they'd take turns looking in on her every few hours in case she wants a drink.'

'Our Steve will make sure she's all right, he's a good bloke.'

'Yes, I know,' Phoebe said. 'He's more sympathetic and understanding than you are.'

'That's because he's two years older than I am. He's had more practice than I have. It's the same with kissing, he's had two years' more experience than me. That's why there's no time to lose. So if yer'll just pucker yer lips for me, I can begin to practise.'

Phoebe held her head away and looked into his eyes. 'And what about the sympathy and understanding? That's just as important as being good at kissing.'

'I'll start that right now. If yer don't enjoy me kisses I'll sympathise with yer and understand.' He cupped her chin in one of his hands. 'That was my idea of a joke, but after the way I acted earlier, I can see why yer might not appreciate it. All I can say is, I'm sorry and I'll try to make it up to yer. So if yer'll pucker those sweet lips of yours I'll begin the process.'

When they broke apart, Paul sighed with the sheer thrill and pleasure. 'They'll be having the interval waltz at Barlow's now, and d'yer know what? I feel sorry for those suckers 'cos they don't know what they're missing.'

Molly arrived at Lizzie's the next morning at half-seven to be told by Jill that the old lady had slept most of the night. 'I came down about two o'clock and she was stirring so I gave her a Beecham's and made her a cup of tea. Steve came down at four and she was fast asleep. I think she seems a bit brighter, but it's hard to tell.'

'Has she been down the yard, sunshine?'

Jill nodded. 'I took her as soon as Steve left for work. I didn't want to embarrass her by asking in front of him.'

'That's a good girl.' Molly closed the front door behind her. 'Let's see for meself how our friend is this morning.' She stood in front of the couch and was heartened to see Lizzie's eyes were wide open and a lot clearer than they'd been yesterday. 'Good morning, sunshine, it's good to see ye're awake and taking notice.'

'Me head's a lot better, Molly, thanks to the powders. I'm still shivering even though I'm hot, but not as bad as yesterday. I've no strength, and poor Jill had to practically carry me down the yard. It's a good job I'm only little and thin or she'd never have managed.'

'Of course she would, she's as strong as an ox, is Jill. Anyway, she can toddle off to work now and I'll get yer washed and put some clean clothes on yer. Yer'll feel a lot better then.'

Jill bent down to kiss the old lady who'd become like a mother to her and Steve. But a thin hand waved her away. 'I don't want yer catching whatever it is I've got, sweetheart, so don't come too close.'

'I'll save all me kisses until ye're better, then, Auntie Lizzie. I'll keep a tally and give yer them all in one go.'

After seeing her daughter off, Molly set to work. And when Nellie came at eight o'clock, it was to see Lizzie resting on pillows with clean slips on, wearing a nice fresh nightdress and with her hair neatly combed. 'My word, things are looking up, girl! Yer look like a film star lying there all done up like a dog's dinner.'

'Molly's been very good, she's washed me from head to toe. And I do feel better with all clean clothes on, I was beginning to smell with all the sweating I've done.'

After a broad wink at the old lady, Nellie turned to her mate. 'Ay, girl, if I was sick would yer wash me down?'

'Don't even think of it, sunshine, I'd need a block and tackle to lift yer. I mean, there's things even a best friend won't do.'

'Yer'd soon get the hang of it, girl, it wouldn't be that bad. All yer'd have to do would be lift a layer of fat at a time. Mind you, there's all the creases as well, they're a bugger to get at. But yer could do it over two days, then it wouldn't be so bad.'

'Forget it, sunshine, and make yerself useful now ye're here. Yer can put the kettle on for a cuppa while I give Lizzie a Beecham's.' She saw the old lady shiver and knew it was because she hated taking the powders. 'I know they don't taste nice, medicine never does. But yer've got to put up with it if yer want to get better.'

'She doesn't half like ordering people around,' Nellie said, throwing her coat over a chair. 'It's a wonder she doesn't have a whip and make us jump to it.'

'It's a case of having to with you, otherwise yer'd never get anything done.' Molly pointed to the coat thrown carelessly over the chair. 'And yer can just hang that up, sunshine, 'cos our Jill tidied up before she went to work.'

'Oh, God, here she goes.' Nellie tutted as she picked up her coat and hung it on the hook behind the door. 'It's no wonder poor Jack looks worn out all the time, he's henpecked.'

Molly chuckled. 'I always think your George looks worn out, but I don't think it's your nagging what does it.'

Nellie pretended to be surprised. 'Molly Bennett, shame on yer! How do you know what goes on in our bedroom?'

'I don't know, sunshine, and I don't want to know. Neither does Lizzie, who like meself would prefer a cup of tea to tales of your marital bliss.'

'All right, slave driver, one pot of tea coming up.' As Nellie waddled to the kitchen they could hear her muttering. 'I wonder if Maisie in the corner shop sells arsenic?'

Molly whispered to Lizzie, 'They don't sell arsenic, but they do a good line in rat poison.'

Nellie's head appeared around the door. 'What was that yer said, girl?'

'I said I was dying for a cuppa, me throat's parched.'

'Oh, I could have sworn yer said Maisie sells rat poison. I was interested because I saw two ruddy big rats in the entry when I came up. They were outside your yard door and I'm not exaggerating when I say they were as big as cats.'

Molly wasn't going to fall for that. 'Oh, yeah, I've seen them. They're playful things, friendly too! I feed them any leftovers I've got.'

Nellie flared her nostrils. 'Ye're a big liar, you are, Molly Bennett.'

'Not as big as you, sunshine. I'd have to go some to beat you for telling fibs.' Molly cupped a hand to her ear. 'Isn't that the kettle I hear boiling? Or is it the two rats singing in harmony outside the back door, hoping yer'll feed them?'

'I wish yer'd stop talking about rats, I hate them. Dirty buggers, they are.'

'None of us likes rats, Nellie, but most us enjoy a cup of tea. Especially when we've had to wait so long for it we're spitting feathers.' Molly clapped her hands. 'Look sharp, will yer, before Lizzie gets up to make it herself.'

When Nellie brought the tea through, Molly sat on the side of the couch to hold the saucer steady for the old lady whose hands were shaking. 'Ye're not out of the woods yet, Lizzie, but yer don't seem to have the high temperature yer had yesterday. Keep this up and yer'll be better for Corker coming home, and for Christmas.'

'Please God, Molly, please God.'

'Yer don't want to miss the party, girl.' There was a cunning gleam in Nellie's eyes as she sipped on her tea. 'It would be a shame if yer missed the party.'

Molly raised her brows. 'Oh, aye, and which party is that, sunshine?'

It was Nellie's turn to raise her brows. 'Why, yours, of course! Who else's?'

'I'm not having no party! I've told yer, I can't afford it this year, what with saving up for Tommy's wedding and everything.'

'But you always have the Christmas party! Every year since I've known yer, ye've had a party at Christmas. Yer can't just stop now when people are relying on yer.'

'I know I've always had the Christmas parties, and the New Year parties, and every other party yer can mention. But not this year, someone else can have it for a change.'

'Yer can't just alter yer mind like that, and leave everyone in the lurch. We're all expecting to come to yours.'

'What d'yer mean, leaving everyone in the lurch?' Molly was getting quite heated. 'I haven't invited anyone to a party this year, so how can yer say I'm leaving them in the lurch? And anyway, who d'yer mean by everyone?'

'The usual crowd.' Nellie tutted. 'I don't know why ye're asking me that, yer know who our friends are. There's Maisie and Alec, the Corkhills, Bridie and Bob, all my lot and yer own family. I can't think of anyone else offhand.'

Molly started counting on her fingers. 'D'yer know how many that comes to, sunshine? The families have grown a lot in the last few years and at a rough guess I'd say over twenty people. There's no way I could fit them all in the house even if I wanted to. But this year I don't want to and I'm not going to! I've told yer dozens of times that I'm counting every penny so I can help Tommy and Rosie. No, yer can just forget it.'

'I can't do that, girl, I've already invited them!'

Molly nearly slipped off the side of the couch. 'Yer've what! Yer've invited people to a party at my house without even asking me?'

Lizzie's eyes moved from one to the other. She was used to this kind of carry-on from two of the people she loved, but had Nellie gone too far this time?

'I've never had to ask yer before, girl so it didn't occur to me. I didn't think yer could be that miserable yer'd spoil Christmas for all yer mates.'

'I won't spoil Christmas for me mates, I'll tell them that you've kindly offered to have the party at your house this year because I've got a lot on me plate and can't afford it.'

'We all know yer've got a lot on yer plate, girl, that's why we've sorted it out.'

Molly locked eyes with her mate. What had she been up to behind her back? Yer couldn't tell whether she was telling the truth or not. 'What have yer sorted out, and who have yer sorted it out with?'

Nellie leaned forward to put her cup on the table then leaned back in the chair with a smug smile on her chubby face. 'Ellen, Maisie and meself. We got together 'cos we know ye're stuck, and we're going to pay for all the food between us. And before yer thank me, girl, let me tell yer the men are clubbing together for the drink.'

'Thank yer? I'll ruddy throttle yer! Yer've no right to discuss my financial state with other people even if they are friends. Seeing as yer've got it all nicely sorted, sunshine, then why don't yer have the party at your house and invite me as a guest? That would make a change, wouldn't it?'

'Because I wouldn't know where to start having a party, that's why. Nobody can do it like you, girl, yer've got the knack for it. If you don't do it, there won't be no Christmas party for anyone and I don't think yer'll let that happen 'cos ye're not really miserable. Not all the time, anyway.'

If I was having a bet, Lizzie thought, I'd put me money on Nellie. Another few minutes and Molly would be throwing the towel in. You could see in her face that she was giving it serious thought, which meant she was weakening.

'So yer'd only be using my house? The party would be held for, and by, everyone? And it wouldn't cost me a fortune?'

'Not a bean, girl, not a bean. After all, as Ellen and Maisie said, we've sponged off yer often enough over the years, it's about time we paid yer back.'

'And you'd help with the preparations and everything? Lend us all your wooden chairs and that three-legged stool yer've got?'

Nellie made a sign on her chest. 'Cross my heart, girl, I'd do anything yer asked.'

'And all the cleaning up afterwards?'

'Scout's honour.'

144

Lizzie's eyes were almost closing and her head was asking to be rested on the soft feather pillows. But with determination and willpower, she stayed as she was. She wouldn't rest proper if she didn't hear the outcome of this.

Molly decided it was time to play her trump card. 'And would yer promise to get yer Christmas dinner over early so the men can carry my table up to yours out of the way?'

Nellie screwed up her face. 'Ah, not that again, girl! There's no room to breathe with that ruddy big thing in our house.'

'Well, I'd never get twenty people in my room with the table in, so I think we're going to have to forget the whole thing. We'll do without a party this Christmas, it won't kill us.'

'I could have the table in me yard, girl, it wouldn't come to no harm.'

'My good table outside in this weather! Not on yer life, sunshine, it's me pride and joy is that table.' Molly thought she'd turn the screw a little. 'There is an alternative if that doesn't suit yer. You have the party and they can bring your table to my house. Now I can't be fairer than that, can I?'

'No!' Nellie's chins jumped with fright. 'I'll have yer bloody table, even though it is a flaming nuisance. But only on one condition.'

'And what's that, sunshine?'

'That I'm yer deputy hostess, like I always am.'

'I wouldn't have it any other way. I'd be lost without you as me deputy, the party wouldn't be the same.'

The two friends looked at each other and burst out laughing. Nellie had known it would turn out like this, and so had Molly. It was what they both wanted anyway. It wouldn't be Christmas without a party at the Bennetts' house.

'I'm glad that's all fixed up,' Lizzie's soft voice broke in. 'I was beginning to worry in case yer asked *me* to have the party.'

'Ah, we've been neglecting yer. Yer can blame Nellie, she started it.' Molly stroked Lizzie's wispy hair. 'Yer don't feel nearly as hot today, thank God. I think yer should get as much sleep as yer can, so d'yer want me to make yer comfortable?'

'Yes, please, Molly.'

'Right, let's get yer bedded down. And while I'm doing it, Nellie, will yer take the cups out and wash them, please, and then bank the fire up?'

Nellie pushed her friend aside so she could bend down to talk to the old lady. 'Did yer hear the orders being given out? Well, that's what it's like being a deputy hostess. The real name for it should be dogsbody, but deputy hostess sounds more posh. And there's nothing I like better than for people to think I've got a bit of class. That I came out of the top drawer, if yer see what I mean.' Carrying the cups and saucers, she swayed towards the kitchen. 'People think I'm as common as muck, but that's 'cos they don't know any better.'

They could hear the china being put in the sink with a heavy hand, and Molly held her breath. Then she and Lizzie both chuckled when they heard Nellie talking to herself. 'Folk around here are so pig ignorant, they don't know ye're supposed to crook yer little finger when ye're drinking tea out of a cup. Common as muck they are, brought up in the gutter. Some of them haven't even got mothers or fathers.'

Chapter 11

Lizzie improved a little each day, and when Molly called on the Saturday morning it was to find her sitting in her rocking chair with pillows at her back and a blanket over her knees. And there was a self-satisfied expression on her face which told how happy she was to be off that couch.

'I hope yer feel well enough for this, sunshine?' Molly said. 'D'yer not think ye're rushing things a bit?'

'No, I do feel better, Molly, honest. I couldn't lie on that ruddy couch any longer, me body and limbs were all stiff.'

Jill had been hovering behind her mother. She would have stayed off work because it would only have meant losing half a day's pay, but her mother had insisted. 'Tell me mam the truth, Auntie Lizzie. Tell her why yer were determined to be back in yer chair today, no matter what I said.'

Lizzie grinned. 'The postman brought a letter from Corker. His ship is docking today and he's hoping to be home by dinnertime.'

'Ah, well, that puts a different complexion on things, doesn't it? Molly wasn't just delighted for the old lady, she was happy for herself. She had a soft spot for Corker who was one of the finest men she'd ever met. 'I'd better get meself all dolled up before he comes, I can't let the side down by letting him see me in me rags.'

'He wouldn't even notice what yer had on, Molly, he'd just be glad to see yer.' Lizzie glanced at the clock. 'Jill's going to be late if she doesn't put a move on.'

'Yeah, yer'd better be going, sunshine, or yer'll be clocking in late.'

'I've told yer, I don't mind taking the morning off, Mam! I could give yer a hand to get the place dusted and polished for Uncle Corker coming.'

'I can do that on me own, sunshine, I don't need any help. Once I've seen to Lizzie I'll go through this place like a dose of salts. Nellie will be up later, she's going to get me shopping in for me so that's one worry less. Now do as ye're told and poppy off.'

Jill gave her a hug and kiss. 'I'll be home by one o'clock.' She put a hand on each arm of the rocking chair and asked, 'Are yer well enough for a kiss, Auntie Lizzie?'

'Leave it for another few days, sweetheart, I don't want to pass me cold on to yer.'

'That's twelve I owe yer now, I'm keeping count. Ta-ra!'

Lizzie waited until she heard the door bang before saying, 'She's an angel, that daughter of yours, and so's Steve. Nothing's trouble to them and I couldn't have been better looked after if I'd been in hospital. I bless the day Corker asked me if I'd ever thought of taking in lodgers. They're more like family to me now.'

'I'm lucky with me children, Lizzie, all of them.' Molly was busy brushing the hearth and the bars of the grate. 'And with me two sons-in-law, they're like me own flesh and blood.'

'That's how I feel about Ellen and the children. I've got to admit I wasn't too keen on him marrying a widow with four children, but that was before I got to know them. Now I love the bones of all of them and don't have to worry about what will happen to Corker when I die. I know he'll live a happy life with a loving family around him.'

Molly put the brush back on the companion set before saying, 'Ay, if I were you, Lizzie, I wouldn't dream of dying for at least another ten years. Think of what yer'd be missing! Four grandchildren to grow up and get married, and imagine how many great-grandchildren they could give yer! Yer've loads to look forward to, sunshine, so if I were you I wouldn't be popping me clogs for a long time.'

Lizzie chuckled. 'I'll have to tell Corker what yer said, he'd be tickled pink. And if Phoebe and Paul are serious about each other, I could end up being related to Nellie! In a roundabout way, of course.'

'It'll be the same roundabout way as I am. But Nellie won't have it that we're not blood relations, and I've given up arguing with her when she introduces me to all and sundry as her sister-in-law. Any time now I'm expecting her to tell folk what don't know us that we're sisters.'

Molly chuckled as her mind went back over the years to the day when her mate had suggested they cut each other on the arm and hold them together so the blood flowed from one to the other. If the Red Indians could do it, Nellie had said, why couldn't they? 'She's come up with some weird and wonderful things in the years I've known her, God knows. But I'll tell yer what, Lizzie, she's the best mate anyone could have. She's enriched my life, has Helen Theresa McDonough, and that of my family.'

'Yer've both enriched all our lives, Molly. Yer make a good pair.'

It was on the tip of Molly's tongue to say she hoped she and Nellie made a pair of good detectives, but she bit the words back. Nothing might come of it and then they'd look silly. 'I'll get the bowl and flannel and give yer a good wash, Lizzie, then change yer nightdress so yer look pretty for Corker coming. After that I'll start on this room and go like the clappers until Nellie comes. Then we'll stop for a break and a cuppa.'

Molly worked flat out. The furniture was polished until you could see your face in it and there wasn't a fingermark anywhere. The black grate shone and the flickering flames from the fire made the room look warm and comfortable. 'D'yer mind if I stand on one of yer chairs to clean the windows, Lizzie, save me dragging the ladder up the yard?'

'Leave the windows, Molly, yer'll wear yerself out! I'll ask Steve to do them tomorrow when he's off.'

'Not on your life, sunshine, I'll do them now. I want this place like a little palace when Corker walks in. Just like you always have it.' So Molly put a cloth on one of the wooden chairs and started on the front windows. It was from this vantage point that she saw her mate approaching the house. And in Nellie's hand there was a Hanley's cake bag. With her mouth watering in anticipation, Molly jumped from the chair and made for the front door.

'Good morning, girl!' Nellie looked decidedly pleased with herself. 'It's a clear day but bitterly cold. Not a day for any monkey what doesn't want to have his things frozen off.' She placed the bag on the table and grinned at Lizzie. 'It's good to see yer looking a lot better, girl. I've brought yer a nice cake to have with yer cup of tea.'

Molly carried the chair back and put it in place. Then she put her hands on her hips. 'I hope ye're not saying there's only one cake in that bag, Nellie McDonough?'

'I didn't think Lizzie could eat more than one.' Looking the picture of innocence, she turned to the old lady. 'You couldn't eat two cakes, could yer, girl?'

Lizzie had found out over the years that you didn't get involved in any conversation between the two friends. So to be on the safe side she shrugged her shoulders and remained neutral. And she was spared being asked the question again because Nellie had caught a movement out of the corner of her eye and turned to see Molly about to open the cake bag. 'If you open that bag, girl, so help me I'll clock yer one.'

It was then that Molly noticed a spot of white at the corners of Nellie's mouth which looked suspiciously like cream. 'You've eaten one on the way back, haven't yer? Yer were too mean to buy three cakes, so yer bought two and ate one on the way back from the shops so I wouldn't know. That's about the most miserable trick yer've ever played, Nellie McDonough, and I won't forget it in a hurry.'

'How was I expected to know yer wanted a cream slice?' Nellie was surprised Molly hadn't noticed her shaking tummy, 'cos it was taking her all her time to keep the laughter in check. 'I'll walk back and get yer one.'

'You most certainly will not! D'yer think I'd enjoy a cake that was begrudged to me? And as for saying yer didn't know whether I'd want one or not, that's a right feeble bloody excuse when yer know they're me favourites.'

'You swore then, girl, and I'm surprised at yer. Always telling me to watch me language and yer come out with it yerself.'

'Nellie, you'd make a saint swear. Now get out of me way while I finish this room off.'

'Aren't yer stopping for a cup of tea?'

'No, I'm not! You can make one for Lizzie and yerself, but leave me out.'

'Ah, come on, girl, don't be like that! I'll go back to Hanley's and get yer a ruddy cream slice, save yer having a miserable gob on yer. It won't take me long.'

'Don't put yerself out, I'll get it meself.' Without further ado, Molly made her way through the small makeshift hallway to the front door. There, she bent down and retrieved the white confectioner's bag which was tucked away at the side of the step. Then after closing the door behind her she returned to the living room and handed the bag to Nellie. 'There yer are, sunshine, didn't take me any time at all, did it?'

Lizzie put a hand to her lips. Well, who'd have thought it? These two could beat Ethel Barrymore for acting any day.

'Yer knew all the time!' Nellie said. 'Yer let me carry on and yer knew all the time.'

'I was cleaning the front windows when yer came up the street and I saw yer bending down. I didn't know what yer were doing then, but when yer came up with the excuse that yer'd only bought a cream slice for Lizzie, I guessed right away. I knew yer wouldn't leave me out, sunshine, it would be more than yer life's worth.'

Nellie's chubby face creased. 'It was a good trick, though, wasn't it?'

'Yeah, it was! Yer had me going for a while until it suddenly struck me.'

'The pair of yer had me fooled,' Lizzie said. 'I thought we were going to cut the cream slice into three to keep everyone happy.' She shook her head. 'It's a mystery to me how yer think these things up, Nellie, and an even bigger mystery how Molly goes along with yer even when she knows what ye're up to. As I said, yer had me fooled. I was expecting yer to come to blows any minute. And me with no strength to be referee.'

Molly chuckled and put her arm around Nellie's shoulders. 'The only time me and me mate nearly came to blows was about twenty years ago, when the kids were fighting in the street. Even then we ended up laughing our socks off, and we've been the best of mates ever since. Isn't that right, sunshine?'

'We never came to blows, girl, even though at the time I did feel like clocking yer one 'cos yer accused our Steve of making Jill cry.'

'Yeah, I remember now, it was more of a tussle, really, even though we'd both rolled our sleeves up. And the upshot of it was, it wasn't Steve who'd pulled Jill's hair, it was another kid.' Molly shook herself mentally. It was nice to reminisce but there was a time and place for everything and now wasn't the time. 'Lizzie's had some good news, sunshine, Corker's coming home today. That's why I was cleaning the front windows and I've still got the back to do. I've given the room a good going over so I want no crumbs when we finally get to eat our cakes. And talking of them, let me pick me own if yer don't mind. I don't fancy the one yer've had yer finger in, 'cos God knows where that finger's been.'

Nellie picked up the two bags and waddled to the kitchen, muttering under her breath. 'She's a fussy bugger, that one. Where the hell does she think me finger's been? Dirty mind, that's what she's got.'

'We can hear what ye're saying, yer know, Nellie, we're not deaf.'

There was no reply for a few seconds, then Nellie's head appeared around the door. 'Did yer say something, girl? I couldn't hear proper 'cos I was washing me finger under the tap.'

When Jill came in at one o'clock, it was to say that Uncle Corker had been walking up with her but he got waylaid by Auntie Nellie.

'Oh, lord, she'll keep him for ages!' Molly groaned. 'Once she gets talking there's no stopping her!'

'No, I don't think so, Mam, 'cos he called into the butcher's to see Auntie Ellen and she told him about Auntie Lizzie not being well. He'll be here any minute.'

Jill had barely finished speaking when the door opened and in walked the gentle giant with his seaman's bag flung over his shoulder. He had eyes for no one but the mother he adored. Dropping the bag, he stretched out his arms and picked Lizzie up from the chair as if she was a china doll. Cradling her like a baby, he smiled down at her beloved face. 'What's this I hear about yer not being well? Yer have no right to be sick while I'm hundreds of miles away in foreign waters.' Swaying gently, he asked, 'Haven't yer got a kiss for yer son?'

Molly turned her head away, feeling she and Jill were witnessing something private. She never failed to be moved by the love shown openly by mother and son. It always brought a lump to her throat. 'I'll put the kettle on.'

'I'll do it, Mam, you sit and talk to Uncle Corker.'

'Let's put her down, Ma, so I can say hello to Molly.' The man with hands as big as shovels gently lowered his mother into her rocking chair and picked up the blanket to cover her knees. Then he turned to Molly with his blue eyes twinkling in his weatherbeaten face. With his hands on her waist, he lifted her high. 'Molly, me darlin', ye're still as pretty as ever.' He kissed her cheek, bringing a smile as his moustache and beard tickled her skin. 'Yer don't look a day older than yer did twenty years ago.'

'Put me down, yer daft ha'porth. I was going to say flattery will get yer nowhere, but it wouldn't be true 'cos it'll get yer a nice cup of tea and a cream slice. And there's a story behind the cream slice which Lizzie will tell yer later.'

His mother grinned. 'I've got a few tales to tell yer, son. It's almost worth being sick to be looked after by Mollie and Nellie. Ye're frightened to die in case yer miss something.'

'Ellen told me how good yer've been, Molly, and not for the first time in our friendship I owe yer a debt of gratitude.' He raised his voice to call, 'And you, princess, I've had glowing reports on how well you and Steve have cared for the woman I love most in the whole world.'

'Ay, I'm going to tell yer wife on you,' Molly said, smiling. 'All this talk about loving another woman more than her.'

'I didn't marry Ellen under false pretences, me darlin', she knew about the other woman in me life and agreed to share me.'

'Tea up, folks.' Jill came in carrying a neatly set tray. 'You pour, Mam, while I see if there's any biscuits. I haven't been shopping yet, so there won't be much on offer.'

'There's a white bag in the pantry, sunshine, with four cakes in. All courtesy of the one and only Helen Theresa McDonough. I'll leave Lizzie to tell yer the tale behind that when I've gone, but right now I could just murder a cup of tea.'

'I won't sit down, Mam, 'cos Steve will be in soon and I want to have his dinner ready. Not that he's getting much, just egg and chips.' Jill placed the cakes on a plate and set it on the table. 'Why did Auntie Nellie buy four cakes, Mam, who are they for?'

'They're for Corker and Lizzie, and you and yer husband. And as for why she bought them, well, I could say she was shamed into it, but yer'll hear all about that after I've gone. Suffice to say yer should never look a gift horse in the mouth, especially when it comes to Nellie. For it may never happen again.'

'Ay, Mam, that's my mother-in-law ye're talking about.'

'Yes, I know that, sunshine, but more importantly she's my best friend and I'm allowed to say what I want about her 'cos everyone knows I don't mean it.' Molly waved a hand towards the kitchen. 'Go and see to Steve's dinner, he'll be in any minute.'

The delicate china cup looked out of place in Corker's hands, and he could have drunk the contents in one gulp. He was used to the huge mugs on board ship, and Ellen had bought one for him after she realised he was drinking three cups of tea to her one. But all he was used to drinking out of in this house was china cups. And he wouldn't have it any other way because his mother prided herself on her china cups. Many of them he had brought home from the foreign countries where his ship docked, and he knew there was enough carefully wrapped in newspaper on the top of the wardrobe to keep her going for years. 'Ellen told me yer had a really bad cold, Ma, and they thought they might have to get the doctor out to yer.'

'I did have a temperature, son, but Molly gave me Beecham's powders every four hours and they were a blessing. In fact Molly herself was a blessing. Half-past seven every morning she's been here to wash and dress me, and then her and Nellie kept their eye on me all day until Ellen came. So what with yer wife, and Jill and Steve, I've been watched over twenty-four hours a day.'

'Her cold was much worse than she's letting on, Corker, there was a time I thought she was heading for pneumonia,' Molly said. 'I think it's the cold in the bedroom that caused it, it's freezing up there. Jack blocked our fireplace over with hardboard to keep the draught out and it really helps.'

'Many's the time I wanted to do that, Molly, but Ma said to leave it in case she ever wanted a fire. But I'll get it done today whether she likes it or not. And I've got ten days' leave so I'll be here to look after her during the day until Jill and Steve get home from work.' His huge hand covered one of Lizzie's. 'I hope ye're taking all this in, Ma, 'cos it's all for yer own good. I can't go away to sea and worry meself sick 'cos yer were too stubborn to let me block the ruddy fireplace up. I wouldn't care, but in all the years we've lived here I've only ever known yer to light that fire once, and that was when I was off colour.'

'Jack's got a piece of wood under the stairs that might just be the right size. If I see Peter in the street I'll send him up with it.' Molly put her cup on the tray and pushed her chair back. 'I'll leave yer to it now, Lizzie, seeing as ye've got plenty of people to wait on yer hand and foot. But I'll slip up tomorrow to see how yer are.' She tugged playfully on Corker's beard. 'Yer've got five days to make her better, sunshine, 'cos she's coming to the Christmas party.'

Corker's loud guffaw filled the room. 'At your house again, is it, Molly? Ye're not half a sucker for punishment.'

As she slipped her arms into her coat, Molly winked at the old lady. 'Yer can tell them about the party and the cream slices, sunshine, that should bring a few laughs. Mind you, I shouldn't find them funny because most of the time the laughs are on me. Still, I can take it, me shoulders are broad.' She walked through to the kitchen where Jill was slicing potatoes ready for chips. 'You and Steve will be calling in to see us later, won't yer? Yer dad doesn't see much of yer, and he doesn't half miss you and Doreen.'

'We'll be there, Mam, seeing as Uncle Corker is here to look after Auntie Lizzie. And we'll be calling to see how Doreen is.'

When Corker got to his feet the room seemed to shrink in size. 'I'll see yer to the door, Molly, me darlin'.'

'Don't be daft, I'm big and ugly enough to see meself out.'

'And what sort of a gentleman would I be if I didn't escort a lady to the door? Ma would think I'd forgotten all the manners she taught me.'

'Oh go on then, spoil me.' Molly winked as she waved goodbye to Lizzie. 'I'll be having words with my Jack tonight about why he never escorts me to the door.'

Corker stepped down and joined Molly on the pavement. 'I can't thank yer enough, me darlin', yer've been more than kind. Tony said

154

he'd have given Ellen time off, but with Christmas only a matter of days away, they're rushed off their feet.'

Molly held up a hand, thinking of all the favours that this man had done for her over the years. 'I don't want yer thanks, Corker, it would be a poor kind of friend who didn't offer help when it was needed. And I haven't done it on me own, Nellie was there to give a hand.'

'I was talking to Nellie on me way up, and she said it was you who did most of the work. She said she's hopeless when anyone's sick and wouldn't know where to turn. And Ellen said yer'd been paying for things out of yer own pocket. I can't let yer do that, Molly, so if yer'd tell me what I owe yer, I'll settle up.'

'Don't you dare offer me money, Corker, don't even think about it. Anyway, it was only a few coppers, not worth talking about.'

'I'll make it up to yer, Molly, some way. And to Jill and Steve. What a good job they're here, otherwise Ma would have been on her own and God knows what would have happened to her.'

'I've told yer before, Corker, that when ye're away yer don't have to worry about Lizzie. Me and Nellie call in most days, and Ellen never misses a night coming up and bringing one of the kids with her. I'd say your ma has more visitors than anyone I know.'

'It's a lucky man I am to have such a loving family and friends, Molly, and I thank God for me blessings. And for giving me the best mother anyone could have.'

'She'll be sitting there on pins, waiting to give yer the news. Well, it's not news really more the antics of Nellie. She surpassed herself a couple of times this week, has my mate, so yer should get a good laugh. And I hope yer'll call in and see Jack when yer get the chance, he'll be made up when I tell him ye're home.'

'I've got ten days' leave, Molly, isn't that a lovely thought? Depending how things go with Ma, I'll be having a few nights out with Jack and George. There's nowhere in the world yer can buy a pint of beer as good as here.'

She stood on tip-toe and kissed his cheek. 'And I'm always glad to see yer, Corker, yer've always been one of me favourite people.' Molly turned away, saying, 'I'd better be getting home to see to the dinner. But I'll see yer later, I hope. Ta-ra.'

It was the morning of Christmas Eve and Molly and Nellie were up and out bright and early, hoping to miss the crowds. But it seemed every woman in the neighbourhood had the same idea, for when the friends reached the butcher's it was choc-a-block. 'Bloody hell,' Nellie

155

moaned, 'we'll be here all day! Let's go to the greengrocer's and come back later when it's not so crowded.'

'It's going to be like this all day, so we may as well get it over with. And don't be making a show of me like yer did last year by saying we should be served before anyone else 'cos we'd ordered our meat. Yer nearly caused a flaming mutiny.' Molly had to grin when her mate stretched herself to her full four feet ten inches to try and count how many people were before them. 'Another thing, sunshine, yer shouldn't be swearing on Christmas Eve. If ye're thinking of going to midnight mass, take a tin hat with yer 'cos the church will probably collapse on top of yer.'

They moved apart to let two customers who'd been served out of the shop. 'That's two less, anyway,' Nellie said. 'You're taller than me, can yer see how many are before us?'

'About twenty at a rough guess, but Tony and Ellen are pretty quick so we shouldn't be here that long.'

'I hope it's not too long or I'll be wanting to go to the lavvy. It's the cold weather, yer see, girl, it has that effect on me.'

'Cross yer legs and hope for the best, sunshine, that's what I do.'

Five minutes passed before another two customers left the shop enabling the two friends to stand inside. 'Yer see,' Molly said. 'We won't be here that long at this rate.' Then she cocked an ear. 'Eh, guess who's in front, sunshine, our friend Elsie Flanaghan. I'd know her voice anywhere.'

Nellie bristled. 'I'll flatten her if I get the chance.'

'You dare make a show of me, sunshine, and I'll never speak to yer again.'

When her friend didn't answer, Molly took it that her words had been heeded. But Elsie Flanaghan herself wouldn't let them forget what a bad-minded gossip she was. Her loud voice could be heard above the chatter, and this time the victim of her vicious tongue was a close neighbour of hers. She didn't worry that there were other neighbours listening who could repeat the nasty things she had to say because she knew no one would tackle her as she was well-known for being handy with her fists. 'She's a lazy, dirty cow, that Hilda Staples. Yer can't see through her windows 'cos it's that long since they were cleaned.' There were a few gasps and heads were shaking because Hilda Staples was a sick woman. She had problems with her chest and could hardly breathe at times. But she was well liked in the streets because she hardly ever moaned and always managed a smile. And she never said a bad word against anyone.

156

'And have yer seen her front step?' Elsie wasn't talking to anyone in particular and more of the women in the shop had their eyes averted or were gazing down at the floor wishing they could be served and away from the wicked tongue. 'Once a month she does it, and it's so dirty it spoils the look of all the other houses.' After hitching her bosom, she carried on. 'And as for that no-good husband of hers, well, if he was mine I'd make him jump through hoops, the lazy bugger!'

Molly's temper was rising as she listened. 'She's a bad bitch,' she whispered to Nellie, 'yer couldn't find a nicer family than the Staples'.'

'I offered to flatten her, girl, for what she said about Steve and Jill, but yer wouldn't have it! So I'm saying nothing right now. But I'll bide me time, and one day I'll have her. You needn't worry yerself 'cos I won't raise me hand to her if I'm with you.'

Molly gave her a dig. 'Just look at Tony's face, sunshine, he's giving her looks to kill. I bet she gets the smallest turkey in the shop.'

'I hope he gives her one that's going off and she spends Christmas in the lavvy. It would be the price of her.'

Several more people had crowded in behind the friends so their conversation stopped. But not so with Elsie Flanaghan who was now picking on another neighbour in her street. This one, a Vera Southall, was, according to Elsie, giving the eye to every man she saw. 'None of our husbands are safe with her, she's a right bleeding trollop if ever there was one. Anything wearing a pair of trousers will do her, she's a slut.' The reason Vera Southall was being picked on was because she was a very attractive widow who drew many admiring glances from the men in the neighbourhood, John Flanaghan included. But she was a quiet, reserved woman who kept herself to herself. 'She's out every night dolled up to the nines, and I'll lay bets she goes to Lime Street to see what she can pick up.'

Tony had had enough. There were one or two women in front of Elsie, but he said, 'I hope yer won't mind, ladies, if I serve Mrs Flanaghan first? Yer see, I think she's in a hurry.'

The women didn't mind, they too had had enough of her. But Elsie was so thick-skinned she thought Tony had chosen her as one of his favourites and she drew herself to her full height and smirked. 'Thanks, Tony, lad, I am in rather a hurry.'

Nellie's screwed up eyes were a sure sign she was intent on something, but Molly didn't think anything of it when her mate said, 'Change places with me, girl, I can't see anything from here and I've got a kink in me neck.'

'Okay, sunshine, if that's what yer want, but yer won't see any better 'cos there's nothing to see, only heads and backs. Unless yer look up and see the turkeys hanging from that iron bar, and yer have to admit they're not the prettiest sight in the world.'

'Not now they're not, girl, but neither would we look pretty if we were dead and hung up by our necks.' Nellie held her tummy in as they changed places. 'But they're a grand sight on the table on Christmas Day. All golden brown, stuffed with tasty sage and onion stuffing and surrounded by roast potatoes.'

'Shut up, sunshine, ye're making me feel hungry.' Molly lowered her voice. 'I asked Tony for a big turkey 'cos Jill and Steve are coming to dinner, plus Doreen, Phil and Victoria. I'm glad they're coming 'cos it wouldn't be the same without all the family together.'

Nellie stopped listening at that point, she was too busy watching Tony pass a bag over the counter to Elsie Flanaghan. And she was working out a strategy to pay the woman back for all the evil things she'd said about people. She had a plan in mind but didn't know whether it would work or not.

'Will yer move out of the way?' Elsie Flanaghan didn't believe in being polite and pushed her way through the crowd regardless. It was when she came level with Nellie that the little woman stuck her foot out and tripped up her unsuspecting victim. Those at the back of the shop moved aside so Elsie fell flat, face forward on the floor. And not a soul went to her aid.

Then Nellie started wailing and hopping around. 'Yer stood on me foot, yer stupid bugger. Ow, I'm in agony!' Hopping on one foot, she kept up the crying while at the same time keeping a close eye on the figure on the ground 'I bet she's broken every one of me toes, and I'll swear she did it on purpose.'

Tony was quite concerned. 'Will yer let Nellie through, please, so she can lean on the counter and take her shoe off?' There were many willing hands to help and soon she was leaning her two arms on the counter with her head bent and giving out noises which told of the great pain she was in. Tony bent down to ask, 'D'yer want to sit in the stockroom, Nellie? It's not very nice out there but at least there's a chair to sit on.'

'No, lad, I'll be all right,' said Nellie, playing the martyr. 'Just give us a few minutes, that's all.' Then she turned her bowed head and surprised him with the devilment shining in her eyes. In a hushed voice, she said, 'That's paid her back for a few people. I've been dying to teach her a lesson.'

Tony was stunned for a few seconds, then he wanted to burst out laughing. But he couldn't do that while one woman was picking herself up off the floor and another one was crying out in pretend agony. So he rubbed his forehead and tried to look serious. 'You stay there until yer feel better, Nellie, and I'll carry on serving.'

Everything had happened so quickly Molly's head hadn't caught up with events. She could see Nellie down by the counter and heard her cries, and she could see Elsie Flanaghan straightening herself up. And somewhere in her dazed mind she connected the two. She watched as the woman with the evil tongue bent down to pick up the turkey which had escaped from the bag and was lying on its back with its legs wide open. And then she sensed trouble as the said woman began to push her way towards the counter.

'You cow! Yer tripped me up deliberate and ye're not getting away with that so don't think yer are. I'm not bleeding stupid, yer know.' Elsie was raring for a fight. That was one way of restoring her dignity. 'I'll wait for yer outside.'

'Now, come on, ladies, let's have no talk of fighting.' Tony thought if anyone imagined working in a butcher's shop was dull they should come here for a day and they'd get all the laughter and excitement they wanted. 'It's obvious what happened, Elsie, yer stood on Nellie's foot and lost yer balance. It could happen to anyone.'

'Yeah,' she agreed. 'If yer had any manners yer'd apologise for nearly breaking me toes. But yer haven't got any manners, have yer, Elsie? Yer don't even know the meaning of the word.'

Oh, my God, Molly thought, she's egging the woman on! Poor Tony's going to have a fight on his hands in a full shop on the busiest day of the year! 'Excuse me, will yer let me pass so I can get down to me friend, please?' A passage was made for her and she found herself at the counter. But it wasn't her mate she faced, it was the woman who was looking for trouble. 'Go home, Elsie, and let the other customers get served. We've all got stacks of work to do at home and don't have time to listen to you. If yer haven't got the decency to apologise to my friend for the pain yer've caused, then go and find someone else to fight with. A mad dog if yer can find one.'

Everyone held their breath as Elsie squared up to Molly. Red in the face and with her nostrils flared, she pressed closer until their noses were almost touching. 'You keep yer bleedin' nose out of it unless yer want a go-along.'

'Oh, aye, and who's going to give it to me?' Molly poked a stiffened

159

finger into the woman's chest. 'You can try, but I definitely wouldn't recommend it.'

Elsie knew she was on a hiding to nothing. The women in the shop were letting their disgust be heard now, and the flaming turkey under her arm was beginning to slip. 'I couldn't be arsed, ye're not worth it.' She stretched her neck to look around Molly to where Nellie was. 'You tripped me up, yer bitch, and I haven't finished with yer by a long chalk.' With that she began to push her way through the crowd of women who jostled and pushed, making her exit far from easy.

Nellie stood up, her toes seemingly no longer hurting her. 'Sod off, Elsie Flanaghan! Go where yer belong. To that place down below where a man with horns will make yer spend yer days shovelling coal on to a bloody big fire. The only difference between you and the devil is that yer can see *his* horns.'

Red in the face now, Elsie left the shop with laughter ringing in her ears. And she spent the night trying to figure out whether she had stood on Nellie McDonough's toes and lost her balance, or whether the crafty cow had really tripped her up.

The two friends were laden down with shopping as they made their way up the street. 'Well,' Molly sighed, 'it's been some day this has. I've never known anything like it.' She glanced sideways to where Nellie was puffing and blowing from the weight she was carrying. 'Yer did trip her up on purpose, didn't yer?'

Nellie put the heavy basket down. 'Let's stop for a minute, girl, me heart's nearly bursting.' She wiped the back of her hand across her forehead, took a deep breath and said, 'Of course I did! She was asking for it, if ever anyone was. And before yer say I broke me promise, let me remind yer that I said I wouldn't raise me hand to her. I wasn't going to let yer down, girl, so I raised me foot. And I'm glad I did, she's a horrible woman.'

'Yer made a lot of people in that shop happy, sunshine, me included. And Tony was over the moon 'cos he can't stand her. And guess what? He's given us both a pound of sausages as a Christmas present. So we can have them with the turkey tomorrow.'

Nellie looked surprised. 'He didn't say nothing to me.'

'He didn't get a chance, did he? Yer were too busy nattering and blowing yer own trumpet. We'll have to thank him after the holidays 'cos the turkeys he'd put away for us are whoppers.'

'I know, I can tell by the weight. Me arm's nearly pulled out of its socket. But we've done well, haven't we, girl? All the shopping in, the tree and decorations up, and the washing and ironing aired and put away. We've never been so organised before.'

'And we've never caused mayhem in a shop before. Poor Tony and Ellen were rushed off their feet as it was without you causing trouble.'

'I didn't cause no trouble, girl! All I did was stretch me foot 'cos I was getting cramp in it. How was I to know that someone was going to pass at exactly the same time? It was pure coincidence and that's the story I'm sticking to.'

'Ye're a smasher, you are. At least life is never dull with you around.' Molly picked up her basket and bags. 'Come on, sunshine, I'm hoping to get the veg and potatoes done for tomorrow. I want this Christmas Day to be special, with all me family around me. And next year we'll have an extra one with Doreen's baby. Life is good, Nellie, and I've got no complaints.'

They began to walk slowly. 'What time d'yer want me tomorrow night, girl?'

'The gang are coming at eight, so say half-seven and yer can give me a hand if I need it. There won't be much to do because Jill and Doreen will be making the cakes and seeing to the sandwiches. They said I can take it easy for a change.' They stopped outside Molly's house and she put her basket down to take the front-door key from her pocket. 'Hang on till I open the door, Nellie, and throw this lot in the hall.'

'Me flaming arms are dropping off, hurry up!'

'All right, give me a chance!' Molly quickly opened the door and put all her shopping inside before taking Nellie's basket from her hand and placing it on the ground. Then she put her arms around her neighbour and hugged her tight before planting a kiss on her dear, chubby face. 'A very merry Christmas, sunshine, the best friend anyone could have. May Father Christmas bring yer lots of presents.'

Nellie forgot her aching arms as her face creased into a smile. 'And the same to you, girl. Me very best mate.'

Chapter 12

'Tommy, give yer dad a hand to put the extension leaf in the table, sunshine, before yer go out.' As Molly spoke she was taking the chenille cloth off the table. She shook it several times before folding it into four and laying it over the back of a chair. 'I don't want to leave everything until the last minute.'

'I'm not going round to Nan's until all the family are here,' Tommy told her. 'I want to see Jill and Doreen to wish them all the best. And their husbands, of course.'

'I'm glad ye're going round there for yer Christmas dinner, I don't feel so guilty now about not being able to have me ma and da here. No matter how I've tried to work it out, there's no way I could get twelve around this table. It's going to be a crush trying to cope with eight.'

Ruthie came down the stairs wearing the dress she'd got from Father Christmas. It was more grown-up than any of her other dresses and she thought she was the whole cheese. 'How do I look, Mam?' She did a twirl to show off the full skirt on the maroon, short-sleeved dress. The richness of the colour suited her blonde hair and gave her complexion a rosy glow. 'It fits me smashing.'

'Yer look lovely, sunshine.' Molly felt her heart swell with pride. 'Yer couldn't have got one to suit yer better. What d'you think, Jack?'

'He leaned back against the sideboard, and like his wife he was feeling proud. His youngest daughter was as pretty as her elder sisters and he could see her breaking a few hearts in the not too distant future. 'Yer look beautiful, love, like a film star.'

Ruthie turned bright eyes to her brother. 'What d'yer think, Tommy?'

His handsome face broke into a grin. 'I'm thinking that if yer weren't me sister, I'd be ditching Rosie and hanging around for a few years while yer grew up.'

All this praise, plus her first grown-up dress, had the girl brimming with happiness. She craned her neck to look in the mirror over the

163

mantelpiece. Stroking her long blonde hair, she asked, 'Can I go over and show Bella?'

Molly raised her brows. 'Now, I think that would look like showing off, don't you? I'm sure Mary will have bought Bella a nice new dress as well.' Then she had a thought that would ease the disappointment. 'Besides, it would spoil the surprise tonight when yer go to the Corkhills. Gordon and Peter will be wearing their new togs, and Bella, so it would spoil the effect if they've seen yours. Leave it until tonight, sunshine, then knock 'em dead.'

A wide grin showed her words had had the desired effect. In her mind, Ruthie imagined she could see amazement on Gordon's face when he saw her all dolled up. And it was Gordon she most wanted to impress. Because he was working now he thought himself all grown up, but when he saw her in this dress he'd realise she was growing up too, and would be leaving school in a few months' time. 'Yeah, ye're right, Mam, I'll knock 'em dead tonight.'

'In the meantime, go and change into something else or wear a pinny over it,' Molly said. 'Knowing you, ye're bound to get it dirty.'

When they heard her running up the stairs, Jack said, 'I'm beginning to feel old, love. What with Doreen expecting a baby, and me youngest daughter growing up quick, they're putting years on me.'

'Go 'way, Dad, we'll keep yer young! By the time yer've got a few grandchildren yer won't have time to grow old.' Tommy gestured for his father to stand at the other end of the table and they both pulled until it was extended to its full length. 'Where's the other leaf, Mam?'

'It's on top of the wardrobe in the front bedroom wrapped in an old sheet so it doesn't get scratched. The size of you, yer won't need to stand on anything to get it. But be careful, sunshine, this table's got to last us a good few years yet.'

'Have we got enough chairs to go round?' Jack asked. 'There'll be eight of us, yer know.'

'I know that, soft lad, I'm not thick. We've got six, with the one out of the bedroom and the one I call Nellie's chair. And Phil's bringing a couple over with him so that's enough to seat everyone for dinner. The table should look nice and colourful when it's set, with the crackers and the presents. I feel quite chuffed with meself.'

With both children upstairs, Jack took the opportunity to put his arms around his wife. 'Can I have a proper kiss now? The one yer gave me when we were exchanging presents was more a peck than a kiss.'

Molly smiled into his eyes. 'Hurry up, then, before they come down.' The kiss held all the love he felt for her and she sighed with pleasure. 'Yer might be getting older, sunshine, but yer can still send a shiver down me spine.'

'Yer do more than that for me, love.' Jack nuzzled her neck. 'I wish it was the kids down here and us upstairs. And we can't even look forward to an early night in bed.'

Molly heard footsteps on the stairs and broke away. 'It'll be a long day today, and I'll be on me feet most of it. Still, never mind, eh, 'cos we can have a nice lie in in the morning.'

Tommy stood the heavy extension leaf down. 'Yer can have a real easy day tomorrow, Mam, 'cos yer won't have any cooking to do. Rosie's over the moon that we're going there for dinner, she's got it all planned.'

'It's a lot to cook for, sunshine, will she be able to manage?'

'Rosie's a wizard at cooking, Mam, so don't worry about that.' Tommy grinned. 'Her mammy taught her how to cook, and a saying to go with it.' He cleared his throat and spoke in an Irish accent '"Me mammy said a cook's only as god as the utensils she's got. And it's true right enough, so it is. For where would a cook be without a knife or a pan?"'

'I can't wait to meet her parents, they sound real characters,' Molly said. 'And I want to see if Rosie's beauty comes from her mother or her father?'

Tommy looked pleased. 'She is beautiful, isn't she, Mam?'

Molly nodded. 'In every way, son, inside and out. You've got yerself a very special girl in Rosie O'Grady. But then, Steve and Phil are lucky, too, they've got special girls. Yer two sisters are very beautiful, sunshine, and I'm not saying that just 'cos I'm their mother either.'

'Yer don't see yer sisters in that same light as yer see yer girlfriend, Mam, 'cos yer've seen them every day of yer life and take them for granted. But that's not to say I don't know how lovely they are, or that they get their looks from you.'

'Oh, the boy deserves a kiss for that.' Molly nearly smothered him. 'It's nice to get a compliment, son, they come few and far between these days.'

'Well, I like that!' Jack scratched his head. 'I'm always paying yer compliments but I notice I don't get any back.'

'That's 'cos I don't want to make yer big-headed, love. There's nothing worse than a vain man who thinks he's God's gift to women.'

Ruthie had heard the remarks on her way down the stairs. 'I hope I get some compliments tonight or I won't speak to Gordon again.'

'D'yer know, I feel heartily sorry for that lad,' Tommy said with a grin. 'Barely fifteen and spoken for already. It's like those arranged marriages yer hear about in foreign countries where the boy or girl is spoken for as soon as they're born.'

'I see Gordon's got friendly with the new boy, Jeffrey, I've seen them talking in the street a few times. In fact, unless I'm hearing things, I think Ellen said he's been asked to go to theirs tonight.' Molly turned her head to hide a smile. 'So with a bit of luck yer might cop off with him, sunshine. He's a nice-looking lad and not to be sneezed at.'

'I don't want to cop off with him!' Ruthie's retort came fast. 'He's not as good-looking as Gordon, not a patch on him.'

'Beauty is in the eye of the beholder, sunshine. You might find someone ugly and another person might find them beautiful.'

'Yeah, this Jeffrey might think you've got a face like the back of a bus and take a fancy to Bella! She's a nice-looking kid.' Tommy concentrated for a minute as he helped his dad to fit the leaf into the middle of the table. Then he went on, 'Anyway, both those lads are too young to be bothered with girls.'

'Ay, you've got a short memory, me lad,' Molly laughed. 'Rosie and you were only fifteen when she put a tick by your name. Yer couldn't stand the sight of her and used to run a mile if yer knew she was coming here.' She looked with affection at the son she loved dearly. 'I don't want to embarrass yer but me and yer dad often talk about those days, and they should bring back fond memories for you. I'll never forget the first night she came here with me ma and da. It was her first day in Liverpool and the poor girl must have felt lost and missing her family. But she took one look at you and said, "Sure, it's a foine figure of a man yer are, Tommy Bennett, and that's the truth of it." And you blushed to the roots of yer hair and asked me to shut her up. And when she wouldn't, yer ran up the stairs with her shouting after yer, "Have yer got a girlfriend, Tommy?"'

'I do remember it, Mam, she used to terrify me. I would avoid her like the plague until the night Ginger asked me to put in a good word for him. He wanted to ask her for a date but didn't have the nerve. And that was the night I started to see Rosie in a different light. I was jealous and wouldn't let poor Ginger get a look in after that.'

'She gave yer a run for yer money in the end, though, didn't she?'

Tommy allowed his mind to go back over the years and he burst out laughing. 'The night I plucked up the courage to ask her for a date, d'yer know what she said? "Yer'll have to ask me Aunt Bridget,

Tommy Bennett." I must have looked a right nit standing there with me mouth open and reminding her that her Aunt Bridget was my nan. It didn't do any good, either! If I wanted a date I had to ask permission.'

Jack's chuckle was loud and hearty. 'And did yer ask yer nan for permission?'

'After a fashion. Me nan and granda took pity on me, I think. Ginger didn't, though, he said I'd played a lousy trick on him. We nearly fell out over it. We had the first fight we'd had since the day we started school together. That's not counting the times he got me into trouble for breaking windows. It was his ball, but he used to tuck it under his arm and run hell for leather, leaving me to take the blame.'

'That's what I meant by looking back and having fond memories. And yer've got a whole lifetime in front of yer to remember them.' Molly rose from her seat on the edge of the couch. 'But I haven't got a lifetime to get the dinner on the go and set this table so it looks a real treat when the family walk through the door. And you can all do yer bit to help.'

'You give the orders, love,' Jack said, 'and we'll carry them out.'

'Right, you get a duster and give this table a good going over 'cos that leaf is thick with dust. Then yer can put the chenille cloth back on and cover it with the white sheet in the sideboard cupboard. That's your job.' Molly looked to her youngest daughter. 'Now, Ruthie, you get all the knives, forks and spoons out and give them a good polish so there isn't a mark on any of them. And fasten that pinny over so yer don't dirty yer dress.'

Tommy stood waiting. 'It's like being back in the army with the sergeant shouting his orders out.'

'I bet your sergeant wasn't as good-looking as me, sunshine, even if he did have a louder voice.' Molly pointed to the grate. 'Will yer bank the fire up for us? Then fill the coal scuttle and the bucket so no one has to run down the yard for coal.' She grinned up at him. 'I bet those orders aren't as bad as the ones yer got in the army.'

Tommy had some good memories of his time in the army, the friends he'd made and the laughs they'd had playing tricks on each other. But he also had nightmare memories, of guns, and bombs, and men dying. These he never let his mind dwell on, except when in the company of Archie, the man who had saved not only his life but those of dozens of other young soldiers by leading them through a minefield which had already claimed many lives. Archie had been given a medal for his bravery but had made Tommy promise he'd never tell anyone because he found it embarrassing.

'I'll do that with pleasure, Mam. And I'll rake the fire, take the ashes out and then clean the whole fireplace. So when yer've sorted the dinner out, yer can have a bit of time to make yerself pretty.'

Phil carried two chairs across the cobbled street, handed them over to Tommy and went back to give Doreen a hand with Victoria and the bag of presents she had clutched in her hand. Immediately on their heels came Jill and Steve. 'Couldn't have timed it better, Mrs B, could we?' Steve said. 'Save yer opening the door twice.'

The room came alive with everyone exchanging greetings and kisses, and Molly's heart was overflowing with happiness. She missed her two daughters more than she'd ever admit, the house didn't seem the same since they'd got married, and it was lovely to have the whole family together now. 'Let's get you settled, Victoria, and out of harm's way. Sit in Jack's chair by the fire and warm yerself through.'

'The room looks lovely, Molly, with the tree and the decorations.' Victoria sank gratefully into the comfort of the armchair. 'Everywhere looks warm and welcoming.'

'Jack and Tommy put the decorations up, and me and Ruthie did the tree. They make the place look more Christmassy, don't they?' Molly was watching Phil help Doreen off with her coat and her heart missed a beat. Her daughter was four months pregnant now, and it was showing. She looked the picture of health and contentment, her happiness there for all to see every time she looked at her husband. 'You look very well, sunshine, yer must be getting well looked after.'

Phil looked so proud. 'She does look well, doesn't she, Mrs B? She suits the extra bit of weight she's putting on.'

'I think she looks lovely,' Jill said, putting an arm across her sister's shoulders. 'Like a flower beginning to blossom.'

'Ay, will yer all take yer eyes off me? Ye're making me blush.' Doreen looked to her mother for help. 'Can we give the presents out now or is the dinner ready?'

'I think we'd better eat first, sunshine, or the turkey will be walking out of that oven and complaining.'

'In that case, Mam,' Tommy said, 'I'll give my presents out and then I can love yer and leave yer. Ruthie will give me a hand with them.'

'Yer shouldn't have bought presents, Tommy, we weren't expecting any,' Jill told him. 'We all know ye're saving up hard and need every penny yer can get.'

'They're only small presents, just tokens really. But it's the thought that counts and I didn't want yer thinking I couldn't be bothered to put meself out.'

'Leave them under the tree, Tommy, and we'll open them after we've eaten.' Doreen was taking wrapped presents from the carrier bag and putting them on the sideboard. 'Half of these are Jill and Steve's, so don't be thinking I've become generous all of a sudden.' She placed several of the parcels to one side. 'These are for yer to take with yer, Tommy.'

There was surprise in his voice. 'All of them!'

'Yeah, yer didn't think we'd leave anyone out, did yer? There's yours, Rosie's and Nan and Granda's. They're all marked so you and Granda won't end up getting a pair of ladies' stockings by mistake.'

'I think yer may as well take ours round as well. I was going to give them tonight but there'll be so many here there won't be room to breathe.' Molly began to point out some of the present lying beneath the tree. 'Will yer pick them up, Ruthie? Yer can bend down easier than me.'

Ruth had that mutinous expression on her face. 'Has nobody noticed me dress? What's the use of getting done up like a dog's dinner when no one even notices?'

'I noticed, sweetheart, as soon as I came in,' Victoria said. 'And I think yer look very pretty in it.'

'I did, too,' Jill said, remembering what it was like to be her sister's age and wishing the years away so she could be grown up. 'No one could miss yer, Ruthie, 'cos yer stand out. As Aunt Vicky said, yer look very pretty.'

'I was only waiting for a break in the conversation to tell yer,' Doreen said. 'The dress and the colour really suit yer.'

Steve's deep dimples were in evident as he told the young girl what she was waiting to hear. 'Yer've gone and got all grown up on us. And ye're getting so like yer big sisters, me and Phil will be kissing yer by mistake after yer've grown a few more inches.'

'I was just thinking the same thing.' Phil had his arm around his wife's waist, holding her close as if he was afraid she'd disappear. 'Yer took the words out of me mouth.'

Ruthie's eyes were humorous as they met her mother's. 'I think that's all the compliments I'm going to get, Mam, so I'll pass yer the presents up.'

Jack chuckled softly. His youngest daughter was like both her sisters in looks, but in temperament she took after Doreen: very outspoken, quick to answer back and would have the last word if it killed her.

Unlike Jill, who was more quiet, gentle and caring. He couldn't ever remember her answering him or Molly back, it wasn't in her nature.

Tommy lifted the bag filled with presents and grinned. 'I feel like Father Christmas. All I need is a sleigh and a reindeer to pull it.'

'If yer had a sleigh, yer wouldn't need a reindeer,' Phil said. 'Me and Steve would pull it for yer.'

'Providing we got paid,' Steve laughed. 'And it's double time on Christmas Day.'

'I'll use shanks' pony, it's cheaper.' Tommy gave Molly a kiss. 'We'll come about eight, Mam, that'll give nan and granda a chance to have a sleep after their dinner.' His eyes went around the room. 'Enjoy yer dinner, folks, and don't be eating too much. Remember there's a party tonight and yer don't want to be too full to dance.'

Molly followed him to the door. 'You enjoy yer dinner, too, sunshine. And give me ma and da a kiss and say I'm looking forward to seeing them.' She was standing on the top step and her eyes were on a level with her son's. Cupping his face, she said, 'My big, handsome son. I don't half love yer, sunshine.'

'I love you, too, Mam, ye're the best mother in the world.' He moved back. 'I'm going now, before we end up crying on each other's shoulder.'

'And I'd better get back to the turkey before it hands in its notice and walks out of the back door. I'll see yer later, son, ta-ra.'

'Ooh, I've eaten too much, Molly,' Victoria said after she'd been helped from the table to sit in the fireside chair. 'It was a lovely meal, but me eyes were bigger than me belly.'

'Well, you sit there and rest, sunshine, and I'll sit on the end of the couch and keep yer company. The men are clearing away and the girls are washing up. I've had strict instructions to stay out of the kitchen, and for once in me life I'm going to do as I'm told.'

'I should think so, yer've worked very hard.' Victoria laid a thin veined hand on Molly's. 'Doreen's like you, she keeps the house like a little palace. I wouldn't know what to do without her now, I've gone past doing any serious housework. Even dusting the sideboard wears me out. And I'd never manage keeping the coal scuttle filled or cleaning the ashes out.'

'Yer've done yer whack, sunshine, and now it's time for taking things easy. I'm sure Phil is a big help to Doreen and the pair of them seem very contented with life. Our Doreen looks the picture of health so I don't have to worry about her. But when she gets nearer her time,

I'll be over there by the minutes to make sure she's all right.'

'There's one thing I feel sad about, Molly, and that's the christening. Phil won't have a solitary member of his family to see his first child christened. He never talks about it, but I know it must be on his mind.'

'You're his family, Victoria, you and Doreen. And the baby when it comes. That's without me and Jack and the children. As far as we're concerned he's one of us.' Molly briefly considered telling the old lady that plans were afoot to find Phil's real father's relations, but thought it would be unwise. Think what a disappointment it would be if they drew a blank, which was very likely as they had so little to go on. 'We treat him like a son, as we do Steve, and always will do.'

Jack tapped his wife on the shoulder. 'D'yer want us to take the extension leaf out of the table and take it back upstairs?'

'If yer would, love, but get one of the lads to help yer 'cos I don't want yer straining yer back. Don't forget to wrap the old sheet around it before it goes back on top of the wardrobe. It won't be seeing daylight again until next Christmas, please God.'

'I'll give yer a hand, Mr B,' Steve said. 'Phil's helping the girls put the dishes away.'

'I wouldn't be too eager to offer me services, Steve,' Molly grinned, ''cos yer might be asked to do something yer wouldn't want to do.'

'Nah, me back's strong, Mrs B, there's not much I can't do.'

'Ah, well, that's a load of me mind. So in about an hour's time, yer won't mind helping Jack carry the table to yer mam's house, then?'

'Oh, no, Mrs B, not that!' Steve slapped an open palm on his forehead and feigned horror. 'Anything but that! I'll get down on bended knee and beg yer to spare me from a fate worse than death. Me mam hates that table 'cos she gets a bruise every time she passes it. She does more swearing when it's in our house than any other time. And that's saying something 'cos yer know how she can turn the air blue.'

Three heads appeared around the kitchen door then and Jill wanted to know, 'What are yer getting down on yer bended knee to me Mam for, Steve?'

Steve winked at Molly before facing them. 'Ay, Phil, ye're just the man for the job. Will yer do Mr B a favour and help him move the table?'

Phil nodded. 'Of course I will! Where d'yer want it moved to? Under the window?'

Jack could see the funny side and went along with it. 'Yeah, under the window, but it'll do in an hour or so.'

171

Phil was eager to help, though, and said, 'We may as well do it now and get it over with.'

'It can't be done for another hour, sunshine,' Molly told him. 'Yer see, it's not this window it's going under, it's the McDonoughs'.'

Doreen pulled Jill back into the kitchen and they doubled up with laughter. Phil was the only one who didn't know the saga of the table and Nellie. 'Oh, dear, oh, dear,' Doreen chuckled, this should be interesting.'

'Yer'll have to tell the poor lad,' Jill said. 'We all know it's a regular performance, and Auntie Nellie doesn't mean it when she takes off, but he doesn't know. And she's such a good actor she'll frighten the life out of him.'

'She might at first, but he'll soon see the funny side of it.'

'I hope so, for his sake.' Jill glanced around the kitchen. 'We're finished here now, all the dishes are washed and put away. So let's open our presents and relax for an hour before we make a start on the sandwiches for tonight.'

Nellie was prepared for the knock on the door. When Paul stood up to answer it, she said, 'It's all right, son, I'll go.' As she opened the door her face was like thunder. 'Where the hell are yer going with that?'

Jack was used to this, he got it every time they had a party. 'Molly told us to bring it here so I thought yer knew about it.'

'Well, yer can just take it back to where it came from, 'cos I don't know nothing about it. She's got a bloody cheek, trying to palm that off on me, what does she think I am! Go on, buzz off and take that ruddy thing with yer.'

Phil's jaw dropped. He'd never seen Mrs McDonough like this before. He lifted his end of the table and said, 'Come on, Mr B, we'll take it back.'

'Hang on a minute, son.' Jack held out his hands. 'We can't take it back, Nellie, we're having a party tonight and there's no room for it.'

'I know ye're having a party, soft lad, 'cos I'm the deputy hostess, aren't I? But that doesn't mean I've got to have that ruddy thing in me house. Stick it in yer yard by the coal-hole, it won't come to no harm.'

Jack was dying to laugh at the expression on Phil's face. He'd fallen for it, hook, line and sinker. 'I'm not taking it back, Nellie, 'cos Molly would kill me.'

'Yer've got a choice then, haven't yer? Yer can go home and be killed by Molly, or yer can try and get that ruddy thing in this house and *I'll* flaming well kill yer. Take yer pick.'

172

Phil heard a sound and turned his head to see Doreen, Jill and Molly standing on the pavement, three doors down, laughing their heads off. It was then that the penny dropped. Oh, aye, he thought, they're playing a joke on me. Well, two can play at that game. 'Come on, Mr B, yer wife's just shouted up to say we're not to argue any more, we've to take the table back.' He turned his head again as though someone had called him, nodded, and looked up at Nellie. 'Mrs B's told me to tell yer she won't be able to have a deputy hostess 'cos there won't be enough room.'

In her eagerness to get outside to see what was going on, Nellie's body moved faster than her feet and she lost her balance. Before Jack or Phil could go to her assistance, she'd banged her hip on the table. 'Damn, blast and bugger it!' She rubbed the sore part briskly, her eyes narrowed in supposed anger. 'I hate this ruddy table, Molly Bennett! I'm in agony now and it's all your fault 'cos yer've put a jinx on me.'

Molly sauntered up, her arms folded. 'Ah, have yer thrown yer dummy out of the pram, sunshine? Well, don't cry, I'll pick it up for yer.'

'I've a good mind to pick this table up and throw it at yer.' Nellie craned her neck to look up at her friend. 'But I'll get me own back, you'll see. My George has got a great big axe under the stairs and I'm going to spend the next hour chopping the legs off the ruddy thing and using them for firewood.'

'Okay, if it makes yer happy.' The wind was bitterly cold and Molly rubbed her arms to warm them up. 'I'll see yer at half-seven then, sunshine?'

'I'll be there, girl, don't worry.' Nellie stepped into the hall and jerked her head. 'What are you two standing like dummies for? Get that thing in here on the double. And mind yer don't scratch it 'cos I'll get the blame.'

'Will it be all right if I scratch me head?' Phil asked. ' Yer see, Mrs Mac, me mind hasn't taken it all in yet. I'm a bit slow on the uptake.'

'I had noticed, son, and I thought to meself, He takes after his father-in-law. I mean, like, yer'd have to go a long way to find two grown men standing on a pavement on Christmas Day with a ruddy big table between them. Still, don't let it get yer down 'cos it takes all sorts to make a world.' Nellie went ahead of them, saying over her shoulder, 'I see yer both got shirts for Christmas, they look nice on yer. My feller bought me a new dress but ye're not seeing it until tonight. I'll introduce meself to yer 'cos yer won't recognise me in it.' With a wicked glint in her eyes she added, 'I got an underskirt off our Lily and stockings off Paul. I asked him to buy me a pair of knickers 'cos I'm short on them, but he said he wasn't going in no shop and asking for a pair of knickers the size of a parachute.'

George's voice came loud and clear. 'In the name of God, woman, will yer shut that ruddy door? We're getting blown off our feet in here.'

Turning the table on its side so they could get the legs through the door first, Jack winked at Phil and chuckled. 'Never a dull moment, son, never a dull moment.'

Corker had carried his mother down to have Christmas dinner with him and Ellen and the kids. Despite her protests that people would think she'd lost the run of her senses, he'd wrapped her in several layers of clothes and scarves to protect her from the cold wind and picked her up as if she was a two-year-old. And now, after a delicious dinner, sitting in front of a warm fire with her step-grandchildren around her, she was glad he'd paid no heed to her protests.

'That was a lovely dinner, Ellen, thank you.'

'Ye're welcome, Ma, we'd have been disappointed if yer hadn't come.'

'I didn't have much choice, sweetheart, I was dressed and carried like a baby. Heaven knows what the neighbours thought.'

'I don't think many people will be spending their Christmas Day looking out of their windows to see what you get up to, Ma,' Corker said. 'We didn't pass a soul, so chances are yer weren't seen.'

'Anyway, Nan, what does it matter if anyone did see yer?' Phoebe asked, sitting on the floor at the side of the rocking chair. 'I bet any woman in this street would be highly honoured to be carried by me dad.'

As Lizzie stroked the girl's hair, she felt a warm glow in her heart. At one time she had given up hope of her son ever marrying and having a family of his own. And here he was with a good wife, and children who loved him enough to call him their dad. 'Yer look very pretty in yer new dress, Phoebe, and so does Dorothy. And what about the boys, don't they look smart? Both of them in long trousers now, proper little gentlemen.'

'Our Peter's only got the loan of his kecks,' Gordon said. 'Me mam said they're going away after the holiday until he leaves school. I'll be glad, too, 'cos he's done nothing but swank all day.'

'What about yerself?' Peter growled. 'You think yer own the place, just because yer've started work. And the tuppence pocket money yer give me is so begrudged it burns me hand.'

'That's enough, boys, cut it out.' Corker didn't raise his voice, he didn't have to. 'This is one time of the year ye're supposed to be nice to each other, so d'yer think yer could pour yer mam and grandma a glass of sherry without coming to blows?'

The boys scrambled to be first in the kitchen while Phoebe asked, 'What about me, Dad? I'm old enough for a sherry.'

'Make that three glasses, boys, and don't fill them too full in case the ladies spill them on their new dresses.'

'Ay, I'm here, yer know, Dad!' Dorothy had been lounging but she now sat up straight. 'I can have a sherry, can't I?'

'Ye're not sixteen yet, love, a bit too young for drinking.' Corker saw the disappointment on her face and relented. 'I'll tell yer what, yer can have a port and lemon, how about that?'

'Oh, yeah, that's the gear.' Dorothy left her seat to give her father a hug. 'You have got to be the best dad in the whole world.'

The boys appeared at the kitchen door. 'If she can have one, so can we,' Gordon said. 'That's only fair.'

'Yer wouldn't want a port and lemon, lads, that's a cissie's drink. But I'll make yer both a small shandy.' Corker saw his wife's raised brows and hastened to add, 'They'll only be small ones, with a drop of beer and plenty of lemonade.' His head turned sharply when there was a knock on the door. 'See who it is, Gordon, please. If it's Molly, ask her in.'

'Ah, ay, Dad, can't one of the girls go?'

'Open the door, Gordon, and do as ye're told, please.'

The boy pulled a face. Why couldn't one of his sisters open the flipping door? Whoever was outside, it wouldn't be him they wanted. So he wasn't too happy when he pulled the door open and saw Jeffrey Mowbray, the new lad from two doors up, standing there. 'What are yer doing here now? Ye're not supposed to come until half-past seven.'

Red in the face and moving from one foot to the other, the lad stammered, 'Me mam and dad are going to a party at a friend's house tonight, but our Joanne doesn't want to go and asked me to see if yer'd let her come here with me?'

'But she's old!'

'She's only seventeen, that's not much older than you. I don't want her to come meself, but it would mean her being in the house on her own on Christmas night. She wouldn't be in the way, honest.'

'I'll have to see what me mam says.' Gordon only knew the girl by

175

sight, he'd never spoken to her. 'Stay there and I'll go and ask her.'

Ellen wasn't very happy when asked. 'The girl's older than you, Gordon, older than all of yer friends that are coming, so I can't see she'd enjoy herself.'

'She can always go home if she gets fed up. Anyway, I don't like telling Jeff she can't come, it doesn't sound very friendly.'

'Oh, let her come,' Corker said, 'the more the merrier.' He saw disapproval on Ellen's face and put a hand on her arm. 'Yer can't see a young girl on her own while we're all enjoying ourselves, love, that wouldn't be neighbourly. And we'll only be next door, so we can pop in every so often to see if everything's all right.'

Ellen sighed. 'Okay, have it yer own way.'

When Gordon left the room to pass on the good news to Jeff, Corker tried a bit of persuasion on his mother. 'Are yer sure I can't coax yer to come to Molly's party, Ma?'

'No, son, I don't feel up to it. Besides, I've said I'll go and sit with Victoria for a few hours to keep her company. We're both past going to parties now, we couldn't stand the noise.'

Gordon came back from closing the door with a smile on his face. 'Jeff said to thank yer, their Joanne will be really pleased.' He rubbed his hands together and smiled at his father. 'Come on, Dad, show me how to make shandy and I can celebrate Christmas in good style.'

Chapter 13

The Bennetts' living room was noisy and crowded. Everyone had had enough drink to make them merry. Not drunk, just happy to be with friends and enjoying themselves. They'd sung every song they could think of, and tried on the spot dancing 'cos there was no room to move. By half-ten Molly was out of breath and her voice was hoarse. 'Let's have a break, eh? We'll have something to eat and a cuppa, then when we're refreshed and cooled down a bit we can start all over again.'

'I'll give yer a hand, Molly,' Ellen said. 'Just tell me what to do.'

'Yer can sit down again, Auntie Ellen, and you, Mam.' Jill linked arms with Doreen. 'We are going to see to everything. We told yer, Mam, that you were to take it easy, so sit down if yer can find a chair and we'll get cracking.'

Rosie moved out of Tommy's arms. 'Another pair of hands will make light work of it, so they will. And it's meself that's got a willing pair of hands.'

'Do as ye're told, sweetheart,' Bridie told her daughter. 'Sit on Jack's knee and rest yer feet.'

'There's no need for that, Mrs B.' Steve pointed to the chair he and Jill had vacated. 'Me and Phil will sit on the stairs.'

'And I'll join yer, seeing as me dearly beloved intended has deserted me,' Tommy said, a grin covering his face. 'We'll leave the old ones in peace to have a natter. Are yer coming, Archie?'

'Eh, less of the old ones, sunshine, we can still dance the legs off you!'

'That's right, girl, you tell 'em.' No one was dancing now except Nellie's chins and they were doing a quickstep as she nodded her head vigorously. 'We've got a damn' sight more life in us than the young ones will ever have.'

'I'll agree with yer there, Nellie,' Corker said. 'You and Molly are as agile as yer were twenty years ago.'

Nellie's eyes narrowed. 'What has he just said we are, girl? Was it a compliment or a ruddy insult? If it's an insult, you can sit on him while I clock him one.'

Lily left her seat on Archie's knee. 'You go and sit on the stairs with the boys and I'll give the girls a hand. We women have to stick together.'

'I could help, yer know,' said Maisie from the corner shop. 'I feel guilty sitting here and getting waited on.'

Her husband, Alec, chuckled. 'Yer never feel guilty when I'm waiting on yer hand and foot. Yer take it as yer right, as though God made man just to wait hand and foot on women.'

'Take no notice of him, Maisie,' Molly said. 'You just stay where yer are and let the girls do all the work. I'm dying for a cuppa to quench me thirst.'

Ellen nudged Corker in the ribs. 'Will yer slip next door and see if things are all right?'

'It's only an hour since you went, and you said they were as good as gold and really enjoying themselves.' Corker's huge hand covered hers. 'If anything had happened in that hour we'd have heard by now.'

But Ellen wasn't satisfied. When she'd gone to see if the children were all right, she'd been expecting to see the Mowbray girl sitting with them, but there was no sign of her and her brother said she'd be coming later. And it was the girl that was making Ellen ill at ease. Joanne Mowbray was two years older than the other children in years, but with her thickly made-up face and her cocky manner she appeared much more. And hadn't the girl's own mother described her as lazy and hard-faced? 'I'll go, I'll feel better in meself if I make sure everything's all right. I'll only be five minutes.'

Phoebe, who'd been listening, said, 'Me and Paul will go, Mam, don't you disturb yerself. Yer've worked hard enough in the shop and at home, yer deserve a break.' She glanced at Paul. 'I'll go on me own if yer don't feel like it?'

'No, I'll come with yer and stretch me legs. And take a few gulps of fresh air.'

As soon as Phoebe entered the house she could feel the strained atmosphere. Apart from Joanne Mowbray whose flushed face was wearing an inane grin, the kids were sitting quietly, some with their beads bowed, and they certainly didn't look as though they were enjoying themselves.

Joanne jumped to her feet the second Paul came into the room. Ignoring Phoebe and the black looks being thrown her way by her embarrassed brother, she waved a sprig of mistletoe in the air and stumbled towards him. 'Merry Christmas, Paul.' She held the mistletoe over his head and stood on tip-toe to kiss him full on the mouth.

Paul moved his head back after a second but he took it in the Christmas spirit. After all that's what people did over the festive season, they kissed each other. He laughed down at her and seemed not to sense the atmosphere or the expression of dismay on Phoebe's face.

'Dorothy, can I see yer a minute?' Phoebe jerked her head to the kitchen. Closing the door, she asked, 'What the hell is going on?'

'That Joanne is what's going on. We were enjoying ourselves until she came. She's not half hard-faced, Phoebe, she doesn't take any notice of anyone. As large as life, she came in the kitchen, found the bottle of sherry and without a please or thank you, poured herself a glass. Then when she'd drunk that, she poured herself another.'

'This is your home, Dorothy, and apart from her ye're the oldest one here. Yer should have asked her what she was playing at! I'm surprised yer let her get away with it. Yer could even have come next door and told me mam.'

'We were playing cards when she came, and having a laugh, but she said playing cards was dull and we'd have more fun playing postman's knock, or that game where one has to count to a hundred while the others find a hiding speck. She's kissed all the boys with that flaming mistletoe, even poor Peter who didn't know where to put himself.'

Phoebe was blazing. 'Why didn't her brother stop her?'

'He tried, honest he did. I feel really sorry for him 'cos yer can see he feels terrible. He told her to sit down and shut up, but she told him to sod off. She said we were all miserable buggers what didn't know how to enjoy ourselves. And just before you came in, she was going to help herself to another glass of sherry.'

'Our mam and dad will go mad when they know,' Phoebe said. 'Me mam said she was too old to be with the others and she was right.' She sighed. 'I'm not telling her to leave 'cos she looks drunk to me and I wouldn't put it past her to let fly with her fists. I think it's best if me mam or dad come and deal with it.'

'I hope I don't get into trouble 'cos it's not my fault she's here. It was me dad what said she could come, me mam wasn't too keen.' Dorothy was feeling really down in the dumps. She'd been put in charge, being the eldest, and this had to happen. 'If I do get into trouble, then I'll batter her.'

There came a tap on the door. 'Phoebe, what are yer doing?' Paul

179

called. 'Will yer come out, there's something I want to ask yer?'

'I'm coming now.' Phoebe put a finger to her lips. 'Not a word to her, Dorothy, let me mam and dad deal with it.' She opened the door to find Paul looking very flustered with Joanne hanging on to his arm and giggling. And this picture didn't please Phoebe one little bit. 'What is it yer want to ask me?'

'Joanne wants to know if she can come to the Bennetts' party with us. I've told her we can't invite anyone, it's not our party, but she's quite persistent. And I think she's had a few drinks.'

Phoebe pushed them both aside and gestured to Dorothy to pass. 'Go and sit down, sis, I'll sort it out.' She faced Joanne. 'No, you can't come to the party. It's not up to us to invite strangers and I think yer've got a cheek asking. So go and sit down, we're leaving now.'

'Don't be so bloody miserable!' Joanne hiccuped and clung to Paul's arm. 'One more wouldn't be noticed. And Paul wants me to come, don't yer, Paul?'

'I didn't say that, Joanne, so don't be making things up.' He prised his arm free from her grip. 'If I were you I'd behave meself and not have any more to drink. Come on, Phoebe, let's get back, they'll wonder what's keeping us.'

But Phoebe was too angry to let it go at that. 'How dare yer help yerself to drink that doesn't belong to yer? Yer've spoilt the kids' party and yer should be ashamed of yerself.'

'Party, did yer say? This is no party, it's more like a bleedin' wake. And you're nothing but a stuck up cow.'

Gordon had heard and put up with enough from Jeff's sister and was sorry he'd talked his parents into letting her come. He felt sorry for Jeff, too, the lad didn't know where to put himself. 'Don't you call my sister a stuck up cow! It's you what's a ruddy nuisance.'

Joanne waved a hand. 'Sit down and keep quiet, little boy, before I smack yer bottom.'

Ruthie jumped to her feet. She wasn't going to let anyone talk to Gordon like that. 'You and whose army? Yer think ye're tough but ye're all mouth. Walking round like the whole cheese when ye're only the maggot.'

Joanne lunged forward, her teeth bared and her arms raised. But Paul moved fast and put himself between the two girls. 'That's enough now, just stop it. You're old enough to know better, Joanne, so sit down and behave yerself.' He turned his head to ask Phoebe what he should do, but there was no sign of her. 'You deal the cards, Gordon, and start a game. Joanne is going to sit on the couch, nice and quiet.'

At that moment, Phoebe was pouring it all out to her mam and dad. 'Yer'll have to do something, Dad, she can't stay there 'cos she's giving the kids a dog's life.'

'Well, she's not coming here and that's for sure,' Ellen said firmly, to nods from those sitting near her. 'The cheeky begger, helping herself to sherry and her only seventeen.'

Corker stood up and stretched his huge frame. 'I'll go and sort it out so don't let it spoil this party for yer, love. I should have listened to yer in the first place when yer were against her coming. But how was I to know a chit of a girl could cause so much trouble?'

'I'll come with yer, Dad, 'cos Paul's still there trying to keep the peace.' Phoebe hadn't told them everything because she was too embarrassed, but once outside she put a hand on her father's arm. 'Dad, she's not a nice person. She wouldn't let them play cards, she wanted them to play postman's knock and that game where everyone hides and the one who lost the toss has to find them. And she's got a sprig of mistletoe and kissed all the boys. She had the nerve to kiss Paul in front of me. And she can't half swear, too!'

'A charming girl by all accounts. Anyway, while there's still time for the kids to enjoy themselves, let's see what we can do with her. She can't stay in our house, that's for sure.'

Paul had never been so glad to see anyone. 'Apart from sitting on her, Uncle Corker, I just don't know what to do. She's behaving very badly.'

Corker stood in front of the couch and looked down on a young girl very much the worse for drink. Her thick make-up was smudged, her hair in a mess and her lips were curled in a sneer. 'Who gave you permission to drink my sherry, might I ask?'

'It was there so I drank it. What did yer buy it for if yer didn't want anyone to drink it? Or was it just for show, to try and look posh?'

'What I didn't buy it for was for a young girl, not long out of her gymslip, to get drunk on. I have a daughter your age and I wouldn't allow her to drink sherry neat. You're too young to go in a pub for a drink and too young to have one in my house. So, young lady, I think it's time you went home and left these youngsters to enjoy themselves because I think ye're setting them a bad example.'

'I can't go home, I've got no key to get in and me mam and dad are out.' The sneer was now covering Joanne's whole face. She thought she was safe, knowing the man as big as a mountain wouldn't throw a young girl out on the street at this time of night and in this cold weather. So if she played her cards right she might just get what she

181

wanted. 'I could come with yer to the other party, though.'

Jeff was shaking his head. Never again would he do his sister a favour, not after tonight's fiasco. 'Don't tell lies, yer have got a key, it's in yer purse.'

She pulled a face at him. 'I haven't got one! I left it on the sideboard. And you keep out of it anyway, nose fever.'

In Corker's opinion, what was missing from this unruly girl's life was discipline. Strong, and metered out in large doses. What on earth were her parents thinking of? 'Empty yer bag and purse on the table, please, so we can see whether yer brother is right about yer being a liar.'

'I'm not emptying me bag for anyone, and yer can't make me. If yer do I'll tell me mam and dad on yer.'

'Oh, I intend having words with your parents first thing tomorrow, you can count on that. But right now I want you to empty your bag. Or I'll do it for you.'

When his sister's lips set in a firm line, Jeff knew no one would shift her. She'd have her own way if it killed her. Mind you, he had to admit he'd never seen her this bad before. 'I'll empty the bag if she won't. She's nothing but a blinking nuisance and she's spoilt the party for everyone.' Jeff sighed as he bent to pick up the black handbag which was on the floor under one of the chairs. He threw it on the couch and growled, 'Ye're dead selfish, our Joanne, yer think of no one but yerself. Now if you don't open that, I will. So please yerself.'

'You do and I'll knock yer block off.' Joanne had been throwing her weight around since she entered the Corkhills' house and thought nothing of it. She was always bossy and pushy. But tonight's behaviour, which was well over the top even for her, had been fuelled by drink and bravado. But now, as she turned to put her hand over her bag so her brother couldn't get it, she noticed Paul standing watching her with a look of disgust on his face. And it was that look which cleared her mind. She didn't particularly worry about anyone else in the room, but she did worry what he thought about her. 'Oh, all right, I've got me key and I'll go home.' She wiggled her way to the edge of the couch and using two hands pushed herself up. 'I'll get me coat and go.'

'I'll come with yer,' Corker said, 'and make sure yer get in safely.'

'Yer've no need to do that, I can look after meself.'

'That's not the impression I got. In any case, I wouldn't dream of allowing a young lady to go into a dark house on her own.'

'We'll go back to the Bennetts', then, Dad,' Phoebe said. 'They'll wonder what's going on.'

'Okay, sweetheart, I won't be long after yer.'

Joanne was putting her coat on when the couple reached the door, and she called, 'Ta-ra Paul, I'll be seeing yer.'

'Ta-ra,' he shouted, but didn't look back as he cupped Phoebe's elbow to help her down the step. 'Thank God that's over.'

'What did yer answer her for?' Phoebe was not best pleased. 'She's a horrible girl who's spoilt the night for everyone.'

'I agree, she's been a bitch. But I think the drinks she had were partly to blame, she didn't know what she was saying.'

Keep quiet, Phoebe told herself. Don't start an argument on Christmas night. In fact don't mention the girl's name again or he'll think you're a nagger. So she smiled up at him. 'I'm jealous, that's the problem. So to make me un-jealous, give me a kiss.' She couldn't see his face clearly in the dark, but she knew his dimples would be showing and the brown eyes that could send her weak at the knees would be smiling. Then when his lips touched hers, she forgot everything and everyone as her spine tingled and her heart flipped. And when she heard his soft sigh of pleasure, it seemed every star in the sky came out to shine down on them. It was bliss. Perfect bliss.

As Phoebe and Paul had done, Corker made light of the Joanne incident. 'Everything's fine, a storm in a teacup. The girl had a couple of glasses of sherry and she couldn't take it. She's in her own home now, sleeping it off.'

'We filled a plate for yer, Uncle Corker,' Jill said. 'And the kettle's on the boil for a fresh pot of tea.'

'Thank you, princess, I am feeling a bit peckish.'

Nellie sidled up to him. 'Yer'd better get it down yer quick, lad, 'cos we're all ready to start the party off again. If yer'd been away any longer, yer'd have missed me party piece.'

The big man stroked his beard as his laughter filled the room. 'Oh, aye, Nellie, what have yer got in store for us tonight?'

'I'm not telling yer, so there! Yer'll just have to wait and see.'

'She won't tell me what she's going to do, and it's my ruddy house!' Molly said. 'There's one thing I know she won't be doing, and that's the dance of the seven veils. She did that in the butcher's the other week, and one thing about me mate, she never repeats herself.'

Alec Porter leaned forward. 'Nellie did the dance of the seven veils in the butcher's? How did she manage that?'

'Never mind how she managed it,' Maisie said. 'Why couldn't she come and do it in our shop? We'd have done a roaring trade.'

Those who had heard the tale were giggling and guffawing. And when Nellie said, 'Would yer like to see me do it, Alec?' there were roars of approval.

He looked to Molly. 'It sounds as though everyone's seen it.'

'No, they haven't, sunshine, but I do a very good impression of me mate. Except I don't go the whole hog like she does. I refuse to take me knickers off.'

Corker was shaking with laughter. 'Oh, this we've got to see. Come on, Nellie, let's see yer latest speciality act.'

There was loud clapping and stamping of feet, and Nellie turned to Molly and spread her hands. 'See how my adoring fans appreciate me?' Then she closed her eyes and looked deep in thought. Tapping her chin, she said, 'I intended doing something else, so it means me changing me repertwory.'

Molly spluttered. 'I think yer mean repertoire, sunshine.'

'I know what I mean, girl, so don't be trying to show off how clever yer are. And I don't think it's going to work unless we pretend this is Tony's shop, do you?'

'I think to do the job properly yer'd need to start before yer got to the shop. I'll help yer out with that, sunshine, and then ye're on yer own.'

Nellie nodded, then laced her fingers together and put on a posh voice. 'Ladies and gentlemen, as deputy hostess it is my duty to see you are hinformed about what is going on. Now Mrs Bennett and myself are going into the kitchen for a rehearsal before the show starts, so there will be a short hinterval. During which time yer are not allowed to drink yerselves legless 'cos I don't want no drunken men tearing the veils off so they can see my voluptuous body. The ladies will keep their men on a leash at all times, please.'

George thought this was hilarious. 'Nellie, I know I've been seeing yer voluptuous body since before it became voluptuous, but just in case I forget ye're me wife, who's going to keep *me* on a leash?'

'I know ye're a passionate man, George, and yer can't help yerself sometimes. So when I'm down to the fourth veil, I'll get Corker to put a blindfold on yer.'

Bridie and Bob were sitting on the couch holding hands. They were both laughing at Nellie's expression and really enjoying themselves. 'Molly, me darlin', I'll have me eyes closed, so I will, 'cos I don't approve of such behaviour,' Bridie said. 'So when Nellie is down to the fourth veil would yer give me a nudge so I can cover yer da's eyes? Yer see, I don't think his heart would stand up to seeing Nellie in all her glory.'

Nellie's mountainous bosom was the first to shake with laughter, followed by her tummy and chins. 'Bob, I can just see yer going up the stairway to heaven to meet St Peter. And what d'yer think he'd say if yer told him yer'd died through watching a woman doing the dance of the seven veils? Yer'd get turned back, lad, they'd never let yer in heaven.'

The laughter was loud, particularly Corker's. 'Nellie, ye're a woman and a half,' he said, 'they broke the mould after you were born.'

'Only 'cos they couldn't find anyone my size to fit it, lad.'

Steve was standing behind Jill with his arms around her waist and his cheek touching hers. And his dimples were deep as he grinned at the mother he adored. 'Mam, yer weren't that size when yer were born, yer were only a little tiddler.'

'I was eight pound six ounces, son, and that's no tiddler. At least me mam, God rest her soul, didn't think so.'

Molly tutted and shook her head. 'Can anyone tell me how we got from the dance of the seven veils, through me da getting to the top of the stairway to heaven and being turned back by St Peter, to Nellie weighing eight pound six ounces when she was born?'

'Keep yer hair on, girl, or it'll go white and drop out.' Nellie rolled her eyes to the ceiling. 'Ooh, she's not half impatient is my mate. She asked me to be her deputy to help out, and when I try to amuse the guests she goes all uppity 'cos I'm getting all the attention.'

Molly jerked her thumb to the kitchen. 'Out there, sunshine, so we can rehearse for yer big scene. The way ye're going on it'll soon be Boxing Day.'

'Oh, come on, then, droopy drawers.' As she followed Molly into the kitchen they heard Nellie saying, 'I don't know what ye're worried about, girl, 'cos yer haven't got many lines to learn. Yer've only got a bit part in this show.'

Phoebe squeezed Paul's arm. 'Your mam is a scream, she's got an answer for everything.'

'Yeah, I've never got the better of her yet. She's always been the same, too, and our house has always been a happy one. We all love the bones of her. Mind you, she's never as good as when she's with Auntie Molly, they seem to bounce off each other.'

In the kitchen the rehearsal was going well. 'I'm all right now, girl,

I know where I'm up to. But I need a couple of men's pullovers and coats.'

'Well, d'yer know the part where you scarper down to the greengrocer's to borrow off Billy?' Molly waited for her friend to nod. 'When we come to that, you run upstairs, and in the bottom drawer of the dressing table yer'll find a couple of Jack's pullovers. And his overcoat is hanging in the wardrobe.'

The two women entered the living room arm in arm. 'Yer'll have to use yer imagination folks,' Molly said. 'This is me and Nellie walking to the shops a few weeks ago. You start, sunshine.'

'What are we having for dinner, girl?'

'I don't know, but if I give mine stew again they'll throw it at me. So let's work our charms on Tony and see if we can wangle a ham shank or some sausages.'

'Yer'll have to do more than work yer charms for two ham shanks, girl. I think that would take the dance of the seven veils.'

'I don't need two ham shanks, sunshine, I only need one. So I'll work me charms and you can do the dance of the seven veils for your shank.'

There was complete silence in the room, rapt expressions on all the faces as the two women walked to the hall doorway. 'Now pretend we're in the shop,' Molly said, dropping Nellie's arm.

'Morning, Tony! Morning, Ellen! How are you both on this fine winter's day?'

Dropping her voice as low as she could, Molly became the butcher. 'Oh, aye, what are yer after, Molly?'

'I'm working me charms on yer to see if I can wangle a ham shank.'

Nellie pulled on her dress. 'I'm just nipping to the greengrocer's girl, I won't be long.'

'Ay, hang on, I've got to go there, too!' But Nellie had now legged it up the stairs as planned, and Molly's expression of surprise was a work of art. 'I don't know what's got into her, she knows I want spuds as well.'

Then, with a sweep of her arm, she bowed from the waist. 'That's me finished in this scene, folks, but I'll see yer later.'

Upstairs, Nellie was trying to pull one of Jack's pullovers over her huge bosom. 'I need a ruddy shoehorn,' she muttered, 'they're always in the bloody way.' Then she heard Molly being applauded and grinned. 'I'm not going to be very popular with Jack 'cos this ruddy thing will be twice the size when I've finished with it. I hope he's got a good sense of humour.' She took a deep breath then blew it out.

186

'God, but it's tight, I can hardly breathe. I'm not struggling into another one of these, I'll pinch his cardigan.'

The Bennetts' parties were always noisy, but this night they surpassed themselves. The roars of laughter could be heard down at the bottom of the street. Nellie did well with making a great play with the overcoat, pushing it off one shoulder at a time while wiggling her hips, and the cardigan was taken off slowly to whistles from her two sons and Tommy and Phil. Everyone was in stitches with tears running down their faces. But the loudest laughter came when she tried to take Jack's pullover off. She huffed and she puffed and did contortions with her body, but she couldn't get the pullover over her enormous breasts. She tried pulling an arm out of one of the sleeves, but the wool was like a second skin and she couldn't move it. Red in the face, she said, 'Damn, blast and bugger it, the flaming thing won't budge. I can see me going to bed in it.'

Jack felt sick with laughing, even though he knew his pullover would never be the same again. 'Oh, no, yer won't be going to bed in it, Nellie, that's me best pullover.'

'It was, lad, but it ain't no more. If I ever get the ruddy thing off, the only way yer'll get any wear out of it is for you and Tommy to share it going to work. By the time I've finished, it'll be big enough for the pair of yer to get in and should come in handy on these cold days.'

'How, in the name of goodness, did yer get into it, me darlin'?' Bridie asked, thinking they'd have to cut Nellie out of the pullover.

'With great difficulty, girl, with great difficulty. But I'm lumbered with it now, I can't see me ever getting it off.' She looked to Molly for help. 'Yer could cut it down the back, girl, and I'd sew it back up again so no one would notice.'

'Mam, you can't even thread a needle, never mind sew,' Lily said from her seat on Archie's knee. 'Besides, yer can't cut wool, the stitches would run.'

'Then someone will have to take a tin opener to it 'cos I can't do any more.' Nellie grunted, more miserable because her act had been spoilt than she was about Jack's pullover. 'I'm worn out trying.'

'Upstairs with yer then, sunshine,' Molly said. 'If yer lie on the bed I might be able to get it off with a bit of patience and plenty of co-operation from you.' She winked at George who wasn't in the least perturbed by his wife's dilemma because she was always getting herself in a tizzy. 'If not yer'll have to go to the hospital and have an operation to have it removed.'

Nellie gave her cheeky grin. 'Would the doctor be young and handsome, girl?'

Molly put her hands on her hips. 'Get up them stairs right now, Nellie McDonough.'

'Aye, aye, sir!' Nellie saluted smartly and made for the stairs. She was halfway up, with Molly right behind her, when the gang heard her say, 'D'yer know what, girl, yer sounded just like George when yer told me to get right up these stairs. He's always saying the same thing to me. I've told yer often, haven't I, girl, how passionate me husband is?'

'Yer've told me so many times, sunshine, I'm beginning to believe yer.'

Downstairs, all eyes were on George, but he didn't even blush. 'If I was as passionate as Nellie says, I'd be the happiest bloke in Liverpool.'

Upstairs, Nellie was lying flat on the bed while Molly stood with her chin in her hand gazing down and wondering what would be the best way to approach the task. Then she nodded, and said, 'Yes, that's about the only thing I can do.'

'What's that, girl? I mean, it's me what's lying on the bed, so I think yer should keep me informed of what yer intend doing.'

'I think the first thing I should do is try to get the pullover over yer breasts. If I can manage that, it should be easier to get yer arms out of the sleeves. Then there's only yer head left to worry about. And the state of Jack's pullover, of course, that has to be taken into consideration as well. After all, yer didn't even ask him if yer could borrow it, did yer?'

'I wasn't expecting this to happen, was I? I mean, like, Jack's a big man, yer'd think his pullover would fit me easy.'

'Ye're overlooking something, sunshine,' Molly said, starting to stretch the wool. 'Jack doesn't have breasts bigger than footballs. Just a little matter that escaped yer attention.'

'Ay, watch what ye're doing, girl, that's hurting!'

'Ye're going to have to put up with a little inconvenience, sunshine, unless yer want to spend yer life in this thing.' Molly let out a sigh of relief when she finally got the pullover over one of the breasts. 'Thank God for that, now the other one.'

'I think ye're enjoying this,' Nellie said. 'Taking yer time and being rough, just to spite me. And I wouldn't care, but yer know how delicate I am.'

'Delicate me foot! Ye're as strong as a ruddy horse.'

Nellie decided the best policy would be to keep quiet, so she didn't say a word until Molly was standing at the side of the bed, red-faced and puffing but victorious. 'Yer did a good job there, girl, ta very much.' She swung her legs over the side of the bed. 'Now, if yer'll find me something else to wear, I'll finish me dance off.'

Molly was holding the pullover up, dismayed at the shape of it. When Nellie spoke, she glared and shook the woolly in her mate's face. 'I'm not going to find yer anything else to ruin, sunshine, yer must think I'm barmy! No more dance of the seven veils for you, not with Jack's clothing, anyway.'

'Spoilsport, that's what yer are. I don't know what ye're taking off for 'cos there's nowt wrong with the ruddy thing.'

'Except that it would fit King Kong, that's all.'

Now she wasn't confined, Nellie began to chuckle. 'Yer could feed yer feller up until it fitted him. He looks as though a good feed would kill him.'

'Go on, yer cheeky article, my feller is what Rosie would call a fine figure of a man.' Molly was trying to think whether the pullover would shrink if she washed it in a warmer water than usual, or would it get even bigger? 'Tell yer what, sunshine, if ye're looking for something else to wear, try our Tommy's overalls, they're massive. Yer'd have to roll the legs and arms up, but I think they would serve the purpose if ye're determined to finish the ruddy dance off.'

So Nellie got her wish and everyone agreed it had been worth the wait. She shimmied and she shook, going to each of the men in turn and stroking their cheeks with her eyelids fluttering, her lips puckered and her wide hips swaying. And she was well rewarded by the response from her audience as they clapped and cheered her on. That they were enjoying themselves could be told from the loud laughter and the tears running down their cheeks. But no one enjoyed themselves more than the little woman herself. She was in her element, loving every minute of it. When Molly stopped her as the third button on her dress was undone, there were loud catcalls and jeers.

'Never mind that,' Molly said. 'I'll not have my home turned into a house of ill repute.' But she'd enjoyed the performance as much as anyone, and as she often had before, she wondered what a party would be like without her little fat friend. Because not many people would be prepared to make a fool of themselves just for the amusement of others.

It was one o'clock in the morning when Molly and Jack stood on the top step and saw their visitors off. As Corker said, 'Molly, what would we do without you and Nellie? It's been a belting night and we've more than enjoyed ourselves.'

There were murmurs of approval and thanks as the party split up and went their separate ways, Doreen and Phil across the street, Corker and Ellen next door and Nellie and George three doors away. Bob and Bridie were escorted by Tommy and Rosie, and Jill and Steve walked behind them, arms around each other as usual.

Lily and Archie, with Paul and Phoebe, were the only ones left standing outside the Bennetts', and this was because they wanted some time on their own and didn't know where to find it.

'I can't take yer in ours, Archie,' Lily said, ''cos the room is choc-a-bloc with Auntie Molly's table.'

'I'm in the same boat,' Paul said, holding Phoebe close. 'There's no space to move.'

Molly gave Jack a dig in the ribs. 'What did we do when we wanted a goodnight kiss without being watched?'

He grinned as memories surfaced. 'We used an entry, where it was quiet, dark and very private. And funnily enough, there's one only three yards away.' He chuckled. 'Yer know, I'm sure they built entries just for courting couples. It would be a shame not to use them.'

Molly began to pull her husband inside. 'Just as long as yer don't start serenading at this time of night. Us old ones need our beauty sleep.'

Chapter 14

Corker was deaf to Ellen's plea on Boxing Day morning not to call on the Mowbrays. He thought it only fair that the parents should know how their daughter behaved in a neighbour's house. Perhaps they were well aware of her bad behaviour and lack of respect, and were the type of parents who couldn't care less what their children did so long as it didn't interfere with their enjoyment. In which case they deserved to be taught a lesson themselves.

It was Beryl Mowbray who opened the door and her face showed surprise and a little apprehension to see him. 'Good morning.'

'Good morning to you, and the compliments of the season.' Corker was bare-headed, thinking it wasn't worth putting his seaman's cap on to walk to a house three doors away. But he forgot he wasn't wearing the cap and his hand was halfway to his head to raise it to the lady when he remembered it was still on the hook behind the door at home. 'I know Boxing Day isn't the time for fighting or arguments, and I certainly haven't come with that in mind, but I would like a word with you and yer husband about yer daughter Joanne.'

Beryl sighed. 'Our Jeff said she'd been a right pain in the neck in your house and he'd never go anywhere with her again, but that's as much as we could get out of him. Anyway, yer'd better come in. Don't mind the place, it's in a bleedin' mess and I'm certainly not doing any housework today. I'll put food on the table and fill their bellies, but that's me lot.'

David Mowbray blinked a few times when Corker walked through the door. My God, he thought, he's some size, I wouldn't like to tangle with him.

'This is me husband, David,' Beryl said. 'And yer know our Jeff, of course. Joanne is still in bed, she hasn't surfaced yet.'

'I'm James Corkhill, but everyone calls me Corker.' He grasped the hand held out to him and his handshake was warm. He didn't want the parents to think he'd come looking for trouble, they were neighbours after all. Better to make friends than enemies. 'I came to tell yer that Joanne really misbehaved herself last night. Me and the wife were next door at the Bennetts', which is a regular thing on Christmas night, and all the young ones were having their own little party in ours. Unfortunately, your daughter helped herself to a few glasses of sherry that she found in the kitchen, and the effect it had on her spoilt the night for the other kids. She was so drunk she was kissing all the young lads, and I don't mean a peck on the cheek either. In the end I had to leave the Bennetts' to go and see what she was up to. She showed no respect at all and wouldn't listen to what I had to say. In fact she was very insolent, which is something I can't abide in youngsters.'

'I told yer, didn't I, Mam?' Jeff said. 'She was dead hard-faced.'

David looked at his wife and sighed. 'It was years ago she should have got the good hidings for being cheeky and giving us both old buck. But Beryl here, she said hitting the children only made them worse. Talk about "spare the rod and spoil the child". It's certainly true in this case. I shouldn't have taken any notice of yer then things might have been different.' He sighed again and shook his head. 'It's too late now, we'll never get her to change.'

'Sit down, Corker.' Beryl pulled one of the wooden dining chairs from the table. 'David's right, it's my fault. I've been too bleedin' soft with her. Now she treats me like a piece of dirt. And David, too! She's a right hard-faced cow, and one of these days she'll bring trouble to this door, I know she will.'

David leaned forward and asked, 'Would yer like a drink, Corker?'

'A cup of tea would be very welcome, thanks. It's a bit too early for the hard stuff and I haven't really got over last night yet.'

'I'll put the kettle on, Mam, you stay where yer are.' Jeff was beginning to see that while he wasn't as hard-faced as his sister, and he didn't give his parents cheek, he could be a better son than he'd been. He could help his mam more, show he did care. 'D'yer take milk and sugar, Mr Corkhill?'

'Yes, please, son, I take both.' Then Corker remembered sugar was still rationed. He was inclined to forget because they never went short of anything in his house with him bringing plenty home with him every trip. 'Just half a spoonful of sugar, thanks.'

When the lad had gone into the kitchen, Corker said, 'It's never too late to correct a child. Joanne's only seventeen, but the way she's going on she'll never make friends. It would be a shame for that to happen. A little perseverance on your part might make all the difference. If you accept the way she behaves because yer think yer can't alter it, then all is lost and yer'll have a daughter who's disliked by everyone.'

'D'yer want me to get her up and yer can have a word with her?' Beryl asked. 'She'd probably take more notice of you.'

Corker shook his head. 'I had plenty of words with her last night, which she may or may not remember. I think any more from me would rub her up the wrong way. I know yer haven't lived here long and she probably hasn't made any friends, but there's plenty of young girls she could pal up with if she changed her attitude. I'll have a word with the wife and children, see if they can act friendly towards her. She can't go through life being rude to everyone, especially those who are trying to be friendly.'

Jeff came through carrying a cup and saucer. He'd filled the cup to the brim and his tongue was sticking out of the side of his mouth as he concentrated on not spilling the tea into the saucer. 'Here ye're, Mr Corker.' He didn't move away after passing the tea over because something on his mind was worrying him. 'Yer won't stop me being mates with your Gordon, will yer? It's not my fault our Joanne's the way she is.'

'Ye're welcome in the house any time, son, so don't worry. And, come to think of it, it might just change yer sister's attitude if she sees yer making friends and enjoying yerself.'

A smile lit up the boy's face. 'That's the gear, 'cos I get on smashing with Gordon.'

Corker stayed for a while talking about how long he'd been going to sea and where David worked. He could see Beryl and her husband relaxing when they realised he hadn't come to cause trouble. Then he had an idea, and asked casually, 'D'yer drink in the corner pub, David?'

'I've been in twice since we moved here, but I miss the local where we used to live and all me old mates.'

'I go in most nights when I'm home, with two mates I've had for over twenty years,' Corker told him. 'That's Jack Bennett and George McDonough, both neighbours that yer've no doubt seen in passing. We'll be going for a pint tomorrow night, so I'll give yer a knock and see if yer want to join us.'

David's face beamed. 'Yeah, I'd like that, Corker, thanks! And I'm sorry about our Joanne, I'll have words with her when she finally decides to get out of bed.'

'I don't think I'd do that if I were you. If she were my daughter, I'd ignore her, no matter what she does. My opinion, for what it's worth, is that she loves being the centre of attention. But she'd soon get it into her head that it's not worth being cheeky and acting tough if no one takes the slightest interest in her.' He handed the cup and saucer over to Beryl and stood up, his massive frame almost filling the room and his head only about a foot from the ceiling. 'I'd better get home or the wife will wonder where I've got to.'

'Ye're married to Ellen, aren't yer?' Beryl asked. 'The one who works in the butcher's?'

'Yes, I'm happy to say. I've got the best wife and family a man could ask for.' He grinned and added, 'My ma lives at the top end of the street, and she's the best mother any man could ask for. So, all in all, I'm a lucky beggar.' He waved a hand. 'I'll see meself out so don't bother getting up. Enjoy the rest of the festive season.'

When the door closed on Corker, David shook his head as though bewildered. 'He's some man, he is. They don't come much bigger than him, his hands are like shovels. But he's a nice bloke and I hope we can get to know him better. And all the other neighbours. We've been here weeks now and I haven't met one of them, only to nod to.'

'If our Joanne carries on like she is, no one will want to know us. Fancy her helping herself to drink in a strange house, and her only seventeen.' Beryl tutted. 'People must wonder what's the matter with us, and I don't blame them. We should have put a stop to her shenanigans years ago instead of giving her all her own bleedin' way to keep the peace.'

David reached for his packet of Woodbines and lit one before saying what was on his mind. 'I think Corker was right and we should just ignore her. So when she comes down and asks for a cup of tea, don't get up to make her one. Tell her to make her own. And if she takes off, pretend yer can't hear her. If she wants a drink bad enough, she'll soon make her own.'

'I won't be doing anything for her,' Jeff said. 'She didn't half make a show of me last night, I was ashamed of her. The way she was carrying on I thought they'd have thrown both of us out. She won't be coming anywhere with me in future, I can tell yer that. She can just take a long running jump.'

A few doors down, Ellen was asking, 'Did yer see the young madam?'

'No, she was still in bed. But I had a good talk to her parents and they don't seem bad people at all. They just don't know how to handle her.'

'Don't know how to handle her? If she was my daughter I'd know how to handle her all right,' Ellen said. 'That's a pathetic excuse for letting their daughter run wild.'

Corker looked towards the kitchen. 'It's very quiet, where is everyone?'

'Gone out for a bit of fresh air. They're calling to see yer ma, then carrying on round to the Jacksons' to wish them the compliments of the season. Apart from Phoebe, none of them saw Bridie and Bob yesterday, or Rosie and Tommy. And yer know they think the world of all of them. I've told them to be back for one o'clock for their dinner.'

As she was speaking, Ellen realised that her and Corker had the house to themselves for a change so she left her chair to sit on his knee. 'It's not often we get a chance for a cuddle, let's make the most of it.' She felt his arms go around her waist and smiled into his face. 'You're my safe haven, love, I always feel I can come to no harm when I'm in yer arms.' She kissed his cheek and giggled as the whiskers tickled her lips. 'I've got a lot to be thankful for, God knows. A husband in a million and four children to be proud of. They're all well behaved and wouldn't dream of answering an older person back.'

'It's not always the parents' fault if their children grow up to be adults who are miserable, inconsiderate, lacking in social graces and sometimes downright bad.'

'I don't agree with yer, love, 'cos I think the parents set an example to their children.'

'I would have gone along with that twelve months ago, sweetheart,' Corker said. 'But that rotter Lily McDonough went out with, he taught me a lesson: that things aren't always as they seem. He was bad through and through. Always surly, a bully who wanted all his own way and would use violence to get it. And what an out and out liar he was! He led Lily a merry dance with his lies and deceit, and nearly broke her heart. And yet his parents were nice ordinary people who lived a good life and never did anyone a bad turn. He started to break their hearts from the time he started school and nothing they did made any difference. For years they walked with their heads down, ashamed of the boy they'd brought into the world. And yet they had another son who was just the opposite. So, as I said, things are not always what they appear to be.'

Ellen was silent for a while, thinking over what Corker had said while she watched the flames lick the coals in the fire. 'Yer know, sometimes that Beryl Mowbray looks as though she's got the cares of the world on her shoulders. My first impression of her was that she

195

was loud-mouthed, swore like a trooper, was as hard as nails and could hold her own with anyone. D'yer think I've been too quick to judge her?'

'I would certainly give her the benefit of the doubt, she deserves that much. And I'm going to have a word with the children and ask them not to rake up what happened last night. The Mowbrays are our neighbours and I'd hate to be at loggerheads with them. If Joanne doesn't improve her attitude then the best they can do is give her a wide berth.' Corker sat back in the couch and pulled Ellen with him. 'Now that's off me chest, can I have a kiss, please?'

And that was a request Ellen would never refuse.

In the Mowbray household, Joanne came down the stairs wearing a dressing gown that had been a present from her parents. It was a lovely warm red colour, but the effect was spoilt by her matted hair, smudged make-up and a surly frown that said she wasn't in the best of moods. 'Where's me breakfast?'

After glancing at her husband, Beryl said, 'We had our breakfast an hour ago. If yer want anything to eat yer'll have to make it yerself.'

'I'm not making me own breakfast, that's your job.'

'In that case, yer mam did her job an hour ago,' David said. 'She shouted up the stairs to tell yer but yer didn't see fit to answer. Yer missed yer chance when it was there, so see to yerself if yer want anything.'

'I told yer, I'm not making me own breakfast!' The girl sounded determined. 'I go to work all week and I pay me mam to look after me. So let *her* make me breakfast.'

David took a deep breath and told himself to keep calm. 'Yer pay yer mam seven and six a week, that doesn't make her your slave. I work a damn' sight harder than you do, and hand over a damn' sight more every week. But I don't expect to get waited on hand and foot, 'cos I know looking after a house and feeding a family is a lot harder than going out to work. And that's the last word on the subject.'

'I'm still not making me own breakfast.'

Beryl was used to the girl's sullen face and the bad temper, she got it every morning, and usually gave in to keep the peace. But Corker's words had struck a chord with her and she vowed she would never again give in to her bad-tempered, ill-mannered daughter. 'Suit yerself. Yer either do it yerself or do without. It's no skin off my nose.'

Joanne looked confused for a while, shocked at being spoken to like that by her mother. She glanced over to the table where her brother was reading a book which had been one of his presents, and saw a way of saving face. 'Make us a cup of tea and a round of toast, Jeff, there's a good lad.'

He hadn't lifted his eyes from the book, but Jeff hadn't missed a word. He knew his sister would turn to him, expecting him to take her side, but she'd blotted her copybook good and proper last night and he was through being her lackey. 'Ye're a lazy beggar, you are. What makes yer think yer only have to open yer mouth and everyone will jump? Make yer own blinking tea, it won't kill yer.'

Joanne jumped to her feet and flounced out of the room, saying, 'Sod the lot of yer, I'm going back to bed.'

Beryl rushed to the bottom of the stairs. 'Dinner will be ready at one o'clock. If ye're not down here then, that's yer own fault. And yer've got a clock up there so yer've no excuse.' She went back to her chair, her nerves shattered. 'D'yer think I should take a drink and a round of toast up to her? She must be starving.'

'Over my dead body,' David said. 'We should have done this years ago, but better late than never. We've got to keep it up now, Beryl, no feeling sorry for her and giving in. It's for her own good, as well as ours. She hasn't got a friend, boy or girl, because of her sarcastic, cocky manner, and never will have if she doesn't change. So don't let me down, d'yer hear?'

'Me dad's right, Mam,' Jeff agreed. 'Yer'll be doing her a favour in the end. I certainly won't be running messages for her any more, she's had it. And if yer give in to her once, Mam, she'll soon have yer dancing to her tune again. She's always been able to get round yer, and she knows if she keeps it up long enough she'll get her own way. So put yer foot down firmly this time and mean it.'

'Okay, okay, I promise! Otherwise I'll have you two coming down on me like a ton of bricks. I promise I won't give in to her even if she gets down on her bleedin' knees to me'

Jeff, whose voice was breaking and covered several ranges, saw the funny side. 'Now *that* is something I'd like to see – our Joanne on her knees. Still, as it says in this book, strange things are happening every day all over the world.'

In the Bennetts' house, Molly was standing patiently waiting for Jack to fasten the top button of his new shirt. 'The ruddy hole is too small, I'll never get this fastened.' He was red in the face and dropped his arms in disgust. Ten minutes I've been at it and me arms are tired.'

'We know how long yer've been, Dad,' Ruthie said, ''cos we're standing here waiting for yer like two lemons.'

'Come here and let me have a go.' Molly grinned into his face. 'Once yer get yerself all agitated yer make it ten times harder.' She pushed the pearl button through the buttonhole and stood back. 'See, it's easy when yer know how.' She patted his cheek. 'Now can yer put a move on because Rosie's probably got the dinner ready and she'll be calling us for everything.'

Happy now, Jack slipped his arms into his overcoat. 'I'm glad I didn't have much breakfast because I've got a good appetite and I'll eat everything in front of me.' He glanced at his reflection in the mirror. 'What's happening to Lizzie if Jill and Steve are going to yer ma's?'

'Corker was picking her up at half-twelve, she's having dinner with them.' Molly opened her bag to make sure she had the front-door key. 'Rosie did invite Doreen and Phil, so all the family would be together, but they couldn't leave Victoria.' She pushed Ruthie towards the door. 'We've wasted enough time, let's get our skates on. It's no joke cooking for seven, Rosie's probably a nervous wreck.'

When Rosie opened the front door she looked anything but a nervous wreck. She was wearing a floral pinny over a sage green dress and her bonny face was beaming from ear to ear. 'It's meself that's glad to see yer. Come away in out of the cold.'

Molly sniffed. 'My, that smells good, Rosie, me tummy's rumbling now.'

'Hasn't she been hard at it all morning?' Bridie said as she lifted her face for a kiss. 'She wouldn't let me help, she had to do it all herself.'

'If that smell is anything to go by, she's done a darn' good job,' Jack said as he draped his coat over Tommy's arm on top of Molly's and Ruthie's. And as he looked into his son's face, he thought he'd never seen anyone looking as happy and proud. 'I don't have to ask how you are, son, yer look like someone who's just come into a fortune.'

'I'm on top of the world, Dad, and that's a fact.' Tommy lifted his arm and nodded at the coats. 'I'll put these on the bed out of the way. Then I'll give me dearly beloved intended a hand in the kitchen.'

'Sit yerselves down,' Bob said. 'I think the dinner's ready, we're only waiting for Jill and Steve now.'

Molly gazed around the room at the brightly decorated Christmas tree in the corner, the coloured bunting criss-crossed overhead and the balloons hanging on string from the picture rail. Then she let her eyes dwell on the table. It was covered in a pure white linen cloth which had a display of hand-embroidered flowers and leaves in each corner and in the centre. Set out on top were shining knives, forks and spoons, each placed with precision, and by each place setting was a brightly coloured Christmas cracker.

'The room looks lovely, Ma, nice and warm and Christmassy. And the table looks very inviting. Someone has been very busy.'

'Your son did it all, me darlin',' Bridie said, pride and pleasure in her eyes. 'He can turn his hand to anything, and him and Rosie refused to let me or Bob lift a finger.'

'Yeah, he's a good lad and I love the bones of him. But he probably wouldn't let yer help 'cos yer look too posh to get yer hands dirty.' Molly felt a surge of love as she gazed down on her parents. They both looked immaculate, happiness and contentment on their faces. And most of this was down to the girl who had come into their lives when she was fifteen and had stolen their hearts as soon as they set eyes on her. 'I must say you both look very prosperous in yer new clothes, all neat and tidy. I'll swear ye're getting younger by the day. Ma, ye're as good-looking now as yer ever were. And as for you, Da, as Rosie would say, sure, it's a fine figure of a man yer are, and that's the truth of it.'

Rosie's head appeared round the kitchen door, her lovely face flushed with the heat from the gas stove. 'What yer say is true right enough, Auntie Molly, but if I were saying it, I'd say he's a foine figure of a man.'

Molly grinned. 'I stand corrected, me darlin', so I do. Wouldn't yer think by now I'd have a perfect Irish accent?'

'Yer do very well, Auntie Molly, and I'm proud of yer, so I am.' Her eyes rolled when she heard the knock on the door. 'Would yer answer that for me, please? It'll be Jill and Steve.'

'I'll go,' Jack said, 'you sit down, love.' When he opened the door and looked into his daughter's smiling face, his mind went back over the years to when he was courting Molly. Jill was the spitting image of her, as were Doreen and Ruthie. Same long blonde hair, blue eyes and slim figure. Molly's hair was peppered with grey now, and her waistline had thickened, but she was still beautiful in his eyes. 'Yer timed it nicely, the dinner's just about ready to be put on the table. And if the smell's anything to go by, we're in for a treat.'

Tommy was ready to receive their coats. 'I think yer can all take yer places at the table now, Rosie's got everything under control.'

Molly did a quick count. There were nine of them, and the table had been set for nine. But they'd never be able to sit in comfort, there'd be no room to move. 'Ma, would yer mind if I moved the aspidistra off that little table so Ruthie can have her dinner on it? Otherwise we'll be squashed like sardines.'

'Move the plant by all means, me darlin', as long as the child doesn't mind being left out.'

'You wouldn't mind, would yer, sunshine? We can pull the little table nearer so yer won't feel as though ye're out in the cold.'

'I don't care where I sit as long as I get everything you get.' Ruthie had been sitting on the floor near her granda and now she winked at him. 'I'll rely on you to tell me how many roast potatoes everyone's got, Granda, and I want yer to count the sprouts as well.'

'I'll make sure yer plate is as full as the others, sweetheart, I won't let yer down.' Bob pulled out a chair at the head of the table and offered a hand to his wife to help her to her seat. 'And if I'm in any doubt about the size of the portions, I'll get a tape-measure out and measure them for yer. How about that?'

Ruthie beamed. 'Ye're a pal, Granda, a real pal.'

Molly popped her head into the kitchen. 'Where d'yer want us to sit?'

'You and Dad are to have pride of place at the end of the table, facing Nan and Granda,' Tommy said. 'And Jill and Steve facing me and me dearly beloved intended. Rosie wants to sit near the kitchen so it'll be easier for her to pop in and out.'

'D'yer need a hand with anything, sunshine?'

'No, thank yer, Auntie Molly, we can manage. It's always you running around after everyone, so today we're going to wait on you. Sit down and let us spoil yer.'

Molly was rubbing her hands as she sat down. 'Sounds good, that does. I could easily get used to being spoilt.'

'It's a pity Doreen and Phil couldn't be here to make the family complete,' Bridie said. 'But I can understand them not wanting to leave Victoria, so I can. And anyway, we couldn't fit any more around the table.'

'Oh, we'd have made room, Ma! I could have brought a little table from our house, it would have served the purpose. But, as yer say, they couldn't leave the old lady on her own. We'll call over there on our way home so I can satisfy meself that all is well.'

Conversation stopped and eyes widened when Rosie came through carrying an enormous platter upon which sat a huge turkey, all nicely golden and surrounded by crispy brown roast potatoes. With a look of pride on her face she placed it in the centre of the table, then stood back while Tommy came in with two vegetable serving dishes in his hands. One was piled high with sprouts and the other with mashed carrot and turnip.

'Oh, yer have been busy, sunshine,' Molly said, full of admiration. 'It looks lovely and very appetising. Yer'll make someone a very good wife.'

Tommy touched his mother's shoulder. 'And that someone is me, Mam! Am I, or am I not, the luckiest bloke alive?'

Ruthie was standing behind her mother's chair. 'That looks the gear, Rosie, it's making me tummy rumble.'

'You've put me to shame,' Jill said. 'My cooking is certainly not up to your standard, nowhere near.'

'You do very well, love.' Steve was quick to defend the girl he'd loved all his life. With his arm across her shoulders he asked, 'Yer've never heard me complain, have yer? And yer haven't poisoned me yet 'cos I'm still here to tell the tale.'

Jill's blue eyes smiled at him. 'I wouldn't poison you, love, I'd rather starve yer than do that.'

'It's too modest yer are, Jill, and that's a fact. Sure, doesn't Steve look the picture of health on yer cooking?' Rosie said. She was very fond of the Bennett girls, never forgetting how they'd welcomed her into the family from day one. They were like sisters to her. 'And now, Tommy's to have the honour of cutting the turkey, seeing as he's me beloved intended. I'll get the gravy boat and then we can start.'

Molly winked across at her mother. 'I haven't seen that big meat plate since I was a girl, Ma, I didn't think yer still had it.'

'Your mother never throws anything away, sweetheart, yer should know that.' Bob reached for his wife's hand. 'The plate has been well wrapped up, with several other things, for many years. She's over the moon that it's being used after all that time.'

Tommy stood with a long pronged fork in one hand and a large carving knife in the other. 'Well, folks, here goes. I've never carved anything before so if I make a hash of it I'm going to pass it over to me dad.'

But he did very well, almost like an expert, and soon everyone was served with turkey and a spoonful of stuffing, and told to help themselves to potatoes and veg.

Ruthie looked on with dismay. 'What about pulling the crackers?'

'Oh, yes, I nearly forgot!' Tommy slapped a hand to his forehead.

'We can't have a party without paper hats.'

There was much laughter as crackers were pulled and paper hats put on heads before the slips of paper were unrolled and each motto read out. Then it was time to eat the food that looked so mouth-watering.

Rosie had worked very hard that morning, sometimes thinking she'd taken too much on. Her head was in a whirl with so many things to think of and she seemed to be meeting herself coming back. It was the first time she'd attempted a meal for nine people, and she wanted so much for everything to be perfect. And now she watched carefully as knives and forks were put to use. Had she put salt in the sprouts? Were the potatoes too crisp? Was the stuffing tasty?

But her fears were all put to rest when the praise and compliments began and she told herself it had been worth all the worry and hard work, because she cold tell by the way they were all tucking in that the compliments were sincere.

Tommy glanced sideways. 'Rosie, why aren't yer eating?'

'I'll not be telling yer a lie, me beloved, that I'll not. I've been worrying meself to death in case I made a mess of the whole meal. Me tummy is all wound up, so it is.'

Jack rested his knife and fork. 'I can honestly say, Rosie, that this is a feast fit for the King. What do you say, love?'

Molly, her mouth full, nodded and pointed to her cheek to indicate she couldn't speak right then. When she could, she said, 'Yer've done us proud, sunshine, the meal is absolutely delicious. It couldn't be bettered.'

Jill said, 'Me mam's right, it's lovely. When we get our own house, Rosie, I'll be coming to you for cookery lessons.'

Steve agreed. 'I don't know why yer were worried, Rosie, everything's perfect.'

Tommy pulled her close. 'And you are perfect, my beautiful wife to be. So come on, eat up and enjoy the fruits of yer labour.'

Bob and Bridie looked at each other and smiled. Rosie deserved every compliment she got because she was a wonderful girl. They said beauty was only skin deep, but not with this lovely Irish girl. She was kind, thoughtful, compassionate and loving, and gave a piece of her heart to everyone.

Steve pushed the empty trifle dish back and patted his tummy. 'I am absolutely stored. Not another crumb could I fit in. But it was really delicious and can I come back tomorrow for another helping, please?'

'Don't talk about tomorrow, son,' Jack said, 'it's back to the grindstone for all of us.' He smiled fondly at his future daughter-in-law. 'But every time I go to moan I'll think about the meal I've just eaten and it'll get me through the day.'

'I hate to be the bearer of bad news, Dad, but I'm afraid it's a case of singing for yer supper,' Tommy said, straight-faced. 'Only it wasn't yer supper, it was yer dinner. Anyway, the men have been delegated to do the washing-up. All except Granda, of course, he's got special dispensation from Rosie 'cos she's got a soft spot for him.'

Steve pulled a face. 'What about me, Rosie? Haven't yer got a soft spot for me?'

'Oh, I have that, right enough, Steve. But sure, the soft spot I have for yer is in me heart, not in me feet. And it's me feet that are telling me to sit down and give them a break.'

'You stay right where yer are, sunshine, and me and Jill will clear the table.' Molly nodded to her daughter. 'We'll take the dishes out and then the men can get cracking.'

'I'll help, Mam.' Ruthie's paper hat was too big for her and had slipped sideways, giving her a drunken appearance. 'I'll collect all the cracker papers and put them in the bin.'

'Okay, sunshine, there's a good girl.'

The table was soon cleared, the men were busy in the kitchen and Bob was sitting in his armchair, ready for a snooze. Within five minutes of his bottom hitting the chair, he was fast asleep and snoring gently. 'Let's keep our voices down,' Molly said, 'and let him have half an hour, he needs it.'

'Time flies, doesn't it, me darlin'?' Bridie said. 'It doesn't seem like six months since the wedding, it's flown over.'

'Ye're right, Ma, it has flown over. And next year I've got a lot to look forward to, the first thing being Ruthie leaving school. Makes me feel old that me baby is only a few months off being old enough to start work.'

Ruthie was sitting on the floor with her knees drawn up to her chin. 'I can't wait to leave school and get out of that gymslip and the thick black stockings.' She put a finger to her lips and whispered so the men couldn't hear, 'And the navy blue fleecy knickers with a pocket in.'

'Don't be wishing yer life away, sunshine, the time passes quick enough. Anyway, that's one milestone in our lives. Then in May, please God, Doreen will be having her baby and me and Jack will have our first grandchild.'

'And for me and Bob it will be our first great-grandchild. That is something we're really looking forward to.' Bridie's still handsome face smiled. 'And only a few months after that Rosie and Tommy will be getting wed.' She leaned forward to take her daughter's hand. 'Yer've got a lot on yer plate in the next six months, me darlin', that's for sure.'

Molly nodded. 'I'll be happy for Ruthie when she leaves school because I think she's ready for it. And I'll be happy for Doreen once the baby's born. But until then I'll be worrying meself sick over her.'

'Doreen will be all right, Mam,' Jill said. 'There's no need to worry. She feels fine and is really looking forward to the baby. And the time can't go quick enough for Phil.'

'I don't want yer worrying about the wedding, Auntie Molly,' Rosie said. 'Sure, me and Tommy have it all in hand. It'll be a grand wedding, so it will, and I'll spend the rest of me life loving him and taking care of him.'

'Rosie, sunshine, I don't have any doubt about that. He's getting the girl of his dreams, and I know he couldn't have chosen anyone better. Ye're like a daughter to me already. But that won't stop me crying me eyes out for weeks before the wedding comes off.'

'Why is that, Mam?' Ruthie asked. 'I know people cry at weddings, but not for a whole week before. It's supposed to be a happy occasion.'

'And I'll be the happiest person there, sunshine, but I think I'm entitled to weep because me only son will be leaving the family nest. I cried over the girls, and I still miss them, so don't begrudge me a few tears for me son.'

While Jill and Rosie moved to hug Molly, Ruthie's face wore a thoughtful frown. Then she brightened up. 'Yer'll still have me, Mam! I won't be getting married until I'm at least twenty.'

Molly smiled as she wiped away a stray tear. 'Is that a threat or a promise, sunshine?'

Chapter 15

'I hate these days between Christmas and New Year, girl, don't you?' Nellie hitched her bosom, rested it on the table and folded her arms around it. 'It's neither one thing nor the other. I don't know why they don't have New Year's Eve straight after Boxing Day so we can have all the parties in one go instead of having us twiddling our thumbs for five days. Yer'd think one of these clever buggers in London would have thought about that by now, wouldn't yer? It would be better all round, I think.'

Molly bit on her bottom lip. Her mate didn't half come out with some things, and most of them were cock-eyed ideas. 'Except that we'd lose five days in every year. That would shorten our lives quite a bit.'

'How d'yer make that out, girl?'

'Well, if yer went from the twenty-sixth of December to the thirty-first, we'd lose those five days in between.'

'Not if we tagged them on after, we wouldn't. We could easy do that.'

'So, yer reckon we could go from the first of January to the twenty-seventh of December, do yer, sunshine? And yer don't think anyone would get confused, like?'

'Nah! I wouldn't get confused, girl, I'd remember that with no trouble.'

'And what about all the calendars?'

'What calendars? I haven't got no calendars.'

'No, but the factories and offices have.' For a second Molly wondered why she was bothering, then decided she had nothing better to do anyway. 'And it would mean we'd be five days behind every other country in the world.'

'That wouldn't worry me 'cos I've never been further than Blackpool, and never likely to. So I couldn't care less what the other countries in the world do.'

Molly shook her head. 'No, it wouldn't work, sunshine, it would send everything topsy-turvy. I'd say that was one of the worst ideas yer've ever come up with.'

Nellie bent an elbow and rested her cheek on one clenched fist. 'Ah, well, it was worth mentioning, wasn't it? I thought of it in bed last night and it seemed a good idea to me at the time. But things seem different in the light of day, don't they?' She ran a finger down the chenille cloth as her mind worked to find something else to talk about. 'What are yer having for dinner tonight, girl?'

'I'm using the rest of the turkey up. We didn't eat it yesterday with going round to me ma's for dinner, so I'm finishing it off tonight rather than it going to waste. I hate throwing food out, it's a sin when there's people going hungry.'

'Many's the time we went hungry, eh, girl? D'yer remember the days when we didn't have two ha'pennies to rub together?'

'I do, sunshine. We don't know we're born now, compared to those days. I don't think any of our kids will ever understand what it is to scrimp and scrape like we did.' Molly reached across to touch her mate's arm. 'But it wasn't all doom and gloom, was it? After we became real mates, we laughed our way through those bad days, even though our tummies were rumbling.'

Nellie's chubby face creased. 'Ay, I'm not half glad I didn't clock yer one that day when we were having a set-to over the kids. Yer wouldn't have wanted to be me mate if I'd given yer a black eye.'

'Oh, I'd have still been yer mate, sunshine, but it would have been after I'd given you a black eye in return. I wouldn't have stood there and let yer clock me one without clocking yer back. And it would have been easier for me 'cos I'm taller than yer.'

Nellie's tummy began to shake and soon the table was bouncing up and down. 'I could have reached yer if I'd jumped up. And twenty years ago, girl, I was good at jumping.'

'And I was good at ducking, sunshine, so we're even. Anyway, down to business. I only want bread from the shops since I'm making do with all the leftovers for dinner tonight. Have you any shopping to get in?'

'I need bread, and I've got nothing for the dinner.' Nellie's eyes narrowed. 'How much turkey have yer got, girl?'

'There's barely enough meat left to feed me own family, never mind yours.' In Molly's mind's eye, she could see the tin of corned beef standing in the larder, and so began a struggle with her conscience. She was trying to stretch her money out so she could save as much as possible. Not only for Tommy's wedding, but to buy something for

Doreen's baby when it arrived. But that tin of corned beef in the larder would haunt her if she didn't offer to help her mate out. 'Will yer promise to pay me back if I lend yer a tin of corned beef?' I need it meself, really, but I can't see yer stuck. So as soon as Tony gets some more tins in, it's payback time. Have yer got that, sunshine?'

With the prospect of tonight's dinner being sorted out, Nellie would have promised anything. And she'd be full of good intentions to pay it back. It was just that she wasn't as good a manager as Molly, and if she had something in her hand that would make a meal for the family she would use it that day and let tomorrow look after itself. 'I always do pay yer back, girl, don't I? Yer may have to wait a bit, but I always get there in the end.'

Molly thought of all the arguing she'd done at times to get back what was owed to her, but it was her own fault, really, for being too soft-hearted. 'Okay, sunshine, let's change the subject, shall we?'

Nellie hitched her bosom to a more comfortable position before saying, 'I'm looking forward to Corker's party on New Year's Eve, girl, it should be good. I've been racking me brains to think of what I can do as me party piece, but I can't think of anything I haven't already done. And a good artiste never repeats her repertwory.'

Molly opened her mouth to correct her mate, but just in time she saw the gleam in Nellie's eyes and realised that she was being baited. As soon as she said something, the little woman facing her would come right back with an answer she had ready on the tip of her tongue. 'I hate to disappoint yer, sunshine, but I'm not falling for that again. If yer want to pretend ye're daft, I'm not going to stop yer. Anyway, back to Corker's party. If ye're looking for something to do to entertain, why don't yer do yer Al Jolson routine? It always goes down well.'

Nellie frowned as she said, 'Nah! It means me putting black shoe polish on me face and it's a bugger to try and get off.'

'Yer could try using soot, yer'd only have to wash yerself to get that off. Or yer could save yerself a lot of trouble by buying a black mask.'

Nellie sat up straight, her face showing interest. 'I didn't know yer could buy black masks, girl, yer never told me.'

'I didn't think it was necessary when the sweet shop have got masks of every description hanging up on the wall. They've got Red Indian ones which would really be something different for yer. If someone would lend yer a tomahawk, yer could do a war dance.' Molly was being funny, but she should have known better.

'Ay, that would be the gear! Tony must have thousands of turkey feathers left, he won't have had time to throw them in the muck midden yet.' Nellie's mind was racing ahead. 'I could put a band round me head and stick the feathers all around. And my feller's got an axe, that would be just as good as a tomahawk.' Chubby hands were rubbed together in glee. 'Ay, that's a brainwave yer had there, girl, I would never have thought of it.' The bosom was hitched and placed on the table again. 'What could I get dressed in?'

'To be authentic, sunshine, to wear the real thing yer'd have to go out and kill a cow so yer could make a dress out of it. Indians all wear animal skins.' Molly was finding this really amusing. Never for a second did she think her mate would take her seriously. 'Yer wouldn't have to worry about shoes, 'cos they don't wear none.'

Nellie bent her head and gazed down at her hands, pretending to be giving the matter some deep thought. Then she looked up and sounding very earnest, said, 'I haven't seen no cows around here, girl. In all the years I've lived here, I've never seen no cows. But would a horse do? I could always ask the coalman how much he'd want for his. I mean, like, it would be worth the money to have a dress of real leather so I look the part.'

'Oh, I'm sure Tucker would be very obliging, sunshine, especially as yer say he's had a crush on yer for years.'

Into Molly's mind flashed a picture of her husband asking what she and Nellie found to talk about. 'Ye're with each other every day, go everywhere together, and the pair of yer never stop talking! It beats me what yer find to talk about.' What would he say if he could hear them now, talking about Red Indians and skinning the coalman's horse? A smile came to her face. He'd find the whole thing hilarious and laugh his head off.

'What are yer smiling for, girl?' Nellie asked. 'Let's in on the joke.'

'It was nothing, sunshine, not worth repeating. Anyway, it's Tucker's day to deliver the coal tomorrow, yer can ask him about his horse then. But I'd stand well back when yer do, 'cos yer've often heard him say he looks after his horse better than he looks after his wife.'

'Yeah, it was a daft idea anyway. I can't even skin a rabbit proper, never mind a ruddy horse.' Then Nellie's face lit up. 'Perhaps he'd lend it to me, though. I could ride up the street at midnight, when the neighbours are out celebrating, and I could wave me tomahawk and make those noises Indians make. That would be something, wouldn't it, girl? It wouldn't half give them something to talk about.'

'Nellie, I couldn't even begin to imagine yer sitting on a horse.'

Molly dropped her head and put a hand to her forehead. 'I don't know about being the talk of the street, yer'd be the talk of every wash-house in Liverpool, and beyond.'

The chubby face across the table creased, and laughter started to surface. 'I always wanted to be famous, girl, and now's me chance. Big Chief Sitting Bull rides again.'

'Big Chief Sitting Bull can get down off his horse and walk to the shops with me. By the time we get there, Hanley's will have sold out of bread.' Molly took her coat down from the hook behind the door, and as she was putting it on, said, 'I'll give yer a word of advice, sunshine, stick to Al Jolson, it'll be far less trouble.'

After Molly had closed the door behind her, they linked arms and began to walk down the street. 'Ay, girl, d'yer know before, when I said I hadn't never seen a cow down here?' Nellie's eyes were bright with mischief. 'Well, I'd forgotten about Elsie Flanaghan. She's a right cow if ever there was one.'

A couple of nights later, Molly and Jack had the house to themselves. Tommy had gone to see Rosie, as usual, and Ruthie had gone over to the Watsons' house to play with Bella. 'It's nice to be quiet for a change,' Jack said, lowering the evening paper, 'but I feel as though there's something missing, don't you?'

Molly nodded. 'We'll have to get used to it, 'cos when Tommy gets married there'll only be us two and Ruthie. But at least we see the girls every day, it would have been worse if they'd gone to live miles away.'

'It all seems to be happening so quickly,' he said. 'Six months ago there were six of us, now there's four, and come the summer there'll only be three.'

'Come the summer, sunshine, we'll have a grandchild, and that's something to look forward to. Our family is growing, even though they might not all live in this house. We've got a lot to be thankful for, Jack, so let's count our blessings.' Molly glanced at the clock on the mantelpiece. 'I want to slip next door, but I'll be quick. By the time yer've read the *Echo*, I'll be back.'

'What d'yer want to go there for?'

Molly was already reaching for her coat. 'Nothing important, I'll tell yer when I get back.' She planted a kiss on his cheek. 'Don't be getting up to mischief while I'm gone, d'yer hear?'

Jack grinned. 'Why don't yer stay in and we'll get up to mischief together?'

But Molly was heading for the door. 'Yer get worse as yer grow older, Jack Bennett.' She hesitated on the top step, then turned back. 'I'll only be half an hour, so contain yerself until then. I told Ruthie she could stay out until half-nine, so we'll have a good hour to ourselves.' Once again she made for the door, this time with a smile on her face. 'We might even have time for a game of cards.'

'Game of cards, my foot!' Jack shouted. 'I'm in the mood for a game, but it certainly ain't ruddy cards!'

When Ellen opened the door, Molly was still smiling. 'Hello, Molly, this is a surprise. Come on in, there's only me and Corker.'

'Oh, ye're like me and Jack, we've been abandoned as well.'

Corker got to his feet, as he always did when a woman entered a room. 'If Jack's at a loose end, why don't we go for a pint? We could give George a knock, see if he's willing.'

Molly thought of her husband, waiting patiently for her return to indulge in a romantic hour. But she couldn't tell Corker that, she'd be too embarrassed. 'I'll ask him when I get back, but it'll be about nine, would that be all right? Yer see, I want to have a talk to yer about the New Year's Eve party.'

'Nine o'clock's fine by me, Molly, me darlin'.' Corker waved her to a chair. 'Sit down and tell us what's on yer mind.'

'Shall I make a cuppa?' Ellen asked. 'It won't take a minute.'

Still thinking of her husband, Molly shook her head. 'No, thanks, sunshine, I've not long had one.' She sat down and pulled her skirt down over her knees. 'I was wondering if yer realise how many there are expecting to come to the party? Yer'll have a hell of a job trying to fit them all in.'

'I've told him that,' Ellen said, 'but he takes no notice. There'll be well over twenty including the kids, with no room to breathe and people being trampled underfoot.'

'Ooh, we couldn't have that, Ellen,' Molly chuckled, 'the undertakers don't work on New Year's Day. No, I've got an idea. I don't want yer to think I'm just a busybody trying to tell yer how to do things, but why don't we split the party up? The very young, which is your three and Ruthie and Bella, could have their own party in Nellie's.'

'Have yer asked Nellie?' Corker thought it was a good idea. 'Wouldn't she mind?'

'I haven't asked her yet, truthfully, 'cos I didn't think of it until an hour ago. But I know she won't mind.' Molly lowered her eyes for a second. 'Actually, I thought it might be a good idea to use the three

210

houses. The young kids in Nellie's, and the two newly-weds and three courting couples in ours. I don't mean for the whole night, just until about ten o'clock. It would give us older ones a chance to sit in comfort, have a few drinks and a good natter. Then when it's time to eat, those in our house could come here and the party could start in earnest. Not the kids, though, 'cos when Nellie does her party piece it's an adults only show.'

'That sounds like a good idea to me,' Ellen said. 'Don't yer think so, Corker?'

There was a twinkle in the big man's eyes as he stroked his beard. 'What has Nellie got in store for us this time?'

'I couldn't tell yer, she's a law unto herself is my mate. And even if I did know, I wouldn't tell yer 'cos she'd skin me alive. But whatever it is, yer can bet it'll be the highlight of the evening. She's never let us down yet.'

Corker nodded. 'She'd be a rich woman if she charged us for her services. We couldn't be better entertained in a music hall.'

'Don't tell her that, for God's sake, her head's big enough. Anyway, Corker, what d'yer think of my suggestion?'

'It suits me as long as you don't have to put yer hand in yer pocket. I'm supplying all the food and drink, no argument. You've paid enough out over the years, it's my turn now.'

'That's fine by me, Corker,' Molly said, her eyes straying to the clock. She'd told Jack she'd only be half an hour and she didn't want to go over that time. 'I know ye're working in the shop New Year's Eve, Ellen, so I'll come down and give yer a hand with the eats when I've fed the family.'

'I'd be grateful if yer would, Molly, 'cos you're a dab hand at giving parties. We'll get our meal over as soon as possible, then Corker's putting the table in the yard. He's got a piece of tarpaulin to cover it with in case it rains.'

'Right, that's sorted that out, then.' Molly stood up and told a little white lie. 'I'll get back and finish the dishes. I'll wash and Jack can dry. I'll tell him yer'll be giving him a knock about nine, then, shall I?'

Corker followed her to the door. 'Yes, and we'll call and see if George fancies a pint.'

Molly sprinted the few yards to her own door. When she'd let herself in she stood in front of Jack. 'If yer ardour hasn't waned, yer've got three-quarters of an hour to prove to me that yer can be as passionate as Rudolph Valentino.' She slipped her arms out of her coat. 'Corker's

211

calling for yer at nine to go for a pint.'

Jack folded the paper and was pushing it under one of the cushions on the couch when a pane of glass in the back window started to rattle. He lifted his head to see Nellie's face pressed close, trying to see through the curtains. 'Yer wouldn't believe it, would yer, love? It's only yer mate come for a natter. I've a good mind to tell her to go home 'cos she's stopping me from having me marital rights.'

'Don't you dare!' Molly hissed, going towards the back door. 'I'd never live it down, she'd tell the whole ruddy neighbourhood.'

Nellie didn't stand on ceremony and hadn't waited to be asked in. She was already standing in the kitchen where Molly almost bumped into her. 'In the name of God, Nellie, couldn't yer wait for me to open the door? I could have been in me nude for all yer knew.'

Her mate was unashamed. 'Oh, I knew yer weren't girl, 'cos I peeped through yer curtains.' She marched through to the living room and grinned at Jack. 'I thought I might catch yer out having a passionate . . .' she rubbed her head, seeking a suitable word but couldn't think of one '. . . I thought I might catch yer at it, but no such luck.'

'Luck and chance would be a fine thing, Nellie.' In his mind, Jack had been calling her fit to burn when he'd seen her face at the window, but who could fall out with that cheeky grin? 'In future I'll make sure the curtains are tightly closed.'

'Ye're a spoilsport, Jack Bennett, that's what yer are.' Nellie plonked her bottom in the carver chair which she always claimed as hers.

'By the way, girl, what were yer saying about telling the whole neighbourhood?'

Molly was caught unawares and couldn't think what to say. 'Oh, it was nothing.'

'D'yer often talk about nothing, girl? Seems a waste of time to me. And yer don't want to let anyone hear yer or they'll send for the men in white coats.'

'I can't remember what it was, so it can't have been important.' Molly knew her mate would probe until she got what she wanted, so the best thing was to change the subject. 'I think yer'd better nip home and warn George that Corker's going for a drink with Jack at nine o'clock and they'll be knocking for him.' And for good measure, she added, 'Go now, 'cos I've got a bit of news that involves you.'

'Oh, aye, what's that, girl?'

'I'm not telling yer now, it'll give us something to talk about when the men go out.'

212

'I'm not moving by backside off this ruddy chair until yer tell me, so there! At least whet me appetite and tell me why it involves me. Is it something that'll please me?'

'Oh, yer'll be over the moon.' Molly couldn't keep it back, she was dying to see Nellie's face when she told her. 'I've offered the use of your house for the kids' party on New Year's Eve. I just knew yer'd be delighted to help.'

Nellie's face was a picture. 'Well, the bloody cheek of you! I'll have yer know I am not over the moon and I'm certainly not delighted!'

Molly had been expecting this reaction and had her answer ready. 'All right, sunshine, keep yer hair on. If yer don't like it, then yer don't like it and that's all there is to it. All yer have to do is explain to Corker how yer feel, and that ye're not prepared to let the kids use your house for their party. Yer could do it now and kill two birds with one stone. Yer've got to tell George to get ready for the pub, so yer might as well call at Corker's while ye're out.'

That and cut her throat were the last two things Nellie would do. 'Well now, girl, I did say I wasn't over the moon, and I did say I wasn't delighted, but yer never heard me say I wouldn't let the kids use me house, did yer?'

'No, I didn't, sunshine, but yer face spoke volumes. And if yer heart's not in it, I'd rather yer told Corker right away and got it over with.' Molly turned away to hide her smile then she gleefully rubbed salt in the wound. 'That'll give us time to find somewhere else for the kids. So go on, misery guts, get yer dirty work over with. But I'm warning yer, don't come crawling to me making excuses 'cos there is no excuse for being so mean and miserable.'

Jack, his face turning from one to the other as though he was watching a tennis match, was fascinated. If a stranger walked into the room now, they'd think there was a row brewing, or a falling out at least. How wrong they'd be.

'Listen to me, girl, I never said I wouldn't have the kids so don't you go saying I did. Yer can be a bad-minded so-and-so when yer like, Molly Bennett, and it wouldn't surprise me if yer hadn't got me a name like a mad dog. I bet that's why people look at me funny sometimes, or cross the road to avoid me. They've been listening to you, that's why.'

When Molly spoke, the tone of her voice had changed. She thought she'd milked the situation for all it was worth. 'Yer'd better get a move on, sunshine, 'cos your feller wouldn't be pleased with yer if Corker knocked and he wasn't ready.'

Nellie used the chair arms to push herself up. 'Yeah, I better had. He'll want to change his working shirt. I won't be long.'

'No, you hurry back, sunshine, 'cos we've got a lot to talk about.'

Jack let his head fall back against the chair and closed his eyes. What a difference there was between men and women, he thought. Now when he met George tonight, the conversation would go something along the lines of, 'Hello, George, how's work, mate?' And the answer would be, 'Just the same, pal, I can't grumble.' After that it would be football and the weather. Corker usually had a tale to tell when he came ashore, but that only lasted the first night out. They definitely couldn't compete with women. Certainly not Nellie and Molly anyway, they were a breed apart.

'Jack!' Molly shook his shoulder. 'Don't be going asleep now, Corker will be here soon.'

'I wasn't asleep, love, I was just resting me eyes.'

'Resting yer eyes! Yer were snoring yer ruddy head off!'

'I was not! If yer must know, I was trying to fathom out what the outcome was with Nellie. Are the kids going there or not?'

'Of course they are, soft lad! Yer didn't for one moment think there was any doubt about that, did yer?'

'Not really.' Jack was pushing himself to his feet when he chuckled. 'Yer mate's peeping through the curtains again.'

'What would yer do with her?' Molly was standing with her arms folded when Nellie waltzed back in. 'Didn't yer think of knocking?'

'Of course I think about it! But that's all I do, 'cos I can't be bothered.'

'It's a pity about you now! Anyway, is George getting ready?'

'Yeah, I've never known him move so fast. As soon as I mentioned the blinking pub, he was off his chair and swilling himself down in the kitchen sink.' Nellie winked at Jack as he passed on his way to the kitchen. 'Men are easily pleased, aren't they? They're like babies, really. If a baby's sucking on a bottle it's as happy as Larry, and men are the same when they're supping beer.'

'Listen, sunshine, before I forget – have yer still got yer black-out curtains?'

Nellie looked mystified. 'I have, girl, but why d'yer want to know?'

'I'll tell yer later.' Molly's eyes went knowingly to the kitchen where they could hear Jack splashing water around. 'In case I forget, just say black-out curtains and it'll remind me.'

There was excitement in the air when Molly took the plates of sandwiches and cakes down to Nellie's. Everyone who passed was happy, looking forward to the jollity that would come later. New Year's Eve was the one night of the year when everyone came out into the street to celebrate. Neighbours could be at each other's throat for three hundred and sixty-four days, but come the last day of the year and all was forgotten. 'Put them in yer pantry, Nellie, and cover them with cloths so the kids can't see them. There's another two to bring down, then that's the lot.'

Nellie's face was beaming. 'It's exciting, isn't it, girl? I'm really looking forward to the party. It can't come quick enough.'

'It's all right for some,' Molly told her. 'But me and Corker have worked like Trojans for the last few hours. We didn't want Ellen to come home after a day's work and have to start making food for about twenty people.'

'I did offer to help, girl!'

'I know yer did, sunshine, and I told Corker yer were willing.' Molly put her arms around Nellie and hugged her tight. 'But yer know what these kitchens are like, yer can't swing a cat around in them.'

The chubby face beamed up at her. 'What are yer swinging a cat around the kitchen for, girl? Ay, we're not having cat sandwiches, are we?'

Molly rolled her eyes. 'Yer won't tell anyone, will yer? We've put plenty of mustard on them so they won't know the difference from rabbit.' She patted her mate's cheek. 'I'd better move, there's still plenty to do. I'll be coming back and forth, sunshine, 'cos there's bottles of lemonade to bring as well as biscuits.' She spun around at the door. 'He thinks of everything, does Corker. There's lemonade, raspberryade, cream soda . . . you name it and he's bought it. Oh, and he's even got a box of crackers for them to pull.'

'He's a smashing feller, isn't he, girl?'

'He is that, he's got a heart of gold. Anyway, I'm off. I'll see yer later, ta-ra.'

Up until ten o'clock it had been relatively quiet in the Corkhills' house. There had been plenty of talk and laughter, and many a glass had been emptied and refilled. Many a tale had been told, too. Mostly by Nellie, who made them up as she went along, encouraged by her audience's chuckles and guffaws. She also gave her own version of what she'd seen when she'd peeped through the curtains of the Bennetts' window. Ignoring Molly's embarrassment, she said, 'Stark naked they were, the pair of them. Honest to God, I didn't know where to put meself. I was glad it was pitch dark and no one could see me blushing. I gave a knock to warn them I was coming in, and yer should have seen them scramble to put their clothes on.' Above the laughter, she said, 'At their age, wouldn't yer think they'd know better?'

Outside, Phoebe knocked for the third time. 'They can't hear me.'

'They're enjoying themselves too much,' Steve said. 'Here, let me have a go.' He rapped hard with his knuckles. 'They should hear that, it was loud enough to wake the dead.'

Corker was wiping his eyes as he opened the door. 'Come on in and join the party.'

With his arm around Phoebe's waist, Paul made straight for his mother. 'Ay, Mam, will yer tell that joke again so we can all enjoy it?'

'Ooh, I don't think I'd better, son.' Nellie's eyes rolled. 'Can yer see yer Auntie Molly's face? It's set in granite. That means she'll batter me if I tell yer any more. Yer see, she thinks ye're too young to learn about the birds and bees.'

Molly was more interested in where they were all going to sit. 'I thought you lads were going to bring a chair each with yer?'

Tommy closed his eyes. 'Oh, we forgot, Mam. We'll go back and get them, I've got me key with me.'

'Call in to Nellie's first, will yer, and see how the kids are doing?'

'We've already done that, Mrs B.' Steve said. 'They're fine, really enjoying themselves.'

'Sure, and we've had a grand time, so we have,' Bridie said. 'Me and Bob have been finding out things about our daughter, so we have. She's a dark one, and that's a fact.'

Molly shook her fist at Nellie. 'Did yer hear that? I could break yer ruddy neck for yer.'

Jack chuckled. 'I don't know, love, I took it as a compliment.'

'You would, wouldn't yer?' Molly jerked her head, tutted and pushed out her tongue. 'That's male ego for yer.'

Nellie pulled on her skirt. 'What's male ego when it's out, girl? Tell me, 'cos I'd hate to be missing out on something what sounds interesting.'

'I'll tell yer when ye're old enough, sunshine, otherwise it might turn yer head.' Molly raised her brows at Tommy. 'Go and get the chairs, please, so everyone can sit down and we can start bringing the food in.'

Archie took his arm from Lily's shoulder. 'I'll go with him, we can carry two each.'

With Doreen's delicate state of health in mind, Alec from the corner shop offered her his chair. 'Here yer are, sweetheart, yer can have my seat.'

'Thank you, Mr Porter, that's very gentlemanly of yer.' Doreen pulled on Phil's arm. 'You sit and I'll park on yer knee.'

'Mam, all the old ones are to sit down and take it easy,' Jill said. 'If Auntie Ellen and Uncle Corker don't mind us taking over the kitchen, me, Rosie, Lily and Phoebe will hand out the food and make the tea.'

'The old ones! Well, did yer hear that!' But Molly was sitting down as she said it, glad to rest her feet and let someone else take over. 'We're not old, sunshine, we're in the prime of our lives.'

'That's true enough, Auntie Molly,' Rosie said, her curls bouncing as she nodded. 'And when *we're* in the prime of our lives, sure, won't we be glad to let the young ones take over now and again?'

Chapter 16

It was a quarter past eleven and Nellie was getting impatient. She still hadn't done her party piece, and by the looks of things they'd be into the year 1947 before she got her chance. 'We both wasted our time and energy, girl, it'll be time for us all to trip out into the street before I do me turn,' she grumbled.

'I'll tell yer what, sunshine,' Molly said, seeing her friend's drooping mouth, 'you go home and get yerself dressed up and by the time yer get back I'll have everything cleared away and this lot calmed down. Go on, go now before it gets too late.'

'I don't have to go home, I brought me change of clothes with me. They're wrapped in a sheet in me basket in Ellen's pantry. All I need is a big of privacy to do meself up.'

'I thought yer were going home to get changed?'

'I had intended to, girl, but not with the kids being there. I'd frighten the life out of them if I went upstairs a woman and came down a black man.'

Trying to keep her laughter at bay, Molly eyed Nellie's mountainous bosom. There was no one on God's earth who could mistake her for a man. But now was not the time for frivolity for her mate took her role as entertainer very seriously. Catching Ellen's eye, Molly beckoned her over and explained the situation.

'Go upstairs to the front bedroom and get changed,' Ellen told her. 'Yer won't be disturbed, we'll see to that.'

'You come with me, Molly,' Nellie pleaded. 'I'll need a hand.'

Molly came down fifteen minutes later smiling and waving them to silence. 'Can we have a bit of hush now, please, it's time for the main attraction.' She waited until she heard footsteps on the stairs and said, 'Put yer hands together for Mr Al Jolson himself.'

The applause was slow in coming as everyone gaped at the figure before them. Molly, with the help of Doreen, had made a full head mask out of the blackout curtains. There were slits for Nellie's eyes, nose and mouth, and on top of her head sat a straw hat. She was wearing a pair of George's trousers, the legs rolled up to fit, one of his best white shirts and a dickie bow. It was only when she bowed to her audience that they came alive and clapped and cheered her.

Nellie had the hand and body movements of the great man off to perfection as she began to sing 'Swanee'.

The rafters rang as everyone joined in when Nellie sang it for the second time. Then she went straight into another of the great man's popular songs, 'Mammy', and the room erupted. As Corker was to say later, he'd swear the house was lifted a few inches from its foundations. Then Nellie asked for silence for the song to end all songs, 'Sonny Boy'. 'Get yer hankies out ladies. Yer'll need them 'cos Ellen hasn't got enough buckets to go round.'

Now Nellie had seen the great man at the picture house, and he always knelt down to sing this poignant song. To do it justice, she thought she should do the same. She looked for a clear space on the floor.

Molly could read her mate like a book, and knew what was in her mind. 'Don't do it, sunshine, 'cos yer'll never get up again.'

But her warning came too late, Nellie was down on one knee and having difficulty keeping her balance. And at the same time they could hear bells chiming. It was twelve o'clock.

'Out, everyone, come on,' Molly shouted. 'It's about two minutes to midnight.'

Steve looked down at his mother. 'I'll help me mam up first.'

'No need to, son,' Corker told him. 'Me and yer dad will see to her. Everybody else out and give us some room.'

George looked down at his wife who was struggling to get to her feet. Her bosom and tummy were in the way. 'Yer don't half get yerself in some predicaments, Nellie, yer always dive in without a thought for the consequences.'

They had the room to themselves now, and could hear the street outside coming to life. 'You and me, George, are going to give yer wife a chair lift out,' Corker said. 'It'll be the throne she deserves for all the laughs and happiness she's given us over the years.'

And so it came to pass that Nellie was the centre of attention at the beginning of a brand New Year. They could hear the sirens and hooters coming from the boats on the river, mingled with car horns blaring and whistles being blown. The youngsters poured out of Nellie's house, filled with excitement as kisses and hugs were exchanged, and hands shaken. Then Molly said, 'Let's form a ring for a knees-up.' She noticed Lily and Archie were still kissing, as were Phoebe and Paul.

'Knock it off, there's time for that later.' So the Bennetts, McDonoughs and Corkhills, together with the Porters and Jacksons, set the pace. Soon they were joined by many other families intent on enjoying themselves.

The Mowbrays, being new to the street, didn't know anyone except Corker who'd kept his word and knocked one night to ask David if he fancied a pint with some friends. Beryl had spoken to Nellie and Molly a few times, but felt she didn't really know them. So they felt shy about joining in the celebrations and stood outside their house looking on. Then Beryl said, 'We'll never get to know our neighbours if we don't make an effort. They'll think we're miserable buggers standing here like lemons. Come on, let's join in.' She, David and Jeff joined the ring near Nellie, but Joanne made it her business to get in next to Phoebe. She put a smile on her face and held out her hand. 'Happy New Year, Phoebe.'

There was a slight hesitation before the other girl told herself it would be churlish to refuse a greeting at a time like this and held out her hand. 'The same to you.' She was taken aback when a kiss was planted on her cheek, thinking she could have done without that. She was even taken more aback when the girl moved from her to Paul.

Joanne held out her hand and lifted her face for a kiss. 'Happy New Year, and all the best, Paul.'

He glanced quickly at Phoebe, shrugged his shoulders and dropped a light kiss on the upturned cheek. After all, he'd kissed everybody else, he could hardly tell this girl to get lost.

Molly had noticed what had happened and thought, What a little minx! That young lady needs her bottom smacking. Then her mind was taken off it when Doreen and Phil came over to her. 'Mam, is it all right if we go? We want to wish Aunt Vicky a Happy New Year and I'm feeling tired now anyway.'

'Yer don't feel sick, do yer?' Molly looked into her daughter's face. 'It's probably been too long a day for yer.'

'Yeah, that's what it is. I enjoyed it, though, it's been great.'

Phil, forever watchful of his new wife, said, 'I told her to have an hour's rest before we came out, but she can be very stubborn when she likes.'

Molly grinned as she hugged her daughter. 'Yer don't have to tell me that, sunshine, she's always been the same.'

'Will yer thank Auntie Ellen and Uncle Corker for us? He's having a whale of a time and we won't interrupt.'

'I'll do that, sunshine, and you have an extra hour in bed in the morning, d'yer hear?' Molly suddenly remembered it was morning already. 'Heaven knows what time we'll get home, Corker wants us to go back for an hour. Still, it only happens once a year so best make the most of it.' She put her arms around her son-in-law and kissed him soundly. 'Goodnight and God bless, son. I'll be over first thing to make sure yer wife's all right.'

Soon afterwards Rosie and Tommy came over. 'We're hitting the road, Mam, 'cos Nan and Granda are really tired.'

'We've told Uncle Corker we're leaving and he understands. And we've thanked him for everything, so we have.' Even the dim light of the street lamp couldn't hide Rosie's beauty. It's no wonder Tommy is crazy about her, Molly thought.

'I'll come and say goodnight to me ma and da. They've stood up to the pace very well for their age. And as ye're both working tomorrow, I'll call in then and make sure they're okay.'

By one o'clock most of the crowd had dispersed, the men thinking they'd only get a few hours' sleep before it was time to get up for work. Many families had young children already asleep in bed. The Porters had been reluctant to leave, but they opened the shop at six o'clock and needed a few hours' shut-eye before they could face the long day ahead of them. So it was only a small group who finally stood outside Corker's house. 'Come in and have one last drink,' he coaxed. 'One for the road.'

Steve shook his head. 'Yer mother will probably be lying awake waiting for us, Uncle Corker, so me and Jill will get off home. But it's been a cracking night, we've really enjoyed ourselves.'

Jill threw her arms around the big man's waist. There'd always been a bond between them and she loved every inch of him. 'Goodnight and God bless, and thank you.'

He stroked her long blonde hair. 'Goodnight, princess, and God bless.'

They watched the young couple walk away, their arms around each other. Then Molly sighed. 'One drink, Corker, and that's me lot. I want to get home and make sure our Ruthie put herself to bed.' She looked at Nellie who still had her black mask on. 'How did yer ever manage to get up off that floor, sunshine?'

'Ah, that would be telling tales out of school. But I don't mind telling tales, so over our cuppa in the morning all will be revealed.'

'Would it be worth me taking the morning off, Mrs Mac?' Archie asked. 'I would do for a piece of juicy gossip.'

'I should be so bloody lucky to have a juicy bit of gossip, lad.'

Lily tutted. 'Yer said yer New Year resolution was to stop swearing, Mam. The year's only an hour old and ye're at it again.'

'Well, I'll be buggered! Is that what I said, girl? Ah, well, I'll try again next year, eh?'

Nellie was shivering and had her arms crossed in front of her when she pushed past Molly next morning. 'My God, but it's ruddy freezing out there, girl, and the sky looks full of snow to me.' She made for the fire and stood rubbing her arms. 'We didn't have a white Christmas but I think we're in for a white January.'

'I've got the kettle on, sunshine, we'll soon have yer warmed up. Take yer coat off or yer won't feel the benefit when we go out.'

'I wish we didn't have to go out, it's not fit for man nor beast.'

'We've got to go out, sunshine, or there'll be nothing to eat for the family when they come in from work.' Molly carried the carver chair nearer to the fire. 'Sit yerself down and I'll pour the tea out. And yer can have a custard cream as a treat.'

'Aren't you having one, girl?'

'Of course I am, I wouldn't leave meself out.'

In a matter of minutes they were facing each other across the table. 'Well, it's back to normal, eh, girl? All over for another year.'

Molly nodded. 'Yeah, Corker joined his ship yesterday, the workers are back to the grindstone and it'll be months before they get another holiday. Mind you, I'm not really sorry, I'd hate to spend me life going to one party after another.'

'The rich people do, girl, they're always having parties and eating out in all the best restaurants. I bet what they spend on food in a week would keep us for a year.'

'They can do what they like, sunshine, I don't envy them. I'm quite happy with me life, even if I am skint now and again. My ma once said that rich people don't appreciate what they've got 'cos they've never known any different. They don't have to save up for anything they want so they don't appreciate it when they get it. She was right, too. Can yer imagine one of these posh families what live in big houses and have servants dancing in the street and throwing their legs in the air?'

'No, girl, I can't. They don't know how to enjoy themselves like what we poor people do. Stuck-up, toffee-nosed buggers, that's what they are. They wouldn't half look down their noses at you and me and think we were as common as muck.'

'I wouldn't care what they thought, sunshine, I'm quite happy with my lot.'

Nellie eyed the plate on the table. 'Why have yer only brought three biscuits in? Surely ye're not tight enough to eat two and leave me with one?'

'Ye're a cheeky article, you are, Nellie McDonough. That's the last three biscuits left in the house, so yer should consider yerself flaming lucky. Here's me thinking I was giving yer a treat, and all yer do is moan! Yer might have known the larder would be empty after Christmas, so why didn't yer bring some biscuits down with yer?'

'I'd have a job, seeing as we haven't got none.' ANY

Molly huffed, 'Yer've got a nerve, you have. Yer haven't got no ANY biscuits in your house, but yer expect me to have an unlimited supply! Cheeky blighter!'

But Nellie wasn't listening, she had her eyes fixed on the plate and the three custard creams. 'What shall we do, then, girl? Cut one in half?'

Molly rolled her eyes to the ceiling. 'God give me strength. She's trying me patience something rotten, but don't let me lose me temper or clock her one.'

Her legs swinging and her face dead-pan, Nellie said, 'While ye're having a conversation with Him, why don't yer ask Him what we should do with the odd biscuit?'

'I don't need to ask anyone, 'cos I know yer've got yer evil eye on me. If I so much as put that biscuit in me mouth, a crumb would lodge in me throat and I'd choke to death.'

'Oh, well, seeing as ye're me mate, I wouldn't like yer to choke to death. So I'll eat the extra custard cream. It's not that I want it, mind, but I can't have yer dropping dead on me 'cos I wouldn't have anywhere to go for me cuppa every morning.'

'Knowing you, Nellie McDonough, yer'd soon find another sucker.'

Nellie chuckled. 'I'd never find as big a sucker as you, girl, they're few and far between.' Her hand streaked out to pick up the solitary biscuit. It disappeared from sight on the second bite, leaving only crumbs on the tablecloth. She licked her finger and picked up the bits one by one. 'Waste not, want not, girl.'

'In that case, there's half a pot of tea left so don't let's waste that. Then we'll have to make an effort and get down to the shops. I want to call in to Hanley's and pay something off our Tommy's reception. With all the extra expense at Christmas, I haven't paid anything to Edna for weeks. But I've got five pound in me purse and it's going in this morning before I get a chance to spend it.'

'Yer haven't forgotten what yer said about us doing a bit of detective work, to see if we can find any relatives of Phil's, have yer, girl? I'm looking forward to that, it should be exciting.'

'It's hardly the weather for that, sunshine, is it? I mean, we've very little to go on, we could be walking the streets for weeks on end. I don't mind traipsing around if the weather's fine, but I don't fancy it when it's bitter cold like it is today. Neither of us have got heavy shoes, our feet would be freezing.' Molly noticed her friend's downturned mouth. 'We will go, though, Nellie, I'm as eager as you are. There's nothing I'd like better than to unite Phil with some of his father's family. It would be the best present we could give him. But let's leave it a couple of weeks and see if the weather improves, eh?'

'Yeah, okay, girl, ye're right as usual. I froze just walking the few steps from our house to here, never mind wandering around for hours. Me chilblains are giving me gyp as it is.'

'Well, keep them away from the fire or yer'll make them worse.' Molly collected the cups and saucers. 'I'll leave these and wash them when I get back. I don't fancy going out into the cold but needs must when the devil drives. We'll go to Hanley's first, get our bread and I can pay the money over. Then we'll see what we can get for the dinners.'

Molly was in for a shock when she handed the five-pound over to Edna Hanley. 'That makes ten pound now, Edna, but I'll be putting something away each week now the expense of Christmas is behind us. I'll catch up over the next few months.' She watched as Edna brought a book from under the counter and turned the pages to where the entry for Tommy's reception was. 'I've got six months, so a couple of pound a week should do it.'

'This five pound makes it up to fifteen, Molly, not ten.'

Molly shook her head. 'No, I think yer'll find it's only ten, Edna.'

'Are yer forgetting the five that Mr Corkhill paid in? He said it was money he owed yer for buying things for his mother when she was ill.' When she saw the surprise on Molly's face, Edna asked, 'Didn't he tell yer?'

'No, he never said a dickie bird! I wouldn't have let him if I'd known. I never spent nowhere near five pound on Lizzie, and in any case I wouldn't have taken any money off him, he's been too good to us over the years. We'd have forgotten what sugar tasted like through the war years if it hadn't been for Corker, and what about how he helped out at the girls' wedding! I wouldn't dream of letting him pay that five pound.'

'Well, I've taken it now, Molly, so there's nothing I can do about it. Yer'll have to see him yerself next time his ship docks.'

Molly pursed her lips. 'I'll be seeing his wife after I leave here to ask her what he thought he was playing at.'

Nellie was further down the counter being served by young Emily when she heard her mate's voice. Not wanting to miss anything, she waddled along. 'What's up, girl, has she given yer a foreign coin in yer change?'

While Molly was in two minds whether to tell her friend, knowing what she was like for repeating things, Edna made up her mind for her. 'Molly's upset 'cos Mr Corkhill paid five pound to me towards Tommy's reception. He said it was for things she'd bought for his mother when she was ill. I never thought anything of it and took the money.'

'Ooh, ay, girl, that's a big help, isn't it? The first nice surprise of the year.'

'He shouldn't have done it, I didn't need paying for helping Lizzie,' was all Molly would say because there were people standing nearby and she didn't want to fill their mouths. But she'd have a word with Ellen about it. Five pounds was a lot of money. 'Come on, sunshine, let's get our shopping in and hurry home out of the cold. Thanks, Edna, ta-ra for now.'

Outside the shop, Nellie's face gleamed with curiosity. 'Ay, girl, if someone had given me a fiver, I'd be dancing for joy. But you've got a face on yer like a wet week! What's up with yer?'

'I don't feel right taking money off Corker, and you're the last one in the world to argue over that. Just think of what he's given to us over the years, both of us. We'd have had lousy parties without all the food he contributed, not to mention the fortune it must have cost him in drinks!' When Molly blew out, her breath lingered in the heavy, bitterly cold air. 'Before our kids started work, money was very tight and the men only ever had enough coppers in their pockets for one pint on a Saturday night. Corker always understood, never once made them feel as though they were taking charity when he mugged them to a few pints every time he came home.'

Nellie was wearing a scarf over her head, restricting her chins when she nodded. 'Aye, we'd have been lost without him, girl, no doubt about that. He's been a very good friend to both our families.'

'Yer can say that again! It's me what owes him, not the other way around.'

'Have a good think before yer say anything to Ellen, though, girl, 'cos yer might just cause a bit of bad feeling if yer go telling her yer don't want the money. Remember, Corker has cause to be grateful to you in many ways. I did me little bit, like, but it was you what got Ellen the job when she was desperate. It was you who went with her to visit Nobby when he was in hospital, you who gave her a few coppers for the fare. And it was you who made her see sense over marrying Corker.' Never before had Nellie been so serious for so long, and Molly listened intently. 'He's never forgotten those things, girl, and never will. Without you, he might never have married Ellen and been father to the kids. And yer know how he idolises all of them. Perhaps he likes to do little things in appreciation of what you've done for him. So don't be so quick to fly off the handle to Ellen, girl, 'cos yer might just upset a good friend.'

'My God, Nellie, that's the longest speech yer've ever made. And not one swear word all the way through it. Your Lily would have been proud of yer.'

'Never mind our Lily, did any of it sink into that stubborn, thick skull of yours?'

'Yes, it did, sunshine, every word. I don't need paying for anything I've done for Ellen or Corker, I only did what many other people would have done. But I'll heed what yer said and accept the money gracefully. I don't know what Jack will say when he finds out but I'll hold me tongue until Corker comes home and then I'll thank him.'

'Why d'yer have to tell Jack? What he doesn't know won't hurt him. I only tell George what I want him to know, and no more. I don't go looking for trouble, girl, I may be cabbage-looking but I'm not green.'

'I usually tell Jack everything 'cos it gives us something to talk about. But I think in this case I'll keep it to meself.' Molly tucked her arm in. 'See, ye're leading me into bad ways, Nellie McDonough. I'll be swearing next.'

'Now that's one thing I am good at, girl. If yer want any help, I can teach yer every swear word known to man. And that's another thing yer don't need to tell yer husband. I don't want to get the blame if yer ever tell him to bugger off.'

They were nearing the butcher's shop and Molly reminded her friend, 'Don't forget I've decided not to let on to Ellen so watch what yer say.'

'Me lips are sealed, girl, have no fear.'

Tony and Ellen both smiled when the friends entered the shop. 'Come to brighten up our day, have yer, ladies?' Tony asked. 'We could do with it 'cos we're not doing much business. I think we've had about four customers in all morning.'

'Everyone's skint, Tony,' Molly said. 'We go mad the week before Christmas buying things we can't afford, and then suffer for it afterwards. Anyway, we're here now so yer day won't be wasted.'

'What have yer got in mind, ladies?'

Nellie moved away from her mate to stand straight, her shoulders back and her bosom to attention. With her hands laced in front of her, she adopted her favourite stance. 'My friend suggested we buy a leg of pork each, but one gets so sick of pork, doesn't one? So we decided on a leg of lamb each instead. Lean ones, with plenty of meat on, if you will, my good man. Lamb is so delicious with mint sauce, don't you think?'

Ellen roared with laughter, but Tony managed to keep a straight face as he answered. 'The only lean legs with plenty of meat on in this shop, Mrs Mac, are yours.'

'Ho, ho, very funny, I must say. But sarcasm does not become you, Mr Reynolds, you do not have the face for it.' Nellie sniffed haughtily as she raised her eyebrows. 'Seeing as you do not have any lamb for sale, can you kindly suggest a suitable substitute for my friend and I?'

Molly bent to look into her friend's face. 'Are yer feeling all right, sunshine? That dictionary yer swallowed must be playing havoc with yer tummy.'

'No, it didn't do me no harm, girl, I made sure of that. Yer see, I tore the hard back off it before I swallowed it. The only bit of trouble I had was when I came to the word "inconsistent". It was a bugger trying to get that page down me throat.'

It was Ellen's turn to keep a straight face. 'What does the word mean, Nellie?'

'Oh, I couldn't tell yer that, girl. Yer see, I was eating it, not reading it.'

'I'll buy yer another dictionary for yer birthday, sunshine, seeing as yer seem to find them tasty,' Molly said. 'It would be a damn' sight cheaper than a box of chocolates.' She patted Nellie's cheek. 'And now d'yer think we can get on with what we came in for? Tell Tony what yer want.'

'You tell him, girl, he'll take more notice of you. Ask him, if we can't have two legs of pork, what can we have?'

Tony got in before Molly could ask, 'How about a pound of pork sausages each?'

Molly was well pleased. 'That's the best offer I've had for months, Tony. We'll be very happy with sausages.'

Nellie craned her neck to look into her friend's face. 'Why d'yer tell lies, girl, when yer know God can hear everything yer say?'

'I'm not telling lies!'

'Yes, yer are! Yer've just told Tony it's the best offer yer've had for months. Well, it's only about ten days since I peeped through yer windows and saw what yer were up to. And from what I saw, yer'd just had a better offer off Jack than a pound of ruddy pork sausages.'

Molly could feel the colour flooding her face and neck. 'Nellie McDonough, I'll strangle yer with me bare hands one of these days. It's a good job nobody believes a word yer say otherwise I'd never leave the house 'cos I'd be too ashamed.' Then she had an idea. 'Anyway even if what ye're about to tell Tony and Ellen was true, you'd be the one to come off worse. No one likes a Peeping Tom.'

'Ay, girl, if ye're going down that road, I'm going to demand me rights. For the record, it's Peeping Nellie, not Peeping Tom.'

Molly scratched her head. 'I can't win so I might as well give in. Serve us, will yer, Tony, and let's be on our way so I can give me mate a good talking to.'

Ruthie had gone to the first house pictures with Bella and her parents, and Tommy was on his way round to see Rosie. So Molly took the opportunity to tell Jack about Corker's five pounds. She told him the lot . . . how she'd been upset at first and was going to have a word with Ellen, and how Nellie's words had stopped her. 'What d'yer think, love?'

'I think Nellie was right! Yer can't throw the money back in his face, Molly, he'd be very insulted and hurt, and it would put a strain on your friendship. I think it was very generous and thoughtful of him, and I'll tell him so when he comes home again.'

'Yeah, so will I. He'll get an extra kiss off me and a big hug.' Molly then considered telling him how she and Nellie were going to try and trace Phil's relatives, but a voice in her head told her not to. If they were successful, then let it be a lovely surprise for everyone. If they weren't then nobody would be disappointed.

Chapter 17

January turned out to be one of the coldest in years with several heavy falls of snow and bitterly cold winds. Although there was no snow in February, it was still very cold with lots of rain, certainly not fit for Molly and Nellie to be traipsing the streets. In fact they wouldn't be very welcome if people had to leave the warmth of their fires to answer a knock from two strangers they'd never seen in their lives before.

It as the first day in March when the two friends faced each other across Molly's table, hands curled around their cups for warmth. There was a fire in the grate but it was banked up with slack to last the day and wasn't giving out much heat. Coal was still rationed and Molly was thrifty with it during the day so she could build it up and the house would be nice and warm for the family coming in from work.

'The baby's due in a couple of months, girl, if we leave it any longer we'll be too late.' Nellie had pulled the carver chair up to the table for comfort, and also, she said, because sitting in it made her feel posh. Someone of importance, like. 'I think we should make a start to try and find Phil's relatives.'

'I've been thinking that meself,' Molly said. 'Doreen said the baby's due in May, but as yer know a baby can come early. So if the weather's not too bad tomorrow, how about us making a start?'

Nellie grinned at the thought of a little excitement. They could do with something to cheer them up after the few bad months they'd had. 'Yeah, I'd like that, girl. Have yer got the name of Phil's dad written down, and the address yer had?'

'I haven't got a proper address, sunshine, just the name of the street. Well, it's not a street, it's Bullen's Terrace, off Marsh Lane. We'll make a start there and see how we get on. But I'm not telling a soul, even Jack, so keep it to yerself, Nellie, not a word to anyone.'

'Not a word will cross my lips, girl, yer have my solemn promise. And I was thinking, in case we're late getting home, shall we make a big pan of stew today that'll do two days? It would be a worry off our minds and we wouldn't have to rush back.'

'That's a good idea, but can we get enough meat to make a stew for two days? And don't even think of getting round Tony by doing another striptease, me heart wouldn't stand the strain. We'll just appeal to his better nature and generosity.'

'I'll be me own sweet self, girl, like butter wouldn't melt in me mouth. I'll kowtow to him and knock him cold with me charms. He won't be able to resist that, girl. When I turn me charms on, no red-blooded man can resist me.'

'It's not that I don't trust yer, sunshine, but I think I'd feel happier in me mind if yer'll just stand next to me with a smile on yer face and leave the talking to me. And now, I'd like yer to finish yer tea so I can take the dishes out. I want to go over the road to see if Doreen needs any shopping. She's six and a half months now and I don't want her lugging anything heavy.'

'I'm ready when you are, girl, I've only got to slip me coat on.'

'Okay, let's go then. And when we come back from the shops I'm nipping up to see Lizzie. We don't know what's going to happen tomorrow, or how long we'll be out, and I don't want to leave it two days without seeing her. Will yer be coming with me?'

'That's a stupid question if ever there was one. As if I'd let yer go anywhere without me! You don't tell me half what yer get up to when I'm not with yer. That's because yer're not a jangler like me. I tell yer everything. Anyway, I'm coming with yer in case I miss something. That would never do.'

The two friends crossed the cobbled street and Molly lifted the knocker on Victoria Clegg's front door. It was Doreen who answered. She was certainly showing her pregnancy now, but it suited her and she looked very well. 'Come in, you two. Yer always remind me of Darby and Joan.'

'Darby and Joan were an old couple, sunshine. We've still got a long way to go before we catch up with them.'

'Besides which,' Nellie said, tossing her head and sending her chins in all directions, 'one of them was a feller.'

'Go 'way!' Doreen closed the door behind them. 'Which one was the feller?'

Nellie gave Molly a dig in the ribs. 'Tell her, girl.'

'Tell her what?'

'Which one the feller was!'

'D'yer mean to tell me yer can't work out for yerself which one the feller was? Well, how many men have yer heard of with the name of Joan?'

'Not many, I'll grant yer that, girl.'

'Name me one, sunshine, before I lose me rag with yer.'

'I can't think, off-hand, so I'll go along with you. You think Darby's the feller, don't yer?'

'I don't *think* he was the feller, sunshine, I *know* he was! He used to live in our street when I was a kid,' Molly said, feeling quite pleased with herself. It wasn't often she got one over on her mate. 'I never met Joan, though, 'cos he'd moved to another area before he met her.'

Victoria was smiling and rocking her chair gently as she listened to the lively pair. The two women had changed in looks from the young newly-weds they'd been when they first came to live in the street, but their character, kindness and generosity hadn't changed. Neither had their ever-present sense of humour. Even in adversity they could always manage a smile.

'Can we forget it now and remember our manners?' Molly crossed to kiss the old lady. 'Ye're looking well, Victoria! And I like the hairstyle, it suits yer.'

'I can't take the credit for it, Molly, it's Doreen's handiwork. She spends more time on me every morning than she does on herself.'

'She's not neglecting herself, though, sunshine, 'cos she looks as fit as a fiddle. She reminds me of meself when I was expecting.'

Molly was elbowed aside to make way for Nellie. 'My mate's always hogging the limelight, Victoria, I can never get a word in edgeways with her.' She planted a noisy kiss on the upturned face. 'Ye're looking well, girl, like a spring chicken.'

'I wish I felt like one, Nellie, but while the heart is willing, the flesh is weak.'

'I don't believe that for a second, ye're pulling our legs. I bet when ye're on yer own, yer get out of that chair and waltz around the room.' She winked broadly. 'I'll tell yer another one who carries her age well, and that's my mate. Because if Darby lived in the same street as her, that means she must be nearing the hundred mark! Yer wouldn't think so to look at her, would yer?'

'Looks can be deceiving, sunshine, 'cos there's times I feel like a hundred. Anyway, let's get on with what we came for. D'yer want any shopping, Doreen? I can get it for yer, save yer going out.'

'If yer would, Mam, that would be great.' Doreen opened a drawer in the sideboard and took out a ration book and her purse. 'Will yer get me three-quarters of mince on this, please? And if yer going to the greengrocer's, I'd like two onions and some potatoes.'

Molly took the book and put it in her basket. 'I'll get yer five pounds of spuds and they'll do yer tomorrow. Yer see, me and Nellie are going into town then to look around the shops, and we might treat ourselves to a cuppa and a scone, so we'd be too late getting back to go to the shops for yer. If there's anything else yer want, sing out now.'

'Yer could get me some carrots and a swede, if it's not too much for yer to carry?'

It was Nellie who answered. 'Nah, it won't be too much, girl, 'cos I'll help her. We always share the load between us.'

'How much d'yer think it'll be, Mam?' Doreen asked, opening her purse. 'I haven't got a clue over prices.'

'Four bob should do it, sunshine. Yer might even get a couple of coppers change.' Molly held out her hand for the two-shilling pieces, and as she was putting them in her coat pocket, she raised her brows at Victoria. 'Is there anything you fancy, sweetheart?'

Victoria didn't even have to think, she knew what she fancied. 'If they've got any pies left in Hanley's, would yer get two? Me and Doreen can have them for our lunch.'

Doreen opened her purse again. 'I'll pay, Aunt Vicky, and yer can settle up with me later.' Not for the world would she say it didn't matter about the money 'cos Miss Clegg was a lady who valued her independence. 'Ask for two with plenty of gravy in, Mam. That's how we like them, with gravy running down our chins.'

'Ooh, yer've got me mouth watering now,' Nellie said, licking her lips. 'Let's go mad, girl, and ask for four.'

Molly huffed. 'Ye're worse than a child, you are! Everything yer want, yer have to have. Our Ruthie used to be like that, but she grew out of it when she was about ten.'

'I can't help it if I'm a slow grower, can I, girl? I'm young in heart, that's what it is, and it gets on your wick 'cos ye're jealous.'

'Yer may be young in heart, sunshine, and in the head. But yer body hasn't been slow in growing, so don't be expecting me to give yer a piggy-back home from the shops. Now come on, let's be about our business.'

Nellie was following Molly to the door when she turned and looked at Doreen. 'I hope ye're not going to take after yer mother, girl, 'cos she's downright mean and hasn't got no sense of humour. I mean, a slip of a thing like me and she refuses to give me a piggy-back. I can't make her out sometimes, even though she is me best mate.'

Doreen was smiling as she closed the door on them. For she knew that nothing in the big wide world could come between those two.

Outside, Nellie asked, 'Shall we go to Lizzie's now, to see if she wants any shopping?'

'No, Jill finishes work before the shops close. She brings everything they need in with her.' They began to walk towards the main road. 'And don't forget we're supposed to be going into town tomorrow, don't let the cat out of the bag.'

'I won't say a word, girl, 'cos I'm not as good a liar as you are. Me face goes all red and gives me away when I tell a fib. But when yer were telling Doreen that lie, I was looking at yer, and yer didn't even turn a hair.'

'That's because it was only a little white lie and it was being told in a good cause. Our Doreen may thank me for it some time, please God.'

Lizzie Corkhill saw her friends passing the window and they barely had time to knock before she had the door open. She was always pleased to see them for their ability to lift her spirits when she felt down in the dumps. Not that Lizzie was feeling down in the dumps, like, she had no reason to be. Since Jill and Steve had come to live with her it had given new meaning to her life, knowing there'd be someone coming home every day.

'Come in, ladies, I'm very glad to see yer. Take yer coats off while I put the kettle on.' From the kitchen she called, 'How's life treating you two?'

'Can't complain, Lizzie,' Nellie answered as she made a bee-line for the chair near the fire. 'And when I say I can't complain, I don't mean I've nowt to complain about, I mean I'm not allowed to. My mate here carries on something woeful when I tell her me corns are giving me gyp, so I don't bother no more. All I get from her is, "There's millions would give anything to change places with yer, so stop moaning."'

When Lizzie came through with the tray, Molly said, 'I don't mind her complaining about her corns, Lizzie, but it's not only them she complains about. She moans about washing the dishes, making the beds, peeling spuds . . . you name it, she complains about it. And they're jobs every housewife in the country has to do! Yer should hear her when she's had to move the couch to clean behind it. She's pathetic!'

'Yer still love me though, girl, don't yer? I mean, what would yer do if yer didn't have me to pull to pieces?' A gleam came to Nellie's

235

eyes. 'Say Elsie Flanaghan was yer best mate and yer had to listen to her every day. Yer don't know ye're born, that's your trouble.'

'There's no fear of that, sunshine, 'cos I wouldn't have Elsie Flanaghan for me mate even if we were the only two left in the world.'

Lizzie stirred the tea in the cups before handing them over. 'She's a bad bugger is Elsie. I don't use me back door any more in case I bump into her. She talks about everyone under the sun, and hasn't got a kind word to say about them.' She put her own cup on the table and pulled out a chair. 'And yer know that as soon as yer manage to get away from her, she'll be pulling yer to pieces to the next poor sod she collars.'

Nellie was nodding her head. 'There's a few times I've gone to strangle her, but Molly always drags me away.'

'She's not worth soiling yer hands on,' Molly insisted. 'Yer'd only bring yerself down to her level, and that's the gutter. Anyway, let's talk about something else. Have yer heard from Corker lately, Lizzie?'

'Yes, I get a letter every week without fail. Same as Ellen and the kids, we all get letters at the same time. It's a twelve-week trip this time, so there's another three or four weeks to go before we see him again. He always asks after you two, and Jill and Steve. And I get strict instructions to keep him up-to-date on Doreen and Phil.'

'Doreen's doing fine, tell him. Me and Nellie were over there this morning and I think she suits being pregnant, she looks lovelier than ever.'

'I agree with yer, she looks really bonny. Her and Phil come up two or three times a week, just for an hour or so to have a natter with Jill and Steve. And me, of course, they never leave me out.'

'My hope is that when Jill and Steve find a house, it won't be far away. My two daughters are like twins, they'd be lost if they didn't see each other often.'

'This might sound selfish, Molly, but I hope they don't find a house for a long time. I love having them here and I'll be sad and lonely when they go.'

Molly and her mate stayed for an hour to keep Corker's ma company. Then they said they'd have to get home to see to the dinner. 'We won't see yer tomorrow, Lizzie, 'cos me and Nellie are thinking of going into town for a few hours. But we'll see yer the day after.'

Lizzie showed them to the door. 'Don't spend all yer money in the one shop, now.'

'We're not going to buy anything, sunshine, we're just going to window shop and pick out what we'd buy if we had the wherewithal to splash out.'

Nellie's bosom stood to attention. 'Yer never know, we might just click with two rich men who could buy us anything our heart desires.'

'Aye, and pigs might fly, sunshine!' Molly linked her arm and began to pull her away. 'Ta-ra for now, Lizzie, we'll be seeing yer.'

When they stopped outside Nellie's house, Molly said, 'I'll expect yer at ours at ten in the morning, sunshine, and don't be late.'

'I'll be on time, girl, and before yer say it, I'll look decent and respectable.'

Molly chuckled as she covered the short distance to her own front door. She was a cracker, was Nellie. You didn't get many like her in a pound.

At a quarter past ten the next morning, Molly was pacing the floor with her coat on. What the heck was keeping Nellie? It wasn't like her to be late, she was usually so punctual. Then Molly had a thought she didn't like. Perhaps her friend was ill, lying in bed with no one to hear her call. But the thought was quickly dismissed. If Nellie was ill, George would definitely have let her know.

After another five minutes, Molly spoke to the empty room. 'This is ridiculous, the day will be gone before we get started. I'm going to give her a knock.' So after making sure she had her keys in her purse, she stepped into the street and pulled the door behind her, 'I'll give her a piece of me mind while I'm at it, keeping me waiting like this.'

But when Nellie opened the door, Molly gasped and took a step back. 'In the name of God!' For her friend stood before her dressed in a pale blue stockinette underskirt over a brassiere which would have gone twice around the gasworks and there'd still be some to spare. The underskirt was designed to come down over a lady's knees, but with Nellie's enormous frontage pulling it out of shape, it finished twelve inches above hers, leaving an expanse of blue fleecy-lined knickers on display.

Molly stood shaking her head in disbelief. 'How did yer know it was me knocking? Yer could have opened the door to anyone . . . a man even.'

'No, it wouldn't be a man, girl, not with my luck.' Nellie swayed into the living room, leaving her friend to close the door. 'I won't be long, I've only got to put me dress on.'

Molly gazed at her, still shaking her head. 'The sights yer see when yer haven't got a gun. Or a camera. If I had one I'd go home and get it

237

so everyone could see yer in all yer glory. They'd have to believe me if I had the evidence to back it up.'

'That would be blackmail, that would.' Nellie's voice was muffled as she strained to pull a navy blue dress over her head first, then her bosom and tummy. 'I could go to the police if yer did that and yer'd have to pay me a lot of money.'

'Some hope yer'd have of getting a lot of money out of me, sunshine, I'm always skint. Anyway, why are yer so late?'

'Well, its like this, yer see, girl. I've only got one pair of stockings what haven't got holes and ladders in, and I forgot to wash them last night before I went to bed. So I rinsed them through this morning and put them over the fire-guard, but they've taken ages to dry.'

'What's the use of putting stockings on the fire-guard to dry when yer haven't got a ruddy fire!' Molly's eyes slid down to the stockings which were being held up by a piece of elastic. 'Are they still wet?'

Nellie began to look pleased with herself, having finally won her battle with the dress. 'No, I dried them, see, so there! I'm not as thick as yer think I am. I rubbed them in a towel first and got most of the wet out of them, then I stuck them in the roasting tin and put them in the oven for a quarter of an hour. Bone dry they are now.'

'Nellie McDonough, I don't know what I'm going to do with yer! One of these days yer'll set the ruddy house on fire. I wonder what George would say if he knew what yer get up to?'

'Well, he won't know if you don't tell him. Anyway, what I had to do this morning is all your fault, and if the house had burnt down I'd have told him that.'

'My fault! How d'yer make that out? I wasn't even here when yer stuck yer stockings in the oven! If I had have been, I wouldn't have let yer.'

'Would yer have gone out with me with ladders running up me legs and holes in me heels? No, yer wouldn't, yer'd have told me off and left me behind. I'm not proud, I don't worry about what I look like, but you do. Every hair must be in the right place, nails clean, stocking seams straight and definitely no holes in the heels. Oh, and shoes polished as well. I feel as though I'm in the flaming army with the sergeant eyeing me up and down.'

Molly's imagination took over. She could see her little fat friend standing in a line of soldiers and looking up at the sergeant. And she could hear her telling him where he could stick his ruddy gun.

'What are yer laughing at, girl?'

'You! Yer wouldn't last two minutes in the army 'cos yer'd never

238

take an order from anyone. And yer'd never get up at five in the morning, get washed in freezing cold water and be ready for parade and inspection by six.'

Nellie was slipping into her coat by this time. 'Ye're right there, girl, I'd be telling them to sod off and going back to sleep.'

Molly spotted the front door key on the sideboard. 'Don't go without that, sunshine, I don't feel like climbing through the kitchen window to let yer in.'

Nellie pocketed the key. 'Let's hope something comes out of today, eh, girl? So shall we wish ourselves good luck.'

'You're my good luck charm, sunshine, I'm relying on you.'

Her friend looked really pleased. 'Yer've never told me that before, girl! D'yer really think I bring yer good luck?'

'I never told yer 'cos ye're big-headed enough. But, yeah, I've always felt that yer brought me good luck. So let's hope it works today, eh?'

Nellie linked her arm and squeezed. 'It might not happen today, tomorrow or next week, girl, but I've got a feeling in me bones that we're going to touch lucky and find someone who knew Phil's father.'

They were walking down Marsh Lane when they passed a picture house. 'Ay, girl, that's the Marsh Lane Palace. They call it the flea pit 'cos no one goes in there without coming out scratching themselves all over.'

'Yer only need a couple of people to have fleas and they could contaminate everyone there. Fleas jump from one person to another, and in the warmth of a picture house they'd be breeding like mad.'

'Ay, there's Bullen's Terrace, girl. We found that easy enough, didn't we?'

'Finding that was the easiest part, sunshine, it'll be all uphill from here.'

They stood on the corner wondering which side of the road to start on. There were large houses on one side. Molly guessed they were eight-roomed, with several steps leading up to the front door. There were iron railings to the front of each house, and they could see windows below street level which meant they had large basements. On the opposite side, the houses were much smaller with only one front door step.

Nellie was looking at the pub on the opposite corner. 'Ay, girl, how about trying the pub when it opens? We'd probably find out more there than we will do knocking on doors'

'I was thinking that meself, sunshine, but I'd rather be knocking on a few doors while we're waiting. We can't afford to waste any time.'

'Okay, girl, I'm game if you are.'

They'd reached the first gate when Molly saw a woman walking towards them, her basket over her arm. She looked to be in her sixties, old enough to remember families who'd lived in the area before the war. There was no harm in trying anyway.

'Excuse me, love, I wonder if yer can help me?'

The woman smiled. 'I will if I can. Are yer not from around here?'

'No, we live a few miles away. But we're trying to trace the family or any relatives of a man named Bob Mitchell. We know he used to live somewhere around here.'

'Oh, Bob Mitchell died about fifteen years ago, queen. They used to live in that house over the road, number eight, the one with the railings painted green. But when the father died, the family moved to a smaller house and that's the last I saw of them.'

'It's a big house,' Molly said, 'they must have been a large family?'

'They were, and they were a lovely family, the salt of the earth. But they suffered a lot of heartache. I was sorry when they moved and I missed them. But where they moved to I have no idea.'

It was Nellie who asked, 'So they don't live around here any more?'

'That I couldn't tell yer, queen, 'cos I don't get out much. I've suffered with rheumatism in me hands and feet for years now and the furthest I can walk is to the shops around the corner. The Mitchells could be living quite near for all I know.'

'Would anyone else in the street know, d'yer think?' Molly asked. 'It's quite important that we find them.'

The woman thought for a while, then she nodded to a house next to the Mitchells' old home. 'Yer could try the Waltons in number ten. They used to be very friendly with the Mitchells, it's possible they've kept in touch.'

'Thank you, we're beholden to yer.' Molly smiled. 'You take care of yerself now.'

The two friends watched as the woman walked away, her pace slow, as though each step was an effort. Then Molly looked down at her friend. 'Well, we haven't really found out anything, but I've got more hope than when we started out. So let's try the Waltons in number ten and see if we can go forward a few more steps.'

Their knock was answered by a small, thin woman. Molly mentally put her age at about seventy, but she wasn't very good at guessing and could be ten years out either way. 'Mrs Walton?'

The woman nodded, her hand on the door latch. 'Can I help yer?'

'We're trying to find a family by the name of Mitchell who lived in this street years ago. We were told you were friendly with them and might know where they're living now?'

The woman came to the edge of the step and folded her arms. 'Yes, I knew them well. We were good friends and neighbours. They'd had a lot of trouble, more than most people, and had to move to a smaller house. The mother, Maggie, said she'd get in touch when they'd settled in, but she never did. I was sad about that 'cos we were good friends.'

'So yer've no idea where they moved to?'

'I'm sorry, love, but I haven't. It could be the other side of Liverpool for all I know.'

Molly's hopes were dashed. But she wasn't going to give in without exploring every avenue. 'I don't suppose yer can think of anyone who might be able to help? We have some news for them which I'm sure they'd be delighted to hear.'

Mrs Walton pursed her lips and looked down. Then, after a minute, she said, 'Yer could try Alf, the landlord of the George on the corner. It's possible he's heard something over the years 'cos the boys used to drink in there. So did their dad, but he died not long before they moved. In fact, I think that's why they went. They couldn't afford to pay the rent here when his wages stopped coming in.'

'We'll try the pub then,' Molly said. 'And thanks for talking to us, it was kind of yer.'

'I'm just sorry I couldn't be more help. Ta-ra, and good luck.'

Molly gave Nellie her hand to lean on as they went down the steps. 'Well, the pub it is, sunshine, they should be open by now.' She began to chuckle. 'What would Jack and George say if they knew what we were up to? Two women going in a pub . . . they'd do their nut.'

The pub was open but there were no customers yet. The landlord turned out to be very friendly when Molly explained why they were there. 'Yeah, I knew the Mitchells well, they were a lovely family, and I know they're living somewhere in the vicinity 'cos the two lads come in now and again for old time's sake. I'm calling them lads, but they're well into their forties. In fact the eldest, Jim, must be knocking on fifty.'

'But yer don't know their address?'

'No, I don't, though for some unknown reason I've always thought they lived in one of the streets going down towards Seaforth Docks. Both the lads work on the docks, so it would make sense to live near

241

them. If yer want to put my hunch to the test, just turn left when yer get out of here, past the entrance to the railway station, and cross over. On yer right, in the distance, yer'll see St James's church. Yer want to turn down the road where the church is and keep on walking through to Knowsley Road.'

'Oh, I know Knowsley Road,' Molly said. 'That's where the Gainsborough picture house is. I've been there a few times.'

'Yer shouldn't have any trouble then. Because just past the Gainsborough, ycr'll come to some streets that were named after poets. There's Eliot, Wordsworth, Scott and a few others. They're only narrow streets of two-up-two-down houses where everybody knows everybody else. If they do live down there it won't take yer long to find them. If I'm wrong, and I'm sending yer on a wild goose chase, then I'm sorry. But it's the best I can do, and it's somewhere for yer to start.'

'We'll take yer up on yer hunch and make a start today.' Molly was thankful they'd got a friendly landlord, not one who would have turfed them out without even listening to what they had to say. 'We're very grateful, aren't we, Nellie?'

'Yes, we're very grateful to yer.' She was thinking if she didn't get something to eat soon, her tummy would be rumbling. Molly might be able to go hours on end without food, but she couldn't. 'I don't suppose there's a café anywhere near, is there?'

The landlord chuckled. Here was a woman who liked her food and showed for it. 'There's one just around the corner, yer can't miss it. It's very clean and they do very good bacon butties.'

Nellie patted her tummy. 'Thanks, mister, yer'll be me friend for life.'

As they were leaving, Alf shouted after them, 'If yer do find them, would yer let me know sometime? I'll be interested in how yer got on.'

Molly nodded. 'We'll definitely let yer know. Scout's honour. Ta-ra.'

Chapter 18

'There's yer pot of tea, me husband's doing yer bacon butties.' The woman in the café placed the pot in the middle of the table next to the cups and milk jug. 'I'll bring them as soon as they're ready.'

'Can yer see me nose twitching?' Nellie asked. 'It's the smell of bacon frying, yer can't beat it.'

The woman's apron was as clean as the café itself. 'Yer'd think I'd be sick of the smell of food cooking by this time, but bacon is the one smell I'll never tire of.'

'How d'yer manage with the rationing?' Molly asked. 'It must be a struggle.'

'We've never been rationed for bread, though everything else was in short supply until recently. But we're finding the other food-stuffs are getting easier to come by.' There was a man standing by the counter waiting to be served, his fingers rapping impatiently, and the woman made her excuses. 'I'd better see what that man wants, he's giving me daggers. Enjoy yer tea, the butties will be along soon.'

'She's nice and friendly, sunshine,' Molly said, pouring milk into each of the cups. 'And the place is so clean yer could eat off the floor.'

'There'll be two cups each in that pot, won't there, girl?' The smells wafting towards Nellie's nose had her tummy rumbling. 'I could eat a ruddy horse, I'm that hungry.'

'Don't mention eating horse meat, it makes me feel sick. I believe they did that during the war and didn't tell anyone. For all we know, half the time we've been buying what we thought was stewing beef, we've been palmed off with horse meat.'

'Well, if we have, it hasn't done us no harm, girl, and I ain't about to worry about something that might have been.' Nellie saw a man coming through a door at the hack of the counter carrying two plates and wiggled her bottom on the chair in anticipation. 'Here it comes, girl, and am I ready for it . . . I'll say I am!'

'Here yer are, ladies.' The man was stocky, well-built, with a receding hairline and a smile that would put anyone in a good mood. 'Eat them while they're hot.'

'They smell delicious,' Molly said. 'I didn't think I was hungry until I came in here.'

'If yer want a round of toast to go with them, ask the missus.'

'Thank you,' Nellie said, hoping he wouldn't stand talking. She couldn't wait to sink her teeth into the bacon she could see sticking out of the sides of the sandwich. He must have guessed what was going through her mind because he raised a hand in salute and made his way back to the kitchen. 'Oh, boy, oh, boy, am I going to enjoy this, or am I going to enjoy this?' As an answer wasn't called for, she picked up half of her sandwich and put it to her mouth. Before Molly had time to pick hers up, Nellie's had been demolished.

'In the name of God, sunshine, what's the hurry? And wipe yer chin, there's fat trickling down and it'll go on yer coat.'

'Oh, girl, I was ready for that. It was the best bacon buttie I've ever eaten. Shall I order another two?'

'Not for me yer won't! This will keep me going until my dinner tonight. Anyway, I can't afford to be throwing me money around, yer know that.'

Nellie looked longingly at the half sandwich left on her friend's plate. 'I wish I could eat slowly, like what you do. But two bites and this will be gone.'

'That's because yer've no control over yerself. Take yer time, take smaller bites and chew it for a while. That way yer'll enjoy it more.'

Nellie gazed down at her plate and muttered, 'You behave yerself. Don't be pushing yerself into me mouth in one go.' She picked the sandwich up and took a dainty nibble. 'Ay, girl, how come yer didn't mention Phil's dad?'

'What, and have it all around Bootle in no time? None of the people we talked to mentioned the son who got killed, so I wasn't going to. What we have to say is for the ears of any family we find, not Tom, Dick or Harry. So you be careful what yer say, sunshine, or yer'll spoil the whole thing.'

Nodding her head, Nellie wiped a hand across her chin. 'I'm me own worst enemy, aren't I, girl? Never know when to keep me trap shut.'

'I'll be keeping me eye on yer today, and if I think ye're going to come out with something yer shouldn't, I'll put me hand over yer mouth.' Molly grinned. 'Either that or smack yer bottom and send yer home with yer tail between yer legs.'

Nellie watched her friend refill their cups, then her eyes slid to the counter and the scones stacked on a glass cake stand. 'I'll mug yer to a scone, girl, yer'd like that, wouldn't yer?'

'No, thanks, sunshine, I've had enough. But you have one by all means.'

'Not if you're not having one.' Nellie tried to sound sincere, but failed miserably. 'Yer'll only think I'm greedy.'

'Of course I won't think ye're greedy! It's your tummy, and you should know when ye're hungry. And it's your money, too, so yer don't have to ask my permission.'

Even before Molly had finished speaking, Nellie was beckoning to the woman behind the counter. 'Could I have a scone, please?'

'Just the one, queen?'

'Yeah, me mate's not hungry. She had a big breakfast, yer see.'

'D'yer want butter and jam on it?'

Nellie thought her ship had come in. 'Oh, yes, please.'

Molly dropped her head to hide a smile. When it came to food, her friend was like a child. It was no wonder she didn't lose any weight. But if she was happy and contented as she was, why should she starve herself? 'That looks nice,' Molly said when the woman put the plate before Nellie. 'Did you make them?'

'Well, me and me husband between us. All the cakes are home-made and we only use the best ingredients.'

'Yer must work very hard. What time do yer open?'

'Seven o'clock in the mornings, queen, and that's our busiest time. A lot of men come for their breakfasts on their way to work, and others buy sandwiches for their carry-out.'

Nellie was eating as she listened, jam lodged in the corner of her mouth. If Molly hadn't been with her, she'd have mugged herself to another scone.

'What time d'yer close then?' Molly asked, wondering how the woman stayed on her feet so long.

'Five o'clock weekdays, six on a Saturday. And I can tell yer, I'm glad to see me bed at the end of the day. But I enjoy the work and most of the customers are regulars so we have a laugh and joke with them. If yer want money in yer pocket, yer won't get it sitting on yer backside, will yer?'

'True enough.' Molly's eyes never left the woman's face yet she still didn't miss the quick flick of Nellie's tongue around her lips to lick up every trace of jam. 'And I bet it's more pleasant than standing in a factory all day behind a noisy machine.'

'Oh, we get the odd moaner who wouldn't be satisfied if yer put a roast dinner in front of them. But all in all they're a good crowd.' The woman noticed Nellie's empty plate and picked it up. It was as clean as it was before she'd put the scone on it. Not one crumb was left. 'I'll take these plates out of yer way and leave yer to finish the pot of tea.'

Molly watched her walk away. 'She's a nice woman, just right for a place like this. And from the look of your plate, sunshine, she makes good scones.'

'My tummy is feeling very pleased with itself, girl, I don't think we'll hear a peep out of it for a few hours.'

After draining her cup, Molly took out her purse. 'I'll pay at the counter and yer can square up with me later.'

Nellie, her tummy full and her heart overflowing with goodwill, raised a hand. 'This treat is on me, girl, I'll go to the counter.'

Molly looked flabbergasted. This was something that never happened. It was always she who paid, with promises from Nellie to settle up later. Which, half the time, she never did. It was like trying to get blood out of a stone. 'Are yer feeling all right, sunshine?'

Nellie wasn't easily hurt and she saw the joke. So did her chins which swayed sideways, and her tummy which went up and down. 'I know it's a surprise, but don't yer go and have a heart attack on me, girl, or I'll be sick and it'll all have been a waste of money.'

Molly watched her friend waddle over to the counter, her hips brushing every chair she passed. And she heard the woman laugh and glance her way when Nellie said, 'If yer think me mate looks a bit white around the gills, it's because I've just given her the shock of her life by offering to pay.'

The woman, whose name was Nora, called over to Molly, 'There's a first time for everything, queen, so if I were you I'd make the most of it.'

'I'll do more than that, sunshine, I'll put the flags out when I get home. But only when I'm sure she won't come knocking on my door in the middle of the night asking for the money I owe her. She's feeling good-hearted at the moment, but the thing is, how long will that last?'

Nellie pretended to look hurt. 'That's a terrible way to talk about a mate, I'm cut to the quick, I really am. I would never come knocking at yer door in the middle of the night and I don't know how yer can say such a thing.' Then her shoulders began to heave. 'I'd leave it until at least ten in the morning so yer'd be wide enough awake to look for yer purse.'

Molly got to her feet and winked at Nora. 'And don't think she wouldn't sunshine, 'cos I wouldn't put anything past her. And now, if yer'll take her money, we'll be on our way. We've got an important message to go on.'

After following the pub landlord's directions, and only stopping one person to make sure they were on the right track, Molly and Nellie found themselves standing in Knowsley Road opposite the Gainsborough picture house. 'That didn't take long, did it?' Molly asked as she stepped to the kerb. 'We've hopped in lucky so far, let's hope it keeps up.' She watched the cars and buses go past, then held out her arm. 'Stick yer leg in, sunshine, and when the road's clear we'll make a run for it.'

Safely on the opposite side, Nellie nodded to the picture house. 'I don't remember ever going there, girl, unless it was donkey's years ago.'

'Well, perhaps yer've never been, sunshine! I went a couple of times with Jack when the kids were little. It was before Ruthie was born so yer know how long ago it was. We could take the children to first house because they were comedy films and children were allowed.'

'Ye're a dark horse, Molly Bennett, yer never said a word to me.'

Molly chuckled. 'It was before we became joined at the hip, sunshine. We were friends but not bosom pals. We didn't tell each other what we had to eat or where we'd been.' She saw a couple of women talking, baskets over their arms, and said, 'I think I'll ask those women for directions, it would save us time.'

'Good idea, girl, my feet are not that keen on walking too far.'

The women stopped talking when Molly approached them. 'I'm sorry to bother yer, but could yer tell us if we're on the right way to the streets what are named after poets?'

One of the women transferred her basket to her other arm. 'Yer won't find them down here, love, but ye're not far away. If yer go down one of the streets opposite yer'll come to them.' She pointed a finger. 'Walk down Percy Street, and when yer get to the bottom yer'll be facing the streets ye're looking for. Five minutes walk, that's all.'

Molly thanked her, then took Nellie's arm. 'Back over the road, sunshine, so keep hold of me. I'm glad we asked, we could have been walking all afternoon and not found what we're after.'

'Yeah, if we'd walked far enough we'd have ended up in the Mersey.'

247

Five minutes later they reached the end of Percy Street and were reading the road signs on the wall of the street opposite. 'Have yer ever heard of a poet called Spenser, Nellie?'

'Fancy asking me that, girl, yer know I'm as thick as two short planks.'

'Let's walk to the next one, then.' But the friends were none the wiser when they came to Shelley Street. 'I've never heard of him, either! God, we must be ignorant.'

But Molly's faith in herself was restored when they came to Tennyson Street. 'Now we've both heard of him.' She stepped into the road to see the sign on the following street and a smile came to her face. 'Wordsworth Street, sunshine, we're definitely on the right track.'

'Ay, girl, I might be ignorant when it comes to poets, but I'm not that daft I don't know we've walked in a ruddy square! I bet if we walked down one of these streets we'd be back in Marsh Lane. That feller in the pub sent us miles out of our way.'

'Let's give him the benefit of the doubt and say he got mixed up. I just hope his hunch turns out to be better than his directions.'

'And where do we go from here? Do we have to start knocking on doors?'

'I can see a little shop on the corner of the next street, I suggest we ask in there before we knock on doors. If it's anything like Maisie's shop, they'll know everyone who lives in these streets. Unless yer have other ideas, sunshine?'

'Not me, girl! You're the senior detective, I just follow orders.'

The smell in the shop reminded them of Maisie's. Mixed with the sweetness of fresh bread were the stronger odours of paraffin and firelighters. This was a shop that sold everything under the sun, from coal to babies' dummies. There were only two customers, and they were being served by a middle-aged woman who, from the friendly conversation, knew her clientele and their families well. Could she be just the one to help them?

After the shopkeeper had filled the customers' baskets and given them their change, she said, 'I'll see yer tomorrow, ladies, ta-ra for now.' Then she turned to the two friends. 'What can I do for yer?'

Molly felt a bit guilty about not having any intention of buying anything, and hoped the woman would understand. 'I was wondering if yer could help us? Me and me mate are trying to get in touch with a family who, we've been told, may live around here. We've got some news for them and it's important we make contact.

We thought you may be able to help as yer probably know most people in these parts.'

'I'll help if I can, love, what's the family's name?'

'Mitchell. They used to live in Bullen's Terrace, many years ago, and the father's name was Bob. But we know he died before the family moved to one of these streets.'

'There's a few Mitchells live around here, but from what yer've said, I think it's Maggie Mitchell ye're looking for. I know her husband was called Bob, and that he died just before they moved into Wordsworth Street. Yer could try her first, that would be yer best bet.'

'D'yer know the number?'

The woman shook her head. 'I don't know the exact number of the house, but it's about halfway up on the right-hand side. Anyone up there will tell yer.'

'Thank you,' Molly said, 'yer've been very helpful. We wouldn't have known where to start.'

'Well, that's my good deed for the day. If it is Maggie ye're after she'll be glad to see yer. A proper nice woman she is.' The shopkeeper was curious but didn't like to pry. 'Yer should catch her in at this time.'

Nellie hadn't opened her mouth since they came in the shop, and so the shopkeeper wouldn't think she wasn't quite right in the head, she spoke the words she knew Molly would if given the chance, 'Thank you, we're beholden to yer.' With that she put her hand on her friend's back and pushed her towards the doorway. Once outside, she said, 'I don't mind yer being chief cook and bottle washer most of the time, girl, but it's beginning to get boring. So from now on, instead of standing like a stuffed dummy, I'd like to be brought into the conversation now and again, if yer don't mind.'

'Well, I like that!' Molly's eyebrows nearly touched her hairline. 'I doubt if I spoke more than about sixty words in there, and yer could have joined in any time yer wanted, no one was stopping yer. And in the café yer were too busy filling yer face to be interested in saying anything of interest.'

'Don't be getting on yer high horse, girl, 'cos yer'll fall off one of these days. I just pass a comment, as yer would, and before I know it I'm getting told off and insulted. I think yer got out of bed on the wrong side this morning.'

'No, sunshine, I think it's you what's losing yer sense of humour. I was going to say be my guest if yer want to do the talking, but I've

249

just had second thoughts. Come on, and I'll tell yer why while we're walking.' Arm in arm they crossed the cobbled street and stood at the bottom of Wordsworth Street. 'If this Mrs Mitchell is Phil's grandmother, we're going to have to be very careful what we say. For all we know, she might not have known the girl her son was going to marry was pregnant.'

'D'yer mean Fanny Bradley, girl?'

Molly nodded. 'She married Tom Bradley very quickly so people would think the baby was his, then they left the area. In that case, this is going to be a big shock to a woman who must be getting on in years. She might not believe us and send us packing. After all, it's over twenty-two years since her son was killed, and us talking about it is going to bring back all the heartache.'

'She might be upset, that would only be natural, but I think in the end she'll thank us for it. But because you can talk better than me, and because I might put me foot in it, I won't open me mouth unless yer ask me to.'

'Right, let's get going before I talk meself out of it. The woman said halfway up on the right-hand side, so we'll start there.'

They didn't count the houses, but when they seemed to be halfway, Molly came to a halt. 'I'm shaking like a leaf, sunshine, and I feel like turning tail and running like hell. But I know I'd regret it for the rest of me life so I'm going to knock on this door.'

A woman about the same age as Molly answered the door. She was pleasantly plump with a round happy face. She eyed the two women, then smiled. 'Can I help yer?'

'We're looking for a Mrs Mitchell, Maggie Mitchell.'

The woman jerked her head. 'Next door, love. And I know she's in 'cos I've just come back from the shops with her.'

'Thank you.' Molly felt like hugging the woman but contented herself with giving a wide smile. 'We'll give her a knock. Ta-ra.'

After knocking on the next door, Molly noted the spotlessly clean windows and net curtains, the highly polished window sill and white step. Then the door opened and Molly felt tongue-tied. Her mouth as dry as sandpaper, she couldn't get her jaw to work. It was Nellie who asked, 'Mrs Mitchell?'

'Yes, that's me. What d'yer want?'

It was Nellie's sharp dig in the ribs that brought Molly's brain to life. 'You don't know us, Mrs Mitchell, but we know something that might interest yer and would be grateful if yer'd spare us a few minutes of yer time?'

Maggie Mitchell was in her late-sixties but the two tragedies in her life had aged her. Snow white hair sat above a face that was heavily lined, and pale blue eyes told of a weariness she couldn't escape from, even in sleep. 'If ye're selling something, or collecting for the church, I'm afraid I don't have the time or the money to talk to yer. So I'll bid yer goodbye.'

The door was half closed when Molly stuck her foot out. 'Mrs Mitchell, we know yer had a son called Bob who was killed in an accident a few weeks before he was to be married. What we have to tell yer is in connection with that.'

Now the door was fully open, but there was suspicion in the tired eyes. 'That was a long time ago and I cried all my tears then. I don't think yer can tell me anything I don't know.'

'I think we can, Mrs Mitchell, and I think it's something that will make yer happy. Just give us a few minutes of yer time, and if ye're not interested, we'll leave.'

'Come in, then.'

The tiny hallway led into a room that was neat and tidy, with furniture and hearth shining. 'Yer keep yer house nice, Mrs Mitchell,' Molly said, 'it's a credit to yer.'

The curt nod told them she wanted to hear what they'd got to say and would they get it over with quickly? 'Sit down please.' Mrs Mitchell crossed the room to her rocking chair and began to rock slowly. 'Now say what yer have to.'

Molly licked her lips. Where was she going to find words that wouldn't upset this woman? Then she felt a hand on her arm and Nellie said, 'Go on, girl, get it over with.'

After taking a deep breath, Molly said, 'I know this is going to be painful for yer, Mrs Mitchell, but I'm hoping there'll be a light at the end of a dark tunnel for yer.'

The chair stopped rocking and the woman leaned forward. 'Ye're not fortune tellers, are yer? If yer are, yer can get out of my house quick, for I'll have none of that.'

'Good heavens, we're not fortune tellers! Like yerself I can't abide them. No, I'll start at the beginning and tell yer what we know.' After taking another deep breath, Molly continued. 'When yer son Bob was killed he was a few weeks off getting married to a girl called Frances, wasn't he? A girl he'd been courting for a few years?'

'That girl's name is never mentioned in our family. Not after what she did. My son thought the world of her, but she couldn't have thought much of him 'cos a month after the funeral she married someone else.

We haven't seen sight nor life of her since. Not that we'd want to after what she did.'

'Yer didn't know that when yer son died, she was pregnant?'

'What! Yer mean she'd been carrying on with someone behind his back?' There was a short pause then Mrs Mitchell said, 'No, she couldn't have, they saw each other every night, she was never away from our house.'

'She was pregnant with yer son's child, Mrs Mitchell, that's why she got married so quick to the first man who asked her.'

'I don't believe yer! And if yer've come here thinking I'll fall for that, then yer must be crazy, the pair of yer. And I'll ask yer to leave my house now, please.'

'Don't yer want to know about yer grandson?' Molly asked quietly. 'From the picture he's got of his dad, he's the spitting image of him. His name's Phil, and he's married to my daughter. He doesn't know Nellie and I are here, we're doing this off our own bat because he deserves some happiness in his life. And he and my daughter are expecting a baby in a few months so it would be wonderful if he had a member of his family at the christening.'

Maggie Mitchell sat back in her chair, feeling as though all the breath had left her body. There was no doubt in her mind that Molly was telling the truth. The woman had an open, honest face and the emotion in her voice was real. 'I need a drink,' Maggie gasped.

Nellie sprang from her seat. 'I'll put the kettle on, girl, you stay where yer are. I'll find the tea caddy and things so don't be worrying. You just listen to what me mate's got to say, and yer can believe every word out of her mouth.'

'What about the man Frances married, aren't they his family now?'

'She married a man called Tom Bradley, the biggest rotter yer could ever meet. She had three children to him, one boy and two girls. They were the lowest of the low and tried to get Phil into their way of life, which was stealing everything they could get their hands on. Even his mother didn't stick up for him, she tried to get him to go out stealing with his stepfather and stepbrother. Phil hated them, and their way of life, and was so ashamed but he had nowhere to go and was forced to live with them. All this was before we knew him.' Molly then went on to tell how the Bradleys came to live in their street and how they broke into their neighbours' houses and stole from them. How Doreen had met Phil at a dance and had fallen head over heels for him. And how devastated she was when she found out he was a Bradley.

Nellie came in with a cup of steaming tea. 'Here yer are, girl, get

252

that down yer and yer'll feel better.' She gave a cheeky grin. 'My mate was that nervous she forgot her manners. She's Molly Bennett and I'm Nellie McDonough.'

'Ye're not letting me drink on me own, are yer?'

'Not likely! I've poured two cups out for me and me mate.'

'There's some biscuits in a tin in the larder.'

Nellie's smile was from ear to ear. 'Ye're a woman after me own heart.'

'Help yerself.' Then Maggie's eyes went back to Molly. 'I can't take it in that I have a grandson. I want to know everything so I can tell the rest of the family tonight. It'll be as big a shock to them as it has been for me. But the nicest shock I've had in twenty years.'

'Well, things came to a head when Phil was coming home from work one night. He always used the entries, never the front door because he was so ashamed of the family and the dirty state of the house. Anyway, he was walking up the entry when he saw his stepbrother, Brian, climbing over an old lady's yard wall intending to break in. He pulled the lad back and a fight broke out between the two of them. The neighbours heard and came out – that's when Doreen found out Phil was a Bradley. It broke her heart and she would have nothing to do with him for a long time after that. Anyway, Brian had been given a good hiding by Phil, and the old lady whose house was going to be burgled said Phil shouldn't go home because Tom Bradley would kill him. Against the advice of all the neighbours, she invited him to stay there the night, and that's been his home ever since, except when he was in the army. Her name is Miss Victoria Clegg, and they idolise each other. She was the only person who had ever shown him love, and he was the son she'd never had. When our Doreen and Phil got married in July, they made their home with her.'

'He was in the army?'

'Yes, sunshine, he joined up. The Bradleys were causing trouble for him, always hanging around and demanding money. He was afraid that as long as he was there, Miss Clegg was in danger. Eventually the neighbours forced the Bradleys out, Phil fought in the war and was discharged early because he'd been wounded. He's happier now than he's ever been, with a wife he loves and the elderly woman who gave him a home when he was destitute.'

'How did yer find out about us?'

'Because at that point his mother did the only decent thing she'd ever done for him. She met him outside his works one day, just before he left for the army and told him the whole story and gave him the

253

photograph that he treasures. It's of her with your son when they were on a day out. Phil is the spitting image of his real dad. He has no idea me and Nellie are trying to find you, I didn't want to tell him and then have to disappoint him if we failed. It was when we found out my daughter was expecting a baby, and realised he'd have no one of his own at the christening, that we decided to move heaven and earth to find yer. He's a fine lad. I love him dearly, and he's a grandson yer can be proud of.'

Maggie wiped away a tear. 'But how did yer find out where I lived?'

Molly's eyes slid sideways to Nellie. 'You tell her, sunshine.'

'We did some detective work. Yer see, my mate thought she remembered Phil mentioning Bullen's Terrace, but we couldn't ask him or we'd have given the game away. So that's where we started.'

Molly took up the tale. 'We asked a few of yer old neighbours but they had no idea where yer'd moved to. They spoke very highly of yer, though. Then we tried the landlord of the George on the corner. He had a hunch yer'd moved into one of the streets that are named after poets. So down we came and made enquiries in yer corner shop. From what the shopkeeper there told us, we ended up knocking next door. It's all a bit complicated, sunshine, but we made it, thank God, and we found yer.' She looked down at her clasped hands for a few seconds then asked, 'Would yer rather we hadn't?'

'Oh, no! I'm sorry if I don't seem to be happy or excited, but it's too much for me to take in! I'll probably cry me eyes out and jump for joy when I'm on me own. Yer see, never a day goes by that I don't think of my son – he was such a wonderful person. I named him after his dad, and he always got Bobby so we'd know the difference. Neither of them are ever far from my mind and my heart.' Maggie lifted the corner of her floral apron and wiped her eyes. 'But I've got a good family and I've a lot to be thankful for.'

'How many children d'yer have, Mrs Mitchell?' Molly asked, her heart going out to the woman. If she lost one of her own children she didn't think she'd ever get over it.

'Two sons, one daughter and five grandchildren. Jim's the eldest, he's forty-nine and his wife's Elsie. They've got two children, both grown-up and working. They live in Percy Street.'

'Ooh, er, we came down Percy Street,' Nellie said. 'Fancy that!'

'The other son, Wally, lives in the next street with his wife Edna and their two children. And the youngest is Beth. She and her husband live with me. They've got a daughter and she goes to work as well. I'm very lucky having my daughter live with me, and the two lads never fail to call on their way home from work.'

'So Phil's got a big family to get to know?'

Maggie leaned forward and didn't try to stem her flood of tears. Her voice thick with emotion, she said, 'They'll be so happy when I tell them, and they'll want to meet him soon. Our own flesh and blood, and I can't wait to hold him. When can I meet him?'

'I'll tell him and Doreen tonight,' Molly promised. 'This is going to come as a shock to Phil, but a very happy one. I'll make arrangements for him and Doreen to come down one night, and you can put yer family in the picture. Me and Nellie will call on yer in the morning and tell yer when they're coming.' She glanced at her friend who had been listening intently, and covered her hand. 'My best mate, Nellie McDonough, can take a lot of the credit for us being here today. She's plagued the life out of me. If she'd had her way, we'd have been tramping through the snow in January trying to find yer.'

'Yer both have my sincere gratitude. And I thank you and yer neighbours for taking care of my grandson. I think we'll be seeing a lot of each other. At least, I hope so.'

'I think I can safely say there's no doubt about that, Mrs Mitchell.'

'Call me Maggie, all my friends do.'

Molly gave Nellie a nudge. 'Come on, sunshine, we'd better be making tracks.' She got to her feet and walked to the rocking chair. 'It's been my pleasure to meet yer, Maggie, and we'll give yer a knock about eleven in the morning.' She planted a kiss on the woman's upturned face. 'You and yer family are going to make such a difference to Phil's life, and that makes me very happy.'

'Me too!' Nellie wasn't going to be left out. 'Ye're going to make a smashing grandma for a smashing lad. We'll see yer tomorrow, ta-ra for now.'

Maggie followed them to the door. 'I'm going to sit in the quiet now and go over it all in me mind. I never dreamt when I got out of bed this morning that it was going to be one of the best days of me life.'

Chapter 19

Even though Molly was dying to share her news with the family, and her nerves were as taut as a violin string, she did her best to act as normal as possible. But her bright eyes and quick, jerky movements weren't lost on Jack. 'What have you and Nellie been up to today? Yer look as though yer've lost sixpence and found half a crown.'

Molly feigned surprise. 'I don't look any different than usual, ye're imagining things. What could me and Nellie get up to but shopping and housework?' God forgive me for that necessary lie, she prayed silently. But Phil has to be told the news before anyone else, even my own husband.

Tommy grinned. 'Anyone listening to yer, Mam, would think yer lead a dull life. But life can't be dull when ye're with Auntie Nellie.'

'No, ye're right there, sunshine, there's never a dull moment. But that doesn't mean every moment is filled with excitement either. Unless yer call cadging a ham shank off Tony exciting, or being early enough at Hanley's to get fresh bread.'

'It's not like you to complain about yer lot in life, love,' Jack said. 'Yer always look very contented and satisfied.'

'That's because I am, soft lad. And I didn't start this conversation off, it was you! I'm fine, happy with me lot in life. I've got the best family and friends in the world, and I know how lucky I am. Now, if that satisfies yer, get on with yer dinner so I can wash up and then nip over to Doreen's to check on her state of health.'

'She's all right, Mam,' Ruthie said, her legs swinging as usual. 'I called in from school before I came home. Her and Miss Clegg were having tea and biscuits.'

'Good for her, she needs to rest during the day. But I still want to see her for meself so I'm going over when I've cleared away and tidied up.'

'I'm going to Bella's, Mam, remember?' Ruthie had something else on her mind but didn't know how to get the words out or whether this was the right time. 'She's going to the first house pictures on

257

Saturday night with her mam and dad. They said I could go with them but I had to ask you first.'

'It's a wonder Mary Watson isn't sick of the sight of yer, yer spend more time in there than yer do in yer own house.'

'I said that to Mrs Watson, but she said it's her way of saying thanks for asking Bella to all the parties we have. So can I go to the pictures with them?'

'As long as Mary will let yer pay for yerself. I'll give yer half the money and yer can get around yer dad for the other half.'

They seemed to be taking ages over their meal and Molly felt like telling them to hurry. But it was no different from any other night, except that she couldn't wait for them to go out so she could slip over the road. She didn't think she could hold it in much longer. Then Tommy laid down his knife and fork and pushed his plate away. 'I was ready for that, Mam, and I really enjoyed it. You stay where yer are and I'll see to the dishes.'

Molly shook her head. 'Thanks for offering, sunshine, but I'll do them. Yer've done a full day's work as it is, yer've done yer whack. Get yerself washed while the sink's not in use.'

'I'll help yer, Mam.' Ruthie was feeling very benevolent now she'd been given permission to go to the flicks on Saturday. Maureen O'Sullivan was on and she was the girl's very favourite film star. 'You wash, I'll dry, and me dad can put the tablecloth away.'

'There's no need, sunshine, I can have it done in half the time by meself. So finish that potato and then go and see yer mate.'

When both Tommy and Ruthie had left, Jack raised his brows at his wife. 'Yer can't fool me, love, I've known yer too long. There's something on yer mind, it's sticking out a mile, so come on, own up, what is it?'

Molly put the dirty plates back on the table and leaned over to face her husband. 'I should have known I wouldn't get away with it, yer know me too well. And, yes, ye're right, there is something on me mind. But I'm not going to tell yer yet, not for about half an hour. It's nothing for yer to worry about. In fact, yer'll be delighted when yer know.'

Jack watched his wife pick up the plates and walk towards the kitchen door. 'Hey, Missus, yer can't just leave me up in the air! What's going on?'

'Half an hour's not long to wait, love, and when yer know what it is, yer'll understand why I couldn't tell yer before. Yer could do me a favour while I'm washing the dishes, though. Yer could nip over the road and ask Doreen and Phil to come over. Tell them to give me twenty minutes, to see to the dishes and tidy around.'

'What d'yer want them for?'

'Yer'll find out when they come.'

'But they're bound to ask what yer want them for.' Jack looked puzzled. 'What's the big mystery?'

'Jack, yer'll find out soon enough. It isn't a mystery, it's something wonderful.'

'Well, why aren't yer asking Jill and Steve down? And why didn't yer tell us when Tommy and Ruthie were in?'

'Because it doesn't concern them, that's why.'

He took his coat down from the peg and slipped his arms into the sleeves. 'I dunno, yer live with a woman for nearly twenty-five years and still can't get to the bottom of her. If yer were a man, yer wouldn't be able to keep something to yerself like this. Men aren't as melodramatic as you women.'

'Will yer get going, sunshine, or it'll be time for bed.'

'I may as well stay over there and come back with them. It's not very often I get to see Miss Clegg. And if they ask me what yer want them for, I'm just going to shrug me shoulders and pretend I haven't got a clue. Which I haven't.'

Molly moved like greased lightning. When she heard Jack's key in the door, the dishes were away and the living room tidy.

Doreen came in first and walked into her mother's outstretched arms. 'Dad said yer wanted to see us. I hope it's something nice, I like surprises.'

'Hi-ya, Mrs B.' Phil kissed her cheek. 'Don't tell me yer want to ask for yer daughter back? If that's it, ye're out of luck, I wouldn't part with her for all the money in the world.'

'I know I'd be wasting me breath, sunshine, 'cos she's more than happy where she is. No, what I wanted to see yer for is very important. So sit yerselves down and I'll tell yer a story. Doreen, you sit in my chair, it'll be more comfortable for yer.'

Her daughter shook her head. If it was something important, she wanted to be near her husband. 'I'll sit at the table with Phil.'

'We'll all sit at the table,' Jack said, his eyes going to the packet of Woodbines he'd left on the mantelpiece. He'd forgotten to take them with him and he was dying for a cigarette. Molly hadn't given him time to have his after-dinner smoke and he was gasping.

She grinned. 'Yer've got ten seconds to get them and light one up.'

'Blimey!' Jack said, hopping to it. 'It must be important.'

Molly waited until the first puff of smoke swirled its way upward, then she turned her eyes to Phil. He was holding Doreen's hand and stroking the soft skin with his thumb. If ever a couple were made for each other, it was these two. 'Phil, this is going to come as a shock, and it might bring back some painful memories, but if yer bear with me I can promise the story has a happy ending.'

'Ah, ay, Mam, I hope ye're not going to drag up things we'd rather forget?' Doreen squeezed Phil's hand. 'Because I can't see how that would have a happy ending.'

'Let yer mam say what she has to, sweetheart, she would only ever do what is best for us. You go ahead, Mrs B.'

A voice in Molly's head told her to get right to the point, so she did. 'Remember the day yer mother met you outside work and told yer all about yer real father? When she told yer his name and gave yer the photograph?' Molly looked down at the table so she wouldn't see the expression of hurt on Phil's face. She would do anything rather than hurt him, but she had to start at the beginning to make sense of what she and Nellie had done. 'Well, around that time, my mate Nellie said we should turn detective and try and trace any of yer dad's family. Anyway, you went into the army and as time went by we forgot about it 'cos we really didn't have anything to go on. All we had was yer dad's name and I thought yer'd mentioned Bullen's Terrace in Bootle.' Molly stopped to draw breath. 'It was when we found out Doreen was expecting a baby that Nellie mentioned it again. I won't go into any of the details now, we can do that later, but we set out today, Phil, with real determination, and I'm happy to say we found Mrs Mitchell, yer grandma.'

His face drained of colour. 'Yer found out where she lives?'

'We did more than that, sunshine, we went to her house and had a cup of tea with her!'

Tears welled up in Phil's eyes, Doreen had a hand to her mouth and Jack had let his cigarette burn down to his fingers. 'Yer saw my grandma?' The lad's voice was thick with emotion. 'Yer mean, yer spoke to her?'

Molly nodded. 'She didn't know about yer mam being pregnant, so she didn't know she had a grandson. And yer've got two uncles, an auntie and five cousins!'

Phil had been biting on the inside of his mouth to keep the tears back because grown men weren't supposed to cry but this news was something he'd dreamed of for years. Only he'd never expected those

260

dreams to come true. So with tears rolling down his cheeks, he asked, 'Does she want to see me?'

'She can't wait, sunshine. She's getting all the family together tonight, to tell them. None of them had any idea yer existed, yer mam never told them. And I'll tell yer what, yer'll love your grandma 'cos she's a real sweetheart.'

Doreen put her arms around her husband's neck and rained kisses on his tear-stained face. 'Don't cry, love, or yer'll make me cry.'

He wiped his cheeks and sniffed. 'I've shed some tears in me life, mostly because I'd been battered by Tom Bradley or hurt when he kept throwing it up at me that I wasn't his child. But I'm happy to be shedding these tears and I don't care who knows.' He took his wife's arms from his neck, stood up and went around the table to Molly. 'Yer've always been like a mother to me, Mrs B, and I've loved yer for it. But never as much as I love yer right this minute.'

Molly got to her feet and held her arms wide. 'Come here, yer daft ha'porth, and give us a kiss. Then yer can sit down and I'll go through a day in the life of the Bennett and McDonough Detective Agency. Or maybe I'll make a cup of tea first, I think we could all do with a drink.'

Jack, full of pride and admiration for his wife, waved her down. 'I'll make the tea, you've done enough. And if we had a bottle of something in, I'd lift my glass in a toast to yer. Miracle worker and mender of hearts.'

'I didn't do it on me own, love, and I don't deserve all the praise. Nellie did as much as me and I hope yer'll all remember that when yer see her. She's the one what spurred me on. I'd still be thinking about it if it wasn't for her. And she encourages yer by being so funny. On the way home she said we were better detectives than Charlie Chan.'

'I won't forget her, Mrs B,' Phil said. 'I'll never forget her. If she was here now I'd kiss and hug her to death.'

'Oh, and wouldn't she love that! She'd tell all the shopkeepers, and anyone else she could get hold of, that yer were after her voluptuous body.' The smile left Molly's face as she thought of her best mate. 'She'll be sitting at home now on pins, driving herself mad 'cos she doesn't know what's going on in here.'

'Well, there's no need for that!' Jack said. 'There's no reason why she can't be here, it's the least she deserves. So while I'm giving yer mam a hand to make a pot of tea, Doreen, why don't yer slip to Nellie's and invite her down?'

261

'I think it would be nice if the whole family were here,' Molly said. 'So I'll make the tea, love, while you give Nellie a knock and then carry on to pick up Jill and Steve. And we can't leave Tommy and Rosie out.'

'What am I supposed to tell them?'

'Just tell them it's a family gathering, there's no need to go into details. But don't stand gabbing to them or the night'll be over before we know it.' After Jack had left, Molly gave Phil a rueful smile. 'I'll tell Ruthie when she comes in, and I'll tell her in me own way. Yer see, although she knows Tom Bradley wasn't yer real father, that yer dad had been killed in an accident, I didn't go into the details or the ins and outs with her. She's a bit young yet to be told about the birds and bees. So if yer ever hear me telling a little fib, that's the reason.' She rubbed her hands together. 'And now to make that pot of tea.'

Once again the Bennett family were all together, this time to hear something that had the women reaching for their hankies. As the story had progressed, they were filled with admiration for the determination shown by the two friends. And of course they were overjoyed for Phil. They made a great fuss over Nellie, too. She was the centre of attention and lapping it up. Sitting on the carver with her chubby elbows resting on the arms, and looking so proud of herself, all she needed to complete the picture was a crown on her head. 'Ay, girl, tell them about the café, yer left that out.'

'Because it had no bearing on what we were discussing,' Molly said. 'Your appetite and rumbling tummy were side issues.'

Nellie grinned. 'When we go down tomorrow I'm going to have another side issue 'cos it was very tasty. And it'll be even tastier tomorrow when it's your turn to pay.'

'Ye're in for a nasty shock, sunshine, 'cos I'm not forking out for a scone for yer. I don't mind paying for the bacon butties 'cos that's our lunch, but I draw the line at scones. They're a luxury.' Molly happened to turn her head and noticed Doreen whispering in her husband's ear. 'Ay, what's going on? We'll have no secrets in this house, not tonight, anyway.'

'Phil's got something he wants to tell yer, Mam.' Doreen squeezed his hand. 'Go on, love, tell them.'

His face was pale, stomach in a knot. Trying to take in the enormity of what his mother-in-law and her friend had brought about had been too much for Phil and he felt physically sick. Tomorrow he'd be jumping for joy and looking forward to taking his wife to meet his grandma and the rest of the family. But right now he just wanted to go back over the road, share his happiness with Aunt Vicky, then hold his wife close and quietly contemplate the difference there'd be in their lives, and in the life of the baby she was carrying. But first he must do as she asked.

'When me and Doreen got married it was the happiest day of me life, a dream come true. But there was one thing which marred the day for me, and that was having to give her the name of Bradley. She said she didn't mind, didn't care about the name as long as we became man and wife. It preyed on my mind, though, because I had cause, as yer all know, to hate that name.

'So one day I took an hour off work and went to see a solicitor in Castle Street. I'd heard about people having their name changed by deed poll, but I didn't know how to go about it or what it entailed. Anyway, the solicitor explained everything to me, charged me five pound and set the wheels in motion for our name to be changed from Bradley to Mitchell. That was four months ago and it hasn't come through yet, but we're hoping it will be before our baby is born. I don't want any child of mine to bear Tom Bradley's name. The solicitor is doing his best to speed up the process so we're keeping our fingers crossed. We didn't tell yer 'cos we wanted it to be a surprise, but nothing could beat the surprise you and Mrs Mac have given us today.'

After a few seconds of shocked silence, everyone started talking at once, Jill and Rosie claimed Doreen, while Phil joined the men, and soon there was a hubbub of conversation, with each one wanting to add their views. And looking on, with a heart threatening to burst with happiness, was Molly. There was nothing in the world that pleased her as much as seeing the closeness of her family, and the smiles on their faces.

She was standing at the side of Nellie's chair. The two women watched and listened. 'We did well today, sunshine, made a lot of people very happy.'

Nellie nodded. 'Yeah, not a bad day's work, girl! I don't half enjoy this detective stuff. I wonder what the next case will be for the Bennett and McDonough Detective Agency?'

Molly closed the door behind her and stepped down right into the path of Paul McDonough. 'I'm sorry, sunshine, did I step on yer foot?'

'No, yer missed by a quarter of an inch.' His brown eyes twinkled. 'I've got an eye for measurements, yer see, I'm never more than a yard out. Anyway, where are yer off to?'

'I'm sitting with Miss Clegg while Doreen and Phil go out. I suppose yer mam told yer what we got up to yesterday?'

'Yeah, she did, and I think yer did a brilliant job. So Phil's off to meet his family for the first time, eh?'

Molly nodded. 'I'm all excited so I don't know how he must fccl. And Doreen was a bag of nerves at dinnertime. God knows what she's like by now.' She raised her brows. 'Where are you going on yer lonesome?'

'Me and Phoebe were supposed to be going to Blair Hall, but Auntie Ellen said she'd come home full of cold and had taken herself off to bed. So I'm going on me own, seeing as there's nothing else to do. I don't fancy staying in all night.' Again the deep brown eyes twinkled. 'I hate playing cards with me mam, she cheats.'

'Is Lily out with Archie?'

'Yeah, they've gone to Blair Hall, too. I was running late and said me and Phoebe would meet them there. I didn't know she was going to be sick.'

'She did the right thing by going to bed, it's the best way to get rid of a cold. And I know yer won't be short of dancing partners, so enjoy yerself.'

'I'll see yer, Mrs B. Ta-ra.' Paul was whistling as he walked down the street. He didn't really fancy going on his own to a dance now, he was used to dancing with Phoebe. But he'd promised Lily and Archie and he didn't want to let them down. Besides, as he'd said, he didn't fancy staying in all night.

When Paul opened the door of the dance hall he was met by the strains of a slow foxtrot. His eyes went around the couples on the floor seeking sight of his sister and her boyfriend, and he nodded when he caught their attention. He was startled when a hand took hold of his arm and a voice said, 'Hello, Paul.'

He turned his head to see Joanne Mowbray standing beside him. He hadn't seen much of her since the New Year and was surprised to find her looking up at him now. 'I've never seen yer here before, is this yer first time?'

Lies came easily to Joanne, particularly if she wanted something badly. 'I've been once or twice, that's all. Me mate from work was supposed to meet me here, but there's no sign of her yet.' She pouted. 'I bet she turns up when it's time to go home.'

'Don't worry, she'll get here.' Paul noticed a girl standing on the edge of the dance floor. He'd danced with her many times before he

264

started going out with Phoebe. 'D'yer mind if I leave yer, I've spotted an old dancing partner?'

'I can dance, yer know.' Joanne laid a restraining hand on his arm. 'My favourite dance is a slow foxtrot.'

Paul was about to make an excuse when he saw a bloke walking on to the dance floor with his old dancing partner. 'Okay, then, but I hope yer really can dance.'

'Yer'll never know if yer don't try.'

It turned out that Joanne wasn't a bad little dancer at all. She was smooth and could match all his steps. The only thing that put him off was the look Lily gave him when she danced by with Archie. It was a look which asked him what the hell was going on. Where was Phoebe and what was he doing with their hard-faced neighbour?

When the dance finished, Paul thanked the girl and excused himself. 'I'll have to join my sister and her friend.'

'What's going on?' Lily asked. 'Where's Phoebe?'

'In bed with a heavy cold. Her mam said her eyes and nose were running and she had a temperature.'

'Yer didn't come with that brazen article, did yer?'

'Hey, hold yer horses, Sis! I didn't even know she came here. I'd just come through the door and was looking around for you two, when the next thing I know she was standing beside me. She said she was meeting a friend from work here, but so far there's no sign of her. Then she asked me to dance and I could hardly tell her to take a running jump.' Paul rolled his eyes at Archie. 'I haven't spoken above six words to the girl since New Year's Eve!'

'I haven't opened me mouth, mate,' Archie said, dark hair slicked back and white teeth gleaming. 'And I've never ever spoken to the girl in me life, but from the sound of things I'd say she's a bit forward.'

If they could have read Joanne's mind at that moment, they would have said crafty and calculating were far more suitable words to describe her. She'd taken herself off to the ladies' room, her plan of action being to take things slowly. So far she'd been lucky in guessing the right dance hall, they could have chosen to go to Barlow's Lane or the Aintree Institute. And Paul didn't have his girlfriend with him which was more than she could have hoped for.

As she looked into the spotted mirror on the wall, Joanne patted her nose with a powder puff before applying fresh bright red lipstick. She might never have another chance to get Paul on his own again, but if she made a blunder and came on too quick, she'd never get a chance anyway. Particularly if that sister of his had her way. She hadn't half thrown daggers Joanne's way when she saw who her brother was dancing with. So as she snapped her handbag shut, she muttered under her breath, 'Just take it nice and easy. Don't let him see that ye're interested.'

It was when the interval came that she set her plan into action. With a shy look on her face, she approached the trio with the lies ready on her tongue. 'Me mate didn't turn up after all and I don't know anyone here. I feel like a lemon standing on me own so would yer mind very much if I stand with yer?'

Paul decided to keep out of it. 'Yer'll have to ask me sister, I'm off to the gents'.'

Lily felt like throttling him. Fancy dropping her in it like that! She'd sound childish and churlish if she told the girl they didn't want her company. 'Please yerself. But once the dancing starts we'll be up for every dance.'

'I don't mind being on me own when the dancing starts 'cos I've been getting asked up for dances. It's just while the interval is on and everybody seems to have someone to talk to. I won't make a nuisance of meself.' And she didn't. She was quiet and well behaved, only speaking when she was brought into the conversation.

Lily wouldn't have admitted to being surprised, though, she still thought the girl was up to something. Probably had her eye on Paul. Well, she'd be wasting her time if that was the case, he seemed to be quite settled with Phoebe.

When the music started up, Joanne excused herself. 'I'm going to comb me hair now, but thanks for letting me stand with yer.' She smiled and turned to weave her way through the crowd of boys who hadn't made up their mind who to ask for a dance, and girls who were waiting and hoping their mates weren't asked up before them. There was nothing worse than seeing a self-satisfied smirk on your friend's face when she was asked up and you were left swinging on yer own, trying to look as though you couldn't care less.

Joanne came back from the toilets and stood near a group of girls. She was asked up for several dances and pretended she didn't see Paul as he waltzed by with a different girl in his arms for every dance. One of the blokes who asked her up wanted to make a date with her, but she told him she already had a boyfriend who wasn't with her tonight because he did shift work. The boy, who was a good dancer and quite good-looking, wasn't put off by this. 'Ye're not old enough to be courting serious so what harm would it do if yer came out with me one night? We could go to the flicks or anywhere yer want.'

Because he was so presentable, Joanne kept her options open with more lies. 'Me boyfriend's on afternoon shift this week and nights next week. So I could meet yer here next week, if yer like?'

'Yeah, that would be great! Me name's Sam, by the way. What's yours?'

'Joanne.'

'That's a nice name,' he said, twirling her around, 'it suits yer. Can I take yer home?'

'Not tonight, I'm going with some friends who live in the same street as me. Perhaps next week.'

When the last waltz was announced, Joanne left the hall quickly before anyone asked her up. She collected her coat from the cloakroom, slipped her arms into the sleeves but didn't fasten the buttons up. Then she lay in wait. As Lily and Archie came through the door followed by Paul, she moved into their path, fastening the buttons as though she'd just put the coat on. 'Oh, I may as well walk to the bus stop with yer. A bloke asked if he could take me home but I'd never met him before so I refused. Yer can't always tell what people are like when yer first meet them. They could act as nice as pie outside but be horrible inside.'

'Yer'll be all right coming with us,' Archie said. 'Safer, anyway.'

Paul had nothing to say. He had no objection to the girl tagging on, she'd be safer than being on her own this time of night, but he knew Phoebe wouldn't see it that way. So best to keep his mouth shut and then he couldn't get into trouble. Or so he thought.

'It's half-past eleven, Victoria, I think yer should go to bed,' Molly said. 'I thought they'd have been in by now but they have got a lot of years to make up. I don't mind if they don't come in until the early hours but it's taking you all yer time to keep yer eyes open.'

'I want to hear all their news, Molly, I couldn't sleep if I went to bed. And I bet they won't sleep a wink, their heads will be swimming.'

'Yeah, it's a pity it's not the weekend and Phil could have a lie-in. Still, we can't always have everything tailor-made for us.' She'd just finished speaking when there was a tap on the window. 'This'll be them,' she said, hurrying to the door, 'I can't wait to hear how they got on.'

'Wonderful,' Phil said, having heard his mother-in-law's words. 'Me and Doreen decided on the way home that wonderful was the best word to describe tonight.' He went straight over to his Aunt Vicky and took her hand. 'They can't wait to meet you, to thank yer for taking me in and giving me a home.'

'Mam, Phil's the spitting image of his two uncles.' Doreen threw her coat over the arm of the couch. 'But it was sad at first, 'cos his grandma started crying when she saw him. She said it was as though her son had come back to life. They all said the resemblance was really remarkable. Phil doesn't only look like his dad, but his voice and laughter are the same, and his expressions and the way he walks.'

'I know it's a daft question, son, but I gather they made yer welcome?'

'Mrs B. I feel as though I'm walking on air. To have found a whole family when I've spent most of me life on me own . . . No one cared a toss for me or showed me affection, until Aunt Vicky came to my rescue, and then you and all yer family. And I can't leave the McDonoughs or the Corkhills out, they've shown me nothing but kindness and friendship.'

'And when are yer seeing them all again?'

Phil shook his head as though bewildered. 'Yer've no idea how good it feels to be able to say these words. Me grandma's coming on Sunday afternoon, with me Auntie Beth and her husband Noel. They're going to take it in turns to come, otherwise they'd never all get in, and anyway it would be too much for Aunt Vicky.'

The Westminster chiming clock on the sideboard struck the midnight hour and Molly reached for her coat. 'I'll come over in the morning and Doreen can take her time telling me and Victoria every little detail. But right now I'll have to get home, Jack will be waiting up for me.' She kissed the old lady first, then Phil. 'Try and get some sleep or yer'll be good for nothing in the morning.' Her daughter came in for a special hug and kiss, with the words, 'You have an extra hour in bed, young lady, yer need plenty of rest.'

'Mam, meeting Phil's family tonight did me more good than sleep. It was the best tonic I could have. But I'll be a good girl and have an extra hour in bed, just to please you.'

Molly opened the front door and called, 'Goodnight and God bless.' Then she quickly crossed the cobbled street and pulled a face when she saw a light on in her living room. Poor Jack, he'd never get up in the morning. She'd better make sure the alarm clock was set or they'd be going out to work without any breakfast. And men needed something inside them to start the day. As she slipped the key in the lock, she reminded herself it was tomorrow already.

Chapter 20

Phoebe came down next morning with eyes and nose red from constant wiping. There were beads of perspiration on her forehead which told of a temperature.

'Yer can't go to work like that,' Ellen said. 'Ye're still full of it.'

'I'll be all right when I've had me breakfast. I'd rather work it off than be stuck in bed for another day.'

'Being stuck in bed for another day would probably do the trick, love. A Beecham's every four hours and I'm sure yer'd feel much better tomorrow. Besides, yer workmates wouldn't thank yer for going in and spreading yer germs around.'

'Do as me mam says, Phoebe,' Gordon said, to nods from Dorothy and Peter. 'Yer look like death warmed up.'

'Thanks, that's cheered me up no end.' But she did feel lousy and was sensible enough to know that bed was the best place for her. 'I think I'd better do as yer say, Mam, but there's no powders left, I emptied the box last night.'

'I'll nip to the corner shop before I go to work, and ask Nellie to pass the message on to Paul that yer won't be going out tonight. Now, up to bed with yer and I'll bring yer a cup of tea and a round of toast.'

'I'll have the tea, Mam, but I'm not hungry.'

'Hungry or not, yer've got to eat. Otherwise yer'll be as weak as a kitten and not fit to go to work tomorrow. Now hurry up while the bed's still warm.'

After seeing the other three children off, Ellen dashed to the corner shop. Maisie served her straight away, knowing she'd be due at work soon, and with the Beecham's came a little advice. 'Tell her to drink loads of liquids, it'll keep her chest clear of phlegm.'

'Will do, Maisie, thanks.' Ellen covered the ground quickly. It was at times like this she wished she didn't have a job. Not that she didn't enjoy working in the butcher's, she did. Tony was a marvellous boss and easy to get on with. But as a mother, she felt her place was with her children when they were sick.

As soon as she got home, Ellen mixed one of the powders and took it up to Phoebe. 'Drink that right away, then I'll bring the tea and toast.'

'I can see to meself, Mam, I don't want yer to be late for work.'

'Five minutes is neither here nor there, love, and Tony won't mind. Heaven knows I'm not one for taking time off or being late.'

'It's only for today, I'll be fine tomorrow to go to work.' Phoebe pulled a face as she drank the potion. 'They're horrible things to take, I feel like vomiting.' She handed the empty cup to her mother. 'But I'll keep taking them 'cos me dad's due home at the weekend and I don't want to look like death warmed up then.'

The words lifted Ellen's spirits. She couldn't wait to see Corker's face and feel his arms around her. She always felt her world was complete when he was here. He'd be upset if he found one of the children not well, even though it was only a heavy cold. 'I'll get something special in for Sunday's dinner, and if yer'd like to invite Paul for tea, I'll put a little spread on.'

'Thanks, Mam! Now, will yer go, please?'

'I'll go after I've brought yer tea up. And that eiderdown should be round yer shoulders keeping yer warm, not halfway down the bed.'

Phoebe snuggled down, saying, 'Ye're a fusspot, Mam, but I do love yer.'

Nellie grinned across the table at her son. 'I'm afraid yer love life's doomed again, lad, 'cos Phoebe's still not well. Ellen said to leave it for tonight, but she should be all right tomorrow. She's hoping to go to work anyway.'

'Ah, not again!' Paul groaned. 'What was she thinking about, getting a ruddy cold? Has the girl got no consideration, leaving me in the lurch again? Well, I'm not going dancing on me own again, that's a dead cert. And I'm not staying in playing cards either. I think I'll inflict meself on Jill and Steve for a couple of hours.'

'Yer'll only end up playing cards there, 'cos Lizzie Corkhill loves a game. So yer might as well stay in and have a game with me and yer dad. Keep us company, like.'

'Yer can take me money off me, that's what yer mean, isn't it? I don't stand a chance of winning a game with you 'cos ye're always cheating.'

Nellie looked suitably hurt. 'Fancy saying a thing like that about yer own mother! D'yer know, I'm cut to the quick.' She glanced at her husband who was quietly eating his dinner. 'I don't cheat, do I, George?'

'I couldn't honestly say, love.' He laid down his knife as though giving the subject some thought. 'I was told once that women were the weaker sex and we should give way to them. That's why I always hand me money over without a quibble. Not that I've found yer any weaker than me, Nellie, far from it. But I'd hate anyone to think I wasn't a gentleman when it comes to dealing with women.'

Paul chuckled. 'Yer mean yer give in, Dad! Anything for a quiet life, that's you. Yer should have sorted me mam out when yer first got married, it's too late to change her now.'

'Ay, you, hardface, ye're not too big to be given a go-along, yer know.' Nellie began to shake her head, then realised she should be nodding. This caused confusion with her chins and in the end they gave up and went their separate ways. 'Yer dad will hold yer hands behind yer back while I clock yer one.'

'There yer go again, Nellie, volunteering me services without asking first. Can't yer pick a day when I'm not so tired? I think ye're forgetting yer son has youth on his side.'

Lily got in from work half an hour before her father and brother. She'd already had her dinner and was upstairs getting changed. She heard part of the conversation on her way down. 'What's our Paul done that yer want to clock him one?'

'Called me a cheat, that's what. Mind you, I'm making allowances for him 'cos his love life's down the spout at the moment. Phoebe's still in bed with a cold.'

'Oh, aye, left on yer tod again, are yer?' Lily opened a drawer in the sideboard and took out a hairbrush. 'Well, I'd keep away from dance halls, if I were you. Yer'd be better off staying in for a change.'

'For yer information, and to satisfy yer curiosity, I've decided to give Jill and Steve the pleasure of me company. I hope that satisfies yer.'

'It doesn't matter whether it satisfies me or not, brother dear, as long as it satisfies Jill and Steve. They're the ones what'll have to put up with yer.'

'There's no need for sarcasm,' Nellie said. 'Let's have a bit of sister and brotherly love for a change. Be like me and yer dad, yer never hear us being sarky. Always nice and polite to each other, we are.'

Lily gave her brother a broad wink before saying, 'Oh, I know! All our lives yer've been perfect role models for us.'

'Yeah, yer've set us a good example all right,' Paul said, deadpan. 'A mother what can swear like a trooper and never fails to cheat at cards, and a father who spends every night in the pub and rolls home blotto. You and me have got a lot to live up to, Lily, d'yer think we'll make it?'

'Of course we will! I'll learn all the swear words and you can learn how to get rotten drunk every night.'

'Ho, ho, very funny,' Nellie said, enjoying it immensely. 'At least we've passed something on to our children. Some parents don't teach their kids nothing.'

'Don't think we're not grateful, Mam, 'cos we are,' Paul told her. 'It's just that if yer were going to pass anything on to us, we'd rather it was a few hundred quid.'

'If I didn't spend all me money in the pub, son,' George said, 'then we'd be able to leave yer some money. As it is, the most yer'll get when we peg out is about ten quid on the insurance. Just about enough to bury us.'

'Ay, hang about!' Nellie put her hands flat on the table and willed herself not to laugh until she'd said what she had to. 'Who was it what said, years ago, that they weren't going to fork out good money for when they die 'cos they wouldn't be here to worry about it?'

George grinned. 'That sounds like something I would say. And it make sense because I wouldn't be here, would I? But I think you should insure yerself, Nellie, to be on the safe side. Yer never know, yer might be short of cash.'

'It's funny how great minds think alike, isn't it?' Nellie was telling herself it was only a minute to go, then she could laugh her socks off. 'Yer see, I took note of what yer said. I mean, as yer explained, if I died I wouldn't have the worry of finding the money to bury meself either, would I? So I didn't insure meself, I insured you instead. If I go first, yer've got yerself a problem, George. But if you go before me, I'll be laughing sacks.'

Laughter filled the room until Lily said, 'We shouldn't be laughing, it's not a laughing matter. It's tempting fate.'

'Ye're right, it isn't a laughing matter.' George kept his face straight. 'I want you two to promise me something. I want yer to help me look after yer mother so she lives until a ripe old age. Left to herself, she's inconsiderate enough to die on me. And in that case I'd have to go round with the hat.'

When Nellie's body shook, her bosom bounced up and down. 'It better hadn't be me three-guinea wedding hat or I'll come back and haunt yer.'

Lily was wiping her eyes when she went to answer the knock on the door. 'What are yer crying for?' Archie asked. 'Has something happened?'

'It's a long story, Archie, so don't ask me mam about it or we'll never get out. I'll tell yer on the way to the pictures.'

Phoebe sighed with relief when she turned the corner into her street. It had been hard going at work today and she felt drained. Another day off would have done her good, as her mam had said, but she was glad she'd made the effort and got it over with. She'd have an early night and would feel better in the morning.

She sensed rather than saw a figure walking behind her, just a step away. When she turned her head it was to see Joanne Mowbray with a huge smile on her face. 'Hello, Phoebe,' the girl gushed, 'are yer better now? Me mam said yer had a cold.'

'I'm fine now, thank you.' Phoebe wasn't in the mood for talking, especially to this girl, but it would be impolite to ignore her. 'I'm back at work now.'

'I wondered why Paul was on his own at the dance the other night. He never said yer were sick.'

'Oh, yer spoke to him, did yer?'

'Yeah, and danced with him. Ay, he's a cracking dancer, I really enjoyed meself. I was supposed to meet a friend there but she didn't turn up. So I was made up to have someone to come home with.' Joanne was fully aware her words wouldn't be well received. That was her intention. 'I don't like being out on me own when it's dark.'

They'd reached the Mowbrays' house by this time and Phoebe didn't want to hear any more so she kept on walking, saying over her shoulder, 'Ta-ra.' Had she turned her head she would have seen the crafty gleam in the other girl's eyes. The seed had been planted and now she'd wait to see if it took root.

Ellen made a fuss when she opened the door. 'Yer shouldn't have gone in, yer look as white as a sheet. It's an early night in bed for you, my girl, and I don't want any argument.'

'Don't worry, I'll be glad to get to bed.' Phoebe hung up her coat 'But I'll wait until Paul comes. I won't bring him in, I'll talk to him at the door.'

'There's no need for that, I'll tell him. He'll understand yer can't help being sick.'

'No, I'd rather see him meself.'

Phoebe was quiet as the family sat around the table having their dinner. No one noticed because Dorothy, always a chatterbox, never stopped talking. She was a vivacious girl, more outgoing than her sister and not in the least shy. If she thought anything, she said it, regardless of the consequences. And she was clothes conscious. Every penny of her pocket money went on clothes, except for the one night she went to the pictures with a friend from work. She was allowed to go to the first house every Saturday, and she went dressed to the nines, looking older than her sixteen years. She turned a few heads, too, but up till now she hadn't really been interested in boys.

'Can't yer put a sock in it?' Gordon asked. 'Yer never even stop for breath and ye're giving me a headache.'

'Yeah, yer sound like a gramophone record what's got stuck.' Peter shook his head in disgust. 'Flipping girls are all the same.'

'Yer won't think that in a few years when yer meet someone yer like,' Ellen told him. 'If she's the one for you, every word out of her mouth will sound like music.'

Peter huffed. He couldn't imagine ever feeling like that about a girl, to him they were all blinking nuisances. 'I've finished me dinner, Mam, can I go up to Dave's now?'

'Give yer hands and face a rinse first or his mother will wonder what sort of a home yer come from. And I don't mean a quick lick, either, ye're not going out of here with a tidemark.'

Peter's departure from the table was a sign for Dorothy and Gordon to follow suit. They could be heard laughing in the kitchen as each one tried to elbow their way to be first at the sink.

'Just listen to them, they still act like kids.' Ellen began to collect the plates. 'Still, better that than having old heads on their shoulders.'

'Leave the dishes, Mam, I'll see to them,' Phoebe said, knowing her mother was on her feet all day. 'Sit down while yer've got the chance.'

'I may as well.' Ellen dropped on to the couch. 'I can't get to the sink to wash up while they're out there.' She stifled a yawn. 'I've been sniffing meself today, I hope I haven't caught your cold. Not with yer dad due home in a couple of days.'

Peter was the first out of the kitchen and he presented his neck for inspection. 'See, no sign of a tidemark. In fact I don't know why yer keep bringing it up, 'cos I haven't had a tidemark for years. I hope ye're not still asking when I'm into me twenties, that would be real embarrassing.'

'I'll make yer a promise,' Ellen laughed, pulling him down so she could kiss him. 'On the day yer get married I won't even mention the word neck.'

'Yer can mention tide, though, Mam, 'cos the ship I'm going on will be sailing with the tide. I'm going to be a sailor, like me dad.'

As Ellen gazed up at her youngest son, she knew a moment of sadness. His black hair and brown eyes reminded her of his real father, Nobby Clarke. The two girls had inherited her mousy colouring, but the two boys took after Nobby. His name was never mentioned now by the children because it brought back unhappy memories. He had never shown them love, not like Corker did, but she'd taught them not to hate their real father because on the day he died he had tried to make amends. 'Yer've got a long way to go yet, son, yer might change yer mind if yer meet a nice girl.'

There was a very definite shake of the head. 'I want to be like me dad and see the world. As soon as I'm sixteen, I'm going to ask him how to go about it.'

Gordon came in from the kitchen. 'Good, I can have the bed to meself then.'

Ellen sighed. 'So yer'd like yer brother to go away to sea for months at a time, just so yer can have the bed to yerself? That's a bit selfish, isn't it?'

'You don't have to sleep with him, Mam!' Gordon was making signs behind his brother's back to let his mother know he was only kidding. 'He snores like a pig for a start, and his arms and legs are never still. It's a wonder I'm not black and blue all over.'

'I'm glad I'm a girl,' Dorothy said, her shoulder-length mousy hair brushed until it shone. 'Boys are all clumsy with long arms and legs. Me and Phoebe don't keep each other awake, we cuddle up and don't move until the next morning. Proper ladylike, aren't we, Phoebe?'

'If you say so.' Usually Phoebe took her sister's side against the boys and there'd be a lot of laughing and teasing. But she couldn't rise to the occasion tonight, her head was splitting. All that was keeping her from her bed was seeing Paul and saying what she had to say. Then she'd climb the stairs, lay down her head in the darkness and hope that sleep wouldn't be long in coming. 'But yer can't put all girls in one class, or all boys. Everyone is different.'

Ellen followed her three children to the door with instructions. 'Peter, no later than half-nine, d'yer hear? And you two, no later than ten. Don't forget I have to wait up for yer.'

'Yer don't have to, Mam,' Dorothy said. 'Yer could give us a key.'

'It'll be another year or so before yer get yer own keys. Now poppy off or it won't be worth yer while going out.'

Phoebe was in the kitchen waiting for the water to boil to wash the dishes when Ellen walked through. 'Go and sit down, I'll see to them.' She put a hand to her daughter's forehead. 'The best place for you is bed, yer look as though yer've no energy.'

'And that's just the way I feel.' The knocker sounded and Phoebe moved away from the sink. 'This will be Paul.'

'Don't yer stand at that door for long or ye're asking for trouble.'

'I won't.' Phoebe was all mixed up. Joanne's words had upset her, making her feel worse than ever. A little voice in her head was telling her this wasn't the time to pick an argument, that she should wait until she felt better. But she felt so sick and weak, so sorry for herself, she ignored the voice of wisdom.

Paul's grin stretched from ear to ear. 'I see ye're back in the land of the living, then?'

She didn't return his smile. 'No, I still feel lousy and I'm going to bed. I only stayed up 'cos I wanted to see yer.'

His face dropped. 'Yer mean, ye're not coming out?'

'No, I'm not. But that doesn't mean you can't go out and enjoy yerself. I'm sure Joanne would love to go dancing with yer. According to her ye're a cracking dancer and she didn't half enjoy herself the other night. And she was over the moon 'cos yer walked her home.'

Paul's expression was one of disbelief. 'And yer believed her?'

'Shouldn't I? Didn't yer dance with her and walk her home?'

'I had half a dance with her because she asked me. I was with our Lily and Archie.' Paul began to get angry. Why should he have to explain himself? He'd done nothing wrong. 'So yer prefer to believe her and I'm a liar, is that it?'

'Well, she wasn't telling lies about dancing or coming home with yer, was she?'

It was on the tip of Paul's tongue to tell her the truth. That he'd been with Lily and Archie all night, and that it was Archie who'd agreed Joanne could walk home with them, not Paul. But he bit the words back. It was all so petty and childish. She was blaming him for something he hadn't done, and it wasn't right he should beg for her understanding. If she didn't trust him then there didn't seem any point in carrying on with the conversation. 'All right, Phoebe, it's obvious yer think I'm a liar so I'm not going to argue. I'll bid yer goodnight.' With that he turned on his heels and walked away.

'That didn't take long, love,' Ellen said. 'Was Paul disappointed yer weren't fit to go out?'

'I couldn't tell yer, Mam, I didn't ask. All I want to do is climb into bed and have a good rest so I'm fit for work tomorrow.' She walked towards the stairs. 'I won't kiss yer, Mam, in case yer catch me cold. Goodnight and God bless.'

'Goodnight, sweetheart.' Ellen had a feeling that all was not well. Paul was someone who laughed and joked a lot, but there'd been no sound of laughter tonight. Not that she heard, anyway. But the young couple couldn't have fallen out, they hadn't seen each other for three days so there wasn't anything to fall out over. 'I'm imagining things,' she said to the empty room as she lowered herself on to the fireside chair. 'It must be me age.'

Paul walked to the bottom of the street and stood on the corner, wondering what to do. He was seething with anger, his hands clenched so tight his nails were digging into his palms. He was angry with Joanne for telling tales, and more angry with Phoebe for believing them. Well, he wasn't going to go crawling to her, not until she'd apologised. And if she wouldn't do that, then blow her. If you didn't have trust in a relationship, then you had nothing. He didn't fancy spending the rest of his life defending himself when he was innocent.

For a few seconds he toyed with the idea of going home where Lily and Archie were playing cards with his parents. He was so mad, he wanted to tell his sister what he'd been accused of. She'd soon put Phoebe straight, but why should she be brought into it? Better forget the whole thing instead of dragging the two families into something they couldn't do anything about. But he wouldn't be calling for Phoebe any more, of that he was certain. If she wanted him then she could do the running.

He saw a tram coming towards him, the indicator showing it was going to the Pier Head. As he didn't fancy going home and having questions thrown at him, he jumped on board. The fresh wind down by the Mersey would clear his mind and it would help pass a couple of hours. He might even feel different when his anger abated.

It was eleven o'clock when Paul came back up his street. He walked slowly, his shoulders drooping. The anger had gone, but it had been replaced with sadness. Although his head was telling him one thing, his heart was telling him another. He didn't want to fall out with Phoebe, he wanted her to be his girlfriend, he really loved her. But his pride wasn't going to let him give in. She'd believed Joanne's lies instead of asking for his version of events, and that was something he couldn't stomach. No, unless she came to him and apologised, then they were through.

* * *

The following night, when the dinner was over and the three young ones had gone out, Ellen eyed her eldest daughter. 'As yer look a bit better today, I suppose yer'll be going out tonight with Paul?'

Phoebe sighed. It was no good putting it off, it was better to get it over with. 'I won't be going out, Mam, me and Paul have had a falling out.'

Ellen's face showed her surprise. 'Yer haven't seen him for three days, how can yer have fallen out?'

'It was something daft, Mam, but I'd rather not say. Anyway, he won't be calling here any more, and that's that.'

The surprise on Ellen's face turned to astonishment. 'But I don't understand, love! Yer were like two love-birds on Sunday, and yer haven't been out since. So how could yer have had a row? Besides which, Paul would never row with anyone, he's not the type.'

'It wasn't a row, Mam, just a difference of opinion. But yer can take it from me that he won't be calling tonight or any other night.'

'Oh, come on, love, it couldn't have been that bad! Ye're a bit down at the moment, that's what it is. But it'll all blow over, you mark my words.'

'It won't, Mam, and I'd rather not talk about it any more if yer don't mind.'

'Phoebe, yer can't not talk about it! The McDonoughs are our close friends, they're bound to wonder what's going on. Nellie's in the shop every day, d'yer think she's not going to mention it and ask questions?'

'Paul will tell her what he wants to, it's not for me to speak for him. What happened was probably my fault, I wasn't feeling well and not thinking straight. But that's as much as I'm going to tell yer. And I don't want to talk about it any more.'

'That's a nice homecoming for yer dad, isn't it? He's very fond of Paul and will be really disappointed and upset. I just hope yer come to yer senses before he arrives.'

'Don't pin yer hopes on that, 'cos it's not going to happen.' Phoebe sighed and pushed herself up from her chair. 'I'm going to get stripped and have a good wash down. Then I'm having an early night in bed.'

Two doors away, Paul was suffering the same fate. 'What d'yer mean, yer've packed up with Phoebe?' Nellie wasn't very happy about what she'd heard and didn't care who knew it. 'Surely to God ye're not childish enough to pack her in 'cos the girl's had a cold and couldn't go jazzing with yer?'

'I didn't pack her in, Mam, we both agreed we didn't want to go out together any more.' Paul couldn't think of anything else to say. 'It was mutual.'

'That was a bit sudden, wasn't it?' George asked. 'I thought the pair of yer got on like a house on fire. She's a nice girl, is Phoebe.'

'I know that, Dad, she's a smashing girl. It's just that we didn't see eye to eye on some things and decided to call it a day.'

Lily had been listening intently while she ate her meal. There was something fishy going on here, it didn't ring true. 'Yer never said anything when we were at the dance the other night, how come? I mean, Phoebe was supposed to be coming with yer so everything in the garden must have been rosy then.'

'Blimey!' Paul was exasperated. 'Didn't you ever fall out with a boy when yer were young, Mam? Or you, Dad? Was me mam the only girl yer ever went out with?'

'No, I went out with a couple of girls, but it was never serious. Yer mam is the only one I ever courted. The others were just dates, nothing more. But we all thought you and Phoebe were courting proper like.'

'Well, yer were wrong, weren't yer?' Paul pushed his chair back. 'I'll get washed at the sink before yer start on the dishes.'

'Are yer going out?'

'Yes, I'm going out,' he said, disappearing into the kitchen and running the tap in the hope of drowning out any further questions. He wasn't feeling very happy and could do without all this hassle.

But Nellie wasn't going to let him off the hook so easily. 'Where are yer off to?'

Paul's head appeared around the door. 'I haven't made up my mind yet, there's dozens of places to choose from.'

George caught his wife's attention. 'Leave it, Nellie, we'll find out eventually.'

'I'll find out tomorrow.' She mouthed the words. 'I'll ask Ellen when I go to the butcher's, she's bound to know.'

But to Nellie's surprise and dismay, Ellen didn't know any more than she did. 'She must have said something to yer, explained why she wasn't going out with him? Girls talk more to their mothers than boys do.'

Ellen shook her head. 'I know as much as you, Nellie, she just clammed up on me.'

'Perhaps if the pair of yer left them alone, they'd sort themselves out,' Molly said. 'All it needs is for them to pass in the street, and one look at each other should do the trick. And God knows, they'd have a hard job not meeting when they only live two doors away.'

'I've told Ellen that, Molly, but she will worry,' Tony said, his eyes on the scales as he weighed out three-quarters of stewing steak. 'True love never runs smooth.'

'I know that, soft lad.' Nellie jerked her head as if to say she wasn't stupid. 'But when they fell out is the mystery. They were all lovey-dovey one day, then they don't see each other for three days but manage to have a row and fall out! It beats me.'

'Corker's home the day after tomorrow, he might have more luck than me.' Ellen wrapped up their meat and passed it over the counter. 'Phoebe thinks the world of him and might just open up her heart. I hope so, anyway, I don't want her and Paul to be out of friends.'

Chapter 21

Molly wiped the floorcloth over the hearth several times, her finger stiffened to make sure she captured every trace of soot from the corners. Then she sat back on her heels and spoke to the empty room. 'That's me lot, thank goodness. Washing done, beds made and rooms dusted and tidied. I'm feeling quite pleased with meself.' Pressing her hands down on the floor she scrambled to her feet. 'I'll just rinse this cloth out and then get meself ready before Tilly Mint comes.' She straightened up with a hand pressed to her back, and pulled a face. 'I can't get up as easy as I used to, me age is beginning to tell.' She grinned as she made her way to the kitchen. 'If anyone heard me talking to meself they'd have me certified.'

She was rinsing the floor cloth out in the sink when she saw a shadow pass the kitchen window. 'Oh, no, not Nellie, it's too early.' With hot words on her lips, she opened the door. But it wasn't Nellie, it was Mary Watson, Bella's Mam, who lived opposite. 'What on earth are yer doing at me back door, Mary? I thought it was me mate and was going to tell her to go home for half an hour 'cos I'm not ready.'

Mary stepped into the kitchen. 'I know it looks like a cloak and dagger mystery, but I didn't want to be seen knocking at yer front door. And don't start panicking when I tell yer what I'm here for 'cos there's no need.'

'If yer tell me quick, Mary, then I won't panic. But keeping me waiting has got me heart in me mouth, so out with it.'

'Well, yer know I slip next door to see Victoria a few times a week, don't yer? I called this morning and sat having a little natter to her. I happened to notice your Doreen rubbing her tummy a couple of times and I asked her if she was all right. She said she was fine, and she certainly looked it, but Victoria said she'd got pains in her stomach. Doreen said it was nothing, and she's probably right, but I thought I'd better let yer know. Don't tell her I told yer, Molly, I don't want her to think I'm a nosy poke.'

'It can't be the baby, it's not due for another two months.' Molly usually kept a cool head in a time of crisis, but not when it concerned one of her own children. 'I'd better get meself ready and slip over to see her for meself. Everything's been going so well for her and Phil, what with him just finding his dad's family and all. I pray to God there's nothing wrong now, it would devastate them. It would devastate all of us.'

'Molly, it's probably what Doreen said, just a pain in the tummy. Yer know what a worry wart I am, yer've told me often enough over the years about wrapping our Bella in cotton wool. But I can't help me nature, it's the way I was born. So don't go dashing over thinking the worst, 'cos yer'll only upset the girl. Just call there, as yer do every morning and don't let on I said anything. Perhaps I shouldn't have, but I thought it best to be on the safe side.'

'Yer did the right thing, sunshine, and this is one time I'm glad ye're a worry wart. Our Doreen's only a kid herself, she might be worried sick inside but afraid of saying anything in case we think she's stupid. Anyway, I'll tidy meself up, give Nellie a knock and let her know where I am in case she has the street up looking for me. But I'll do everything on the double and be over the road in ten minutes.'

Mary stepped down into the yard. 'D'yer want me to give Nellie a knock for yer, save yer time?'

'That would be a help, if yer don't mind. Tell her to stay put in her own house until I call for her. She's not to follow me over, 'cos if Doreen thinks we're all worried, it'll put the fear of God into her.'

'I'll tell her, Molly, but yer know Nellie is so unpredictable I can't guarantee she'll take a ha'porth of notice of me. She'll probably tell me to mind me own business and bugger off!' Mary began to walk down the yard. 'I hope I'm not worrying yer for nothing, but if I hadn't got it off me chest I'd have been on pins all day.'

'I'm glad yer came, sunshine, 'cos knowing our Doreen, she wouldn't have said a dickie bird to me and worried herself to death until Phil came home from work. Anyway, I'll let yer know if there's anything wrong, and thanks once again for telling me.'

Her heart and tummy reacting to her anxiety, Molly gave her face a cat's lick and a promise before pulling her coat on. After making sure she had the front door key with her, she let herself out and made haste across the cobbles.

'Hello, Mam!' Doreen peeped either side of her. 'On yer own this morning? Where's me Auntie Nellie?'

'She wasn't quite ready.' Molly kissed her daughter's cheek as she squeezed past. 'I was feeling full of beans and got me work over with early.'

Victoria leaned forward in her chair and dispensed with formalities. 'I'm glad to see yer, Molly, 'cos Doreen doesn't feel very well.'

'It's just a tummy ache, that's all.' Doreen's face flushed. She felt embarrassed whenever she discussed the baby with her mother or Aunt Vicky. She didn't mind with Jill 'cos they were the same age and neither had a clue about what happened when yer had a baby. 'There's no need to fuss, it'll go away soon.'

'Sit down, sunshine.' Molly knew exactly how Doreen was feeling because she remembered how difficult she'd found it to tell her own mother that she was expecting. 'There's no need to blush or feel shy because don't forget I'm the one what gave birth to you. I know all about the birds and bees. So be sensible and tell me what sort of pain it is, where it is and when did it start?'

'It started when I was getting out of bed this morning. And it's not really a pain, it's just a funny feeling in me tummy.'

'It wasn't the baby kicking to let yer know it's still there?'

Doreen shook her head. 'I'd know if it was that. I can't explain properly, Mam, it's just that I feel different, as though I want to vomit.'

Molly took her hand. 'Listen, sunshine, it's probably nothing at all to worry about. But to be on the safe side, I'm taking yer to the doctor's. If Phil was here, it's what he would do. And it's no good yer shaking yer head at me like that because we're going right now, before he leaves to go on his rounds. So get yerself ready while I nip over for Nellie. She can sit with Victoria until we come back.'

There were only two patients in the waiting room besides themselves, and Molly hoped Doctor Greenshields wouldn't be called out on an emergency before they were attended to. That had happened to her once before and she'd had to sit for an hour until he got back. And not only her but about ten other patients, too. She'd been fidgety with impatience for the whole hour until she was told later he'd been called out to a dying man.

'Will yer be able to come in with me, Mam?' Doreen asked, her nerves getting worse the longer they sat there. She'd only been to the doctor's twice in her life, and that was in the last six months to make sure the pregnancy was going as it should. 'He's very nice, the doctor, but I'd feel better if you were there.'

'We'll see, sunshine,' Molly said, patting her knee. 'If he wants to examine yer, I think yer'd be less embarrassed if I wasn't there.

Anyway, we'll see what he has to say.'

Twenty minutes later they were the only ones in the waiting room. 'Not long now, sunshine, and we'll be in and out in no time.'

The door opened and a voice called, 'Next, please.'

Molly took her daughter's arm and held her tight. 'I'll come with yer, sunshine, but I can't promise he'll let me stay.'

The doctor was a small thin man with sandy hair. Some people said he was an eccentric because of the old-fashioned clothes he wore, but no one doubted he was the best doctor in the area. He sat behind a desk cluttered with papers, and raised his brows when he saw both mother and daughter. Molly quickly explained why they were there. After he'd asked Doreen a few questions he nodded his head. 'I'll have to examine you, Mrs Bradley, so if you'll go behind the screen and strip from the waist down, I'll be with you in a minute.'

'D'yer want me to leave, Doctor?' Molly asked.

Doctor Greenshields had known the family for years although he'd never had much cause to call on them. But he knew them to be a caring family, and understood Molly's anxiety. 'No, you can stay, it won't take long.'

When the doctor disappeared behind the screen, Molly started to bite her nails. When she heard a low moan from Doreen she had the urge to run to her daughter. Instead, she closed her eyes and said a little prayer that everything would be all right and that the tummy upset had nothing to do with the baby. Then she heard the doctor saying, 'You can get dressed now, Mrs Bradley.'

He came from behind the screen and walked to a small sink in the corner of the room where he washed his hands. He didn't speak and Molly was too afraid to question him. After drying his hands, he sat behind his desk and smiled at her. 'We'll wait for your daughter, save me having to repeat myself.'

When Doreen appeared she was shaking all over with nerves. She had her lips clamped together because she couldn't control them. Molly wanted to run to her and hold her but was conscious that the doctor would be wanting to be out and about on his calls. He was a kindly man but noted for not wasting words. 'The reason for your discomfort is because the baby has turned. It hasn't come to any harm, I could feel its arms and feet moving. But for your wellbeing, and that of the baby, it needs to be turned back as soon as possible.'

Doreen licked her lips. 'How can that be done, Doctor? And I know my husband will want to know what yer mean by the baby's turned, so could yer explain it to me and tell me how yer can turn it back?

And if the baby's going to be all right?'

'It isn't unusual for a baby to move, my dear, and while it might be an unpleasant procedure for you, it should have no ill effect on your unborn child. I'll arrange an appointment with a specialist at Walton Hospital as soon as possible.'

The colour drained from Doreen's face. 'I won't have to stay in hospital, will I?'

'I shouldn't think so, but that depends upon the specialist.' The doctor allowed a small smile to appear. 'It also depends upon how stubborn your baby is.'

'But how could it have happened? I didn't do anything to cause it, I'm very careful about lifting and stretching.'

'It's nothing you've done, my dear, it's one of those things that nobody can explain. Now, if you'll excuse me a minute, I'll ring the hospital and arrange an appointment.'

After he'd left the room, Doreen turned to her mother. 'I'm frightened, Mam! What will they do to me? I don't understand how it's happened 'cos I've been so careful and really looked after meself.'

'There's no need to worry, sunshine, yer'll be fine. I've often heard of babies having to be turned, it's not something new.' Molly was trying to reassure her daughter, but she couldn't reassure herself. She had heard of cases where a baby has been turned to avoid a breech delivery but Doreen still had a few months to go. 'Don't start getting yerself all upset 'cos that could upset the baby. They can sense these things, yer know.'

The door opened and Doctor Greenshields came in. 'Eleven o'clock tomorrow morning, Mrs Bradley. If you go through the main hospital doors, you'll see an enquiry window on your left. If you give your name in there, they'll tell you where to go and who to ask for. I visit the hospital nearly every day to see patients of mine so I'll find out how you got on. And I think it would be wise if you came to me for an examination every two weeks now so I can keep an eye on you.' He saw Doreen's eyes widen with fear. 'That is quite normal and has nothing to do with the present situation. Once an expectant mother gets to six months I ask them to come every fortnight, then at eight months I like to see them every week until the baby is born.'

'But what for?' Doreen's voice was shrill. 'I'm going to be all right, aren't I? And the baby?'

'Of course you are! You and the baby are perfectly healthy and you can assure your husband there is absolutely no need to worry. It will not be a pleasant experience for you tomorrow, but if it's any consolation you'll feel much better afterwards.'

'Thanks, Doctor.' Molly handed Doreen her coat. 'I'll go with her to the hospital tomorrow, she'll be all right.'

He nodded. 'And please see she comes to the surgery every fortnight from now on.'

'I'll bring her meself.' Molly cupped her daughter's elbow. 'Come on, sunshine, let's get yer home, Miss Clegg will be worried about yer.'

'Oh, how is Miss Clegg?' The doctor showed interest. 'It's a long time since I've seen her so I hope that means all is well?'

'For a woman of her age, she's amazing, Doctor. She can't do what she used to do, and she seldom goes over the door, but she has all her faculties about her. Her hearing and sight are fine, and she's got enough on top to beat us all at cards.'

'Give her my warm regards.' Doctor Greenshields opened the door for them then went back to the papers on his desk. He had about twelve calls to make, some of them urgent, which meant he'd be out for most of the day. His evening surgery started again at five o'clock so chances are he wouldn't have a proper meal until supper. Still, he was doing the only job he'd ever wanted, helping the sick and needy. A strictly religious man, he believed that is what he was put on earth to do.

'Where the hell have yer been to all this time?' Nellie demanded when she opened the door. 'Me and Victoria have been worried sick about yer.'

'Well, for your information, sunshine, we haven't been on a ruddy picnic! Where the hell d'yer think we've been?'

'Don't bite me head off, girl, I only asked. I've worn Victoria's lino out walking to the window and back, looking for yer.'

Molly looked fondly at the old lady who was leaning forward, her eyes filled with anxiety. 'We had to wait our turn, and then Doctor Greenshields examined Doreen. And, by the way, he sent yer his warm regards.'

Victoria waved this aside, more important things on her mind. 'What did he have to say after he'd examined her?'

'Yer can ask me, Aunt Vicky,' Doreen said. 'I'm the one what had to get undressed behind the screen and I have got a tongue in me head.'

'I'm sorry, sweetheart, but I've been so worried about yer. Sit down and tell me what he had to say.'

'I'll make a pot of tea,' Nellie said, heading for the kitchen and muttering, 'the kettle's been boiled that many times it's got no backside left.'

Molly grinned. Knowing how much her friend hated to miss anything, she said, 'We'll hang on and wait for yer, sunshine, we wouldn't leave yer out.'

So, while they were having a cup of tea, Molly sat back and let her daughter do the talking. And it turned out to be a good thing because as she spoke Doreen seemed to gain more confidence and understanding of what the doctor had told her. 'So I've got to go to Walton Hospital in the morning. Me mam said she'll come with me.'

Throughout the explanations, Nellie's eyes had been narrowed. Now she asked, 'So the baby has turned upside down?' She waited for Doreen's nod, then asked, 'Eh, yer haven't been doing handstands, have yer, girl?'

This brought the first smile of the day to the girl's face. 'Hardly, Auntie Nellie. I was never good at that when I was at school, so I'd definitely not make it in my condition.'

Nellie thought on this for a while. 'Well, after yer get sorted out tomorrow, and the baby is where it should be, would yer mind having a word with her? Just say that in future, if she feels like moving house, would she wait until me and yer Mam have got our shopping in. To choose a more convenient time, like?'

'Ye're saying "she", Auntie Nellie, but it could be a "he".'

'Nah, it won't be a boy, 'cos boys are too lazy to move around. It's girls what have got more go about them. They'll have something done while the boys are still thinking about it. Mind you, my old ma, God rest her soul, used to say girls were too bossy and had too much to say for themselves.'

'Your ma said that, did she, sunshine?' Molly raised her brows. 'I wonder who she had in mind when she said it? I mean, you were the only daughter she had!'

Nellie chuckled, the chair groaned and the three onlookers waited for it. 'Yeah, she said I was enough to put her off having any more. She said when I was born, the midwife handed me to her so she could have a little cuddle before they washed me down.' The chair was being put under more pressure now. 'Now I never believed this, 'cos me ma was fond of pulling me leg. But she said as soon as she looked down at me, I opened me eyes and said, "It's about time yer let me out of there, I'm starving and I want me dinner."'

'Why didn't yer believe her? From what I know, yer haven't changed

287

a bit from the minute yer were born, sunshine! Yer mouth is still an ever-open door.'

'That's charming, that is! Ye're supposed to be me best friend!'

Doreen had her eyes on the cup and saucer Nellie was holding on her lap. There wasn't a lot of space on her lap because her tummy took most of it up, and the last thing Doreen wanted was to have part of her wedding present tea-set chipped or broken. 'If yer've finished with yer cups, I'll take them out.'

'You stay where yer are, I'll take them out and rinse them. And ye're to take it easy for the rest of the day, sunshine, d'yer hear? Don't bother making a dinner, it won't hurt to have fish and chips from the chippy for once. Ruthie will run down for them when Phil's due home.' Molly collected Nellie's cup and saucer and took it out to the kitchen with her own. 'And I happen to know that Victoria is very partial to fish and chips, so that's one worry less for yer.'

'Leave those few dishes, Mam, I'll wash them. I'm not an invalid, it's better if I keep on the go. Sitting on me backside won't do me any good. You and Auntie Nellie go and get yer shopping done.'

She's right, Molly thought. It's best if she keeps active, as long as she doesn't overdo it. 'Okay, sunshine, we'll leave yer to get on with it. Apart from yer usual loaf, d'yer want any other bits and pieces from the shops.'

Doreen nodded. After the frightening morning she'd had, she decided she deserved a treat. 'Yeah, yer can get us two cream cakes. Me and Aunt Vicky will go mad and spoil ourselves. It doesn't matter what they are, 'cos there won't be much selection left at this time, as long as they're nice and gooey.'

Nellie licked her lips and rubbed her tummy. 'Sounds just the job to me. Shall we mug ourselves, girl?'

Molly clicked her tongue. 'See what I mean about believing what yer ma told yer? Yer were hungry the minute yer were born and yer've been hungry ever since.'

'This day seems never-ending,' Molly said as she and Nellie walked back from the shops. 'I feel as though I've been on the go for twenty-four hours.'

'And yer've got another long day ahead of yer tomorrow, girl. Sometimes yer can be hours in the hospital before yer get seen to.'

Molly could see the distance between herself and the gutter becoming narrower. 'Nellie, will yer stop pushing me towards the kerb, sunshine? I've got half a dozen eggs in me basket and if I trip and break them, I'll break your ruddy neck.'

'Honest to God, ye're not half a moaner. Let's swap places and then yer'll have nothing to cry about. Unless, of course, yer decide to clean the window sills of the houses we pass with the sleeve of yer coat.' Nellie came to a halt to allow her mate to pass in front of her. 'Ay, girl, was it this year yer cleaned those window sills or was it last year? The time's going so quick I can't keep up with it.'

'It was last year, sunshine, and that was only 'cos yer will insist on pushing me. On me own I can walk a straight line, but not with you on me arm.'

'It's not as though I mean to, girl! I can't help it if I've got sexy hips what like to sway from side to side. They go with me voluptuous body, yer see. Yer can't blame me for being built to attract the opposite sex. I mean, yer must have noticed how that man in the sweet shop couldn't keep his eyes off me, and how he wouldn't move away from me. I was drawing him like a magnet.'

'Yer know why that was, don't yer?' Molly quipped. 'Yer were standing on his ruddy foot and he was too much of a gentleman to say anything.'

'When I tell George tonight, it'll be my version he hears 'cos . . .' Nellie turned her head when she heard a shout. 'Ooh, it's Corker!'

Molly's face lit up when she saw the giant of a man walking towards them. His peaked cap was set at a jaunty angle, his seaman's bag slung over his shoulder, and his weatherbeaten face, behind the beard and moustache, was beaming. 'Good morning, ladies.' He swung the bag from his shoulder and put it on the ground. 'It's good to see yer.'

'And it's lovely to see you, Corker.' Molly lifted her face for a kiss. 'Don't be picking me up and twirling me round like yer usually do, 'cos I've got eggs in me basket.'

Nellie gave him a cheeky grin. 'I haven't got no eggs in me basket, Corker, if yer feel in the mood for twirling someone round.'

'I'll settle for a kiss, Nellie, I know me limits.'

'We were in the butcher's shop not long ago, Ellen never mentioned yer were coming home today. Have yer seen her?'

'Yeah, I've just come from there. She said yer'd not long been in. And she told me Doreen was poorly. What's wrong with the lass?'

'Nothing serious, according to the doctor, but I'm to take her to hospital in the morning so we'll know more then.'

'D'yer want me to come with yer, me darlin', for some moral support?'

Molly looked at him and chuckled. 'You in a maternity clinic? It's

289

hardly the place for men, Corker, but thanks for offering, I appreciate it. I don't think Doreen would, though, she'd be very embarrassed.'

'Well, if there's anything yer think I can help with, yer know yer only have to ask.' He turned his eyes to Nellie. 'I believe your son and my daughter have had a falling out?'

'Yeah, pair of silly buggers.' Nellie's disgusted shake of the head set her chins swaying in agreement. 'They passed each other in the street last night and didn't even let on. Passed each other like strangers when they've known each other all their lives. I've told our Paul, they both want their bumps feeling.'

'And neither of them will say what brought this about?'

'No, they won't even talk about it. I think our Lily knows more than she's letting on, but all she'll say is that she believes that Joanne Mowbray's got something to do with it.'

Corker picked up the ropes of his seaman's bag and tossed it over his shoulder. 'I'll see if I can get anything out of Phoebe. If I have any luck I'll let yer know.' The three of them began to walk up the street. 'I'll give Jack and George a knock about half-eight, to see if they fancy a pint or two.'

'Have you ever known a time when they didn't fancy a pint?' Molly asked. 'Every night they ask if there's any word when yer'll be home.'

'It's good to be home, Molly, I've got to say. I'm getting to the stage now where I think I've had enough of a life on the ocean wave. I want to settle down and be with me family more. Every time I leave home it gets harder, 'cos I miss them so much when I'm away.'

They came to a halt outside Molly's door. 'Ellen and the kids would be delighted if yer packed in the sea. Not that anything's ever been said, but I know they miss yer a lot.'

'I'll have to give it some serious thought. Anyway, I'll see you two ladies tonight when I call to take yer husbands off yer hands.'

'Go on, sunshine, walk with Corker!'

Nellie's mouth dropped. 'He only lives next door!'

'I know that, soft girl, and you only live another two doors away. But if yer don't go at the same time as Corker, I'll be lumbered with yer and I can't have that, I've got work to do.'

The big man bent his elbow. 'Come, Mrs McDonough, I'll see yer to yer door.'

Nellie stuck her tongue out at her friend. 'See, I told yer, didn't I? I'm a ruddy magnet to men, they can't resist me swaying hips and voluptuous body.'

* * *

290

Corker waited for the right moment to speak to Phoebe. The other three children had gone out and Ellen was rinsing a few clothes through in the kitchen. After lighting one of his Capstan Full Strength cigarettes, he sat back on the couch. 'What's this I'm hearing about you and Paul falling out, sweetheart? D'yer want to tell me about it?'

Phoebe's shoulder-length hair swung about her face as she shook her head. 'There's nothing to talk about, Dad. We've agreed to disagree and that's about it.'

Corker watched the smoke ring rise to the ceiling then asked in a low voice, 'And did yer agree that yer were not even going to be friends? That yer would pass each other in the street without a second glance?'

'They don't miss much around here, do they? It's a pity they've not got more important things to do than jangle about me. I wish they'd all mind their own business.'

'Does that include me, me darlin', and yer Mam?'

'No, of course not! But there's nothing to tell, except that we're not going out with each other any more. We're just not suited, that's all.'

'Yer looked very suited to me last time I was home. I would have said yer were made for each other. So something must have happened to change yer feelings, Phoebe, and I'd very much like to know what it was.' When his daughter lowered her head and didn't answer, he went on, 'Did Joanne Mowbray have anything to do with it?'

'No, of course not!' But the tell-tale blush belied her words.

Corker patted the empty space beside him. 'Come and sit here, sweetheart, and tell yer dad exactly what's gone on. I'm not being nosy, but ye're my daughter and I want to know about the things that happen in yer life.'

Phoebe loved the gentle giant so much she couldn't refuse. So as he held her hand, she poured out her heart. And when she'd finished, she wiped away a tear and gulped, 'Yer won't say anything to Paul, will yer? I know I shouldn't have called him a liar, that wasn't very nice of me. But he didn't deny he'd danced with the girl, or that he'd walked her home. And I'm not ever going to chase after a boy, Dad, I'll never do that.'

There was such feeling in her voice, Corker knew she was remembering how Nobby Clarke had treated his wife and children like slaves. She didn't want that sort of a life for herself. 'No, I wouldn't want yer to chase after a boy. You keep yer pride, sweetheart, that's very important. But I think yer should have given Paul the benefit of the doubt. Still, it's your life and yer must do as yer see fit. I'll not interfere.'

And when he was sitting in the pub later with Jack and George, he didn't intend to interfere as such. It was just a friendly conversation with two of his oldest mates, and it was only natural to ask how their families were.

'Yer don't have to ask how Jill and Steve are, does he, Jack?' George put his glass down before wiping the froth from his mouth with the back of his hand. 'They are the perfect couple and always will be.'

'George is right, they are perfect.' Jack felt his heart surge with pride. 'So are Doreen and Phil, I'm dead proud of them. My girls have turned out like their mother, very sensible and good housewives. And they're pretty like their mother, too.'

Not to be outdone, George had to do his share of bragging. 'The way things are going, Corker, it won't be long before Lily and Archie get engaged. I'm glad about that 'cos he's a fine bloke and will make her a good husband.'

Corker stroked his beard. 'And Paul?'

'Ah, well, he's a mystery, doesn't say very much. Him and Phoebe pack in and neither of them will say why! I can't fathom them out.'

'I had a word with Phoebe, and although I didn't get it word for word, she did admit she was feeling under the weather and harsh words were spoken. As far as I can gather, that young Joanne Mowbray told her things to cause trouble between her and Paul. They were probably lies but Phoebe was understandably upset. I've got a sneaking suspicion she regrets being so hasty but it's no good closing the stable door after the horse has bolted. She'll not be the one to give in, she's got her pride, has my daughter.' Corker pushed his chair back and reached for the glasses. 'Anyway, whatever will be will be. If there's still feelings between them, it won't be long before they're back together again.' With the three pint glasses in one of his huge hands, he made for the bar. 'Same again, eh?'

Watching the barman filling the glasses, Corker was hoping George would repeat what had been said. If he did, it might encourage Paul to make the first advance.

And George did repeat it, to Nellie, Lily and Paul. But his son just shrugged his shoulders and said if Phoebe was waiting for him to make the first move, she'd be waiting a long time.

So it came about that by the end of Corker's ten days' leave, the couple were still passing each other in the street like strangers. Not a glance nor a word exchanged.

292

Molly was linking her daughter's arm as they walked up the long path to the hospital. 'How d'yer feel now, sunshine?'

'Mam, I am petrified. Me legs are like jelly and I don't know how they're carrying me up this path. If you weren't with me, I'd turn tail and run.'

'Listen, sunshine, no one carries a baby for nine months without any problems. And it's worse when it's yer first, 'cos yer don't know what to expect.'

'Were you frightened, Mam?'

'I was terrified, sunshine. To listen to me, yer'd think I was the only one who had morning sickness. And every time the baby kicked I thought there was something wrong. My Mam was no help, she used to go all red and flustered if I asked her anything, and the only thing she said was, "Leave things be, nature will take its course." That wasn't much help. But I wasn't afraid when I was expecting you 'cos I knew what was happening by then.'

They walked arm in arm through the main doors and Molly motioned for Doreen to wait while she made enquiries. Soon they were entering a room where there were about ten other pregnant women. Some looked as though they were ready to give birth there and then, others were barely showing.

'Sit down, sunshine, it looks as though we'll be here quite a while.' Molly looked around and saw most of the women were laughing and joking with each other. The only one in the room who looked scared to death was her daughter. This fact wasn't lost on the woman sitting next to Molly.

'Is this yer first time here, love?'

'Yes, I've come with me daughter. It looks as though we're in for a long wait.'

Just then a door on the opposite side of the room opened and a nurse came out holding a white card. 'Mrs Bradley?'

Molly jumped to her feet. 'That's us.'

'Are you Mrs Bradley?'

'No, I'm her mother.' Molly pushed Doreen forward. 'This is Mrs Bradley.'

'You'll have to wait here. Mr Winstanley will call you if necessary. Come, Mrs Bradley.'

Two hours later Molly was on her own in the waiting room. All the expectant mothers had been attended to and no one had been near to tell her what was happening with Doreen. Her nerves were shattered and tears weren't far away. If she could, she would have changed places with her daughter and suffered the fear and pain for her. For the umpteenth time she got up and paced the floor. What in the name of God was going on? The next time a nurse passed the window she'd stop her and try to find out.

Molly was so deep in anxious thought, she didn't hear the door open and jumped when her name was called. 'Mrs Bennett?'

'Thank God for that! I've been worried sick! Where's me daughter?'

'She's resting on a bed at the moment, but Mr Winstanley would like a word with you.' The nurse covered the ground quickly, not giving Molly time to ask questions. 'In here, please.'

The man sitting behind the desk got to his feet. After checking the name on a paper in front of him, he held out his hand. 'Mrs Bennett, I'm Mr Winstanley.'

'Just tell me me daughter's all right, Mr Winstanley, before I have a heart attack and yer've got another patient on yer hands.'

He smiled and waved her to a seat. 'Doreen will be fine. She's resting in one of the side wards at the moment, feeling sickly, with a sore tummy and probably hating me. I had to put her through the mill, I'm afraid, because the baby was in an awkward position and I had great difficulty in turning it. But it had to be done for the baby's welfare and your daughter's.'

'Can I go and see her?'

'Of course. As soon as she feels up to it, you can take her home. I would suggest a taxi if you can afford it. It would be far more comfortable and she'd be home more quickly.' He pushed his chair back and crossed his legs. 'In the unlikely event of its happening again, please bring her straight here. I'm not expecting it, but just in case. And now you can go and see her.'

Doreen was very tearful. 'Mam, it's been terrible, please take me home.'

'Of course, sunshine, I'll ask them to ring for a taxi.' Molly stroked her daughter's long hair. 'It's over, thank God, and you and the baby are fine. We can all rest easy in our beds tonight.'

Chapter 22

It was during a slow foxtrot at Blair Hall that Paul found himself being excused by Joanne.

'Doesn't yer boyfriend mind yer cutting in on me every week? It's not very flattering to him, is it?'

'I don't care whether he minds or not, he's not me boyfriend.' Joanne fluttered her eyelashes as she'd seen film stars do. 'He'd like to be, but I'm not really interested.'

'He pays for yer to come in so he must think ye're his girlfriend. Otherwise why would he waste his money?'

'That's his worry, not mine. If he wants to pay for me then I'd be daft to refuse. He keeps asking me to go to the pictures with him but I haven't done yet.' Once again Joanne fluttered her eyelashes. 'I'd go with you if yer asked me, though.'

'That's never going to happen, Joanne, so forget it. Ye're lucky I speak to yer after what yer did.' Four weeks had gone by since Paul last went out with Phoebe and this girl was partly to blame. He would never like her but didn't see any point in ignoring her. After all, if Phoebe had believed and trusted him, they'd never have fallen out. 'Yer told a lot of lies, Joanne, and I'll never forget that. So go out with Sam Welsby and consider yourself lucky. I've known him since we were at school together and he's a really good bloke. He's far too good for you though it's not my place to tell him that.'

She wasn't going to give in that easily. 'But I didn't tell lies, I just didn't tell the whole truth and that makes a difference. And I only did it 'cos I like yer.'

'Yer cost me me girlfriend, Joanne, and I wouldn't go out with you if yer were the only girl in the world. I don't hate yer, I don't know yer well enough for that, but I certainly don't like yer. And I'd be grateful if yer wouldn't excuse me every week. I don't want yer to, and I'm sure Sam doesn't either.'

When the dance was over, he didn't do the gentlemanly thing and walk her back to where she'd been standing. He didn't think she deserved to be treated like a lady.

Joanne put a smile on her face when she approached Sam. 'It's the interval waltz next, and you like a waltz, don't yer?'

Sam wasn't very happy with the situation. 'I don't know why yer have to excuse Paul every week and leave me standing here like a lemon. If I'm good enough to bring yer to the dance, then I should be good enough to stay with. I'm not going to be made a fool of, Joanne, so make up yer mind. If yer come with me, yer stay with me. If not, ask Paul to bring yer.'

'I don't know why ye're getting so het up about it. I've told yer, I only live a couple of doors away from the McDonough family and we're friends. And anyway, I feel sorry for him 'cos his girl's packed him in.'

'Yer feel sorry for him, or yer've got yer eye on him?' Sam Welsby had the feeling he wasn't hearing the full story. There were dozens of girls in the hall who would give their eye teeth to be Paul McDonough's girlfriend, there was no need for anyone to feel sorry for him. 'Just say the word if yer don't want to go out with me. I'd rather be told the truth than be used as a stand-in.'

Joanne forced a look of surprise to her face. 'I'm not using yer!' After what Paul had told her, she knew she didn't stand a chance with him. Not now or ever. 'What d'yer think I am? If I didn't like yer, I would certainly say so!' Like hell I would, she thought. Not when he pays for me to come here. Besides, Sam was a nice-looking bloke, even if he wasn't in the same class as the dark-haired, brown-eyed boy she really wanted. And he treated her well, always polite and attentive. 'I'm not a gold-digger, yer know.'

Sam smiled and reached for her hand. 'Yer see too many films, Joanne. There's not many gold-diggers come to Blair Hall, they only go after men with bags of money.' The interval waltz was announced and he led her on to the dance floor. 'How about coming to the pictures with me on Friday? I'll take yer in the best seats and buy yer a box of chocolates.'

'Yeah, okay, that sounds good. As long as I can choose which film we go to see.'

'How's Doreen?' Nellie asked as she pulled the carver chair over to the table. 'I suppose yer've been over?'

'Yes, sunshine, I've been over. Eight o'clock every morning without fail. She's fine and looks really well. But there's only a couple of weeks to go now, so I'm watching her like a hawk. Phil's had strict instructions that if Doreen has any pains during the night, he's to come over for me. Even if she says it's nothing, he's got to come.'

'I hope it happens during the day, girl, so I can help yer get her to the hospital. It's a pity we don't know anyone with a car what could take us.'

'None of our friends are well off enough to afford a car. Except Alec Porter, he's got his van. But I can't see our Doreen getting in there, she's as big as a house now.'

'Ay, just think, girl, yer'll be a grandma soon. I'll be dead envious of yer, yer know that, don't yer? I hate you having something I haven't. I don't know why your Doreen couldn't have waited for Jill and Steve, then we'd have both been grandmas.'

'Yer know why Doreen didn't wait, her and Phil were thinking of Victoria. They wanted her to see their child before God decides he wants her in heaven.' There was fondness in Molly's eyes as she gazed across at her friend. 'Just think, sunshine, if it hadn't been for our Doreen getting pregnant, we wouldn't have been so keen to find Phil's family. As it is, Victoria will not only see his baby, but she's met all his family as well. And as she said to me yesterday, she's happier than she's ever been in her life. So don't be envious, Nellie, 'cos your turn will come soon enough. Yer'll be a grandma three times over before yer know it.'

'I'll be waiting a hell of a long time for our Paul to make me one, he hasn't even got a girlfriend. Not that we know of anyway. But that doesn't stop him going out every night. He goes dancing with Archie and Lily about once a week, but where he gets to the other nights, well, God only knows.'

'I would never have thought of him and Phoebe breaking up, not in a million years. I said it was a lovers' tiff and would be over in a week, but how wrong I was. Ellen said she thinks Phoebe's pining for him, she's gone so quiet and seldom goes out. But she's too stubborn to do anything about it. It's six weeks now, and the longer it lasts the less chance there is of them making it up.'

'Huh! Our Paul's not a barrel of laughs, either. Oh, he might laugh, but not like he used to, if yer know what I mean. It never gets as far as his eyes. And he never pulls me leg like he used to, and I don't half miss that.'

'There's nothing we can do about it, sunshine, we can't force them back together again. All we can do is hope they come to their senses before it's too late.'

'I feel like knocking some sense into him, but George has told me to do and say nothing. Yer know what my feller's like, anything for a quiet life. But it's breaking me heart to see the way our Paul's changed. He's not the happy lad he was before all this. If I thought it was that Joanne Mowbray what caused it, I'd clock her one. I did mention it to her mother but Beryl says she knows nothing about it. And yer can't blame the mother for what the girl did.'

'Tommy and Rosie get married in two months so Phoebe and Paul are going to have to meet each other then. Unless they turn down the invitations.' Molly sighed. 'I've just thought on, Phoebe can't refuse to come, she's a bridesmaid.'

'Yer've got a lot on yer plate, girl, what with worrying about Doreen *and* the wedding. If I had all that on me mind I'd leave home.'

'A fat lot of good that would do, sunshine, leaving someone else with all the worry.' Molly smiled as an image came to her mind of Nellie scurrying down the street with a case in her hand. Halfway down the street the case burst open and brassieres the size of barrage balloons tumbled out, accompanied by lisle stockings with the elastic garters still attached and blue fleecy-lined bloomers.

'What are yer smiling at, girl?'

Molly shook her head. 'Nothing exciting, it was just something Jack said this morning. Anyway, I don't have to worry about the wedding, everything's organised. I've got to say that Rosie is the most organised person I've ever met. She's sent the money over to Ireland for the boat fare for her mam and dad to come over. She's booked a photographer, ordered the flowers and the cars, and is now busy writing out place cards for the table so everyone will know where they're sitting. In fact I've got very little to do. But I suppose it is easier when a son gets married 'cos most of the arrangements are done by the girl's family. All me and Jack have got to fork out for is the reception. Oh, and a few bottles of port.'

'How are yer getting on with the reception, have yer nearly paid up?'

'I've still got fifteen pound to pay, that's all. But our Tommy doesn't know that so mind what yer say when ye're talking to him. Him and Rosie were over the moon when we told them the reception was our wedding present, 'cos apart from Rosie's dress, it's the biggest outlay.'

'Yer are still wearing the same hat as yer had for the girls' wedding, aren't yer? Everyone will know I'm wearing the same one, so I don't want you waltzing round in a new creation.'

'Of course I'm wearing the same hat! The price it was, I'll be wearing it to every wedding for the next ten years. And I don't care what anyone thinks, either, 'cos I'm not made of money.'

Nellie smiled at the words. 'That's right, girl, you tell 'em! They'll all be jealous 'cos we'll be the best dressed women there. And my feller will fall for me all over again.'

Molly pressed her hands down on the table and pushed herself up. 'It's time we were making a move, sunshine, or the shops will be closing for the dinner hour. And please don't stop and talk to all and sundry, Nellie, 'cos I don't want to be out for long. Until our Doreen's had the baby I want to be on hand all the time.'

When they were walking down the street arm in arm, Nellie said, 'Ay, girl, I hope ye're not going to be one of these women who never stop talking about what a lovely baby yer daughter's had. I mean, I don't mind hearing once how much it weighed, and how like it's dad it is, but it would get on me wick if I had to listen to it over and over.'

'I'll bear that in mind, sunshine. In fact, just to please yer, I'll stand in the middle of the street and shout all the information out at the top of me voice so everyone can hear and I won't have to repeat it.'

Nellie grinned. 'I knew yer'd understand, girl, 'cos yer know me inside out.'

'Oh, I do indeed, Nellie! I know yer well enough to know yer've got a head like a sieve and will have forgotten all these things ye're telling me not to do by the time your own first grandchild arrives. But don't you worry yer little head about it 'cos I'll be here to remind yer.'

Nellie changed foot to keep pace with Molly. 'See, it's just like I tell everyone, girl, ye're a mate in a million. I'd never get another one like yer.' Under her breath but just loud enough to be heard, she muttered, 'Not that I'd bloody want another one like her, she's a bossy bugger.'

Ten days later, Doreen began to have twinges in her tummy just after Phil had left for work. Not wanting to worry Aunt Vicky, and not being sure whether they were labour pains, she said nothing until they became more frequent and more severe as she was making some sandwiches for lunch. She told herself not to panic or she'd upset the old lady and the baby.

'I'm having pains in me tummy, Aunt Vicky, so I'm nipping across the street to see what me mam has to say. It might be just a false alarm.'

A frail hand fluttered to the old lady's face. 'D'yer think it's the baby, sweetheart?'

'I don't know, that's why I want to see me mam. I'll come straight back, I won't leave yer on yer own for long.'

'Don't go rushing over the cobbles in case yer slip, sweetheart.' Victoria left her chair to take up a position by the window. She watched as Molly opened the door and Doreen disappeared inside. Then the old lady began to pray. This was something she'd been looking forward to, but now the time had come she felt afraid for the girl who had become like a daughter to her.

As soon as Molly opened the door she could tell by Doreen's face that this wasn't a social call. 'Have yer started having pains, sunshine?'

Doreen licked her dry lips before nodding. 'I had little niggling pains when yer were over this morning, but they kept going away so I didn't mention them. But they're getting stronger now and coming more often.'

Molly was reaching for her coat and keys as she asked, 'Have yer waters broke, sunshine?'

'Me knickers feel wet, Mam, so they must have done.'

'I'll see yer across the street, then I'll call for Nellie. I know yer've got a case packed ready, so all yer need to do is change yer knickers. Yer can be doing that while I knock for Nellie, and I'll run up and ask Maisie to ring for a taxi.' Molly took her daughter's elbow and led her across the cobbles. 'Don't worry, sunshine, ye're going to be fine. Just keep remembering that very soon yer'll have yer little baby in yer arms. And when yer look down into a beautiful new face yer'll think a miracle has happened.'

Nellie was already at her door with her coat on. 'I saw Doreen crossing over, girl, and I had an idea that her time had come.'

'I want yer to come to the hospital with me, sunshine, so while I run to ring for a taxi, will yer call at Mary Watson's and ask her if she'll sit with Victoria until we get back, or until Phil comes in from work?'

'Yeah, I'll do that.' Nellie pushed the door closed behind her. 'And I'll ask Mary to let Jack and George know, in case they get in from work before we get back.'

The taxi came fairly quickly, so there was no time for nerves to take over, and no time for tears. But when Doreen looked through the taxi window to see Aunt Vicky standing on the step being supported by her neighbour, Mary Watson, there was a lump in her throat as she waved goodbye.

Doreen's first bad contraction came when they were halfway to the hospital. When she groaned and clutched her tummy, Molly forgot all the things she'd promised herself over the last few weeks about staying cool, and began to panic. Oh, please God, she prayed, let us get to the hospital on time. She knocked on the glass sliding window which separated them from the driver and he slowed to a crawl before turning his head. When he saw Doreen doubled up with her arms holding her tummy, he didn't need Molly's warning to get them to the hospital as quickly as possible. While he was a family man and loved children, he didn't like the idea of one being born in the back of his cab. Not when he'd spent hours on Sunday giving it a thorough clean out.

Molly had half a crown ready in her hand. When the taxi pulled up outside the hospital entrance, she thrust the money at the driver without even asking how much the fare was or noting the look of relief on the man's face. 'Move out of the way, Nellie, while I help Doreen down. Mind yer don't bang yer head, sunshine, and come out backwards, it'll be easier for yer. Leave yer case, I'll see to it.'

Once they were in the entrance hall, Nellie took hold of Doreen's arm. 'I'll walk her down the corridor while you fetch someone.'

'Don't leave me, Mam,' Doreen cried, 'I'm frightened!'

'A nurse will be more use to yer than I am, sunshine, and I'll get one quicker on me own.'

And Molly was true to her word. In no time at all she was hurrying ahead of a nurse who was used to the ways of mothers. They'd raised families themselves but were still afraid when the time came for one of their daughters to start their own family.

'I'll attend to Mrs Bradley now.' The nurse was kind and efficient. She took the case from Nellie and told them, 'If you want to wait in the waiting room, I'll be along to see you when she's been examined by the doctor. I'll let you know if she's being kept in.' As she led Doreen away, she said over her shoulder, 'You must be prepared for a long wait because we're very busy at the moment.'

There was a look of pleading on Doreen's face when she glanced back. 'Don't go home, will yer, Mam? Not without seeing me?'

'I'll be here, sunshine, don't you worry about that. No matter how long it takes, I'll wait until I know what's happening.'

'Getting yerself all het up isn't going to help Doreen,' Nellie said for the umpteenth time. 'I know we've been here an hour, but the nurse did say it would be a long wait. So will yer stop pacing the floor, girl, 'cos ye're turning me into a nervous wreck.'

'Just wait until it's your Lily expecting a baby, yer'll be singing a different tune then. And it's only natural for me to worry. Yer should understand that instead of telling me to shut up and sit down. My daughter is not here to have a tooth out, yer know.'

The door to the waiting room opened and the nurse came in. 'Your daughter is in labour, Mrs Bennett, and we're keeping her in. We're preparing her now before taking her through to the labour ward.'

'Is she all right?' Molly asked, and without giving the nurse time to answer, blurted out more questions. 'How often is she having the pains now? How long d'yer think it will be before the baby's born?'

The nurse raised her eyebrows. 'Doreen tells me she has two sisters and a brother. After having four children, you should know that is a question no one could answer. Babies will come when they're ready and not before.'

'I know all that, Nurse, but having had four meself, I know what Doreen's going through. And you'll have seen enough mothers to know it's not unusual for them to be as worried as I am. So I'm asking yer to let me see me daughter before yer send me packing off home.'

'Go on, Nurse,' Nellie said, coaxingly. 'A couple of minutes isn't going to hurt no one.'

'You will be allowed to see Doreen as soon as she's been gowned. But the labour ward is not the best of places to sit in as many of the women are in the process of giving birth and are quite vocal.'

'Nurse, when I was having each of my babies I used to scream the place down, so I'm the wrong one to criticise.' Molly managed a weak smile. 'Mind you, if any of them frighten me daughter I'll put a sock in their mouth.'

Nellie tugged on her coat. 'Yer haven't got a sock with yer, girl, so yer'll have to use yer fist.'

'Anyone causing a disturbance will be evicted from the ward, so bear that in mind.' The nurse was joking as she made for the door. 'And for your punishment you will be made to sit in the labour ward until you've learned to behave yourselves.'

'Hang on, please.' Seeing the nurse was in a happy frame of mind, Molly thought she'd try her luck and hopefully get some information. 'You must have seen hundreds of babies born and probably have more experience than the doctors. So in your opinion how long has Doreen got to go?'

'I would say she'll be a couple of hours at least, but I'm only hazarding a guess. It could be any minute or it could take until tomorrow. I'm sorry, that's the best I can do.'

Molly and Nellie returned to their chairs, both looking down in the mouth. 'We could be here this time tomorrow,' Nellie grumbled. 'Trust you to have a slow daughter.'

'I'll have a bet with yer to pass the time away,' Molly said. 'I'll bet yer a tanner that Doreen has her baby before midnight.'

'Okay, girl.'

Molly tutted. 'What d'yer mean, okay, girl?'

'I mean, I understand that if Doreen doesn't have her baby before midnight, yer owe me a tanner. That's all right with me, girl, I can buy meself a quarter of Liquorice Allsorts and a quarter of Mint Imperials.'

'But yer do understand that if I win the bet, yer owe me a tanner?'

'Oh, yer never asked me to have a bet, girl, so don't be trying to get one over on me. Yer said you'd bet me a tanner, yer didn't say anything about me having a bet. I mean, yer never asked me when I thought the baby would be born, did yer?'

'Ye're a tight-fisted so-and-so, Nellie McDonough, honest to God, yer are. Yer'd take my tanner but wouldn't take a chance on having to give me one!'

'Oh, stop yer flipping moaning! I'll have a ruddy bet with yer 'cos it would be worth a tanner to shut yer up.' Nellie jerked her head back and rolled her eyes. She was only acting to keep her mate's mind occupied and away from her daughter. 'I bet your Doreen has her baby before ten o'clock tonight, so there!'

'Okay, ye're on! If the baby's born before ten I owe yer a tanner. If not then the Mint Imperials and the Liquorice Allsorts are mine.'

Nellie's bosom rose as she gave a deep sigh. 'It's a mug's game, this having babies lark. God should have invested another pastime which was as exciting as having sex, but without the problem that goes with it. Or He could have made intercourse horrible, then red-blooded women like me wouldn't be chasing our husbands around the bed every night.'

'Every night, Nellie? Aren't yer exaggerating somewhat? Or is that why George always looks worn out, as though he's carrying the cares of the world on his shoulders?'

'He's the happiest man in Liverpool, is my feller. I know he may look tired all the time but can yer think of a nicer way of wearing yerself out? It beats joining a rambling club, I can tell yer. Not that I've ever been in a rambling club, like, but I knew a bloke who was and he was the most miserable sod imaginable! I wouldn't have been chasing him around the bed every flipping night.'

'How can yer talk about rambling clubs when the furthest I've know yer walk is to the shops and back?' Molly said before remembering. 'Oh, I was forgetting the time I coaxed yer to walk to Walton Vale. Yer moaned about it for a month afterwards.'

'It's all right for you, yer haven't got corns on yer toes what give yer gyp. Bloody murder they are, and not a word of sympathy do I get from you.' Nellie gave another deep sigh. 'Ay, girl, I'm running out of things to talk about. How about a game of "I Spy"?'

The appearance of the nurse had Molly jumping to her feet, childhood games forgotten. 'How is Doreen? Can we go and see her now?'

'Yes, she's still in the main ward so you can see her. But only for a few minutes because it's a busy ward and the nursing staff can be run off their feet so visitors are not welcome.'

Molly's face dropped. 'Yer mean, I can't sit with her?'

'I'm afraid not. And even when she's had the baby, only fathers are allowed in for the first few days. So come and see your daughter now because it may be seven to ten days before you see her again.' The nurse walked from the room, her freshly starched uniform making a rustling sound. She was followed by Molly, with Nellie coming up behind, her little legs moving fast to keep up. 'Don't let her see you're worried, she's nervous and agitated enough already. Try to cheer her up.'

'Can't I wait in the waiting room until she has the baby? I won't be no trouble, I just want to know she's all right.'

'Good grief, you could be there all night! I suggest you go home and ring up in about four hours. And the husband will be allowed in once Doreen's had the baby and been taken to the maternity ward.' They reached the entrance to a ward and the nurse waved her hand. 'Third bed down on the right. Remember, five minutes only or you'll get a ticking off from the Ward Sister. As I said, they're strict about visitors.'

Doreen's arms were lying flat by her sides on top of the white sheet. Her eyes were wide with trepidation. She was amazed that some women were relaxed enough to hold a conversation with the person in the next bed. All she wanted was to curl up under the sheets and cry. And when she saw her mother coming towards her, a broad smile on her face, the girl wanted more than anything to hold out her arms and beg to be taken home. But she didn't. Because when she saw Auntie Nellie behind her mother, waddling down the ward with a face red from the exertion of trying to keep up, Doreen actually managed a smile. 'Hello, Mam! Auntie Nellie!'

304

'Hello, sunshine! We're under strict instructions to stay only a few minutes so we'll have to be quick.' Molly stroked the blonde hair before kissing her daughter. 'Only husbands are allowed to visit, even after the baby's born, so yer won't see me for a while. But I'll be getting Maisie to ring in every couple of hours to ask how things are, and I'll be thinking of yer all the time.'

Nellie moved closer to the bed. 'I won't get too near, girl, in case it's catching. But we'll all be thinking of yer, all yer family and friends what love yer. And yer can tell the doctor I said we don't want a baby what's always crying so he's to pick a nice quiet one.' Her chins agreed with her nodding head. 'Otherwise we'll bring it back and exchange it for another.'

Molly could have kissed her friend for bringing a smile to Doreen's face. 'Phil will be here as soon as he's had a bite to eat, sunshine, and we'll all be waiting for him to get back with his news. If there's anything you want bringing in, let him know and I'll get it for yer.'

A nurse appeared at the food of the bed. 'I'm afraid you'll have to leave now.'

Molly nodded. 'We're just going.' She bent for a last kiss. 'Yer'll be fine, sunshine, and it'll all be over in no time.'

When Nellie bent for her kiss, she whispered, 'Try and have it before ten o'clock, girl, 'cos I've got a bet on with yer mam.'

The nurse overheard and was smiling when she escorted the two women from the ward.

It was eleven o'clock and Victoria Clegg's living room was full. All the Bennett family were there, even Ruthie who had flatly refused to go to bed. Jill and Steve had been there since seven, as had Tommy, Rosie and Nellie. They were all on pins waiting for Phil to come home from the hospital.

'I thought he'd have been well home by now,' Molly said, her eyes on the clock for the umpteenth time. 'Doreen must still be in labour.'

'Calm down, love,' Jack said. 'It could be hours yet.'

Then they heard the key turning in the lock and all eyes were on the door when Phil walked in. He hardly had time to close it behind him before Molly was clutching his arm. 'How is Doreen?'

His eyes went around each of them before his face broke into a wide grin. 'Doreen and I are the proud parents of a beautiful son.' That was all he was able to say before the hugs, kisses and hand-shakes started. All the women were crying with happiness, and in Molly's case with deep relief.

305

'Can we have a bit of quiet now?' Jack asked. 'Give the lad a chance to tell us more about the baby and Doreen.'

Phil pulled a chair over to where Victoria was sitting. He took her hand in his before telling them, 'The baby weighed seven and a half pound, has a good set of lungs and is perfect. Doreen was very tired when I left her, but happier than she's ever been. And I can't put how I feel into words. I'm dizzy with happiness, bursting with pride and ten feet tall.'

His Aunt Vicky squeezed his hand. 'Have yer had time to think of a name for your son?'

Phil nodded. 'We chose the name when we first knew Doreen was expecting. We had two names, one for a boy and one for a girl. The baby's going to be called Bob, after my father.'

'Oh, I'm so happy,' Molly said, tears sliding down her cheeks. 'Yer'll have to let yer grandma know as soon as yer can.'

'I promised Doreen I'd go in me dinner hour tomorrow. She'll be over the moon, particularly when I tell her what we're calling our son.'

'Will yer give Doreen a big kiss for me tomorrow night?' Jill was feeling very emotional. 'Tell her me and Steve can't wait to see the baby. And we've got stacks of baby clothes for her so she won't need to worry on that score. And we stuck to white, thank goodness, in case it was a boy.'

'Didn't meself have the same idea?' Rosie said. 'Blankets, sheets, pillowcases and matinee coats, all in white.' She turned her beautiful Irish eyes on her dearly beloved intended. 'And we both send Doreen a kiss, don't we, sweetheart?'

'I'll say – a whopper!' Tommy was still getting used to the idea of his sister becoming a mother. She was only a year older than him! 'Tell her we're all very proud of her.'

Nellie had been quiet up till now. 'Just out of curiosity, Phil, what time was the baby born?'

'A quarter to ten, Auntie Nellie.'

The chubby face that turned to Molly was creased in a wide grin. 'That's a tanner yer owe me, girl.' Then she rubbed her hands and said to Phil, 'Tell Doreen I'm not only proud, but richly proud. And tell her the timing was perfect.'

There was much laughter when Phil said, 'She knows that, Auntie Nellie. She told me to tell yer she wants half of that tanner for making it on time.'

Molly gave a deep sigh. 'If she can crack jokes then I don't have to

306

worry about me daughter. I'll rest easy in me bed tonight, thank God.'

'If I don't get me tanner tonight, girl,' Nellie told her, 'I'll charge yer a penny a day interest.'

'Sod of, Nellie McDonough! I'm a grandma now or had yer forgotten? Yer'll treat me with respect from now on.'

Chapter 23

Ten days after the birth, Doreen and the baby were discharged from hospital and Phil took the day off work to bring them home by taxi. No man had ever looked happier or more proud as he helped his wife and child down the high step of the cab. Molly, Nellie, and Mary Watson were waiting outside Miss Clegg's house and a few of the neighbours came out for a peep at the new baby and to offer their congratulations.

'I knew he'd be blond,' Mary said, gently stroking the cheek of the sleeping child with a finger. 'He couldn't be anything else with his mam and dad both being blond. I bet he's got blue eyes, too!'

Molly fussed around her daughter. 'Let's get inside, sunshine, yer don't want to be on yer feet too long. And Victoria's been a nervous wreck waiting for yer.'

Doreen made straight to where the old lady sat in her rocking chair. 'Here yer are, Aunt Vicky, you can have first hold.'

Victoria searched Molly's face. 'You should be first to hold him, Molly, he's your grandson.'

'No, that's all right, sunshine, I held him that time I sneaked into the hospital. I managed a quick cuddle before the nurse told me off for being there.'

Victoria's faded blue eyes were blurred with tears as she held the child of the couple who'd made her house into a home. 'He's beautiful. Look at those tiny hands and fingernails, they're perfect.' Slowly she set the rocking chair in motion while softly singing a lullaby. This was the first time in her life that she'd held a new-born baby in her arms. If the man she'd loved hadn't been killed in the First World War, she too would have know the joys of motherhood and of rearing a family.

'Yer make a lovely picture, Aunt Vicky,' Paul said. 'You and the baby look so contented with each other.'

'Yes, we're going to get along fine.' There was a knowing look in her eyes when she said, 'Will yer bring his present down now, please?'

The present turned out to be a cradle in dark polished wood with ornate carving on the sides and spindles. And it had a handrail for rocking the cradle from side to side. It was a very handsome present and a complete surprise to everyone. Doreen was stunned for several seconds, her hand to her mouth. 'Oh, it's beautiful! How and when did yer get it, and why wasn't I told?'

Phil was wondering how much happiness a body could take. He'd said so many times over the last few months that he couldn't be any happier, and yet things kept happening to prove him wrong. Right now, he felt as though his heart was ready to burst. 'Aunt Vicky bought it as a present for the baby. We had it delivered to the back door so no one would see, and we didn't tell you because we wanted it to be a surprise.'

'That's a surprise and a half, that is,' Molly said. 'Baby Bobby is a very lucky child. None of my children had anything so grand. It really is beautiful.'

'Yer can say that again.' Nellie and her chins thought it was very grand. 'I haven't never seen one so posh.'

Doreen, the pain of childbirth forgotten, was clasping her hands. 'Ooh, can I go and bring some bedding down and make it look pretty?'

'You, young lady, can sit on the couch and rest yer legs.' Molly didn't give her daughter a chance to argue as she pressed her gently on to the couch. 'A week of taking it easy, sunshine, then we'll let yer do a little bit more each day. So do as ye're told and I'll bring everything down that yer need. I'm just as eager to see me grandson in his posh cradle as you are.' She was halfway across the room when she heard Nellie speaking. 'What did yer just say, Nellie?'

It was Phil who answered. 'She was just saying how lucky the baby is, Mrs B.'

'Don't be telling no lies, son, or God will punish yer.' Nellie's hands went to her hips and she pretended to glare at her friend. 'What I said was that there'll be no stopping yer now ye're a grandmother. Ye're going to be bragging all the time and getting on me bloody nerves. I dread the day he starts teething and I get a running commentary from yer every day on how bad his pains are. I just hope he grows them all in one night and gets it over with, otherwise me life won't be worth living.'

'Ah, me heart bleeds for yer, yer poor thing.' Molly sniffed up and wiped away an imaginary tear. 'But yer won't be left out, I'll see to that. For every night I sit up with the baby while he's teething, we'll let you have him the next night. Now I can't say fairer than that.'

'Nah, I wouldn't be arsed, girl. I'll hang on till your Jill has a baby. Then, 'cos my son will be the father, we'll be on equal terms. We can spend out time each trying to outdo the other with bragging.' Nellie shook her head and tutted in mock disgust. 'No, our lives have changed forever, girl, they'll never be the same. I can see it all now. Instead of trying to coax a leg of lamb off Tony in the butcher's, yer'll be saying, "The baby's gained two ounces this week, Tony, isn't that fantastic! And he smiled at me this morning. He's far more advanced for his age than most babies."'

Molly chuckled. 'I'm one ahead of yer, sunshine! I'm going to ask Jack to put his name down for a job in his works when he leaves school.'

It was Phil's turn to chortle. 'I'm sorry, Mrs B, but I beat yer to it. I've sorted it out with me boss and the lad's coming to work with me when he leaves school.'

Nellie had a smirk on her face when she waddled over to Molly. 'Go on, girl, let's see if yer can go one better than that.'

'I'll give it some thought later, sunshine, 'cos at the minute me mind's full of getting the cradle ready for my grandson.' Molly had her foot on the bottom stair when she said, 'I'm sure when he's settled down, Doreen will let yer rock it.'

'Ay, yer know what yer can do with yerself, don't yer, girl?'

'No, and I don't want yer to tell me, either! I'll not have yer swearing or using naughty words in front of me grandson. He's going to be a little gentleman, so there!'

'I'll come upstairs with yer, then, and whisper it in yer ear.'

There was silence in the room as the two women climbed the stairs. Everyone had their ears cocked, and they could hear Nellie puffing as she pulled herself up by the banister. Then they burst out laughing when they heard Molly saying, 'No, I will not bugger off, Nellie McDonough, there's work to be done here. So behave yerself or I'll send yer home with yer tail between yer legs.'

Molly cast an anxious eye at her daughter. There had been a constant stream of visitors since six o'clock and Doreen looked exhausted. It had been a long and over-exciting day for her; too long, in her mother's opinion. After all, she'd only come out of hospital that morning. It hadn't been so bad with her own family, 'cos Jill and Tommy understood when she'd explained that Doreen was still weak and mustn't over-exert herself. They'd produced their presents of baby clothes and bedding and left after half an hour. She'd even chased away Jack and Ruthie, much to the disgust of her youngest daughter who wanted to sit and rock the baby in his cradle. Mind you, Molly could understand the young girl because the baby looked adorable in his new white clothes, lying on sheets and pillowcases hand made and embroidered by Bridie and Rosie, and covered with a pale lemon blanket lovingly made by Jill.

Molly shook her head mentally to clear her mind. It was no good sitting here being all sentimental when she could see her daughter's smile becoming more forced and her eyelids drooping. But she couldn't be so outspoken to the visitors who were here now because they were Phil's family. Maggie Mitchell had been brought to see her new great-grandson by her daughter Beth and her husband Noel. And Maggie's happiness knew no bounds when she was told the baby was to be christened Bob. She would have smothered the child with love if Beth hadn't stepped in.

'Mam, I think the baby's been handled enough now, let Doreen put him down.'

Molly saw her chance to say what was on her mind without sounding impolite. 'Yes, I think mother and baby have both had enough for one day.'

Phil agreed. He'd seen his wife growing more tired but didn't like to say anything because he didn't want to upset his grandma. 'Yeah, the nurse told me Doreen should get plenty of rest for the next two weeks. In fact, she should have gone straight to bed when we got home from the hospital, but we've had a lot of visitors and she didn't want to miss anything.'

'I was so pleased to be home and to see all my family again,' Doreen admitted, 'and it's true I didn't want to miss anything. Besides which, I wanted to swank and show me beautiful baby off to everyone.' She stifled a yawn. 'But I'm ready for bed now.'

'Are yer feeding the baby yerself, sweetheart?' Maggie asked.

Doreen dropped her head to hide the blush she knew would cover her face. Young and inexperienced, she found it embarrassing to discuss anything so personal. 'Yes, every two hours I take him upstairs. For now anyway, but as Bobby grows older the times between feeds will be longer.' She raised her head. 'The Ward Sister told me to feed him when he's hungry and not to keep watching the clock. She said he'll soon let me know when he's hungry or wants his nappy changing 'cos he's got a great pair of lungs on him.'

'She's got a lot of sense, that nurse,' Maggie said, nodding in agreement with a woman she'd never meet. 'There's too many folk

312

around these days with fancy ideas. They think they know more on how to bring a baby up than the mother does. Silly stuff and nonsense they talk. Nobody knows better what is right for her child than the mother. And as the days go by and yer come to know each other better, yer'll get along just fine.'

Beth laughed. 'After passing all that knowledge over, Mam, d'yer not think it's time we left so Doreen can see to the baby and then get herself off to bed? From the sound of things there's been loads of visitors calling and the poor girl must be worn out.'

Maggie pushed herself from the chair and leaned over the cradle for one last look at her great-grandson. She couldn't help a stray tear escaping as she remembered the son she'd lost. How happy and proud he'd be if he were here now. Then she took a deep breath and pulled herself together. 'Yes, we'll leave yer in peace to get some rest. But I want yer to know, Doreen, and you, Phil, that yer've made an old lady very happy.'

'I'm not half getting soppy in me old age,' Molly said as she and Jack were cuddled up in bed that night. 'If I've cried once today, I've cried a hundred times.'

'Well, I've got to admit to being more than a bit emotional meself, love. After all, it's not every day yer daughter gives birth to a baby and yer become a granddad. Sitting there watching Doreen, me mind went back over every stage of her life, from a baby and toddler to her first day at school.' Jack pulled his wife closer. 'And as clear as day, I could see her in her teenage years. She could be wilful and as stubborn as a mule at times, and outspoken when she thought she was in the right. Her and Jill were as different in nature as chalk and cheese. But from the time she met Phil, Doreen changed. He's been a good influence on her and it's easy to see they love the bones of each other.'

Molly sniffed. 'Every time I looked at her today I got a lump in me throat. My little girl is now a mother herself. It takes some getting used to but I know she's going to make a perfect one.'

'She did very well for presents for the baby, didn't she? I couldn't believe it when I saw them all stacked up on the sideboard. There's enough matinee coats to last the lad until he starts school.'

'You weren't there when me ma and da came. I cried me eyes out when me ma handed Doreen the christening shawl she knitted for my christening. She's had it wrapped in tissue paper for all those years and it looks as good as the day she finished knitting it. Our Doreen was in floods of tears, and she wasn't on her own because me and

313

Victoria joined in. And I saw Phil turn to wipe his eyes.'

'It's been a day for tears, love, but they were tears of happiness. And it's a day we'll remember all our lives.' Jack removed his arm to plump his pillow. 'It's turned midnight and I have to be up for work. I've set the alarm and just hope I hear it ringing.'

'Before yer go to sleep, sunshine, just let me tell yer about me last bout of tears. It was when I saw Doreen putting the baby down in his new cot. Everything was perfect, from the embroidered pillows and sheets, to the soft blankets. And Doreen did it so gently, with so much love, I had to turn away so she wouldn't see her mother blubbering like a big soft kid.' Molly turned her head and kissed Jack on his forehead. 'Goodnight and God bless, sunshine. It won't be so hectic tomorrow, we'll have more time to get to know our grandson.'

'Mam, d'yer think it will be all right if me and Archie call and see the new baby?' Lily called from the kitchen where she was getting washed. 'We've kept away for three days because Auntie Molly said Doreen was tired with all the visitors, but I'd hate her and Phil to think we weren't interested. Besides, I'm dying to see the baby.'

'Yeah, of course yer can call! It's not as though yer'd be making a night of it.' Nellie pushed herself up and swayed to the kitchen. 'Did yer ever buy a present for the baby? It'll look terrible if yer don't take anything.'

'Yer said Doreen had got stacks of presents, Mam, so me and Archie decided not to buy anything. Instead, we've opened an account at the Post Office in the baby's name and we've put five pounds in. That way, Doreen can keep the account open and put a few coppers in each week, or she can draw it out whenever she likes.'

'Ay, that was a good idea.' Then Nellie frowned. 'How can Doreen draw it out if it's in the baby's name?'

'We've put her name on the book as well, as guardian. She'll have no trouble if she wants to take it out.' Lily gave her face a good rub with the towel. 'I don't think she will, though, 'cos Phil's on good money and they're not short.'

Paul left his seat to join them in the kitchen. 'I'll come over with yer. But, sad to say, I won't be bearing gifts because I wouldn't have a clue what to buy for a baby.' He pulled a face. 'It'll look a bit mean not taking anything, won't it?'

Nellie folded her arms across her tummy and puckered her mouth. 'I know what yer could buy, son, if the sweet shop is still open. They've got money boxes in the shape of animals and I think they're only

314

about two bob. Yer could buy one of those and put a few bob in. That would be a good present.' Then she had a brainwave. 'Ay, yer dad hasn't put his hand in his pocket yet, he'd give yer a few bob to put in it.'

'I heard that, Mrs Woman!' George called. 'Don't be so fond of giving my money away 'cos I'm not loaded.'

'Just listen to the tight-fisted so-an-so,' Nellie said, winking broadly before shouting back, 'Keep yer flaming money, yer lousy nit! I just hope yer get a hole in yer pocket and it all falls through. It would be the price of yer.'

'Now then, Nellie, can't yer take a joke? Yer know darn well I wouldn't begrudge giving the bairn a few bob.'

Nellie's whole body began to shake with laughter. 'Ten bob did yer say, George? Well I think that's very generous of yer.' She jerked her head at Paul. 'Run down to the shop pronto, before they close.'

He was out of the back door like a whirlwind, shouting over his shoulder, 'Don't go without me, Lily!'

Phil opened the door and greeted them warmly. Until he saw Paul, then his smile seemed to flicker for a brief second. 'Come in, it's nice to see yer.'

Lily was the first to enter the room and her footsteps faltered when she saw Phoebe holding the baby in her arms. Oh, dear, she thought, this should be interesting.

Paul came in, laughing, saying, 'Where's this baby I've heard so much about?' Then his eyes met Phoebe's and he stopped dead in his tracks. The room was so silent you could have heard a pin drop. Then he seemed to shake himself. 'Hello, Phoebe, how are yer?'

'Hello, Paul. I'm fine, thank you.' She dragged her eyes away from him and turned to Doreen.

Handing the baby over, she fought to keep her voice even. 'I'll leave now yer've got more visitors. But he's lovely, Doreen, you must be very proud. If you and Phil ever want a babysitter, I'll be more than willing. And as yer know, I'm used to looking after babies.'

'Yer don't have to leave on our account,' Paul said, willing her to stay.

'I'm not leaving on your account, I'm meeting a friend to go to the pictures.' Phoebe smiled her goodbyes and left a room that was quieter than it had been all day.

Lily was the first to speak when the front door was heard to close.

'Paul McDonough, ye're a stubborn beggar. Why don't yer go after her?'

'I'm not running after her, Lily, so just leave it, will yer?' He regained his composure and his smile, handing over the paper bag containing a money box in the shape of a cute piglet. 'It's not much, but I haven't had much experience buying for babies.'

'Oh, it's lovely!' Doreen made a great fuss to try and ease the awkward situation. 'And it's got money in it, too! When Bobby's old enough, he'll be able to thank his Uncle Paul.'

'It's got a rubber stopper in the bottom so yer can take the money out when yer want.'

Victoria held out her hand to inspect the money box. 'We'll make a habit of putting our spare ha'pennies and pennies in it. It'll soon mount up.'

Archie had been given the Post Office savings book by Lily, to hand over. 'Me and Lily didn't buy anything because we knew yer'd be getting plenty of baby clothes and stuff. We've opened an account for the baby in the Post Office.'

While all this was going on in Victoria's room, Phoebe was walking with a heavy heart to meet her friend. She thought she was getting over Paul but when their eyes met tonight she realised she was only kidding herself. He was the only boy for her and had been for as long as she could remember. She'd never thought she stood a chance with him because he was so handsome she knew he could have his pick of any girl he chose. When he'd started to take an interest in her and finally asked for a date, her cup of happiness had overflowed.

Phoebe kicked at a small stone on the pavement, the ferocity of the movement far exceeding the size of the stone. It was to vent some of the anger she felt. Why did she have to run away from him? Because that's what she'd done. She was far too early to meet her friend from work, so she'd cut off her nose to spite her face. The same as she'd done when she chose to believe what Joanne Mowbray had told her rather than Paul's version. Just a few little words and she'd lost the love of her life. However, knowing she'd got what she deserved didn't make the longing any easier to bear.

Nellie and George were in bed when the threesome got home from the dance, and not wanting to play gooseberry, Paul made the excuse of being tired and took himself up the stairs to give his sister and Archie some privacy.

'The baby's gorgeous, isn't he?' Lily smiled up into Archie's eyes.

They were sitting on the couch and his arm was around her shoulders. 'He's going to be blond and good-looking like his father.'

'Would you like to have children when yer get married?'

'Oh, yes! Holding Bobby in my arms tonight brought out my motherly instincts.'

Archie reached for her hand. 'And when will that be?'

'When will what be?'

'When were yer thinking of getting married?'

'That's a daft question, Archie Higgins. How do I know when I'll be getting married? It's manners to wait until ye're asked, and chance would be a fine thing!'

Archie took a deep breath and told himself not to be a coward. 'How would the idea of marrying me appeal to yer?'

Lily averted her eyes as a blush covered her face. 'Is that just a general question, Archie, out of curiosity, like, or are yer proposing?'

'If yer'll look me in the eyes, Lily, I'll tell yer.' He waited for her head to turn and her big hazel eyes to meet his, then he said, 'I think yer know how I feel about yer, Lily. How I've felt since the moment I first saw yer. Some people say there's no such thing as love at first sight, but there is. I fell for yer hook, line and sinker then, and my love for yer has grown deeper over the months. I'd give anything to hear yer say yer feel the same way about me.'

Lily pulled back and lifted a hand to stroke his cheek. 'You are such a dear, kind, sweet man, Archie, it would be very hard not to love yer. And if ye're proposing to me, then yes, I will marry you.'

'Yer will!' Archie was beside himself. He cupped her face between his hands and rained kisses on it. 'When will yer marry me?'

'Well, not tonight 'cos it's a bit late.'

They burst out laughing and clung to each other. 'Let's tell yer mam and dad, I want them to know how happy I am.'

'Me mam would skin yer alive if yer woke her up now! Besides, we've got a lot to talk about before we tell anyone. For instance, will we be getting engaged in the near future?'

'We can go for the ring on Saturday, if yer like. Anything yer want to do is all right with me, as long as yer don't change yer mind about marrying me.'

'There's no fear of that, love, I know when I'm well off. When yer come tomorrow night we'll tell me mam and dad, and Paul, of course. Then if yer like we can look at the rings on Saturday. But it doesn't have to be an expensive one, Archie, I don't want yer to skint yerself.'

'I'm all right for money, sweetheart, so you're to choose a ring that yer really like. I want yer to have the very best.' Archie was so full of happiness he wanted to share it. 'I wish there was someone we could tell, my heart is bursting to share the news with someone.'

'Yer can hold out until tomorrow. I won't tell the family, I'll leave that for you to do when yer come.' Lily put her arms around his neck and held him close. 'We've got a lot to discuss . . .' Her words were cut short when Archie's eager lips covered hers.

Nellie's eyes were suspicious as she looked across the table to where her daughter was eating her meal with a smile on her face. 'What's got into you, Lily? Yer've had a grin on yer face since yer got in from work. Have yer had a pay rise or something?'

'Oh, aye, and pigs might fly. No, I was just thinking of something one of the girls in work said today. She's a scream at times and has us in stitches.'

'Well, don't keep it to yerself, let us all in on the joke.'

Lily began to eat quickly. 'I'll tell yer some other time 'cos Archie's coming early tonight and I want to be ready.'

'Blimey! Yer don't have to shovel yer food in, five minutes is neither here nor there!'

'I want to get to the sink before Paul, he takes ages getting ready.'

'I'm in no hurry tonight,' her brother told her, 'I don't even know where I'm going yet.'

'In that case I'll have a swill and then help wash the dishes.' Lily wanted everywhere looking nice for when Archie came. The news he had for her parents wouldn't sound right told over a table strewn with dirty plates. 'I'll make a start, and by the time I've washed, yer'll all have finished yer dinners.'

Nellie was shaking the tablecloth in the yard and Lily was putting the glass bowl back in the middle of the table when the knock came. 'This'll be Archie, I'll open the door.'

George looked up from the *Echo* when Archie came in, and it struck him that the lad looked very pleased with himself. He must have heard a good joke in work, too, he thought, as he greeted his daughter's boyfriend. 'Has that lazy so-and-so yer work with been up to any more of his tricks, son?'

Archie looked surprised. 'No, he hasn't had a day off for two weeks now, why?'

'It's just that our Lily has had a smile on her face like a Cheshire cat since she came in, and you have that same look. I thought perhaps

318

yer'd heard the same joke she had.'

Nellie came in from the kitchen and pulled out a chair. 'Sit yerself down, son, there's no charge.'

'I will in a minute, Mrs Mac, but I've got something to tell yer and I'd rather do it standing up.' Archie held out his hand to Lily. 'Come and stand next to me, love.'

Nellie's eyes were like slits. 'What the hell d'yer need her to hold yer hand for? What's going on?'

'I've got a job to do, and I need to do it proper. I want to know if you and Mr Mac have any objection to me and Lily getting engaged?'

The *Echo* was dropped on to the floor at the side of George's chair as he sprang to his feet. Grasping Archie's hand, he shook it soundly. 'That's marvellous news, son, and me and the wife will be delighted. Won't we, love?'

Nellie folded her arms to hitch up her bosom. 'Ay, not so flipping fast, George. As Lily's father, ye're supposed to ask some questions before agreeing to give yer daughter away. Like, for instance, how much Archie has in the bank, and can he keep her in the manner to which she's been accustomised?' But she couldn't keep up the pretence, she was too excited and happy now her wishes had been granted. Pushing herself to her feet, she held her arms wide. 'Come here, yer daft ha'porth, and give yer future mother-in-law a kiss.'

Paul was smiling and his congratulations were hearty. He thought the world of Archie and knew his sister would be in safe hands with him. But he couldn't rid himself of the ache in his heart when he remembered how he and Phoebe had talked about getting engaged when they'd saved enough money. Still, this was a joyous occasion and not one to be thinking about what might have been. 'I hope yer realise what ye're taking on, Archie? Ye're not only getting our Lily, but me mam as well. Tommy always said yer were a brave man, and yer must be to take on Helen Theresa McDonough.'

Nellie was standing beside her husband and they had their arms around each other. The happiness on their faces said it all, they didn't need to put it into words. They were both mentally comparing this fine, upstanding young man with the boy Lily was courting last year. How different their feelings would be if it was Len Lofthouse standing in their living room now asking for her hand. 'When were yer thinking of getting engaged?'

'We're going to look at some rings on Saturday,' Lily said from the shelter of Archie's arms. 'But I've been having a good think about it today and I'd rather we didn't tell anyone for a week or so.'

319

Nellie's mouth gaped. She was already planning to go down and tell Molly as soon as the love-birds went out. 'Why not? It's no big secret, is it?'

'Of course not! But everyone is still celebrating Doreen's baby and I'd hate them to think we were stealing their thunder. Phil's taking the men out for a pint on Saturday to wet the baby's head, let's not spoil things for him. We can leave it just for another week until the excitement has calmed down.'

Nellie's voice came out in a high squeak. 'Yer mean I can't even tell Molly?'

Archie stepped in quickly. 'Lily, love, I don't think there's any need for that. It's not as though we've got the ring and are having a celebration party. All we need to say is that we're getting engaged soon. I would like to go round the Jacksons' tonight and tell Tommy. Yer know he's torn between who to ask to be his best man – me or Ginger. He's afraid of upsetting one of us. Well, I think it should be Ginger 'cos they've been mates for eighteen years. And I can smooth things over now by telling Tommy that I'd like him to be my best man when we get married. That should make everyone happy.'

Lily's face lit up with joy and mischief. 'I'll give in to yer tonight, but don't take that as a sign yer'll get yer own way with me when we're married.'

'Thank God for that!' Nellie's chest heaved. 'I couldn't have kept it to meself if I'd tried. As soon as you two go out I'll be down to Molly's to give her the news. It'll make a change for her to sit listening to me bragging rather than the other way round. And, oh, boy, am I going to brag!'

'Mam, ye're past the post, you are,' Lily laughed. 'Yer'd be no good in the Secret Service, yer'd be giving all the secrets away to the enemy.'

'Oh, I don't know, girl! Anyway, I don't think you and Archie getting engaged is enough to start another war, do you?'

Chapter 24

'Ay, girl, isn't it the gear about our Lily and Archie getting engaged?' Nellie did a little jig with her shoulders. 'Me and George haven't stopped smiling for the last three days, we're so pleased.'

'I don't blame yer, sunshine, 'cos I'd be exactly the same,' Molly told her sincerely. 'Lily's got a good one in Archie, he's a helluva nice bloke. Yer'll not have any worries as far as yer daughter's concerned, he'll take good care of her. And our Tommy's over the moon about it! As yer well know, Archie is his hero and he's delighted he's coming into our extended family.'

Nellie looked puzzled. 'What d'yer mean, girl, our extended family? He's marrying into our family, not yours.'

'The names may be different, sunshine, but the Bennetts and McDonoughs have always been like one big family and they always will be. I mean, Phil's not really one of us, but as far as we're all concerned he's a member of our large and happy family.'

This pleased Nellie no end. 'Yeah, ye're right, girl. We've always shared everything, haven't we? The bad times and the good, the laughter and the tears.'

'I think on the whole there's been more good times than bad, and more laughter than tears. But whatever, you and me have always shared them.' Molly winked across the table. 'We couldn't be closer if we were sisters.' She began to chuckle. 'Anyone listening would think we spend our time paying each other compliments. And I shouldn't even be here, I should be across the street helping me daughter with the baby.'

But Nellie didn't fancy going back to an empty house so she tried delaying tactics. 'Ay, did Jack tell yer about the good laugh they all had on Saturday night, when Phil took the men out for a drink?'

Molly nodded. 'He said Phil was like a dog with two tails. All the neighbours were slapping him on the back and shaking his hand, and he was lapping it up. Some of the men have three or four children of their own, but Phil was talking as though he was the only one who'd

321

been clever enough to perform this miracle. And Jack said he remembers feeling the same when Jill was born.' She spread her hands on the table in readiness to push herself up. 'That's it now, sunshine, so don't be thinking of anything else to keep me back. I'm late getting over there as it is.'

But Nellie was still reluctant to budge. 'Have yer heard whether Jack's brother from Wales is coming for the wedding?'

'Yes, we had a letter on Saturday to say he and his wife are looking forward to it.' Molly tried to keep a straight face but couldn't. 'It's seven weeks to the wedding, sunshine, and if yer had your way, yer'd keep me talking all that time. So just get off yer backside and let me go about me business.'

'I'll come with yer and give yer a hand.'

'Oh, no, yer won't! Doreen's got her hands full with seeing to Victoria and the baby, she doesn't want visitors this time in the morning.' She saw her friend's mouth open to object, and got in first. 'Yer can ask till ye're blue in the face, sunshine, but ye're not coming over to Doreen's with me. Now will yer vamoose, please?'

'Ye're a miserable bugger, Molly Bennett. I bet your Doreen wouldn't mind at all, she'd be glad to see me.' Nellie lifted her bosom from the table and pushed her chair back. 'I hope yer won't be late for us going to the shops?'

'If you don't stop talking and scram, I won't be back in time! So, on yer way, sunshine, and I'll see yer later.'

Molly still had a smile on her face when Doreen opened her front door. 'You look as though yer've had some good news, Mam! Either that or yer've got a feather in yer knickers.'

'It's that mate of mine! Honest, she's a cracker, she really is.' Molly walked into a room which was a lot tidier that the one she'd left. Victoria sat in her rocking chair smiling a greeting and looking very neat and tidy, and a peep in the cradle showed the baby fast asleep on spotlessly clean sheets and pillows, with that sweet smell all babies have, coming from him. 'Ye're very organised, Doreen, I must say. My place looks like a muck midden compared to here.'

'That's because yer sit gassing to yer mate instead of getting on with it. I do the work first and then relax.'

'I don't have much option, sunshine, 'cos when Nellie's bored at home with nothing to do, she takes a trip down to our house and we both take a trip down Memory Lane. The truth is, Nellie doesn't see why the furniture should be polished more than once a week. So every other day it's just a quick flick of a duster and Nellie's finished. She's

322

very clean, but she'd be the first one to tell yer that she's not house-proud.'

Molly's fit of the giggles started slowly and built up. 'I'm going to tell yer something that ye're not to repeat to a living soul, and I want yer to know I'm not laughing at me mate, I'm laughing with her, 'cos at the time she really did see the funny side. Anyway, one morning the hem on Ruthie's gymslip was hanging down and I couldn't find a needle to sew it. So I nipped out to the back entry and up to Nellie's to borrow one. I knocked on the back door but couldn't get an answer so I peeped through the net curtains. I could see she was in, so I knocked again. When she still didn't answer, I did no more than open the door and walk in. And yer'd never guess what she was doing. She was jumping up and down to blow the dust off the mantelpiece so she wouldn't need to stand on a chair and dust it proper. I couldn't believe it and told her she wanted her bumps feeling. I mean, she wasn't getting rid of the dust, just blowing it around. And when I told her, she said, "If some nosy bugger can be arsed looking up there for dust, then they deserve to find some."'

Victoria was laughing behind a hand while Doreen had her arms around her tummy and was doubled up. 'Ye're making that up, aren't yer, Mam?'

'Am I heckerslike! I'd never think that up in a month of Sundays! It was so funny, I laughed about it for weeks. Yer know how big Nellie's bust and tummy are? Well, I think her bust reached higher than she did! She's not half a case, the things she gets up to.'

'Yer wouldn't have her any different, would yer, Molly?' Victoria asked, even though she knew what the answer would be.

'I wouldn't change a hair of her head, sunshine. She may be daft, but she helps me keep my sanity. The day can be dark, with black clouds overhead and rain tipping down, but when Nellie walks through my door she brings the sun with her.' Molly slipped her coat off and hung it behind the door. 'That's enough about Nellie's shenanigans for today, we'll have another instalment tomorrow.' She rubbed her hands together and asked, 'What needs doing? Are the baby's nappies in steep?'

'Yes, they're in the bucket. But I can do them, Mam, I've got all day.'

'I came over to help, and help I will, So you get on the couch and put yer feet up for an hour while yer've got the chance. In a couple of weeks, when yer've got yer strength back, I'll leave yer to get on with it 'cos I'll be busy sorting things out for the wedding.

Until then, make use of me while yer can.'

'I wish I could do more to help Rosie with the dresses, Mam, but I'm tied with having to feed Bobby every two hours.'

'Rose is managing very well, sunshine, she's got everything under control. Jill, Lily, Phoebe and Ruthie have had a dress rehearsal and I believe they looked lovely. Rosie bought new head-dresses so the outfits look a bit different than they did for your wedding, and apparently all the girls are more than happy. No one has been allowed to see the wedding dress, though, not even me. Tommy said they want it to be a surprise.' Molly tutted and pointed a stiffened finger. 'Ye're doing an Auntie Nellie on me, keeping me talking! Now get those feet up on the couch and let me see to the nappies. There's a good blow out, so they shouldn't take long to dry.'

An hour later, eight nappies were on the washing line being whipped by the wind, the stove had been given a thorough clean and the sink and draining board washed down. 'The kettle's on for a cuppa, it won't be long now.' Molly was drying her hands when she heard a low whimper. Throwing the towel down, she rushed into the living room. 'Let me pick the baby up, please? I know he's ready for a feed, but it won't hurt him to wait two minutes while I have a little cuddle.'

Molly felt a surge of love as she gazed down into the face of her first grandchild. How perfect he was with his pink baby skin and bright blue eyes. He was lively, too, with his arms waving and feet kicking. 'Hello, little feller! I'm yer grandma, and yer'll be seeing a lot of me from now on. And yer granddad, too! He'll be so happy taking yer to the park to play on the swings and roundabouts, just like he did with yer mammy when she was young.' Her eyes wide with wonder, she stared at her daughter. 'Look at the way he's got hold of me finger! He's got a really strong grip.'

Doreen swung her legs off the couch. 'He's also got an appetite, Mam, and he's ready for a feed. So yer two minutes are up.'

Molly handed the baby over reluctantly. 'He could have waited until yer'd had a cup of tea. Yer can tell him from me that he's very inconsiderate.'

'I'll take him upstairs to feed and change him. Will yer make Aunty Vicky a drink, though? She's probably dying of thirst. I'll make a fresh pot when I come down.'

'Yeah, I'll do that, sunshine. Then I'll have to be on me way to get to the shops before they close. Nellie will be laying duck eggs by now.'

'Tell her I'll buy two off her,' Doreen said with a grin. 'Phil is fond of duck eggs but I don't like them, they're too strong.'

'D'yer need anything while I'm at the shops?'

'I fancy liver and onions if it's possible. Oh, and a large loaf, please. I've got potatoes in, and if I need anything else I can nip to the shops later when the baby goes down for his nap.'

'Me mouth's watering now.' Molly licked her lips. 'I'm rather partial to liver and onions meself so I think we'll have it for our dinner as well. That's if the butcher can oblige, of course. But Tony doesn't often let me down.'

When the window frame rattled, Molly screwed up her eyes and rubbed her forehead. 'I'm fed up telling Nellie what the brass knockers on the doors are for. She prefers to use the windows 'cos then she can see if ye're in, and announce herself at the same time.'

'It's a good job the baby was awake or she'd have frightened the life out of him. Tell her I said that, Mam.'

'Doreen, sunshine, I'm sorry to go back to the subject of ducks, but if I was to say anything to Nellie it would be like water off a duck's back. She'd have an answer on her lips before I had a chance to get the words out.' Molly slipped her arms into her coat. 'I'll lift the curtain and tell her to give me a minute while I pour Victoria's tea out.'

Molly moved the net curtain aside, chuckled, then pulled it right back. 'Will yer just look at the state of her!'

Nellie had her hands on her hips and a ferocious look on her face. 'Are we going to the ruddy shops today or not?'

Molly lifted a finger and mouthed, 'I'll be one minute.'

'Then open the door and let me in.'

'No! I'll be right out.'

'Molly, I'll pour me own tea,' Victoria said, 'I'm quite capable.'

Molly shook her fist before dropping the curtain. 'Yer've heard the song "Me and My Shadow"? Well, that was written for me and Nellie. If I didn't put me foot down, she'd be sleeping in our bed between me and Jack.' She jerked her head at her daughter. 'Go on up and feed the baby, sunshine, it's way past his time.'

As she poured out Victoria's tea, Molly couldn't help chuckling as she wondered what the neighbours must be thinking. Nellie couldn't speak softly if she tried so they'd have all heard her asking to be let in. And as she was still on the pavement outside the window, they'd be trying to guess what was happening. What they didn't understand was that Nellie had no sense of time and her minute would have stretched to half an hour.

'Here's yer tea, sunshine, and don't let Nellie's shenanigans spoil it for yer. She doesn't mean no harm.' After handing the cup over, Molly dropped a kiss on Victoria's wrinkled forehead. 'Tell Doreen I'll call later with her shopping.'

'Don't yer ever tell me again that I talk too much, girl, 'cos *you* would take some beating.' Nellie had her arm through Molly's and leaned heavily on it as she skipped a step to keep abreast. 'Yer can talk till the cows come home, you can.'

'Nellie, I don't go over to me daughter's to jangle, I go over to give her a hand. God knows she doesn't ask me to do much, she's coping very well for a girl of her age with a first baby. Just wait until your Lily has one, yer'll know what I'm talking about then.'

'I was going to say I wouldn't keep you standing in the street like a lemon, but I won't 'cos yer'll only get a cob on.' Nellie squeezed Molly's arm. 'Ay, can yer imagine me as a grandmother? D'yer think I'll make a good one?'

'Yer'll make a smashing one, sunshine. And if the baby takes after you, it'll be born with a smile on its face and a joke on its lips.'

That put Nellie in a happy frame of mind and she was laughing when she said, 'I hope so, girl. If it looks up at the midwife and starts swearing, our Lily will have me guts for garters.'

When they reached the butcher's, Tony was serving a customer and Ellen came over to them. 'Did yer see Corker?'

'No, is he home?' Molly was surprised because she didn't know he was expected. 'I've been over at Doreen's, that's how I've missed him.' She noticed the brightness of Ellen's eyes and said, 'It's easy to see how pleased you are, it's written all over yer.'

'I'm always pleased when he's home. He's got some news for yer so give him a knock when yer've got a minute.'

'Why can't you tell us?'

'I think he'd like to tell yer himself, I'm saying nothing. But I'll serve yer if yer tell me what yer want.'

'I'm hoping yer've got some liver in.' Molly kept her voice down in case the other customer decided she fancied liver as well. 'Enough for me and our Doreen.'

'Ay, what about me?' Nellie looked highly indignant. 'Or d'yer want my family to starve?'

'How was I to know yer wanted liver as well?' Molly rolled her eyes. 'I'm not a ruddy mind-reader.'

'Can I have yer ration book?' Ellen raised her voice as another

326

customer came into the shop. She daren't show favouritism or there'd be murder. 'And yours, Nellie?'

As Nellie passed the tattered ration book over, she whispered to Molly, 'It looks as though we're in luck, girl.'

Ellen tore the coupons out of the books and passed them back. Leaning over the counter, she said, softly, 'I can only let yer have half a pound each, but I'll throw a few sausages in as well.'

Molly smiled her thanks. 'Ye're a pal, Ellen.'

Tony was still serving as the two friends were leaving the shop. 'Have yer been up to anything exciting, Nellie? I could do with a laugh.'

'Sorry, Tony, but today's been very dull so far. In fact, I don't think I've cracked me face since I got out of bed. And me mate hasn't helped, she's been as miserable as sin. But I don't like letting yer down, so if yer give me a penny, I'll go to the newsagent's and buy yer a copy of the *Beano*. Yer'll get plenty of laughs out of that.'

'Yeah, but they're not slapstick like yours are. I mean, I get all the action from you.'

Nellie was chortling as she linked Molly's arm and they made for the door. 'You don't get all the action, Tony, my feller gets that in bed.'

Tony got his laugh after all, though. Because Molly, her face red with embarrassment, pulled Nellie out of the shop with such force the little woman's feet left the ground.

'Molly, me darlin', it's good to see yer. Come on in.' Corker held the door wide. 'Did Ellen tell yer I was home?'

Molly lifted her cheek for a kiss. 'Yeah, she asked if I'd seen yer, but I go over to Doreen's every morning so if yer did knock, that's where I'll have been.' She opted for one of the fireside chairs. 'Ellen said yer had some news for me. She was very secretive, wouldn't tell me what it is. And Nellie's practically fallen out with me for the second time today because I wouldn't let her come here with me. But I've got me hands full, Corker, and she can't understand that. I try to help Doreen as much as I can, and of course that's interrupted our whole routine. We're later going to the shops, and we can't make the time up because it's like a day out to Nellie, she talks to everyone. Anyway, I'm here now and eager for yer news.'

'I've finished sailing the seven seas, Molly, I'm home for good.'

She gaped at him. 'Go 'way! No wonder Ellen looked pleased with herself. Oh, I'm so happy for yer and for the kids, they'll be cock-a-hoop.' She sat back in the chair and smiled at the giant of a man who meant so much to her. She'd go so far as to say she loved him, but not with the same kind of love she had for Jack. 'So yer'll be looking for a shore job now, eh?'

'I'm fixed up, Molly! I start work on Monday with a firm down at the docks, overseeing the loading and unloading of their ships. They've offered me a job a few times before but I wasn't ready to leave the sea. But I'm ready now. So as soon as we docked this morning I went to see the boss at this firm, confirmed there was a job there waiting for me, then went back to the ship and signed off for good.'

'I'm glad, Corker. Glad for you, and Ellen and the kids. And it goes without saying that all our families and friends will be delighted. Wait until Jack and George know they've got their drinking partner home for good, they'll be over the moon.'

'I'll give them both a knock tonight and take them for a pint to celebrate. But before then, when can I see Doreen's baby? From what Ellen said, he's a beauty.'

Molly laughed. 'He is, but then I'm biased.' She glanced at the clock. 'Come over with me now, Doreen and Victoria would love to see yer. And I don't care whether yer think I'm bragging or not, but I'm so proud of my daughter because she's turned out to be the perfect wife and mother. And a good little housekeeper into the bargain.'

When Corker stood up he dwarfed everything in the room. 'I'll come as I am, it's only over the road.'

Molly took him across to Victoria's house but didn't intend to stay because time was marching on and she had a dinner to get ready. Not that the family would mind if they had to wait ten minutes for their meal. However, she felt that after working a full day they were entitled to be waited on when they got home. She was glad she hadn't rushed off, though, because the sight of Corker holding the tiny baby was really a sight she wouldn't want to have missed. The six foot four inch mountain of a man could have held the baby in the palm of one of his massive hands. But he gently rested him in the crook of his arm and looked down at the scrap of humanity with such joy and wonder on his face, the three women could be heard sniffing back the tears.

'He's a bonny little feller, Doreen, you and Phil must be very proud.' Then he spoke to the baby in soft tones. 'Yer'll be seeing a lot of yer Uncle Corker, me darlin', because I'm home for good now and will have the pleasure of watching yer grow to be a fine lad.'

Doreen looked at her mother with a puzzled expression on her pretty face. 'What does Uncle Corker mean, Mam, that he's home for good?'

'I'll leave him to tell yer himself, sunshine, 'cos I really have to go and see to the dinner. I'll tell Jack to expect yer, Corker, and perhaps Phil would like to go for a pint with yer, seeing as yer missed the wetting of the baby's head.'

Corker took his eyes off the baby to answer, 'It'll be my pleasure to toast the little feller with his father. And I hope I'm still around when Bobby here is old enough to come to the pub with us for his first pint. Like I've been for every boy in the Bennett and McDonough families.'

'Of course yer'll be around,' Molly said, making a determined effort to walk to the living-room door. 'Where d'yer think yer going? Me and Nellie will be keeping our eye on yer and yer'll not be going anywhere unless we say so.' With a definite nod of the head, she opened the door. 'I'll see yer all later. Ta-ra.'

'One of the girls from work's calling for me, Mam,' Lily said, 'so can we try and get the dinner over early?'

'What's she coming for?'

'Well, she works on the machine with me and we're really friendly, so when I told her about getting engaged, she suggested having a drink to celebrate. Me and Archie are taking her for a drink, then she's coming to Blair Hall with us.'

'But yer not engaged yet so what are yer celebrating?' Nellie shook her head. 'That's what I call putting the cart before the ruddy horse.'

Paul laid down his knife and fork. 'And where do I come into all of this? Yer knew I was coming to Blair Hall with yer.'

'I know! And it doesn't make any difference, yer can come for a drink with us first.'

'I hope ye're not going to try and palm me off with some girl I've never seen in me life before? I can get me own girls, thank you very much.'

'Oh, grow up, will yer! Ginny's got a boyfriend of her own so she wouldn't look twice at you. She's a smashing-looking girl, like a film star.'

Nellie chortled. 'I know some ugly film stars.'

'Don't you start, Mam, or she'll be here before we're halfway through our dinner.'

But when Ginny arrived everything had been cleared away and the room looked neat and tidy. And as Lily had said, she was a smashing-looking girl and very friendly. She chatted away with Nellie and

George as if they were old friends, and even Paul couldn't find fault with her. So it was a happy, laughing foursome who left the house intent on having a good time.

Phoebe happened to be facing the front window as she slipped her arms into her coat. She heard the laughter before Lily and Archie became visible. A second later Paul passed, accompanied by a very glamorous stranger who was smiling up into his face. Phoebe's heart lurched but she managed to put a smile in her face when she turned around. Her parents were sitting close together on the couch, and her brothers and sister were seated around the table. It had been a joyous two hours for the children had gone wild when told their father wouldn't be going away again. They all adored him. This was the first night for a long time that they hadn't dashed off to meet their friends straight after they'd had their dinner. Phoebe would have liked to stay in on this special night, too, but she'd arranged to meet a friend from work and there was no way she could contact her.

'I wouldn't be going out if I didn't have to, Dad, but I can't let Elsie down.'

'There's no reason why yer should stay in, me darlin', 'cos I'll be here every night from now on. Yer can't stand yer friend up, it wouldn't be right. So you go ahead and enjoy yerself and yer can tell me about it tomorrow.'

'I don't know where we're going yet, but don't wait up for me if I'm late.' Phoebe smiled as she got to the door. 'It's going to be great to have yer home, Dad, I'm delighted. But don't be getting the neighbours drunk tonight, will yer?'

'No chance of that,' Ellen said. 'Two pints and that's his lot. Anyway, enjoy yerself sweetheart. Ta-ra.'

Phoebe walked to the main road with her head down, deep in thought. She'd told her parents she didn't know where she was going, but that was a lie. She'd promised to go to the Astoria to see a film Elsie's sister had been raving about, and she'd been quite content with the arrangements until she'd seen Paul in the company of another girl. It had shaken her and she couldn't get the significance of it out of her mind. She'd blown her chances with him. Through her own stupid pride she'd lost him.

It was a quarter of an hour's walk to where she was meeting Elsie, and she had plenty to think of in that time. But thinking it and trying to explain it to her friend were two different things.

330

'What d'yer mean, yer'd rather go dancing?' Elsie asked. 'We're supposed to be going to the pictures, and anyway, I haven't brought me dancing shoes.'

'Neither have I,' Phoebe said, looking down at her high-heeled court shoes. 'But I can dance in these just as well.'

'What made yer change yer mind? It's only a couple of hours since I saw yer in work so something must have happened to bring about this change of heart.'

'I saw Paul with another girl and it really shook me.' Phoebe decided she didn't have time to make excuses, she may have left it too late as it was. 'I'd like to go to Blair Hall to see if he's there.'

'What good will that do if he's with another girl? Yer wouldn't lower yerself to excuse him, would yer?'

Phoebe shook her head. 'No, I wouldn't excuse him. But if he saw me and ignored me then I'd know we're through for good. But if I never give him the opportunity I might regret it for the rest of me life. I'm crazy about him, Elsie, I can't help the way I feel. And because I'm the one that caused the break-up, I should be the one to make the first move.'

Elsie had seen Paul and she'd thought her friend was crazy for falling out with him. She'd have hung on to him like grim death if he was her boyfriend. 'Okay, if that's what yer want to do. I can go to see the picture tomorrow night.' She linked arms. 'I just hope yer don't make a fool of yerself and get hurt into the bargain.'

Ginny turned out to be a good dancer and Paul was quite happy to have the first two dances with her. She had a really good sense of humour and he was laughing as he twirled her around. Then his eyes happened to light on the door of the dance hall just as Phoebe and her friend came in. The smile dropped from his face and he stumbled, treading on one of Ginny's toes. 'I'm sorry, did I hurt yer?'

'No, not really.' She raised her brows. 'Yer look as though yer've seen a ghost, Paul, or is my dancing that bad?'

'No my ex-girlfriend has just walked in and it gave me a surprise. She hasn't been here for ages and she's the last person I was expecting to see.'

'Still carrying a torch for her, are yer?'

'I suppose yer could say that. It was her fault we fell out and so I didn't see why I should be the one to make it up. We've both been stupid and stubborn, I suppose, but neither of us is prepared to give in.'

331

'You said she doesn't usually come here so perhaps this is her way of taking the first step towards making up.' Ginny glanced towards the door. 'Which one is she?'

'The one in the blue dress with the long mousy-coloured hair.'

'She's very pretty.' The dance came to an end Ginny walked with Paul to where Lily and Archie were standing. 'Too pretty to let go without a fight.'

Lily grabbed her brother's arm. 'Have yer seen who's here?'

Paul nodded. 'I saw her coming in. She's with her friend from work.'

'Are yer going to ask her up?' Archie was very fond of Phoebe and had a sneaking suspicion that Paul was still smitten with her. He'd certainly shown no interest in any other girl since they'd fallen out. 'If not, I'll ask her, just to be friendly, like.'

'I'll ask her.' Paul tried to sound nonchalant but his heart was pounding. 'That's if Ginny doesn't mind being left?'

'Of course I don't! Never let it be said I stood in the path of true love.'

As the first strains of a slow foxtrot filled the air, Paul excused himself, afraid that someone else might beat him to it. 'Hello, Phoebe, I'm surprised to see you here.'

'Hello, Paul. I think yer met me friend, Elsie, at Millington's once? We were going to the pictures but at the last minute we fancied a change. So here we are.'

'Would yer like to dance? I remember yer used to like a slow foxtrot.' He held out his hand and a shiver ran down his spine when Phoebe touched him. 'Yer don't mind, do yer, Elsie?' He would never know whether Elsie minded or not because his eyes never left Phoebe's face. And when she was in his arms, his whole body tingled. They glided over the floor, their beating hearts matching their perfect footwork. His lips close to her ear, he whispered, 'How have yer been, Phoebe?'

When she looked up, it was her intention to say she'd been fine. But those deep brown eyes gazing into hers brought the truth to her lips. 'I've been very lonely. And although me and Elsie had arranged to go to the pictures, I talked her into coming here instead because I'd seen yer pass our window with a girl. I came here to get yer back, Paul, and I'd have put up a fight with the girl ye're with.'

He pulled her closer. 'I've been lonely, too! I've missed yer that much I've been as miserable as sin. And the girl is a friend of Lily's from work, I've never seen her in me life before. There's no one else

332

for me but you, Phoebe, and after the dance is over can I take yer home, please?'

'We'll have to walk part way with Elsie, I can't leave her swinging. But, yeah, I'd love yer to walk me home. I've spent the most awful few weeks of me life, Paul, but one kiss from you will make me sleep with a smile on me face tonight.'

He squeezed her hand. 'Are yer still me girlfriend?'

'If yer'll have me.'

When Phoebe's shy smile spread across her face, Paul had to fight the urge to kiss her. With his dimples on display, he said, 'Oh, I'll have yer, Phoebe Corkhill.' The music died down and he squeezed her hand. 'I'll come and stand with you and yer friend, but I'd better show me manners and tell the gang first.'

Elsie was grinning as Phoebe walked towards her. 'Yer don't have to tell me, it's written all over the pair of yer. Just look at him, anyone would think he'd won the pools.'

Paul's pleasure and excitement were plain for all to see. 'Me and Phoebe have made it up.' He shook Archie's hand, kissed his sister and thanked her for bringing her friend along tonight. Then he kissed Ginny. 'Yer'll never know why, Ginny, but if it weren't for you, this stupid quarrel of ours might never have been resolved.' With that he turned on his heels and hurried to the back of the hall where a pair of hazel eyes, full of eagerness and love, searched for his return.

Chapter 25

'Mam, when yer go to the shops, will yer get me a baby's bottle from the chemists?' Doreen could tell by her mother's expression that the request was not being well received. But she carried on, 'And a teat, if yer would.'

'What d'yer want to start him on the bottle for, sunshine? Yer know they told yer in the hospital that babies are far better being breast-fed.'

'I'm still going to feed him meself, Mam, but I thought if I could bottle feed him once a day it would make things easier for me. He's going longer between feeds now. Yesterday he went a full three hours.'

Victoria could see Molly wasn't convinced so she spoke up in favour of the young mother. 'I think it's a good idea, Molly, particularly with the christening on Sunday. If Doreen fed Bobby herself before she left for the church, she could give him a bottle later. After all, it will be difficult for her to feed him with the house full of people.'

'And there's Tommy's wedding as well, Mam,' Doreen pressed home her point. 'Phil's grandma has offered to come for the day to mind the baby for us, and I'd be able to enjoy meself if I didn't have me eye on the clock all the time.'

Molly was feeling more reasonable now she'd had time to think it through. 'Yeah, yer've got a point, sunshine, it would be better all round for yer. But would Maggie Mitchell be able to manage?'

'I'll be here with her most of the time,' Victoria said. 'I'll go to the church because I wouldn't miss seeing Tommy and Rosie getting married, but I won't go to the reception if yer don't mind, Molly, because it would be too much for me. After all, I'm no spring chicken and I tire very quickly. So I'll come here straight from the church and keep Maggie company.'

'I understand, sunshine, and I know Tommy and Rosie will. We won't leave yer out, though, we'll make sure two plates of food are brought up to yer.' Molly breathed in deeply. 'I feel a bit guilty not inviting any of Phil's family to the wedding, but yer have to draw the line somewhere. Money is tight as it is.'

'The Mitchells wouldn't expect to be invited, Mam! They know there's a lot of us, and the McDonoughs and Corkhills. After all, yer can't invite everyone. And anyway, they'll all be here on Sunday for the christening.'

'I don't know how ye're going to fit everyone in here, it's going to be a tight squeeze.'

'We'll manage, Mam, don't worry. I mean, look at the number of people yer've had at your parties and yer've always managed. And they're not all coming here from the church, some are going straight home.'

'At least yer don't have to worry about the food, sunshine, that's all in hand. Me and Jill will make the sandwiches and cakes in our house and carry them over. And there'll be jellies, trifles and biscuits, of course, all the usual party things. The drinks are Phil's department, and he said e's got it all in hand.'

Doreen grinned. 'Tell Auntie Nellie she can be yer deputy hostess, she'll like that.'

'Like it? She'll love it! Honest, she's breathing fire because she said I'm getting all the excitement! She practically said I'm greedy, as though I'd made it me business to have all these things happen so close together.'

Victoria smiled. 'Her day will come, Molly, and then she'll find out for herself that's it's more worrying than exciting.'

'Yeah, I can't wait. Next year their Lily will probably be getting married and I'll be able to sit back and watch Nellie do all the running around. I won't half get a kick out of watching her, she won't know whether she's coming or going.'

'Don't be daft, Mam,' Doreen laughed, 'Auntie Nellie will know exactly where she's going. Right down to your house, that's where she'll be going. And don't say she needn't bother, 'cos yer won't see yer mate stuck. And stuck she would be, because I think we'll all agree that she is never organised over anything.'

'Don't be fooled by Nellie, not like I was twenty years ago. Believing she wasn't very good at coping was my downfall. I started helping her out, doing favours for her, like, and I've been doing it ever since. She's as crafty as a box-load of monkeys.'

'She's paid yer back in laughs, Mam, yer can't deny that. Where you've been the organiser, she's been the entertainer, the comedienne.'

'Yeah, yer've got a point. But when Lily gets married, Nellie can

336

do all the organising. She can be hostess and I'll be her deputy. That'll make a change.'

There was a movement from the cradle and Doreen was up like a shot. 'I'm sure this feller can tell the time, he always wakes when he's due to be fed.' She lifted the baby out and swayed as she held him in her arms. 'I could eat him, I really could. He never cries, yer know, Mam, he's as good as gold.' She wrinkled her nose. 'He doesn't smell very sweet at the moment, he needs his nappy changing. I'll do that before I feed him.'

'I'll get the nappy out for yer, we don't want yer banging his head.' Molly opened the door of the cupboard in the wall recess. 'And then I'll be on me way to the shops.'

'Don't forget the bottle and the teat, will yer, Mam? And will yer ask in the chemist's which baby food he should be on at his age? If yer get me a tin I'll pay yer for the lot when yer come back.'

Molly nodded. 'Let's have a look at me beautiful grandson before I go.' She made cooing noises as she stroked the smooth, pink cheek. 'He's not half filling out, I bet he's put some weight on since he was born.'

'I'm taking him to the clinic tomorrow so we'll find out then.' As Doreen took the nappy, she smiled into her mother's face. 'D'yer know what yer said before about sitting back and letting Auntie Nellie do all the running around for Lily's wedding? Well, yer were talking through yer hat, 'cos there's no way yer'd do that. She'd be running around like a headless chicken if you weren't there to help her.'

Molly chuckled. 'I know, sunshine, I'm all talk. But I wouldn't offer, wouldn't push meself forward unless she either asks me to help or I see her making a right mess of things. The latter being the most likely.' She dropped a kiss on the baby's head and picked up her bag. 'I'll be back in an hour or so – Nellie permitting.'

'Tommy, I'll come round to me ma's with yer tonight, I want to check that I've got the list of guests right. I keep thinking I've left someone off, and I can't be adding to the numbers once I've told the Hanleys or they'll think I'm a ruddy nuisance.'

'Okay, Mam, I'll wait for yer. Rosie's got a list so yer can compare them.' Even just saying the name of his dearly beloved intended brought a smile to Tommy's handsome face. 'In fact, she's got dozens of lists. Red carnations for the men's buttonholes, white for the women. Special pink carnations for the mothers of the bride and groom, and double red carnations for her father, who is giving her away, and the

337

same for Ginger, as best man. Then she has another list for who is to go in the first car and who in the second. Also who has to wait for one of the cars to come back for them, and who is to make it to the church on foot.'

Jack pushed his plate away and reached for his packet of Woodbines. 'Yer've got a good one in Rosie, son, like I got a good one in yer mam. Yer'll never have to be worried about rent arrears or being up to yer neck in debt. There's a few men I know who are old before their time with worry, 'cos their wives have no idea how to manage a home.'

'Rosie's had two good teachers, Dad, and they've taught her how to be economical with money. There's her mam and me nan. Her family were poor, and being thrifty is second nature to her. But she's not tight, far from it. She'd give yer her last ha'penny if yer needed it.'

When Jack saw Molly gathering the plates together, he said, 'Leave them, love, me and Ruthie will tidy up and wash the dishes, won't we?'

Ruthie pretended to pull a face. 'Ye're making an old woman of me, doing housework at my tender age.'

'All good practice, sunshine!' Molly took Tommy's coat down and put it over the back of a chair before reaching for her own. 'It'll stand yer in good stead for when yer get married.'

'Who's top of the list this week, Ruthie? Is Gordon still hot favourite or is Jeffrey Mowbray in with a chance?' Tommy put his coat back on the hook. 'I don't need to put that on, Mam, it's warm out.'

Ruthie, who couldn't make her mind up which of the boys she liked best, gave him a cheeky grin. 'Neither of them, clever clogs. I'm going to write to Mickey Rooney in America and ask if he fancies a beautiful young English girlfriend.'

'I think he's on his third wife, sunshine, so don't waste yer stamp money. Stick to the devil yer know, it's better than the devil yer don't.' Molly tugged on Tommy's arm. 'Come on, let's get going, I don't want to be out too long 'cos yer dad misses me when I'm not here.'

Jack followed them to the door. 'I would have thought yer'd be happy to know I miss yer. It's better than me being glad to see the back of yer.'

'Well, I'm getting a bit worried about yer coming to the door to see us off. Makes me think that as soon as I go out the front, yer'll be bringing yer fancy woman in the back.'

'After a hard day's work, love, yer must be joking! Anyway, tell

338

Bridie and Bob I was asking after them.'

Molly linked her arm through her son's. 'If you and Rosie are as happy as yer dad and I have always been, then yer won't go far wrong. It's grand if yer have a nice house, coal in the shed and food in the larder, but none of that counts for anything if there's no love.'

'Don't be going all soppy on me, Mam, please. I'm beginning to be a sentimental fool as it is, and I'm only twenty-one! I mean, it's all right for Granda to cry when he sees anything that gets to him, like Doreen's baby, 'cos of his age. But folk would talk if I kept getting me hankie out to wipe me eyes.'

'It doesn't hurt to be soppy now and again. Even men are entitled to have feelings.'

'I've found that out, Mam, but I just hope I don't start blubbering at me wedding. If yer think I'm showing signs, pinch me hard.'

Rosie opened the door to them, and after giving Molly a hug, she put her arms around Tommy and smiled into his eyes. 'How is me dearly beloved intended today?'

'Happy now I'm with you.'

'Oh, my God, it's enough to make yer sick!' Molly winked at her mother and father who were sitting in their favourite chairs to either side of the fireplace. 'Me and Jack were never that sloppy.' She winked again. 'At least not in front of you, Ma. Yer never saw us throwing ourselves at each other, not like these two.'

'We might not have seen it, me darlin', but we heard yer right enough,' Bridie said. 'Sure the springs in the couch were very noisy, so they were. And with our bedroom being right above yer, couldn't we hear every movement, word and kiss?'

Bob chuckled. 'My dear wife is exaggerating, Molly, so don't look so shocked. We didn't hear a thing, only the springs of the couch.'

Molly's hands covered her cheeks. 'Yer've got me blushing! At my age, I'm blushing like a teenager after her first kiss.'

'That's because yer feel guilty, Mam,' Tommy said, setting Rosie down on her two feet. 'But fancy being caught out by the springs on a couch.'

Out of the corner of Molly's eye, she saw her parents smiling across at each other as though conspirators in a secret. And then the reason for their smiles dawned on her. She stood in the middle of the living room, a hand to her chin and a puzzled expression on her face. 'Ay, Ma, this is the same couch, isn't it?'

'It is, me darlin', and the springs have got louder over the years, so they have.'

Rosie couldn't understand why Tommy went into fits of laughter. 'What's so funny about that, Tommy Bennett? Sure, doesn't it mean that me Auntie Bridget must take good care of her furniture for it to have lasted so long?'

Running the back of a hand over his eyes, Tommy chuckled. 'Sure, it does mean that, me darlin'. But it also means that every time *we're* on the couch, kissing and cuddling, they can hear the springs playing a tune.'

The light dawned and Rosie's beautiful face beamed. 'Oh, that's it, is it? Well, don't I have the very thing for that now? Sure I'll be putting cotton wool in yer ears every night before yer go to bed, Auntie Bridget, and you too, Uncle Bob. Sure, it's a foine thing when a courting couple can't do their courting without someone listening in. But I'll be generous with yer, so I will. Every night I'll keep count of how many kisses me dearly beloved intended gives me, and I'll let yer know the next morning.'

'That'll be fine, sweetheart, 'cos me and my dear wife like to be kept up-to-date. Yer see, our hearing isn't as good as it was when Molly and Jack were courting.' Bob began laughing at his own joke before he got the words out. 'It's either that, or you and Tommy don't make as much noise as they did.'

Molly feigned disgust. 'Just wait until I tell Jack that me ma and da used to stand with their ears to the door listening in. I'd never have believed it of yer.'

'Well, Auntie Molly, as me mammy would say, yer should never do anything yer'd be ashamed of anyone seeing.'

'And yer mammy is quite right.' Molly pulled a chair out and plonked herself down. 'Now, can we go through the list of guests for the wedding so I'm sure I've got everyone down? I get a different total every time I do it.'

Rosie opened a drawer in the sideboard and took out a notepad. 'I've got them all written down, Auntie Molly, d'yer want me to read them out to yer?'

'Just add them up and tell me how many yer've got. See if the number tallies with what I've got written down.'

Rosie's mouth worked silently as she moved the pencil down the list. Then, tapping it on the pad, she said, 'I get it to twenty-eight.'

Molly breathed a sigh of relief. 'That's exactly what I get it to. Until I get to bed and go over it in me head, then I'm miles out.'

'Have yer got Uncle Bill and his wife from Wales down?' Tommy asked. 'And Ginger and his girlfriend?'

Molly nodded while Rosie said, 'Now I'd hardly be forgetting yer best man, would I?'

'I'll give that number in to Edna Hanley tomorrow,' Molly said. 'It won't matter if an odd one or two extra turn up, she'll fit them in.'

'It's a lot for yer to pay for, Mam, can yer manage it? We've offered to help yer, and we'd rather do that than have yer worrying.'

'Who said I'm worrying about money? Me and yer dad want to pay for it, like we did for the girls. Anyway, I'll be paying the last few pound in on Saturday, and then I'll be straight.'

'I'm looking forward to the christening on Sunday, Auntie Molly,' Rosie said. 'And to meeting all Phil's family.'

'Our first great-grandchild.' There was a catch in Bridie's voice. 'Me and Bob are going to feel really proud.'

'Not as proud as me and Jack, Ma! I'm taking six hankies with me, just in case.' Molly grinned. 'No matter how proud we are, it won't be a patch on how Phil and Doreen feel. Just think, a year ago Phil didn't have a soul in the world, and now he's not only got his dad's family but a baby of his own. And it's no more than he deserves, he's one smashing lad and I love the bones of him.' She touched Tommy's arm. 'Almost as much as I love you and the girls.'

'We're very lucky as a family, Mam, I'll say that. There's not one of us ever fallen out or even had sharp words. Oh, I know when we were kids we used to fight, me and the girls, but it was only ever in fun. We never kept an argument up or sulked. And I've never heard me nan or granda even raise their voices. Just one big happy, loving family. And Steve and Phil have fitted in as though they've always been part of that family. Same as my Rosie has – only she's prettier than they are.'

'I should hope so,' Molly laughed. 'If either of them heard yer saying they were pretty, they'd clock yer one. It's handsome lads they are, both of them.' She suddenly remembered something and twisted in her chair to face her mother. 'Ay, Ma, did Tommy tell yer Lily and Archie are getting engaged? And that Phoebe and Paul have made it up?'

'We knew about Lily and Archie, but Tommy hasn't said anything about Phoebe and Paul.'

'I'd have had a job to tell yer when I didn't know meself,' Tommy said. 'Yer only told us about it when we were having our dinner!'

'Yeah, well, it only happened last night. Nellie did think of waking me up at midnight to tell me, but I'm happy to say she resisted the urge.' Molly's eyes covered each of the faces. 'I've been here nearly

341

an hour and no one's asked if they should put the kettle on. Me mouth is as dry as a bone.'

Rosie jumped to her feet. 'Sorry, Auntie Molly, we'll rectify that right away, so we will. Me dearly beloved intended will be delighted to give me a hand, won't yer, Tommy? And he won't have to worry about stealing a kiss or two, 'cos it's meself that's thinking there'll be no springs in the kitchen floor.'

'Lily, can me and Phoebe come into town with yer? I know you and Archie would probably rather be on yer own when ye're choosing an engagement ring, but I promise we won't get in yer way.' Paul's brown eyes were appealing. 'It's just that we'd like an idea of how much a ring will cost.'

'Ah, ay, Paul, that's a bit much, isn't it? Taking me kid brother with me and me boyfriend to choose a ring? Archie would think I was crazy!'

'Of course he wouldn't think yer were crazy! And knowing Archie, he wouldn't mind in the least!' Nellie, her arms lost from view beneath her bosom, was taking sides with her son. After all, big as he was, he was still her baby. 'They know better than to be nosy or get in the way. And there's more than one window in every jeweller's shop I've ever seen. They can be looking in one window while you and Archie have got yer noses pressed against another. It wouldn't do yer no harm to let them go along with yer.'

Once her mother had taken up the cudgels on Paul's behalf, Lily knew she was beaten. But she couldn't give in without a fight because Archie mightn't like the idea. 'But they're not getting engaged yet so why do they want to be looking at rings?'

'As soon as I've saved up enough money, we will be getting engaged,' Paul told her, 'and I just want an idea of prices!'

'How much have yer got saved, son?'

'Only ten pound, Mam.'

George gasped. 'ONLY ten pound! When me and yer mam were courting, we could have bought a wedding ring *and* an engagement ring for that. And got change into the bargain.'

Nellie rolled her eyes. 'My God, listen to the voice of wisdom! Ye're talking about twenty-five years ago, yer silly bugger! Things have shot up in price since then.' After clicking her tongue on the roof of her mouth several times, she lowered her voice to speak slowly and coaxingly to her daughter. 'How much is Archie forking out for your ring?'

342

George coughed, Paul grinned and Lily gasped. 'Mam! Yer shouldn't be asking things like that! Even if I knew, I wouldn't tell yer. And if yer have the nerve to ask Archie, I'll walk out of the front door in shame.'

'I don't know,' Nellie said, as though she'd been insulted, 'people get upset at the least thing these days.'

'Yer were out of order, Nellie,' George told her. 'Yer have no right to ask a question like that, now or after they've bought the ring. It's none of your business.'

A knock on the door brought the subject to a close. But not before George had wagged a warning finger at his wife. 'Don't you dare, Nellie.'

Archie came in smiling. 'It's a lovely day to go shopping for a ring, don't yer think? And if me girlfriend is ready, we'll be on our way. From what I've been told, a girl can take hours and hours before deciding on the one she wants.'

'Archie, can I ask yer something?' Nellie wasn't to know that her words brought three hearts to a standstill. 'If yer don't like the idea just say so.'

'Fire away, Mrs Mac, I'm all ears.'

'Well, it's like this, yer see, son. Our Paul and Phoebe will be getting engaged soon and they were wondering if yer would mind if they went into town with yer. Just to get an idea of prices, like, yer know.'

'Of course I wouldn't mind, they're welcome to come along.' Archie smiled at Lily. 'We'll be glad of their company, won't we, love?'

Lily was so relieved her mother's enquiry wasn't to ask Archie how much money he had in his pocket, she readily agreed. 'Yer'd better go and get Phoebe, otherwise the afternoon will be over before we get into town.'

Paul wasted no time, and within five minutes he was back with his girlfriend. Looking the picture of happiness, he asked, 'Well, what are we waiting for? Let's go!'

Brown's the jeweller's was a small but well-known shop in Liverpool's London Road. They offered a wide selection of attractive engagement rings at prices which ranged from five pounds to five hundred. Lily's eager eyes lit on a cluster which had an amethyst stone in the centre surrounded by six small diamonds. 'That's nice, Archie.'

'Take yer time, love, 'cos it's got to last yer. Why don't we go inside and ask to see a selection? Yer'd have more idea if yer saw them at close quarters and could try them on. And if there's nothing that takes yer fancy here, we can try another shop. There's plenty of them in the city so yer'd be hard pressed not to find a ring yer like.'

Lily looked across to the other window where Paul and Phoebe were gazing wide-eyed at the vast selection. 'We're going in for a closer inspection, d'yer want to come?'

'No, we'll wait here so we won't be in the way.' Paul was thinking he could save up enough in a few weeks if they didn't go out so much. Not that Phoebe was the one who wanted to go out, it was him. 'If yer want us, though, give us a call.' Then he put his arm across Phoebe's shoulder. 'Can yer see anything yer like?'

She pointed to one of the velvet pads which held about twenty rings. 'The second row down, fourth on the left. I think that's nice.'

Paul pursed his lips. 'It's not very big, is it?'

'I always thought that when I got engaged I would like a solitaire diamond. I don't want a big showy one, and I like the claw setting on that. And the diamond isn't that small anyway, it's just right. It doesn't have a price on, though, so it probably costs the earth.'

'None of them have prices on so that doesn't mean a thing. We'll wait for Lily and Archie to come out, then we'll go in and ask how much it is. Yer might see something yer like better inside.'

'We don't have to wait for them to come out, there's a woman standing behind the other counter, she can serve us.'

But when they got inside, Lily called them over. 'Come and have a look, Phoebe, see what yer think. There's so many it's hard to choose, but three have taken my eye.'

The three rings were quite similar, all clusters with a different gemstone in the centre surrounded by small diamonds. 'They're all very pretty, Lily, it's hard to say which is the nicest. It's a question of taste, really. Try them on and that way yer might be able to make up yer mind.'

'I've tried them, but I'd like you to put them on so I'll get a better idea what they look like.'

With the two men becoming impatient and moving from one foot to the other, Phoebe was asked to show off each ring by putting a hand to her mouth, then on to her chest, and finally flat on the counter. 'I think they all look nice.'

After further debate, Lily decided on the ring which had first taken her eye, the cluster with the amethyst nestled in the centre of six small diamonds. She moved away from the counter and put her hand on Archie's. 'I still like this one, but yer haven't asked him the price of any of them. If it's too dear, we'll leave it and look in other shops.'

344

Archie turned to the man behind the counter, who was waiting and hoping for a sale. 'How much is this ring?'

'Twenty pounds, sir. But we do have a cheaper range if you'd care to see them?'

Archie shook his head. 'Lily, are yer sure? And does it fit properly?'

She spread her hand out for him to see. 'Look, it's a perfect fit. And I really love it.'

'Then you shall have it.' Archie reached into a pocket for his wallet. 'Ask the man to put it in a nice box for yer.'

Phoebe gave Paul a nudge. 'Ask the woman how much the solitaire in the window is.'

The assistant brought the velvet pad from the window, and after Phoebe had pointed out the solitaire ring, she took it from its nesting place and handed it over. 'A very pretty ring, if I may say so.'

Phoebe slipped it on to her finger. 'It's lovely. How much is it?'

'Eighteen guineas, dear.'

Lily, the small red padded box containing her engagement ring safely in her bag, came to see what was going on. 'That looks nice on yer, Phoebe.'

Paul, thinking the male assistant was probably senior to the woman, walked over to the counter where the unsold rings were being put back on display. 'Excuse me. If I put ten pound deposit down on a ring, would you hold it for me until I came with the rest of the money? I don't have enough on me right now.'

'Of course, sir, that would be fine. Give the details to Miss Holdsworth and she'll give you a receipt for your money.'

Paul turned to find himself confronted by Phoebe and Archie. 'I've got money on me, Paul,' Phoebe told him, 'enough to pay for it outright.'

'What! Let yer pay for yer own engagement ring! No chance, love, I'll pay for it meself. It may take a couple of weeks, but we weren't expecting to get a ring today, anyway.'

Then it was Archie's turn. 'Paul, I've got enough on me, I can lend yer the money.'

' No, no, a thousand times no! This is one thing I want to do on me own. I asked Phoebe to get engaged and I'm the one that wants to, and should, pay for the ring.'

So when the foursome left the shop, there were smiles on all their faces. Lily had the ring she'd fallen for and which cemented her relationship with Archie. And Phoebe was delighted that the solitaire ring she'd always dreamed of would soon be hers and she could tell the world that she and Paul belonged to each other. As for Paul, he felt like jumping for joy. There'd be no going to dances or the pictures for two weeks, he was really going to pull his horns in. Of course he could have borrowed the money off Archie and Phoebe would have had her ring today, but knowing her, she wouldn't have been happy in the knowledge it wasn't paid for. It was far better to do it this way, both of them with their pride intact.

Chapter 26

Father Kelly looked surprised to see so many in his church for the christening. Usually it was just the parents of the baby and the godparents, but there were at least thirty people sitting in the pews today. More than he got at mass on most mornings. Since the war had finished, it appeared religion and attending mass were the last things on people's minds. It was as though they blamed God for allowing the bombing and killing which had affected many families in Liverpool and surrounding areas. But it wasn't God who'd brought such horror to so many, it was the greed and wickedness of men.

The font was at the front of the church near the side altar from which the statue of Our Lady looked down, so those sitting in the pews would be able to witness the christening. Doreen was standing swaying gently as most women do when holding a sleeping baby in their arms. Phil was as close to her as he could get, his cup of happiness overflowing.

As Father Kelly approached the font he beckoned the young couple closer. 'You're very lucky having so many friends.'

Doreen smiled. 'Yes, Father, we do have a lot. But most of these people are members of my family or my husband's.'

'Who are standing as godparents?'

Doreen turned to where Jill and Steve were beside Doreen's best friend, Maureen, and her fiancé, and waved them over. Baby Bobby was to have two sets of godparents.

'What name are you giving the child, Mrs Bradley?' Father Kelly asked.

'Robert James Bradley.' That was the only blot on a perfect day for Phil. He'd been hoping to hear from the solicitor saying the change of name from Bradley to Mitchell had been finalised, but it wasn't to be and his son was being christened a Bradley. Although the solicitor said the name could be changed on most things, like rent books and for voting purposes, a birth certificate could not be altered.

'Will you remove the shawl, please?' As the priest held out his

347

arms for the sleeping baby, Doreen was feeling really pleased with her son. He'd been an angel, not a peep out of him. But she was congratulating herself too soon, because the cold water being poured on his head was not to his liking and he soon proved to everyone that he did indeed have a good set of lungs.

The Mitchell family had turned out in force and nearly everyone remarked on the likeness of Phil to his uncles. The younger members had never known their uncle who had died, but for the rest of the family it was an emotional time, bringing back many memories of a son and brother who had been dearly loved. But as Maggie had said to them, the first day Phil came into their lives, 'My Bob will never be dead while Phil is alive.'

As Father Kelly said a prayer over the baby, all the men in the congregation had smiles on their faces while the women held hankies to their eyes. Corker whispered to Ellen, 'You women like nothing better than to have something to cry over. This is supposed to be a joyous occasion, not sad.'

'I know,' she sniffed. 'These are tears of joy.'

Molly, sitting next to Phil's grandma, Maggie, was crying unashamedly. And Jack was biting on his lip to keep the tears at bay.

Doreen held out her arms to take the baby when the short ceremony was over. 'Thank you, Father.'

'I hope when Robert James is older you will set him a good example by bringing him to church every Sunday. If the parents fall away, very often the children will too. And that is not fair to the child because they haven't been given the choice of believing in God or not believing. Don't deny your child that choice, bring him up to be a good Catholic.'

Doreen felt guilty, remembering it was months since she'd been inside the church. But that was due to circumstances and she'd see it didn't happen again. 'I'll do my best, Father.'

Jill was standing nearby, her face radiant with happiness for her sister, and eager to hold the baby. 'Can I have a hold of my godson, please?'

'Oh, aye, that's favouritism, that is,' said Maureen who had been a friend of Doreen's since the day they'd started work in Johnson's Dye Works at the age of fourteen. She'd been engaged to Sammy for eighteen months and they were to be married in September. 'I'm a godmother, too, but I can't get a look in!'

'Let's go outside, shall we? Father Kelly's got another christening in a few minutes.'

Young Bobby's cries had died down now, and as they walked out into the sunlight he was his usual placid self. The strange faces bending over him and the strange voices talking baby talk, seemed to amuse him. He gurgled away happily. Although he'd cried at the cold water being poured over him, he certainly hadn't disgraced himself. And who wouldn't cry if they were only two months old, in a deep sleep, and so rudely awakened? It was enough to frighten anyone.

'Can I have me cuddle now?' Jill asked, her arms held wide. 'And then I'll pass him over to Maureen.'

Molly came up behind them. 'Ay, just hang on a minute. It's age before beauty and I think Mrs Mitchell should be first in line. Followed by yours truly.'

So while the ladies gathered around the baby, all making the sounds they think babies can understand, the men stood together in a group, most of them glad to be out in the fresh air to smoke a cigarette. Jim Mitchell, the eldest of Maggie's children, took Phil to one side. 'We didn't buy anything for the baby because me mam said he had plenty of everything. But she said he had a Post Office savings book so we all chipped in to give yer this to put in it.' He slipped a ten-pound note into Phil's pocket. 'It'll come in handy if he needs anything.'

'I can't take that off yer, Uncle Jim, it's far too much!'

'It's not just off me, it's off me mam, our Wally and our Beth. It only works out a couple of pound each, and yer can't buy much for that. Anyway, seeing what a difference there is in me mam since you came into her life, and then young Bobby, well, we want yer to know how much it means to us.'

'I'm the one who's gained most, Uncle Jim. A few years ago I was the boy with nothing and no one. Now look at me, I've got three families – the Bennetts, the Mitchells and the person who made all this possible, me Aunt Vicky. And on top of that, I've got me lovely wife and beautiful baby. The richest man on earth, I am.' Phil grinned as he patted the pocket in which the ten-pound note lay. 'Although the way things are going, me son is going to be richer than me before he's much older.'

Molly was tutting as she walked towards the group. 'Why do they say it's women who talk too much? You lot take some beating. Anyway, it's time to make our way home before young Bobby starts getting hungry.'

'Me and our Wally and the wives are going straight home, Molly, and we're taking the children with us. Beth and Noel are staying with me mam, but yer'd never get us all in the house, there's far too many.'

'Ye're welcome, yer know, Jim! There's enough grub to go round.'

349

'No, we decided weeks ago it was too much to expect.' Jim had only met Molly and her family twice but they were people he knew he could get on with. 'One of these days we'll hire a hall and have one big do. A real knees-up, jars out, old-fashioned do.'

Corker, who had heard what was said, slapped him on the back. 'That's a very good idea, Jim, and one we'll give some thought to. Molly here knows of a place that would do just fine, and around Christmas would be an ideal time for us all to get together.'

'It sounds good to me,' she said. 'But the ladies have already started walking home so I think those who are coming back should follow on. We'll see yer soon, though, Jim, and yer brother and wives. Look after yerself now, ta-ra.'

When Molly caught up with the women, Nellie glared and flared her nostrils. 'Trust you to make a bee-line for the men. Man mad, that's what yer are.'

'Nothing yer say can affect me today, sunshine.' Molly waved a hand in the air. 'Today is a milestone in me life and I intend to enjoy it.'

'Ye're having too many ruddy milestones in yer life lately, it's going to yer head.' Nellie waddled on, keeping up with the younger ones in front. 'There's no living with yer these days.'

'Are yer giving yer notice in, Nellie? Resigning from yer job as deputy hostess?'

'No, smart arse, I wouldn't let Doreen down by doing that.' Nellie's short legs moved faster. 'It's not her fault her mother's a big-head.'

Jill turned around at that moment and called, 'I'll hurry on ahead with Maureen, Mam, and we can start getting the cups and saucers ready, and the plates. Doreen's given me her key so Miss Clegg won't have to answer the door.'

'Victoria will be looking out of the window, sunshine, waiting for us. It would have been too much for her coming to the church, but I bet she's dying to see the baby in all his finery. She only got a quick look before we came out.' As the girls began to race ahead, Molly called after them, 'Tell her we're right behind yer.'

'Me and Bob haven't seen anything of the baby.' Bridie and her husband had gone straight to the church with Tommy and Rosie. 'I did notice that the shawl looked brand new, though. No one would dream it was forty odd years old.'

'Yer were being kind to me there, Ma,' Molly laughed. 'Forty odd sounds much better than forty-six.'

'Forty-six and a half, girl,' Nellie grinned. 'Don't forget the half.'

'I'd have a job to forget it when yer keep reminding me, wouldn't I?' Molly turned to see where the rest of the gang were. Not far away were the young couples who didn't want to be separated. Rosie was laughing up into Tommy's face, Lily and Archie were holding hands and swinging their arms between them. They hadn't mentioned the engagement ring, except to their mam and dad who had been sworn to secrecy. Behind them came Paul and Phoebe, linking arms and whispering sweet words to each other. They didn't have their ring yet, but they had the thrill of knowing that in two weeks they'd be officially pledged to each other.

The older men were lagging behind: Jack, George, Corker and Beth Mitchell's husband, Noel. Molly swore to herself that Jack had grown six inches in height since the baby was born, he was so proud to be a granddad. She could tell, even from this distance, that he was bragging to his mates.

'Look, Mam, Aunt Vicky's standing at the door,' Doreen said, as they turned into the street. 'She's talking to that Mrs Mowbray, I hope she's not tiring herself out.'

'Jill and Maureen are there now, sunshine, and I think they're taking her in. Besides, Victoria isn't daft enough to overdo things. She knows her limitations.' Molly put her hand under Nellie's elbow and urged her forward. 'I don't know about anyone else but I'm dying for a cuppa. Me mouth thinks me throat's been cut.'

It wasn't like any other party the Bennetts had ever had, there was no singing or dancing and no party piece from Nellie. But after the food had been eaten, and the dishes cleared away, Steve helped Phil to pass the drinks around and very soon the conversation became lively and laugher was in good supply. Ruthie was the only young one there. She soon got fed up not being able to join in so she asked her mam if she could go down to Bella's. When Molly gave her consent, the young girl was out of the door like a shot.

The baby had been fed and put down to sleep in his cot at three o'clock. They hadn't heard a peep out of him since. Doreen and Phil were taking turns to go up and see if he was all right, but Molly said it had been a tiring day for the child. What with the christening, then everyone wanting to hold him, he'd been passed from one to the other and was bound to be tired out.

It was seven o'clock when Bobby finally woke up. Doreen said she'd change his nappy and feed him upstairs. It was then Maggie Mitchell decided it was time to go. 'We'll be on our way now, love, but I'll be up again in a few days. It's been a lovely day and I'm really happy and proud. The christening went off very well, thank you for inviting us all.'

Beth agreed. 'Me and Noel have just been saying how much we've enjoyed it. The occasion was great, and so was the company. But we'll get me mam home 'cos she's beginning to look tired.'

Phil showed his relations out while Doreen took the stairs two at a time, shouting over her shoulder, 'Mam, will yer bring a clean nappy up, please? Oh, and the baby's bucket, if yer would.'

Molly chuckled. 'Ay, Jack, doesn't this take yer back a few years? Up every few hours through the night and nappies everywhere.' Her laughter grew louder. 'I can remember me digging yer in the ribs one night and saying it was your turn to get up. But would yer? Would yer hell! Yer flatly refused, and I was told in no uncertain terms that it was your job to go out to work to earn the money to keep us, mine to see to the house and family.'

'Molly, I think that's a slight exaggeration 'cos I can't remember refusing to get up to see to any of the kids when they were babies. Especially when they were teething and crying with the pain. Many's the night I sat on the side of the bed nursing them.'

'Yes, I know, sunshine, but what yer seemed to forget was that babies don't only have teething pains, during the night, they have them all day as well.'

'Excuse me,' Tommy said, removing Rosie's arm from around his neck so he could speak. 'Are yer saying that me and me sisters cried day and night? That neither of yer could get any sleep because we were bawling our heads off?'

'Not all in one go, son,' Jack told him. 'We did have a year's grace in between. In fact, after you we had seven years' grace.'

Bridie leaned forward to say, 'I may be telling tales out of school, but yer mam could do her share of crying when she was a baby.' And pinching her dear husband's hand to let him know that what she was about to say was in fun, she said, 'In fact, the neighbours used to complain, she cried that loud.'

A voice came floating down the stairs. 'Mam, are yer bringing that nappy up or not?'

'Oh, dear, I'd forgotten about the poor thing.' Molly reached across Corker to the cupboard in the recess for a nappy. 'Don't any of yer dare to talk about me while I'm upstairs.'

'I'll talk about yer,' Nellie said. 'I'll tell them a few tales that'll make their hair curl.'

Molly turned with her foot on the bottom stair. 'I don't mind you talking about me, sunshine, 'cos no one believes a word yer say.'

She was near the tiny landing when she heard her mate say, 'Well, did yer hear that? She's got a ruddy cheek, she has. Here's me, a God-fearing woman what never talks about anyone and wouldn't do no one a bad turn.'

'Nellie,' George said through a haze of cigarette smoke, 'how can yer say yer never talk about anyone when ye're pulling Molly to pieces?'

'Pulling her to pieces? I said she had a ruddy cheek, that's all!' Nellie was getting red in the face with the injustice. 'And I don't call that pulling someone to pieces.'

Steve knew one surefire way of calming his mother down, and seeing as Phil was still at the door with his relatives, he decided to take over as barman. 'Are yer ready for a milk stout, Mam?'

Nellie's expression changed so quickly to one of sweetness and light it brought forth gales of laughter. 'Oh, that's nice of yer, son, a milk stout will go down very well. And while ye're at it, bring one for me mate 'cos she'll be down in a minute. She'd do her nut if yer left her out.'

'I know that, Mam, and I want to keep on the right side of me mother-in-law. So it's two milk stouts coming up.'

When Doreen came down after getting the baby off to sleep, Victoria told her there'd been two visitors for her. 'Maisie came down with a present for the baby, sweetheart. I didn't tell yer before because there was so much going on. She was sorry she couldn't get to the church but the shop was busy and she didn't like to leave Alec on his own. I put the present in the right-hand drawer of the sideboard.'

'Ooh, that was nice of her,' Doreen said, making a dive for the drawer. Her eyes widened when she saw the square, flat parcel which was beautifully wrapped in paper which had teddy-bears all over it and a big satin bow on the top. 'Oh, just look at it! I'm dying to see what's inside, but it seems a shame to tear the paper.'

'There's no other way of finding out, love,' Phil said, coming to stand beside her. 'Let me open it and I'll be as careful as I can and not tear the paper too much.'

Inside there was a silver-plated picture frame with a leaf pattern running down both sides. And there was a card enclosed which said it came with love from Auntie Maisie and Uncle Alec for baby Bobby's first photograph. It was too much for Doreen, and while Phil passed the frame around for everyone to admire, his wife stood sniffing into a handkerchief.

After praising Maisie's present, Nellie sat up straight and folded her arms under her bosom. There was very little she ever missed, and now she wanted to know, 'Who was the other visitor, Victoria? Yer said there were two.'

'She lives in Vera Harwick's old house, I think she said her name was Beryl Mowbray. Anyway, she said it was a custom to give something silver to a new baby, so she gave me two half-crowns for his money box. They're on the mantelpiece, I thought you'd like to put them in the piggy bank.'

'That was neighbourly of her,' Jack said, to nods from everyone present. 'Considering the Mowbrays don't know us very well, it was a thoughtful gesture.'

'The father, Dave, has always struck me as being a decent bloke when he's been in our company in the pub,' George said. 'Always friendly and never shirks paying his way.'

Corker nodded. 'Yes, they seem a decent family. I thought the young girl, Joanne, was a bit of a hard case at first, but I was talking to Dave yesterday and he said there's been a big change in her.' What he was saying now was for Phoebe and Paul's benefit. 'Apparently she met some bloke at a dance about six weeks ago and they're courting now. She brought him home to meet the family and Dave said him and the missus are delighted 'cos he's a nice bloke and has certainly tamed Joanne.'

The conversation was general after that until Molly noticed Archie and Lily had their heads together and were whispering. 'Ay, no secrets are allowed tonight. If yer've anything to say, let's all hear it.'

Archie's face was one huge grin while Lily went the colour of beetroot. 'Thanks for the opening, Mrs B. Lily's gone all shy on me.' He dipped into his pocket and brought out a dark red square box. 'In here is an engagement ring, I would very much like to put it on her finger while all her family and friends are around us.'

The news livened up the proceedings somewhat. There was clapping and laughter as Archie dropped down on one knee in front of Lily. 'Miss McDonough, would you do me the honour of becoming my fiancée, with a view to marriage in the not too distant future?'

There was so much laughter and happiness around her, Lily's shyness disappeared. How lucky she was to have found a man as good as Archie. She spread out the fingers of her left hand, and said, 'I would be honoured, Mr Higgins.'

After the ring had been slipped on her finger, Tommy shouted, 'Do the job properly, Archie, and give her a kiss.'

Rosie caused a fresh burst of laughter when she poked Tommy in the chest. 'Never tell anyone to do something yer won't do yerself, me dearly beloved intended. I'm sitting here with me lips all ready and willing, so what are yer waiting for?'

Steve claimed Jill's lips without waiting to be asked, and Maureen pulled her boyfriend Sammy towards her. 'Blow that for a joke, I'm not going to be left out.'

Phoebe tapped her father on his shoulder. 'Dad, is it all right if Paul kisses me?'

'Of course it is, sweetheart! And as it seems to be catching, I'll be partaking of a kiss from yer mam.'

Nellie was tutting when she saw Phil give Doreen the eye and they made for the privacy of the kitchen. 'Bloody hell!' Her chins tried to keep up with her shaking head but gave it up as an impossibility. 'It must have been something they ate.' She cast her eyes on Bridie and Bob who were sitting on the couch holding hands. 'Don't you two start or I'll pack me case and sign in at the lunatic asylum. They say there's more nutters outside than there are in.'

'I may as well come with yer, sunshine,' Molly said, ''cos my feller can't be bothered getting off his backside to cross the room to give me a kiss.' She saw Jack making a move and held up her hand. 'No, don't bother, yer've left it too late. A thing is not worth having if yer've got to ask for it.' Then she slapped her forehead with an open palm. 'Oh, I've just thought on, Nellie, I won't be able to come to the asylum with yer! I haven't got a ruddy case!'

Chapter 27

It was the Thursday evening before Tommy and Rosie's wedding, and all those taking an active part in the ceremony were sitting round Molly's table. 'We'll go over everything tonight because it'll be the last chance we get. With Rosie's mam and dad coming tomorrow, it's going to be a very busy day.'

'What time are they getting here, Rosie?' Ginger asked. 'And is someone going to meet them?'

Rosie's excitement was proving too much for her and her usually pink cheeks were pale. 'Me and Auntie Molly are going to meet them, so we are. I'm due for a week's holiday from work so I'm off from today which means I can spend as much time as possible with me mammy and daddy. Tommy's on holiday as well so they'll have time to get to know him, and then they'll understand why I think he's the foinest man in the whole world.'

Molly looked at her future daughter-in-law with concern. The girl was a nervous wreck, and although it was understandable as she'd be seeing her parents for the first time in six years, it was happening before the biggest day of her life – her wedding day! That was enough to try the nerves of anyone, let alone one who was already sick with anticipation and excitement. 'Rosie, sunshine, if yer don't try and calm down, yer'll not only make yerself sick, yer'll feel like a wet rag on Saturday and won't have the energy to enjoy yer wedding.'

'Oh, not at all, Auntie Molly! Won't I be as bright as a button on Saturday when I marry the man of me dreams?'

'Well, promise me yer'll go to bed very early tonight and try and get a good night's sleep? We've to be down at the Prince's Dock by eight o'clock at the latest in the morning. The boat might even get in a bit earlier if the crossing has been smooth.'

'As soon as we've finished here I'll take Rosie home and me nan can make sure she goes straight to bed.' Tommy's love was plain for all to see. 'I don't want me bride to have bags under her eyes.'

'Then can we go through the details now and get it over with?'

Molly lifted a sheet of paper from the table. 'The four bridesmaids are to be here for twelve o'clock to have plenty of time to get ready. And at twelve Tommy's going up to Ginger's and getting changed there. One of the cars will be picking him and Ginger up at half-past one, and calling for me ma and pa and Mrs O'Grady. After dropping them off at the church, the car will come back for me and Jack, Nellie, George, Doreen and Miss Clegg. At half-past one the bridesmaids will be collected, and a quarter of an hour later Rosie and her dad.' Molly folded the piece of paper. Everyone else is making their own way to the church.'

Ruthie was like a cat on hot bricks. 'Mr and Mrs Watson are coming to the church with Bella. I wish they could come to the reception.'

'Don't keep on about that,' Molly said, 'we couldn't invite everyone to the reception, it wouldn't run to it. But they've been invited to come in the evening and Mary was very happy with that.'

'I don't know about Rosie being a nervous wreck, Mam,' Jill said. 'You look tired yerself. And hot and bothered.'

'I've had a lot on me mind, sunshine, but I'll be all right. I was worried about where Mr and Mrs O'Grady were going to sleep, but Lizzie Corkhill helped sort out that problem. It was her suggestion that Jill comes back here for the night, and Steve goes back to his old bed, while Rosie's mam and dad have their room. Otherwise we'd have been in a right pickle.'

It was Ginger's turn to air his worries. 'Apart from getting Tommy to the church on time, and having the ring in me pocket, am I down for anything else?'

'Yer've got to give a speech, soft lad,' Lily said. 'That's the main job of a best man.'

Ginger gave a nervous laugh. 'In the last month I've written six speeches and I don't think any of them are any good.'

Molly looked at the freckled face beneath a mop of red hair and the years rolled back. Ginger at five years of age knocking on the door asking if Tommy could play out. He always had a runny nose in those days, and was never without a tidemark. But he'd been a good mate to her son and she was very fond of him. 'Ginger, you are the best person to give a speech because yer know Tommy better than anyone. And yer've known Rosie for six years. All yer have to do is remember the laughs and the good times, and tell us all about them. I recall yer've always been very good with jokes so, as long as they're clean ones, tell them. It's a wedding and everyone will be happy so yer have a head start.'

Molly tilted her head and smiled at the two Corkhill girls who so far hadn't said a word. 'Are you two looking forward to it?'

'Oh, yes, Auntie Molly,' Phoebe said, 'very much so. Me and Dorothy talk about it in bed every night, don't we, kid?'

Dorothy beamed. 'Oh, yeah, and I've been bragging to all me mates in work. Some of them are coming along to see the wedding and they're bringing confetti.'

'That's nice.' Molly closed her eyes for a second. She was so, so tired, and was longing for her bed. 'I think we've covered everything so I suggest we call it a day. I've told Jack he's to have no more than two pints, he should be in any time. Then I'm up those stairs to my bed. I'll sleep without rocking tonight.'

'I'll take Rosie home and come straight back, Mam, I'll only be fifteen minutes.' Tommy scraped his chair back. 'Let's all go and give me mam a bit of peace.'

Jill hung back after everyone had gone. 'Steve said he'd come down for me so I may as well wait. It'll be funny coming back here tomorrow night to sleep, like old times.'

'It's only for the one night, sunshine, that's all. I don't know how long Rosie's parents are staying, but she said it won't be long because they have the farm and cattle to see to. If it's only for a few days more, I'll ask Mary Watson if Ruthie can sleep with Bella and they can stay here. Anyway, it'll be handy for yer, seeing as ye're matron of honour and yer dress is here. And I can rely on yer to make sure the others are ready in time for the cars coming. Oh, and don't forget to make sure the front door is closed properly when yer leave . . .'

There was a tap on the window and Jill jumped to her feet. 'This will be Steve, Mam, but I won't ask him in, yer've had enough visitors for one day.' She kissed her mother's cheek. 'I love you, Mam.'

'And I love you, sunshine. Explain to Steve that I'm really bushed, and it's not because I don't want to see him.'

'He'll understand. Goodnight and God bless. Ta-ra, Ruthie, and don't forget ye're sharing yer bed with me tomorrow night.'

'I hope yer don't snore and keep me awake.'

Jill had her hand on the front door. 'If my memory serves me right, you can send them up with the best. So if I do snore, I'll try and keep in harmony with yer.'

Steve tucked Jill's arm through his. 'I met Tommy and Rosie so I know everything's been sorted, right down to the last detail.' He squeezed her hand. 'Did yer get a chance to tell yer mam yer'd been to the doctor's?'

She shook her head. 'Me mam is worn out, Steve. She's got enough on her mind without me telling her I'm expecting a baby. I don't want to tell her while she's tired, and with so many other things to think of.' Jill smiled up at him. 'I know ye're dying to tell everyone but when I tell me mam and dad, I want to see them jumping for joy, full of happiness. And, anyway, the next few days belong to Rosie and Tommy. Let's wait until their big day is over before breaking the news.'

'You're right, of course, love, I shouldn't be so selfish. It's just that I want the whole world to know how thrilled and proud I am. And another thing, we'll have to tell Mrs Corkhill soon, 'cos we'll have to start looking for somewhere else to live.'

'I know, it's only right she should be told. She's been so good to us, and I won't half miss her when we've got to leave. If yer like, we can tell her tonight and ask her to keep it to herself until next week? We'll both feel better once she knows.'

'Yes, okay. Will you tell her, or shall I?'

'I'll tell her, it's only right. But if I go all shy and get stuck, you help me out.'

Lizzie Corkhill was listening to a play on the wireless but she turned the volume down when she heard the couple coming in. 'It's not much good, so don't worry. A murder mystery they said it was, but I'll bet a pound to a pinch of snuff that it was the feller next door what did it. It's sticking out a mile.'

'You go ahead and listen to it,' Steve said. 'We don't mind. Besides, if yer don't listen to the end yer'll always wonder whether it *was* the feller next door.'

'Nah! I don't really care who did it, 'cos the bloke what got killed was a rotter and he deserved to die.' Lizzie put her hands on the wooden arms of her chair and pushed herself up. 'I'll make us a nice cuppa.'

'Would yer leave it for a minute, Mrs Corkhill? We've got something to tell yer.'

Lizzie let herself drop down into the chair again. 'Oh, aye, queen, is it about the wedding?'

Jill looked down at her clasped hands as she felt her face colouring. Then a voice in her head reminded her she was a married woman now, and an expectant mother to boot. It was about time she gave shyness its marching orders. 'I took time off work this morning, Mrs Corkhill, to go to the doctor's. I wasn't sure, yer see, but he confirmed that I'm expecting a baby. I'm only nine or ten weeks, but me and Steve thought we should let yer know that we'll be looking for somewhere to live, save yer worrying.'

'Oh, I am glad for yer, for both of yer.' But Lizzie's happiness was tinged with sadness. She'd come to love this young couple, they were like family to her now and she couldn't imagine the house without them. She dreaded the thought of being lonely, with no one to watch for coming home from work every night. Then she took a deep breath. She was being selfish, just thinking of herself. 'I bet yer mam and dad are over the moon?'

'We haven't told them yet, Mrs Corkhill,' Steve said. 'They've got enough on their plate right now so we've decided to leave it until after the wedding. We're hoping yer won't mention it to anyone just yet, not until we've told our parents. We just thought you should know what's going on, and to put yer mind at rest, so yer won't worry.'

'And why d'yer think I'll worry, son?'

'That we don't find somewhere to live before the baby's born. But we will, Mrs Corkhill, we'll start looking first thing next week.'

The old lady looked thoughtful for a while then she asked, 'Do either of yer want to live somewhere else?'

'It's not a case of wanting to,' Jill told her. 'But we can't expect you to let us stay here with a baby.'

'Why ever not?'

'It wouldn't be fair on yer! Yer've been so good to us, taking us in when we had nowhere to live and letting us treat the house as if it was our home. We wouldn't expect yer to put up with a baby as well.'

'Listen, queen, do I have any say in this matter?'

'Of course yer do, Mrs Corkhill, but me and Steve understand how concerned yer must be. And we don't want yer to feel embarrassed or worried.'

'Listen to me, the pair of yer. Answer me truthfully. Do yer really want to move out of here and live somewhere else?'

Jill and Steve looked at each other before answering. Then Steve said, 'I don't want to move, I've been very happy here. But, unfortunately, needs must.'

'I don't want to move either!' Jill was close to tears. 'But having a baby here would disrupt yer whole way of life, Mrs Corkhill, and we wouldn't put yer through that.'

Lizzie sat up straight and folded her arms. 'Now let me have my say. I love having yer here and don't want yer to leave. I'd be very lonely without yer. And having a baby in the house would be a

361

wonderful tonic for me. Yer see, a baby brings love with it, not worry or disruption. So now yer know how I feel, yer can make up yer mind what yer want to do. The decision is entirely up to you.'

After one glance at each other, Jill and Steve moved quickly over to Lizzie's chair. And for one moment, the old lady thought she was going to topple backwards. Then she was just righting herself when she thought she was going to be smothered under an avalanche of kisses and hugs. When she could speak, she gasped, 'I take it ye're staying then?'

'Oh, yes, please, Mrs Corkhill!' Jill was so relieved she felt light-headed. 'Both me and Steve were dreading the thought of leaving yer, weren't we, Steve?'

The dimples in his cheeks deep, he said, 'Yer see before yer the happiest man in the City of Liverpool.'

As Molly watched Rosie bobbing up and down and moving from side to side so she wouldn't miss any of the passengers coming off the Dublin boat, her mind went back six years. It was in this very spot that she'd stood with her ma and Nellie, waiting for Rosie's arrival. At the time she'd thought her mother was doing the wrong thing by taking in an unknown girl of fifteen. In fact she'd tried to talk her out of it. But she'd been wrong because Rosie had brought happiness and love to her parents, and to everyone else who came to know her. Particularly Tommy.

'There they are, Auntie Molly!' Rosie darted forward, and because there were so many passengers coming off the boat, Molly had a job to keep up with her. When she saw three people with their arms around each other, crying with happiness, she remained at a distance. How those parents must have missed their beautiful daughter! She couldn't imagine what it would be like if she didn't see one of her girls for six years. But they'd parted with Rosie for her own good. The family were poor, there was no work, and they'd wanted to give her a chance in life. A big sacrifice to make for someone you love.

'Auntie Molly, this is me mammy, and this is me daddy.'

Molly found herself looking in to a beautiful face. The black hair had many strands of white running through it, but the deep blue eyes were the same as Rosie's and so were the rosy red cheeks. 'I can see where Rosie gets her looks from, she's the image of yer.' It seemed natural to hold out her arms to give and receive a kiss. '*Cead mile failte*, Mrs O'Grady. A hundred thousand welcomes to Liverpool.'

'Sure, me name's Monica, so it is, and doesn't it sound more

362

friendly? And this handsome man standing here is me darlin' husband, Mick.'

Under a mop of mousy-coloured hair there was a weather-beaten face that told of the many hours out in all weathers tending to animals and the vegetable plot that had often saved them from starvation in the bad years. It was an open face, one to which you took an instant liking, and the twinkle in his eyes warned of a wicked sense of humour. 'It's glad I am to meet yer, Molly, we've heard so much about yer in Rosie's letters.' His handshake was firm. 'And it's grateful we are to yer for taking such good care of our daughter.'

'Oh, that has been our pleasure, I can assure yer. Rosie is loved by everyone.' Molly eyed the battered case he was carrying. 'We'll get going because me ma will be pacing the floor. She can't wait to meet yer. The tram stop is this way.' She held out her hand. 'I'll carry the case for yer, Mick, to give yer a break.'

'Not at all, not at all!' Monica said, waving an arm. 'Sure, he's as strong as an ox, so he is.'

'If that's true,' Molly laughed, 'I'll not tangle with him.'

They were soon sitting on the tram leaving the Pier Head, Monica and Mick wide-eyed. 'Will yer look at the foine buildings? Sure, I've never see anything like them in me whole life.'

'It's grand they are, right enough,' Mick said, turning in his seat to get a better view of the Liver Buildings. 'Sure, Liverpool must be a very big city indeed.'

But as the tram trundled on its way, Rosie pointed out to her parents the damage inflicted on the city by the German bombs. Open spaces where blocks of offices had once stood, and the department stores which were now empty shells. Houses which were once happy homes now lay in ruins, and whole communities were split up.

Monica was wringing her hands. 'Oh, dear God in heaven, how could anyone be so wicked as to bomb all those buildings and people's homes? But, sure, won't they be punished when the time comes? They'll not get into heaven, and that's a fact.'

It was on the tip of Molly's tongue to say that buildings could be replaced while the thousands of lives lost in the raids could not. But she didn't say what was on her mind because the O'Gradys had come over for a joyous occasion and not to be made sad. 'Well, we've dusted ourselves off since Hitler, and in a few years Liverpool will be rebuilt and thriving again.' She changed the subject. 'Me ma is really looking forward to seeing yer. You're a little bit of the land she still calls home.'

'Does she now?' The face that was so like Rosie's broke into a smile. 'Bless the darlin' woman for not forgetting dear old Ireland. Sure, I always say that no matter how far yer travel in life, yer never forget the place where yer were born. Especially somewhere as beautiful as the Emerald Isle.'

Rosie, who was sitting in the seat behind with her father, tapped Molly on the shoulder. 'Me mammy was always saying that, and it's true, so it is. I love Liverpool, and the people who have been so kind to me here, but part of me will always be in Glendalough.'

'Then ye're going to have to save up and go over for a holiday, sunshine. I'm sure Tommy would love to see the place yer were born.' Molly looked through the window of the tram and realised the next stop was theirs. 'This is where we get off.'

Bridie was standing on the step waiting for them. When they turned the corner of the street she dashed back inside. 'They're here, me darlin', so I'll turn the light up under the kettle.' After a quick look around to make sure everywhere was tidy, she stood in front of the mirror over the fireplace and patted her hair, excitement on her face and in her movements. 'Will I do?'

'Yer look lovely, as always, sweetheart,' Bob said. 'Now go and greet them at the door.'

Monica looked around the small living room and took in how neat and tidy it was, and how spotlessly clean. Then she turned to the two elderly people who had given their daughter a home and plenty of love, who had lain with her when she was crying because she missed her family and was home-sick. All this they'd been told in letters from Rosie, and the kindness she saw in their two faces told her these people had a lot of love to give.

Rosie's eyes were bright with happiness. 'This is me Aunt Bridget, Mammy, and me Uncle Bob.'

'It's very welcome to our home yer are.' The two women shared a long embrace while Bob thought Mick would surely shake his arm out of its socket.

It was a lovely, heartwarming scene which had Molly feeling in her pocket for a hankie. 'I'll make us a cuppa. I think we could all do with one.' The delicious smell in the kitchen had her popping her head around the door. 'What have yer got in the oven, Ma, it's got me mouth watering?'

'It's a steak and kidney pie, sweetheart, and don't be opening the oven door or ye'll spoil it. I thought we'd have a very early dinner 'cos I bet Monica and Mick haven't had a hot meal since early yesterday.'

'Oh, I packed a load of sandwiches, so I did, and they kept the hunger at bay. But I'd not be saying no to a piece of that heavenly smell.'

While Molly was waiting for the kettle to boil, she put a light under the pan of potatoes on the stove. Then she leaned back against the sink and listened to the lilt of Irish voices. Her ma was in her element, asking question after question about folk she could remember who would be the same age as herself now. And Rosie wanted to know all about her brother and sister, and clapped her hands in joy when she heard they were both courting.

Molly left them to it and got on with making the dinner. When it was ready to serve, she called through to ask Rosie to set the table. 'I'm giving meself some, Ma, I can't resist it.'

'It was a noisy meal, with everyone happy to be together and the conversation non-stop. There was praise and appreciation for Bridie's baking, and when the meal was over everyone sat back with a full tummy.

'I'll have to get home and see to a dinner for me family now,' Molly said, 'but I'll be around later to take yer to meet Lizzie Corkhill, whose house yer'll be sleeping in tonight. Then I want yer to come to my house and meet me family. They're really looking forward to meeting Rosie's mam and dad. And at eight o'clock my husband and two of his mates are taking yer to the pub for a drink, Mick. They won't keep yer out late 'cos it's a big day for yer tomorrow. Yer want to look yer best when yer walk down the aisle with yer lovely daughter on yer arm.'

'It's a proud man I'll be, Molly, and that's the truth of it. Oh, I'll be nervous, right enough, but I hope I won't put a foot wrong. I'll not spoil Rosie's big day.'

'If there's anything yer want to know, Mick, then ask Jack. He walked down the aisle with a daughter on each arm last year, and yer'll be meeting yer future son-in-law tonight so yer can have a good chat with him. And although I shouldn't be the one to say it, sure me son is a foine figure of a man – beef to the heel like a Mullingar heifer, so he is.'

Molly's excellent attempt at the Irish lilt brought forth a burst of laughter, and also a hug from her future daughter-in-law. 'Auntie Molly, yer have a son to be proud of, and I thank yer for giving me a husband I love with all my heart.'

Monica met her husband's eyes. They knew now that although they'd always miss their daughter, they would never have to worry about her. These were good people, they'd take good care of her.

Chapter 28

Molly woke at six o'clock on Saturday morning, and try as she might, she couldn't drop off to sleep again. She slipped her legs over the side of the bed and tip-toed to the window. Lifting the curtain, she saw a bright blue sky with a splash of gold which meant the sun was waking up. It was going to be a lovely day. 'Thank you, God,' she said softly.

Creeping across the floor and stepping over the floorboards she knew would creak, she opened the door without making a sound. There was no point in waking Jack, he may as well have another hour. Molly grinned as she made her way down the stairs. He hadn't half enjoyed himself last night when he, Corker and George had taken Mick to the corner pub. He said the Irishman had a wonderful, dry sense of humour and had them in stitches. Tommy had gone along, too, but he'd stayed for just one pint because the only thing he could concentrate on was the wedding.

Molly closed the living-room door so no sound would go up the stairs to waken Jill who was a very light sleeper. 'Thank goodness it's summer and no grate to clean out,' Molly said aloud as she made for the kitchen to make herself a cup of tea. 'A quick dust around and the place will do.' Once again she smiled, but this time it wasn't for any particular reason, it was for all the good things that were happening in the lives of her family. Jill and Doreen settled down with fine husbands who had never given her one moment's doubt, and whom she loved dearly. And today her only son was marrying Rosie, a beautiful girl who would make him a perfect wife. It only left Ruthie at home now, and it would be quite a few years before she wed, so Molly and Jack would have a breathing space. They might even save up and go to Ireland for a holiday, she'd like that. Monica and Mick had invited them, and apparently when they were in the pub, Mick had invited Corker and George as well! How Jack had laughed when he told her the Irishman had said, with a straight face, that they'd have to sleep in the pig-sty, but sure they weren't to worry because although the pigs might smell a little, they were very friendly.

Molly poured milk into her cup, stirred it, then carried it through to the living room and plonked herself down on a fireside chair. How quiet and peaceful it was now, but in a couple of hours it would be like a mad-house. The cup was to her lips when the door opened quietly and Jill crept in. 'I thought I heard yer, Mam, and I knew there'd be a pot of tea on the go.'

'Pour yerself a cup while it's still fresh, sunshine, and come and relax for a while. It might be the only chance yer get, so make the most of it.'

But Jill had disturbed Ruthie when she'd got out of bed, and the youngster couldn't settle. After all, she was going to be a bridesmaid today, and both Gordon and Jeffrey would see her all dolled up. She opened the door with a big grin on her face. 'Today's the day, Mam! Are yer all geared up for it?'

Molly couldn't help but smile. What it was to be young and without a care in the world. 'I'm as geared up as I'll ever be, sunshine. But you should have stayed in bed for another hour, it's only seven o'clock.'

'I opened the curtains, Mam, and the sun's coming up. So I thought to meself, if the sun can get up early, then so can I.'

'Get yerself a cup of tea, then, and try not to talk too much, there's a good girl. I want to give me head a rest while I can.'

Ruthie had no sooner squatted on the floor with her cup of tea, than Jack popped his head around the door, his eyes bleary and his hair standing on end. 'You're all crazy, getting up at this time when there's no need for it.'

'Then what are you doing up, sunshine?' Molly asked. 'Nobody asked yer to.'

He came into the room rubbing his eyes. 'I knew there'd be a pot on the go, and me throat is dry. Be an angel, Ruthie, and pour yer dad a drink.'

'I hope yer didn't wake our Tommy up? He needs all the sleep he can get to be nice and fresh for his big day.'

'I didn't make a sound, love, I was as quiet as a mouse.'

'It wasn't you what woke me, Dad, it was the creaking stair.' Tommy stood there, a broad grin covering his handsome face from ear to ear. 'I'm going to miss that stair, it's always been like a warning system.'

Molly tried not to think about it but she couldn't blank it from her mind. This was the last time she'd see her son's face in the morning, the last time he'd be having breakfast and leaving with his dad. When she could feel herself filling up, she pushed herself out of the chair.

This was no time to be going all sentimental. 'I'll make us some toast and a fresh pot of tea. Then at eleven we can have some sandwiches to tide us over. I don't want to hear rumbling tummies in the church.'

Nellie gave Molly a dig in the ribs. 'Ay, girl, our side of the church is filling up.' As she turned her head, the ostrich feather on the side of her hat tickled Molly's nose making her sneeze. But her mate was so excited she didn't even notice. 'I feel sorry for Monica, though, 'cos on her side there's only Bridie and Bob.'

'Not to worry, sunshine, it's all in hand. The Corkhills and the Watsons are going to sit over there, to even things up a bit.'

'Oh, that's a good idea, girl.' Nellie couldn't keep still and kept swivelling in her seat. Every time she did, the feather tickled part of Molly's face. 'Ay, the bridesmaids are here, I can see them standing outside.'

'Well, they'll be waiting for the bride.' Molly scratched her nose. 'It's no good them walking down the aisle without Rosie and her dad.'

'Your Tommy looks dead handsome, girl, I could fall for him meself.'

'Nellie, if yer don't keep that feather to yerself, so help me I'll snap it off.'

'Ye're only jealous, girl, 'cos your hat hasn't got no feather.' Then Nellie relented. 'It looks nice on yer though, girl, dead smart.'

Jack and George, sitting next to their wives, looked across the two women and raised their brows. Would the day ever come when these two ran out of things to say? Then they grinned, both thinking it would be a sad day for all if that happened.

'Ay, girl, we haven't half got a lot of family and friends.' This time it was Molly's mouth the feather tickled and she pulled a face. 'I think half the street is here.'

'I'm glad there's a good turnout for Rosie's parents. It'll be something for them to look back on.' Molly jerked her head quickly when she saw the deadly feather coming her way again. 'Nellie, when your Lily gets married, will yer buy another hat, please?'

'What! Three guineas and only been worn twice! No chance of that, girl, I'll be wearing this creation for your Ruthie's wedding.'

The organist began to play and all heads turned towards the door. As Rosie began the walk down the aisle on her father's arm, everyone was stunned into silence by the sheer beauty of her. Never had a bride looked so lovely, with a face radiating happiness. The dress she'd kept secret from everyone was magnificent with a four-yard train being carried by the bridesmaids. And never had a father looked as proud as Mick O'Grady, who had never in his life walked so tall.

Molly felt for Jack's hand as the tears ran. 'My God, have yer ever seen anyone as beautiful? She looks like a fairy princess.'

'She does that, love, she's a credit to her parents. And our Tommy is a very lucky lad.'

When Tommy turned around, he thought he was going to faint. Rosie looked so lovely she took his breath away. He'd been nervous sitting in the front pew with Ginger, but when she smiled at him his nerves evaporated. And throughout the whole ceremony the smiles never left their faces. They spoke their vows in voices that could be heard by everyone in the church, never faltering once. Ginger was more nervous than they were. The fingers that handed over the ring were shaking and he swore to himself he'd never be best man again. Looking at Tommy, it wasn't as nerve-racking being the bridegroom.

When the priest said, 'You may kiss the bride,' there wasn't a dry eye in the church as the couple, beautiful bride and handsome groom, joined their lips together for the first time as man and wife.

'I don't know why I bothered borrowing our Jill's powder and lipstick, I've wiped it all off with crying so much,' Molly said. 'But only someone with a heart of stone would not be moved by that sight. She looks like a princess and he is Prince Charming.'

Nellie wasn't easily moved to tears. When she started sniffing she tried to cover it up with a joke. 'Rosie looks just like I did on the day I got married.' She gave her husband a dig. 'Isn't that right, George?'

He put his arm across her shoulder. People fall in love for different reasons. Perhaps looks, perhaps personality. He'd fallen in love with Nellie because he knew his life would never be dull with her. She was brimming over with personality, was warm, passionate, and had a heart of gold. And no man could ask for more than that. 'Sweetheart, ye're just as pretty today as yer were then.'

'Ay, don't be getting soppy, you two,' Molly said. 'Leave that for the young ones today.'

When Nellie winked at George, her eyes were filled with mischief. In a whisper just loud enough to reach her mate's ears, she said, 'Yeah, we'll leave it until we're in the privacy of our bedroom, love, where no one can see us.'

'Don't you dare mention your bedroom in church,' Molly tutted. 'Honest, yer've got it on the brain.'

Jack tugged on her arm. 'We're needed to go through for the signing of the register, love, come on. And we'll have to take Monica with us, 'cos Mick has gone through with Tommy and Rosie, Jill and the best man.'

Monica's face was tear-stained, but her eyes were bright with the wonder of it all. The church, the number of people who had come to see the wedding and the fine clothes they were wearing, the likes of which she'd never seen in her life before. But above all it was her daughter, looking like an angel, who had affected her most. 'Molly, did yer ever in yer life see anything so beautiful? Sure, wasn't me heart ready to burst with love when I saw her? Yer'd travel far and wide and never see such a foine-looking couple.' She was being hurried to a room at the back of the side altar, but was so excited she couldn't stop talking. 'It's a day I'll never forget as long as I live, and that's a fact, so it is. I's just sorry I am that her sister and brother couldn't be here to see it.'

'There'll be a photographer outside the church taking photographs,' Molly said, leading the highly excited woman into a room where the registrar would be waiting to fill in the marriage certificate. 'I know Rosie will send you some.'

The next few minutes were very emotional as Rosie rushed forward to her mother, and Tommy hugged and kissed Molly before being slapped on the back and congratulated by his father. This was the day they saw their son turn into a man. Then Tommy kissed his new mother-in-law, thanked her for having such a beautiful daughter and promised to take care of her for the rest of her life.

It was Father Kelly who restored order. 'If those of you who have to sign will do so now, please, as the registrar has another wedding to attend.'

After the documents were signed, Jill handed Rosie her bouquet back before helping to arrange her train. 'The girls are waiting outside, Rosie, so we walk back as we came in, with them holding the train.' Then she smiled and kissed her new sister-in-law on the cheek. 'Yer look lovely, Rosie, and welcome to the Bennett family.'

Although a few people had gone to stand outside so they could throw their rice and confetti, the church was still quite full. And now the ceremony was over, friends and neighbours called out their congratulations, with many saying they'd never seen such a handsome couple. And Rosie, her arm through her new husband's, had a smile on her face that lit up the dim church.

As they stepped through the church doors, they were greeted by bright sunlight and a photographer with his tripod and camera ready.

After taking several photographs of the bridal couple from different angles, the bridesmaids were called over, together with the best man. Ginger was feeling much better now, and was grinning as he stood with his arms across the shoulders of two of the bridesmaids. He wouldn't allow his mind to dwell on the speech he had to give at the reception because he knew he'd want to turn tail and run. Then he turned to see Tommy looking so happy, and he knew he couldn't let down the best mate he'd had since childhood. He'd do Tommy and Rosie proud if it was the last thing he ever did.

The photographer cleared the church steps, and after a quick word from Tommy, called on Bridie and Bob to stand by their grandson and his bride. The old people looked so happy, and so proud, Molly mentally thanked the young couple for being so thoughtful.

After that it was the bride's parents, followed by the groom's, then the nearest family members. It was a happy occasion with much laughter. But the loudest laugh of the day came when the photographer was arranging people for a group photograph. Nellie insisted she wanted to stand near the front, and when Nellie made up her mind about anything, if you had any sense you would surrender rather than fight a losing battle. 'I'm not standing there, and that's that!' And as her chins were enjoying themselves, they agreed with her. 'How daft I'd look standing next to Corker when I only come up to his belly button! Nah, I'll stand in the front next to Ruthie, she's more my size.'

George very seldom lost his temper with his wife, and he didn't now. He was chuckling when he said, 'Come on, love, stand next to me.'

But Nellie folded her arms and stood her ground. 'There's more to this than just me, yer know. What about me ruddy hat? No one is going to stick me and me three-guinea hat where we can't be seen.'

Everyone was howling with laugher, and young Ruthie used her imagination and the opportunity. Pulling her Auntie Nellie over to where she was standing on the front row, she called to the photographer, 'Quick, take it now!'

So it turned out that Nellie and her ostrich-feathered hat were the cause of everyone on the photograph having huge smiles on their faces.

Edna Hanley had once again done them proud. The tables looked attractive with vases of flowers at intervals, and at the side of every place setting was a paper serviette with wedding bells printed in the corner. In pride of place on the centre table, in front of where the bridal couple were sitting, was the wedding cake. It had been made by Tom Hanley, decorated by Edna, and everyone agreed it was a work of art.

It was an enjoyable, happy meal, with many conversations being conducted at the same time, often from one side of the room to the other. In fact, there was so much going on, nobody noticed how quiet the best man was. The nearer the time drew to his toasting the happy couple and delivering his speech, the more nervous Ginger became. The words that were on the piece of paper in his pocket had seemed funny last night but now he wasn't so sure everyone would appreciate them. He wished his girlfriend, Josie, was sitting next to him instead of on one of the tables running down from the centre one. She was more outgoing than him and would give him some moral support.

Then suddenly he didn't have any more time to worry because Steve was whispering in his ear that all the glasses had been filled and he should now stand up, propose a toast to the bride and groom and get that piece of paper out of his pocket. Too late to worry that his jokes might raise more eyebrows than they did laughs. So Ginger pushed his chair back, raised a glass and said, 'Ladies and gentlemen, I would like you to join me now in toasting the happy couple and wishing them a long life and all the luck in the world.'

When everyone but himself was seated, Ginger reached into his pocket for his notes. But as his hand touched the paper, he suddenly thought, Blow it, I don't need that to talk about me best mate! 'Tommy, remember the day we started school together and you were whingeing 'cos yer wanted to go home to yer mam? I called yer a cry-baby and yer thumped me one? Well, matey, here's where I get me own back.'

Tommy's laugh was the loudest. 'Lies, lies and more lies!'

'Okay, yer didn't whinge, and I didn't call yer a cry-baby 'cos yer were always bigger than me and I didn't want me face rearranging. But when we moved up to Miss Dickson's class, who was it that threw a screwed up piece of paper at her, sat there like an angel and let me take the blame? Oh, yer owned up in the end because yer had to – the piece of paper was out of your exercise book and had your name on it!' Ginger lifted his glass and drank deeply to whet his thirst. 'And remember when me mam bought me a football for me birthday? Yer wouldn't play down in your end of the street in case yer got in trouble, so we were playing footie by our house when the ball bounced on Mrs Corkhill's window and she came out shaking her fist at us.' He began to laugh as the memories flooded back. 'I picked up me ball and the pair of us legged it, hell for leather, down the entry. I don't think there's a woman in our street who hasn't chased us at some time or another. But Mrs Kinsale was the only one who ever chased us with a sweeping brush. She didn't miss us by much, either, we were dead lucky that day.' He noticed Nellie laughing and said, 'One woman even took the ball off us and wouldn't give it back until we said we were sorry and that we wouldn't play by her house again. Her name was Mrs McDonough, do any of yer know her?'

Never one to be outdone, Nellie said, 'I remember her, lad! She was a lovely-looking woman with a figure like Jean Harlow. She had every man in the street after her.'

Ginger waited for the laughter to die down then went on, 'Me and Tommy have been best mates all our lives and have never once fallen out. And I hope we will always be best mates and always there for each other. Today he married the only girl he's ever loved, and I'm happy for him. And Rosie . . . what can I say about Rosie that everybody doesn't know? She's really beautiful in looks and nature. Full of warmth and laugher, she's a wife to be proud of and I know their marriage will be perfect.' He lifted his glass and faced the couple. 'To two of me best mates, and a marriage made in heaven.'

His speech was so well received, Ginger sighed with relief when he sat down. And when Josie came across to kiss him, he said, 'Thank God that's over, I was scared stiff.'

'Ginger, yer were brilliant.' She gave him another quick kiss before returning to her seat for the father of the bride's speech.

It wasn't easy for Mick O'Grady because the only two people he knew well in the room were his wife and his daughter. But his Irish lilt and his humour helped him to find the words to describe how much he loved Rosie, what a good daughter she'd always been, and how proud he'd been of her today. And he spoke of how happy he and his wife were that she'd married a foine lad like Tommy, and how heartening it was to see how she'd been taken into the hearts of such good, friendly people. The clapping as he sat down showed how much his words were appreciated.

Edna Hanley and her daughter had been waiting in the background. Once the speeches were over they moved in to clear the tables while the guests formed small groups to go over the events of the day. They'd be drifting off now, going home to freshen up and maybe put on a change of clothes. But they'd be back, with more guests, at half-seven for drinks, a buffet and dancing to records on the gramophone the Hanleys had kindly provided.

* * *

374

Molly was sitting with Tommy, Rosie and her parents, and they were having a good natter when Molly nodded to the dance floor where Nellie, complete with hat, was pretending to be holding an imaginary partner while she waltzed around the room. She kept looking up and saying, 'Ye're standing on me ruddy foot, yer awkward so-and-so.'

'What would yer do with that mate of mine? I'm sure she'll go to bed in that ruddy hat tonight.' Molly covered her mouth with one hand when she took a fit of the giggles. 'I'll tell yer something funny about that hat – she bought it when Jill and Doreen got married last year, and it was too big for her. Every time she turned her head, the hat stood still. It was so comical it took me all me time to keep me face straight. She'd look sideways to talk to me and the hat would still be facing the altar. Anyway, she bought a hat pin last week and it anchored the blinking hat to her head and it's been as good as gold today. But she must have forgotten it tonight 'cos just look at it. She's danced straight down the room, on her lonesome, and when she got to the bottom she spun around to come back. But as yer can see, she's facing north while the hat is still facing south.'

Monica and Mick thought this was hilarious. 'Oh, Molly, me darlin', she's a broth of a woman, so she is,' Monica said. 'It's lucky yer are to have a friend like her, and that's the truth of it.'

Just then Jill and Steve sauntered over. 'Have yer seen me mam?' When Steve smiled his deep dimples showed. 'I suppose I should go and ask her for a dance, save her making a fool of herself, but I don't think the hat would like me taking her away from it.'

'Leave her alone, sunshine, she's enjoying herself.' Molly glanced towards the door. 'Have Doreen and Phil not arrived yet?'

'We knocked for them, but Doreen was upstairs feeding Bobby. Phil said the baby would sleep for a couple of hours once he's been fed so he was walking Mrs Mitchell to the bus stop so she wouldn't be out too late. He said they shouldn't be long.'

'Will you two sit with me ma and da while I take Monica and Mick to meet the Watsons? They're sleeping there tonight, and I'd like to introduce them to break the ice.'

'Yeah, we'll sit with nan and granda. They seem to be enjoying themselves watching the dancers.' Jill grinned. 'One thing about my mother-in-law, she can keep everybody happy.'

Molly pushed herself from the chair. 'Yer've got a smashing mother-in-law, and Steve's got the best mam he could have.' She reached for Monica's arm. 'Come on, sunshine, I want yer to meet the people who are putting yer up for the next two nights.'

Jill sat down beside Bridie and linked her arm. 'It's been a lovely day, hasn't it, Nan? It went like clockwork, not a hitch anywhere. And didn't Rosie look a picture in that dress?'

'Just like you and Doreen looked pictures in your wedding dresses a year ago.' Bridie patted her hand. 'It's been a wonderful year all round for me and Bob. Three of our grandchildren married and our first great-grandchild born. Not many people at our time of life have so much, or so many people to love. It's lucky we are, and we thank God every day.'

Jill noticed her sister coming through the door. 'Here's Doreen and Phil, I'll call them over.'

Doreen waved aside the offer of a chair. 'Nan, I haven't had a dance for over a year so I'm going to make up for it tonight.' She reached for Phil's hand. 'Come on, love, let's make the best of it while we've got the chance.'

After the O'Gradys had had a chat with Mary and Harry Watson, Molly took them to sit with her parents. She thought they would feel more comfortable with someone who came from their country. All the young ones were on the floor dancing, and it was with a feeling of contentment and a job well done that Molly sat down next to her husband. 'A lot's happened since last year, hasn't it, love? Just looking on the dance floor. There's Archie now engaged to Lily, our Doreen with a baby, Ginger engaged and getting married soon. And I've heard a whisper that Paul and Phoebe are getting engaged next week.' She leaned sideways to kiss his cheek. 'And, of course, there's our Tommy and Rosie.'

'It's not only the young ones dancing, love, look at Corker and Ellen. He's not half light on his feet for such a big feller. And Maisie and Alec aren't making a bad job of it, either.' Jack leaned forward to rest his arms on his knees. 'Now there's a sight I never thought I'd see. George is up dancing with Nellie! Ay, we can't be the only ones left out or we'll never hear the last of it. Come on, love, let's give it a go.'

'Jack, me feet are nearly dropping off, I'd never make it.'

'I'll prop yer up, love, just for this one dance. Go on, be a sport.'

'Oh, okay, but it's only 'cos I love yer, Jack Bennett. I wouldn't put up with the pain for anyone else.' When the record finished, Molly made for the nearest chair. 'Be an angel, Jack, and get me a glass of sherry, will yer? Then yer can go and have a chin wag with George and Corker.'

376

Her husband had no sooner walked away than Jill and Steve came to sit by her. 'Are yer very tired, Mam?'

'Yer can say that again, sunshine, me feet are killing me.'

'Never mind, Mrs B, yer can have a lie in in the morning,' Steve said. 'Yer deserve it after the hard work yer've put in today. But it was well worth it 'cos it's been one great day.'

Then Molly said something she'd had no intention of saying, and to this day she doesn't know why she did. 'By the way, sunshine, I'm going to tell our Doreen to put the christening shawl away safely in tissue paper. So it'll be as good as new when you and Steve need it.'

Jill's mouth gaped. 'Yer know! How did yer know?'

'How did I know what, sunshine?'

'That I'm expecting a baby! I only went to the doctor's on Thursday, and I didn't want to tell yer until after the wedding 'cos yer looked so tired.'

Molly looked at her daughter blankly for a few seconds, and then she saw the huge smile on Steve's face and her tummy lurched with a mixture of love, excitement and happiness. 'Will yer bring yer mam over, Steve, 'cos she'll go mad if she thinks yer've told me and not her?'

Nellie came waddling towards her. 'What is it, girl?'

'Your son's got something to tell yer, sunshine.'

'Mam,' Steve said, 'me and Jill are expecting a baby.'

Nellie looked at her mate to see if she was having her leg pulled, but Molly's moist eyes told her this was no joke. A few seconds ticked by while she digested the news and then the little woman erupted. She dashed into the middle of the dance floor, lifted her skirts to reveal stocking tops, elastic garters, an expanse of bare leg and a couple of inches of light blue fleecy knickers, and broke into an Irish jig. And in a voice with no tune in it, she began to sing, 'I'm going to be a grandma, a grandma, a grandma, I'm going to be a grandma and what d'yer think of that!' Twirling around she kept singing, 'I'll have to learn to brag now, to brag now, to brag now, I'll have to learn to brag now, to keep up with me mate.'

George shook his head as he looked on. 'What's she up to now?' He put his glass down and walked across to his wife. 'Nellie, will yer behave yerself, please? And what brought all this on, for heaven's sake?'

Someone had turned the gramophone off and everyone was watching with interest when Nellie grinned up at her husband. 'I'm going to be a grandma, love, and unless I'm very much mistaken, that means you'll be a granddad. But if yer don't want to celebrate, I'll do it on me own.'

George looked over to where Steve was standing, and when his son nodded, he punched the air as he covered the space between them. Then, of course, the hall came alive with chatter, back-slapping, congratulations and laughter. The couple were surrounded by family and friends, and only Corker stood on the fringes looking on. He waited until most people had drifted off for a drink then he approached Jill and lifted her in the air. The eldest of Molly's children, she'd always been special to him and there was a bond between them. Looking up at her with eyes twinkling, he said, 'My princess has gone and grown up on me. But I'll love yer baby as I've always loved you. Except that no one but you could ever be my princess.'

It was eleven o'clock and still the youngsters danced on while the older guests sat talking in small groups. Molly and Nellie sat together as they surveyed the scene. 'It's been quite a year, hasn't it, sunshine?'

'Yer can say that again, girl! And it looks like another busy one ahead, for me anyway. Archie and Lily have decided on an Easter wedding, and I've a feeling our Paul and Phoebe won't be far behind. But I'm really looking forward to being a grandma, girl, I'm thrilled to bits. So is George, he's cock-a-hoop.'

'No more than Jack, he's never had a smile off his face since he heard. And me poor ma and pa don't know what's hit them, they look dazed. It'll be a few days before it all sinks in with them.' Molly put a hand on her mate's arm. 'We're both very lucky with our husbands and our families, sunshine, they don't come any better.'

'And we're lucky being mates, aren't we, girl? It's not many people have best mates as good as us.' Nellie's chins jumped up and down in agreement as she nodded her head. 'And we always will be, won't we, girl?'

'Nellie, I wouldn't swap you for all the tea in China or the biggest clock ever made. You're irreplaceable.'

'What does that mean, girl?'

'It means no one could ever take yer place and I love yer. And after this dance is over, you and me are going to stand in the middle of the floor and thank our husbands, our children and our friends, just for being who they are.'